A CONGREGATION OF JACKALS

Center Point
Large Print

**This Large Print Book carries the
Seal of Approval of N.A.V.H.**

A CONGREGATION OF JACKALS

S. Craig Zahler

CENTER POINT PUBLISHING
THORNDIKE, MAINE

This Center Point Large Print edition
is published in the year 2010 by arrangement with
Dorchester Publishing Co., Inc.

The text of this Large Print edition is unabridged.
In other aspects, this book may vary
from the original edition.
Printed in the United States of America
on permanent paper.
Set in 16-point Times New Roman type.

ISBN: 978-1-60285-912-8

Library of Congress Cataloging-in-Publication Data

Zahler, S. Craig.
A congregation of jackals / S. Craig Zahler. — Center Point large print ed.
p. cm.
ISBN 978-1-60285-912-8 (library binding : alk. paper)
1. Large type books. I. Title.
PS3626.A625245C66 2010
813´.6—dc22

2010035115

Dedicated to my pals:
Jeff Herriott, William M. Miller,
Fred Raskin, Julien Thuan,
& Graham Winick

Chapter One

They Should Have Paid Attention to Otis

1888

Otis Boulder had what some people in the San Fortunado area referred to as a rumble gut, a stirring in the juices of his stomach that warned him of impending danger, akin to the nerves in the tip of a dog's nose that warned it of bad weather. This was a helpful sense in the sprawling Southwest.

When the two swarthy, sun-bronzed strangers entered the largely empty saloon, Otis's gastric fluids intimated with a low growl that he should leave. Without even finishing the watered-down drink for which he had been overcharged, the thirty-nine-year-old blacksmith stood, grabbed his hat and walked toward the exit. The final thought he had before he passed through the open door and entered the San Fortunado dusk outside was that these two fellows smelled not like men, but like vultures.

The denizens of the saloon glanced furtively at the sun-bronzed arrivals and then returned their gazes to the collections of diamonds and royal personages that they would only ever know in card games. The beeves had been ridden northeast that morning and for the next two months the saloon would be peopled by drunken tradesmen with little to do, and sour fellows too old to ride and too ornery to marry.

Amongst these disenfranchised locals sat an anomalous pair, a young handsome couple from Arizona, married not more than three weeks prior: Charles and Jessica Lowell. When the two sun-bronzed strangers entered the saloon, the newlyweds did not glance furtively as did the others—they openly looked. The couple from Arizona gazed upon the weathered arrivals, surveying the guns in their holsters, the spurs that were long and unnecessarily cruel, the yellow gloves that were stained brown with what might have been dried blood, the dark coats ragged with wear, the cracked faces submerged beneath prickly beards and the long black hair that twined and trailed from beneath their broad brown hats and dripped like candle wax in oily tangles about their shoulders. Their striking resemblance was beyond coincidence: they were identical twins.

Charles squeezed his wife's hand and, a moment too late, whispered to her, "Do not stare." The newlyweds had looked; the twins looked back. The one on the left pointed at the couple with his prickly chin and the other nodded while removing his hat. Their heavy boots elicited groans from the floorboards as they strode toward the Arizonians.

Charles felt his muscles tighten with apprehension; his wife sidled close for protection. The twins, limned by the dusty blue light of the gloaming, closed the distance between the door and the newlyweds. Charles was reminded of standing beside train tracks when a locomotive arrived, though he was not exactly sure why.

He said, "Might I offer you fine gentlemen a drink?"

The twins did not acknowledge the inquiry; they pulled weary wooden seats from the table, legs scraping upon the planks of the saloon floor, and sat themselves. The smell of these men reminded Charles of butcher's offal left a day too long in the bins.

The Arizonian inquired amenably, "Which particular drink is your preference?"

The twins looked at Charles and then over at Jessica. Their obsidian eyes coolly fixed upon the finely dressed blonde woman.

Charles cleared his throat and asked, "What would you gentlemen care to drink?"

"Ain't gentlemen," the one across from Charles said. The man pointed to his own dingy brown hat. "I still got it on. You want my hat off, you just try and take it off."

"I am not overly concerned with hats," Charles

replied. Jessica giggled, perhaps too loudly because of her agitated state.

The talker, the one with the hat, looked at his brother and then back to Charles. "You havin' fun at us?"

"I can assure you, Mister . . ." Charles waited for a name. Receiving none, he continued. "I can assure you, I am not having anything remotely resembling any form of fun at this present time."

"You talk smart. That's how you got her, I s'pose?" The talker looked over at Jessica, upon whom the eyes of the silent brother remained fixed like black moons too stubborn to rise or set.

"I was lucky." Charles turned in his seat and faced the bartender, a nervous bald man of thirty who could pass for fifty, and said, "Three bourbons and a glass of wine."

"Get us whiskey instead."

Charles turned back to the bartender. "Make two of the bourbons glasses of whiskey."

"We'll take a bottle," the talker amended. The bartender looked at Charles; the Arizonian nodded in assent; the rapidly aging drink slinger disappeared to fetch the liquids of his trade.

Charles, his fear allayed by being able to involve some of his considerable inheritance in his current predicament, leaned back comfortably in his chair and asked, "Where are you fellows from?"

"Ain't none of your mind," said the talker. He

then looked over at Jessica. "She's got good breeding. You can tell she ain't done much in the way of work with those hands she got. And all that softness."

The bartender appeared beside the table, set down a glass of wine, a glass of bourbon and a bottle of whiskey.

He reached for the two empty cups upon his tray, but the talker shooed him off and said, "You ain't gettin' this bottle back."

The swarthy man uncorked the whiskey, put the neck to his chapped lips, swallowed a cupful and handed the bottle to his sibling. The silent brother opened his mouth. His gums were wholly bereft of teeth and grossly swollen. At the sight, Charles's stomach dropped and Jessica shuddered; the couple averted their eyes.

"Now that ain't polite—lookin' away from a man while drinkin' with him."

Charles and Jessica raised their gazes and watched the silent brother tip the bottle neck. The Arizonians ineffectually tried to hide their repulsion.

"Since you're buyin', I'll tell you what happened to Arthur, why he can't talk none."

"I am sure it is a fascinating tale," Charles said, disguising his sarcasm enough so that it went unnoticed.

"We was captured by some Indians. Don't at all matter how it happened, but it did. And so there we was, hidden in some cave in some gulch in Indian country, bound up, our backs tied to a damn boulder that weighed more than a fat elephant. Them savages left to go do some scalping or whatever they had a mind to do that day, but only they never did come back. And there we was, tied up expertlike, 'cause if there's one thing those Indians know, it's how to tie a knot that won't never give. Dig up some thousand-year-old Comanche and I bet his moccasins is still tied smart."

A third of the bottle already ingested, Arthur returned the vessel to his brother. The talker drank, smacked his mouth, exhaled gruffly, handed the bottle back to his brother and, properly lubricated, continued the tale.

"A day passed. And then another. And then a third and a fourth day. And there we was, in that cave, starvin' to death 'cause those Indians left us. If it hadn't of rained, we would've gone thirsty, but it did rain and some water dripped from the cave ceiling right there onto our heads and we drunk all of it that ran from our scalps down onto our faces, every little bit, even though it tasted like sweat and lichens. But we drank it all.

"And then the fifth day come and we're both crazy with hunger, delirious, starving, only I'm a little better off than Arthur, 'cause the day we got took by the Indians I had a giant breakfast and dinner, but Arthur overslept and missed his breakfast and he missed his dinner too. So I'm a day behind him in starving to death, if you follow."

"Indeed. Please continue."

Arthur handed his brother the bottle. Again the talker drank, smacked his mouth and cleared his throat. Jessica, calmed by the warming influence of her wine, leaned on her husband's shoulder. Charles looked around and did not think overly upon the fact that most of the saloon denizens had vacated the establishment.

"So we get to arguing. 'I ain't gonna die,' 'It's your fault,' 'Mom said you was gonna get me kilt,' 'It's your fault Dad got kilt'—that sort of stuff that brothers argue 'bout. So Arthur says, 'We was born at the same time and I ain't gonna let you outlive me. I'm gonna last as long as you. Longer even!'" The talker looked over at Arthur. The silent man's eyes were glazed in either recollection or inebriation, Charles could not decide which. "That was the last thing Arthur ever said."

Charles and Jessica were perplexed by the conclusion of the tale. The talker nodded his head and drank another swallow from the dwindling supply in the bottle.

"I am afraid that I do not understand what happened," Charles said.

"He ate his tongue. Bit it off, chewed it up and

swallowed it so he wouldn't starve before me."

Arthur opened his mouth widely for another swallow of whiskey; amber liquid splattered upon the waggling nub within, the tiny remnant of his tongue that was no larger than an olive. Charles stared on in disgust; Jessica, nauseated, placed her wineglass down and clasped her shaking hands.

"My God," Charles muttered. "How did he not bleed to death?"

The talker turned to his brother and with admiration said, "He pulled off his kerchief with his teeth, gulped it in his mouth and pressed it 'gainst the gash to stop the bleedin'."

"My God," Charles repeated.

"Arthur was chewing at his bottom lip the next day when we was rescued. I was just startin' to contemplate my tongue."

Jessica, pale, attempted a weak smile; she said, "That is so . . . so savage."

A coldness descended upon the siblings; beneath hedges of dark eyebrows, four glinting black orbs fixed upon the blonde woman.

"He ain't a savage. He did what he needed to. I know you think you're better than us, but you'd've done the same. We all got the animal within us, even your gentleman husband there."

Jessica stammered, "I didn't m-mean t-to—"

Her sentence was cut off by the slam of the whiskey bottle upon the table. "Shut up. Just 'cause you're pretty don't mean you can call us savages. You'd've done the same if it was you."

Charles was keenly aware that—excepting the far-off bartender and an inebriate with his head upon a table—the bar was unoccupied other than by the brothers, his wife and himself.

With as calm a countenance as he could manage, he said, "My wife is affected by drink. Please pay her no mind."

"We ain't savages. You'd've done the same in that gulch."

"Yes, you are correct."

The talker removed his hat and set it upon the table. A curved scar like a corded pink rope ran from his forehead to the back of his skull; no hair grew from the raised flesh.

"That's what savages do," he said. The talker placed his hat back upon his head. "We ain't savages."

"I am very sorry for offending you," Jessica offered.

"Women says things they don't mean. I know it." The talker looked over at his brother. "You accept her apology?"

There was a glimmer of light by Arthur's hip; the silent man thrust his right hand beneath the table; his gun holster was empty. Terror like the flames of a brushfire leaped across Jessica's features; Charles better hid his fear (though his palms and forehead admitted beads of cool perspiration).

15

"He don't accept it."

Charles pushed back in his seat; a metallic click sounded near Jessica's knees.

"You ain't got his permission to go."

Charles looked at his wife; her eyes coruscated with tears that would soon overflow her bottom eyelids and spill down her cheeks.

"Arthur wants to make a point."

The Arizonians looked at the mute sibling, as if expecting him to grow a new tongue and speak with it. Arthur did not move or even blink; his arm, thrust beneath the table holding his pistol, did not waver; the silent man just stared forward with reptilian eyes.

"What's your name?" the talker asked.

"Charles."

"You got more names than that."

"Charles Alan Lowell."

"And hers?"

"Jessica Parcedes Lowell."

The talker cleared his throat and said, "Mr. Lowell."

"Yes?"

"Open up your mouth."

"What do you intend—?"

Jessica yelped; Charles looked over at his wife.

The talker explained, "Arthur poked her with the barrel. You ain't supposed to ask questions while making him your apology. Open up your mouth."

The Arizonian swallowed dryly, parted his lips and lowered his jaw.

The talker looked at Jessica. "Put the tip of your little finger in Mr. Lowell's mouth."

Charles would have traded his mansion in Arizona and both of his prized stallions for a pistol at that moment. Jessica raised her trembling right hand toward her husband's mouth and extended her pinky finger.

To the husband, the talker said, "Bite down on the knuckle just below the tip. Don't hurt her though—just hold it there with your teeth."

Charles carefully closed his jaw; his upper and lower incisors pressed into the soft skin covering the last joint of his wife's pinky. Jessica's hand and arm dangled from her husband's mouth like an absurd circus-animal tongue.

The talker surveyed the Arizonians and seemed pleased with what he saw. To Arthur, he said, "That to your liking?"

His sibling nodded, his prickly chin moving up and down less than a quarter of an inch.

"Mr. Lowell. I'd advise you, strongly advise you, not to let go of your wife's little finger."

Charles nodded minutely. The talker looked over at Jessica. His eyes surveyed her swollen chest, her long pale neck, her full lips, her upturned nose, her cheeks smeared with rouge (now streaked with tears) and ultimately fixed upon her leaking eyes. The appraisal was like a cold wet hand.

"You love your husband, don't you Mrs. Lowell?"

Without hesitation, Jessica nodded her head.

"But I bet he wasn't the first one you laid with, now was he?"

Jessica stared at the talker, but did not respond. Charles's face reddened, his wife's long fingernail pressed into the wet flesh of his tongue.

"You was with other men before you was with Mr. Lowell, wasn't you?"

Jessica opened her mouth, hesitated and then looked over at Charles, her hand hanging ridiculously from his mouth.

"Don't do no fibbin'. Arthur's hard to fool and don't at all care for fibs."

Charles nodded to his wife; she returned her gaze to the talker and said, "I have."

"How many others you been with, Mrs. Lowell? Lots?"

"One other." Jessica's embarrassment made her face shine bright and red.

"What was his name?"

"Burt."

"Did you love Burt?"

"I was just a girl. I didn't know anything then."

"Did you tell him you loved him?"

"I did."

The talker looked over at Charles and said, "You hear this? Watch out." He pulled an errant twine of oily hair from his prickly beard, set it behind his right ear and inquired of Jessica, "What was Burt's prick like?"

Jessica cried out and yanked her pinky from Charles's mouth. She looked at her husband, frightened.

"You bit me," she said.

"I did not mean t—"

The empty whiskey bottle struck Charles in the face, smacking loudly as it connected with the man's right cheek. In the instant that he tumbled from his seat, he saw that the saloon was deserted. He impacted the floor; his unbalanced chair hesitated on two legs and then fell beside him.

"Get up." Charles righted his chair and reseated himself.

The talker said to Jessica, "You put your finger back in his mouth or my brother's gonna lose his temper. He's an angry one." Arthur stared on, aloof and inscrutable.

Jessica raised her right hand; Charles clamped his teeth to his wife's pinky; her long fingernail settled against the tip of his tongue. His cheek smarted where the bottle had struck him, and his entire face stung with the heat of his embarrassment. He felt his wife's heartbeat within the soft flesh of her fingertip—it was as quick as his own.

"What did Burt's prick look like?"

"I don't know. I didn't look at it."

"Afraid, huh? You one of them that just lies there, eyes shut, feet to the ceiling and takes it like cough syrup?" He looked at Charles and said, "Sorry." He returned his gaze to Jessica. "So you just lie there with your eyes closed, huh? Maybe a buncha fellows was on top of you, takin' turns and you didn't even know it?"

"It was just him."

"What did Burt's prick feel like? Bigger than Mr. Lowell here's? Got a lot of veins or hair?"

Charles felt his wife's fingernail dig into his tongue and realized an instant later it was because he had unconsciously bitten her again. Jessica winced and shut her eyes.

"Stop biting your wife, Mr. Lowell. She don't much like savages."

The talker looked at the Arizonians pointedly.

Charles, embarrassed, nodded minutely and, with ungracious, finger-obfuscated enunciation, said, "We understand your point."

"Good. But that don't mean you learned your lesson." The talker turned to his brother. Arthur shook his head; the arc of his chin traversed only an eighth of an inch, but the gesture twisted Charles's stomach into a knot. "He says you ain't learned." To Jessica, the talker said, "Was Burt's prick bigger than the one dangling between Mr. Lowell's legs? Don't lie."

Charles (unsuccessfully) attempted to ignore his wife's response.

She said, "I'm not sure. It hurt because it was the first time."

"The next time you done it, it feel good?"

"It didn't hurt as much, though I didn't like copulating with him."

"But would you go back looking for old Burt if your husband got himself killed?"

A silence like winter dawn settled upon the quartet. Charles felt his wife's pulse race through her captive digit. Arthur yawned, saliva glinting upon his swollen gums and the limp stub within. Tears rolled down the cheeks of the Arizonians.

"I plan to spend the rest of my life with Charles."

"So you'll forgive him then?"

"For what?"

The talker punched Charles's chin; his jaw snapped shut; the tip of his wife's pinky and a gout of crimson flavored like copper and honey flooded into his mouth. Jessica shrieked and fell from her seat; Charles vomited upon the table.

The sun-bronzed siblings stood up, guns in their right hands. Jessica's shrieking became hysterical sobbing; Charles wiped bile from his mouth and knelt beside his agonized wife. The shadow of the twins fell upon the Arizonians, but neither looked up at their persecutors. Charles wrapped Jessica's finger with a handkerchief to stop the bleeding and thought about Jesus Christ for the first time since their wedding.

A deep voice with a thick Irish accent said, "It's never hard to locate you boys. Let's go."

"Yessir," the talker responded. Without preamble or delay, the siblings strode from the Arizonians toward the door.

Charles and Jessica looked up. Night had fallen on San Fortunado and against that blue-black sky, beyond the reach of the saloon's oil lanterns, stood a tall, extraordinarily lean man with a curved back wearing a gray suit, a gray hat and a matching scarf tied over his face. Through the tears in Charles's eyes, the man looked like a cane made of smoke.

The siblings exited the saloon and disappeared into the night, but the slender man in gray remained.

He spoke to the Arizonians, his Irish brogue deceptively cloying. "Don't take this to the sheriff."

Charles, emboldened by the absence of his persecutors, heatedly replied, "I certainly will— those men attacked us!"

"You are both alive. Your wife still has her clothes on. Nothing serious happened."

The tall gray shade turned away; Charles opened his mouth to respond.

With her good hand, Jessica squeezed his shoulder and said, "I don't want to be a widow."

Humiliation replaced the anger burning within Charles, but he said nothing. The narrow gray wraith twisted weirdly and was welcomed into obscurity by the night.

Chapter Two

Troublesome Boots and Telegrams

The rancher remembered a time not so very long ago when he could remove his boots without sitting down. Even as recently as his early forties, he was able to place the palm of his left hand upon a wall or a tree or a calm horse for support, twist a leg up at the knee and pull off the lifted boot with his right hand. He currently found that—in addition to forty-seven years—the dexterity and flexibility required to become shoeless while standing was behind him.

The strong, hard man sat upon a flat rock beside the creek and removed his left boot and then his right—a low grunt accompanying each endeavor—and set the pair upright beside him, as if awaiting a spectral inhabitant to step into them. He arched his back, eliciting a dozen cracks like wagon wheels on pebble, and inhaled the moist sweet air that only blew in this dell at the edge of his property line. He removed his socks, set them upon the sun-baked stone to dry and then plunged his callused feet into the running water.

Even though he was not a tall man, within this private sanctuary he was a giant, and the animals of his ranch and his house and his wife and his children were but thoughts. The rancher loved all of these things deeply and thoroughly, but he had lived a very different life for many years and still required time to be a solitary giant, time during which the only world that existed was a simple, wordless place.

He leaned back upon the warm rock and observed the surroundings. The shadows of dragonflies slid across the creek; the water broke in foaming complaints as it struck protuberant stones; the leaves turned in the moist wind, caught sunlight and illuminated like emeralds. The aches in his feet dissolved in the cool water; his face warmed in the golden twilight sun; his back melted into the stone. For an instant, all of his mundane concerns, all of the names he knew and treasured, as well as those he would prefer to forget, were borne away by the wind and he simply was.

Then came a sound that touched the melting giant—a person speaking, calling out. He recognized his wife's voice and a moment later the thing that she was uttering, a thing which solidified and returned him to himself. That thing was his name.

"Oswell," she repeated.

Oswell Danford, the forty-seven-year-old rancher with a wife and two children, sat up, grunting at the exertion. He turned his head on his broad shoulders, wiped the light brown hair from his hazel eyes and scratched an itch in his mustache. (He never had itches when he was the melting giant.)

"Oswell, are you down there?"

It took him a moment to find his voice, as if he had misplaced it in a shirt pocket or the dog had snatched it up and run off with it. Upon the escarpment he saw his wife, the sky purple and gold behind her fine full figure, her red hair and yellow hem pulled east by the western wind.

"I'm down here," he said.

Elinore looked at him, her bright green eyes agleam with the lowering sun, and said, "You received a telegram."

"What'd it say?"

"I didn't read it. I didn't know if you'd want me to, so I brought it out here for you."

One of the seventeen reasons Elinore made such a good wife was that she did not snoop. Another was her Oklahoma accent that sounded like honey to Oswell even after fourteen years of marriage. The thirty-nine-year-old woman's right hand disappeared into the folds of her yellow dress and then produced a small white card that appeared no larger than a tooth from where Oswell sat.

"Where's it from?"

"Montana Territory."

Oswell's guts froze. There was only one person he knew in the Montana Territory, and he had not heard from him in more than sixteen years.

25

"Do you want me to read it to you?"

"I'll come up there and read it." As Oswell pulled on his stiff, sun-baked socks and his warm, sun-softened boots he looked at the dragonflies circling atop the water and had an atypical urge to swat them.

Winded from his climb up the dell, Oswell huffed and then kissed his wife on the mouth. She handed him the white card affixed with cut-out pieces of typeface. He read it.

"I need to get back to fixing supper," Elinore informed him.

"I'll come with you. Rabbit?"

"Yes. And turnips."

Oswell took his wife's hand and they walked in silence toward the wooden gate that marked the perimeter of their Virginia ranch. He saw one brown cow grazing in the distance.

"She's eating again," he remarked.

"You think we should leave her out tonight or get her back in the barn?"

"Let's leave her be. It's not cold and we've got to get some weight on her before those cowboys come on through." He untied the post and swung the log gate wide for his wife; the hinges creaked; the distant cow looked up and assessed the bipedal intruders.

"I've gotta fix that. Scares the girls." Oswell spat upon the top hinge and then the lower one;

he slowly closed the gate. The metal groaned longer and no less loudly than when he had opened it. "I'll oil it tomorrow," he said as he shut and tied the post.

Elinore scrutinized the hinges, shook her head and said, "We might need new ones altogether— I believe they're rusted inside."

"You might be right."

The couple walked up the wide flat field upon which they grazed their cattle, through another gate and then across the wolds upon which seventeen sheep chewed, bleated and considered grass. During this walk, Oswell read the telegram two more times; after his third perusal, he spoke of its contents to his wife.

"I've been invited to a wedding."

"In the Montana Territory?"

"Yeah. James Lingham's."

"I've never heard you mention him before."

He shook his head and said, "I haven't."

"Do you intend to go?"

Oswell did not yet know the answer to the question, and presently, in his silent ruminations on the matter, forgot that it had been asked aloud. The couple approached the house in which they had dwelled for the past eleven years—since the day Elinore quit teaching and gave birth to their first child, Benjamin. They walked toward the side porch, their shadows preceding them onto the wood; Oswell shook his head irritably and muttered something he did not wish his wife to hear.

"I'll tend to supper," Elinore said. She leaned over and kissed her distracted spouse on the cheek, opened the door and entered the house. Oswell stood there, the telegram cradled in his hands like a dead infant. He sat heavily upon one of the two rocking chairs and read it again.

MR O W DANFORD
13 CUTTER WAY HARRISFIELD VA=

DEAR OSWELL
I AM TO WED BEATRICE JEFFRIES ON 12 AUGUST
PLEASE JOIN US AT CEREMONY
ALL OLD ACQUAINTANCES WILL BE IN ATTENDANCE=

J LINGHAM
TRAILSPUR, MONTANA TERR

Though the pasted words were of a uniform typeface, the phrase "all old acquaintances" seemed printed in far darker ink. There was nothing he wanted to do less than travel to the Montana Territory and witness this ghost from his past get married—but there was a reason the invitation had been sent.

"You got the telegram, I see."

Godfrey hitched up the warped rawhide belt that waged an internecine struggle with his potbelly; he climbed onto the porch, the rolled cigarette in his mouth not yet alight. Oswell saw a similar telegram clutched in his older brother's right hand and nodded.

"Yeah. I got it," the rancher said.

The beefy man sat in the adjacent rocking chair, adjusted his denims and said, "Should we inquire what he meant by the phrase 'all old acquaintances'?"

Oswell looked at the window behind him. Elinore cleaned a rabbit in the kitchen and then quartered it. The sound of the knife impacting the wood was silenced by the glass.

"She can't hear us," Godfrey said as he struck a match and lit his cigarette, rocking his chair forward as if the flame might escape him.

"You know what Lingham meant," Oswell said. "You know who he meant. He wouldn't have invited us otherwise. I didn't invite him to my wedding, and you didn't invite him to yours."

Godfrey scratched his red and silver beard, drew thoughtfully upon his cigarette as if it might contain wisdom and said, "Do you suppose that he could have been coerced into contacting us?"

"I hadn't considered that." Oswell brooded upon his older brother's suspicion and shook his head. "Nah. Lingham wouldn't."

"The Lingham we knew wouldn't, but we don't

know this one—it's been decades. We're all different than we were."

"You are fatter, that's for certain."

"You always call me fat when I've outsmarted you."

"Lingham was solid. I don't think he'd be part of a trap, no matter what. I can't reconcile that suspicion with him." Oswell turned and through the window watched his wife quarter an onion. To his brother's reflection in the glass, he said, "You're like Ma that way, always suspicious. The way she made the butcher weigh the meat before he charged her and then again after, to make sure he didn't sneak any for himself."

"You think we should go? Travel across the whole damn country and get tangled up in this old mess?"

Oswell turned from the window and looked at his brother directly, "I don't think we've got a choice."

Two small figures strode up the dirt road, excitedly discussing some subject, but the distance dissolved their words into unintelligible squawks by the time they reached the ears of Oswell and Godfrey.

The rancher continued, "It's our mess as much as Lingham's—or maybe more. And even if you're right, even if he was coerced into contacting us, the man who coerced him is alive and likely knows where we live. Better to meet him out there." Oswell glanced pointedly at his children coming up the road; Godfrey looked at his approaching niece and nephew and nodded.

In a quiet voice, the plump man said, "All these years, I prayed that he was dead."

"So did I. Lingham and Dicky said the same prayer, I bet."

"Do you think Dicky will go?"

"I don't know. He wasn't one for responsibility, but he's no coward."

The children walked closer to the house, the words "not" and "hogs," "licorice" and "penny" dimly audible to Oswell. Even from this distance, it was clear that they were his children.

Godfrey asked, "You've still got our gear?"

"Buried beneath the porch." The children, a skinny brown-haired boy of eleven and a chubby redheaded girl of nine with freckles and a smile, reached the edge of the Danford property. "I put it down there when I built this place." The brothers watched the children approach the house.

In a quiet voice that begat a coiled serpent of smoke Godfrey said, "You better dig it up."

Chapter Three

He Knows How to Talk to Ladies:
He Read the Dictionary Thrice

As a child, Richard Sterling had hated the nickname Dicky. When he was only three years old, his father had died of tuberculosis, leaving him in a New York City apartment bursting with women: three sisters (Peggy, Sam and Girdy), a mother and her mother. The absence of a male figure and the ubiquity of women had not made young Richard Sterling an especially masculine boy, nor did his delicate, pretty features, which his mother and her mother regularly referred to as "girl-handsome." The nickname Dicky emasculated him further.

The lone male Sterling, with only eleven years behind him, had taken his first job working for a fishmonger on the east side near Park Row; when he came home, fetid with fish oil, pinched by blue crabs, iridescent scales in his black hair from when he scratched himself after handling carp, he looked at his mother and said, "Please call me Richard."

Despite his request, no member of his family (excepting the deceased father) called him Richard. His grandmother died without ever once uttering the name. He resented being infantilized in a family where he and his dead father's bank account provided almost all of the income (two sisters would hem dresses on occasion), and his ire at being saddled with the name Dicky only grew with its longevity.

Contrarily, as a strikingly handsome man of forty-four years, there was no other name he would have preferred over Dicky. No matter what he said to a woman, no matter what promises he made to her, no matter what fantastical shared future he promised her, he could not be wholly accountable: he was a guy named Dicky. Ladies should not take an adult man named Dicky too seriously, and if they did, who should they blame but themselves?

Several women on several different rainy days in several different bars said roughly, "He told me that he had never before been so truly in love with a woman as he was with me, that my voice was the sound he hoped to hear call him to dinner each night and read to him by the fireside. He asked me the size of my ring finger and also which type of caviar I most enjoyed.

"On Thursday, after we . . ." (The women trailed off here, embarrassed, momentarily excited and then ashamed of that brief excitement.) They continued, "On Thursday"—they leaned close and whispered—"afterwards . . . while we laid intertwined, he said that he was going to send his driver and carriage around to pick me up and take me to Connecticut. He intended to introduce me to his family."

"What was the name of this man?"

"Dicky."

Once that name was said, the listeners, the comforting confidants of the disenchanted ladies, began to lose their sympathy. The world of caviar and pearls and diamonds and champagne and dancing gowns and polo fields and Connecticut mansions is not offered to women by a man named Dicky.

With kind voices, the listeners asked, "Did you really believe him? Did you truly believe that he could offer all of that to you?"

The women pondered their confidants' inquiry and realized how silly, how absurd the whole affair was, and soon learned to laugh when they thought of this idyllic fantasy proffered them by a grown man who went by a child's name. There was also the memory of that Thursday, the women thought as heat suffused their tear-stained cheeks, that secret evening about which their future husbands would never know . . .

Dicky liked to think of that memory as his gift.

The casino was Dicky's second-favorite place in the world (although he admitted that "wrapped in the arms and legs of a woman" may not be considered a place by some). Casino attendees were inclined toward thoughtless behavior—

inspired by the free money gained or the hard-earned money lost—and there was always an angle to be played on people willing to take risks.

Wearing a finely-tailored brown three-piece suit, a matching top hat inlaid with silk, loafers, a maroon bow tie and matching gloves, the handsome man strode across the Oriental rugs that protected the burnished wood floor of Callington's over to a roulette table around which were seated two sweaty, plump men, greed like a weird light in their eyes, and the pretty young woman upon whom he had been focused for the time it took him to crack the shells of and slowly chew nine rugose walnuts. Though occasionally a pretty lady did wander into the casino alone, the single woman found in such an establishment was most often a daughter who had been dragged out by her folks (and then abandoned) or somebody's sister that nobody had any idea what to do with. If a fellow brought his wife and did not hate her, she sat near him; if a fellow brought his girlfriend, she sat near him; if a fellow brought both (Dicky saw that twice in Charlotte), he held his wife's hand while he winked suggestively at the other.

"Would you find it an impropriety for me to sit beside you, madam?" The young woman looked up at him; from this distance he could see that she was just north of twenty and unaccustomed to consorting with strange men. Her mouth was a tiny bit slack—her tongue and upper teeth showed in a way that suggested continual befuddlement—but her eyes were not those of a simpleton, which was good: an unintelligent woman knew that everyone else was smarter than she was and consequently mistrusted people. A fairly smart woman who mistook herself for a genius was far easier game.

"You may sit there," she said. Dicky could not yet tell where she was from—he needed to get her to say something more before he could divine her town of origin from her dialect (a skill he had cultivated in the shops of Park Row and later at bars in Louisville). He removed his top hat and purposely let it slip from his fingers onto her lap. A nervous woman would have been startled or perhaps exclaimed, but this woman had only blinked and looked at the dropped item.

"I apologize," he said as his fingers whisked along her thigh and pinched the brim of his fallen hat.

The croupier looked at Dicky and said, "Final wagers please."

"I'll sit this one out, Alabama." (The croupier's accent was a thick proclamation of his state of origin.)

The pretty young woman beside Dicky rearranged her orange skirt, her dark eyes furtively assessing the handsome man now seated on her left while his cologne invaded her nostrils.

The little silver ball hopped and skipped and clicked and leaped as the squares beneath it flickered black and red and black and red and black and red. The porcine fellows leaned toward the spinning wheel as if emanations from their foreheads might alter the sphere's destiny. The pretty young woman watched, but with less interest. Either she was wealthy or she had not wagered substantially on the spin, Dicky presumed.

The wheel slowed, and after a desperate hop, the roulette ball took up its place of residence in black eleven, changed its mind and skipped back to red thirty.

As Alabama said, "Red thirty," the weird light of greed dulled in the eyes of the porcine gentlemen. Dicky looked at the table. The woman had placed her bets upon red and even and was a winner twice over. The croupier stacked progeny upon her half dozen chips and looked at her; with an index finger twice tapping the air, she indicated for him to replace her bet; he nodded. Dicky was about to advise her differently when a hand landed upon his left shoulder so heavily that it raised the opposite one in an inadvertent shrug.

"Your name is Dicky." This was not a question, but an imprecation. The handsome man recognized the enervated, sullen tone and the loathing that roiled deep within it. This was the voice of a cuckolded man or an outraged father.

"My name is Oswell," Dicky said without turning around. He placed a chip upon the green felt and slid it toward the number box; the fingers tightened upon the sinews of his shoulder.

Dicky said, "You've mistaken me for somebody you may touch without consequences." He swatted the man's hand from his shoulder and continued to slide his chip across the green felt, a round blue barge across a tranquil sea of green.

"Turn around, Dicky. I'm not one for games."

"A strange comment to make in a casino. And let me reiterate: my name is Oswell, and I'm playing roulette."

The croupier looked up at the man behind Dicky and said, "Sir, we are about to play. I cannot allow you to disturb my customers. Make a wager or step away from the gaming area." The man sat beside Dicky. He was a tall, broad-shouldered man in his late fifties with a silver beard, white hair, a blue long coat over his striped blue suit, a tall white hat and humorless narrow eyes on either side of an aquiline nose that could cut the air with a sneeze. Dicky's furtive appraisal told him this man was an outraged father (one who originated in Maine).

"You are supposed to remove your hat when seated beside a lady." Dicky motioned to the woman beside him.

The father placed his hat upon the table; the croupier asked for final bets; the father disinterestedly tossed a chip onto the felt; the Alabamian spun the wheel and dropped the silver ball; the sphere danced across a game of checkers with a clacking tattoo. As the ball hopped along the dial, the man from Maine reached into his blue vest and pulled out a folded sheet of paper.

He looked at the pretty woman beside Dicky and asked, "Are you here tonight as a companion of the man seated to your left?"

"I am not."

"Then I would like you to witness this." The hairs on Dicky's neck tingled.

The Alabamian admonished the father with a glare and said, "Quiet."

The father accepted the warning and silently unfolded his paper. Upon it was the drawing of a man's face—Dicky recognized the visage as the one he shaved every morning. The ball hopped along the inner rail. The porcine men leaned forward. The pretty woman glanced at Dicky. The father flattened the illustration with his meaty palms. The roulette wheel slowed. The ball clicked like a slowly dripping faucet.

Dicky stood up and walked away.

Rain poured onto the cobblestone streets of New York City; the only carriages upon the drear avenues were covered ones guided by soggy drivers bearing persons not too troubled by thoughts of an employee catching pneumonia.

Dicky emerged from the doors of Callington's onto a deck protected from the deluge by a two-yard overhang. He stepped beside the door, pressed his back to the wall and waited.

The door shut and summarily reopened; the father burst upon the deck and ran to its edge; he stared out into the rain for his quarry. Dicky rushed him from behind and pushed him into the downpour; the man spun around, his hat falling to the cobblestone; Dicky punched him in the jaw before the rain even had time to flatten the man's wiry white hair.

Standing beneath the cover of the porch, looking at the dazed and wet man, Dicky said, "Do not pursue this."

"She's with child! You lied to her and took advantage of her, and now she's swollen up with your leavings. You're going to do right by her, yessir!"

Dicky did not impregnate women. Even when they requested (or begged) for him to spill his seed deep within their loins, he denied them without exception. (Additionally, he treasured the slow deliberate movements they made when they—with warm, moist towels—slowly wiped the white ichor from their bellies or thighs or buttocks.)

"What is her name?"

The father was aghast; water pooled inside his agape mouth.

He spat the fluid out and yelled, "How many women have you spoiled this way, you wretch?"

"What is her name?"

"The woman you dishonored—my daughter—her name is Candace."

Dicky remembered Candace. She was a brown-haired woman with breasts a fellow needed two hands to hold and a bottom that wore his handprints very well, and she was ten miles from virginity the first time he had wedged himself in between her pale thighs. Apparently, one of her other lovers had been far less careful with his seed than he.

"Candace lied to you. That child is not mine."

Rage flared in the eyes of Candace's father; he reached his hand into his jacket; Dicky threw his right fist into the man's nose; his knuckles cracked the cartilage. The man grunted and stumbled back; tendrils of crimson swung pendulously from his nostrils. Dicky returned to the porch, sheltering himself (and his suit) from the rain; the deluge hissed between the two men like a serpent with limitless lungs.

Candace's father spat blood into the rain that had filled the gaps between cobblestones and the cylinder of his overturned hat. He looked up at Dicky as if awaiting a coup de grâce.

The handsome New Yorker said, "I know why you are upset, but I know for certain that that child is not mine. I can tell you things about your

41

daughter that you would rather not know, but I would like to keep this encounter polite, brief and, most importantly, singular."

As if he had suspected his daughter's wayward nature all along, the man nodded his head and sighed. His blue jacket, now three tones darker with absorbed rain, clung to his heaving chest. His hand came away from his crooked, purpling nose slick with blood.

"Go home."

Dicky reseated himself beside the pretty woman at the roulette table, hiding his bruised knuckle from view. The Alabamian spun the wheel.

The woman looked at Dicky and asked, "What did that gentleman want from you?"

"He is my great-uncle's retainer. He came here to inform me of my inheritance. I just now learned that I own a mansion in Connecticut."

Later that evening, Dicky returned to the brownstone in which he rented a room, the taste of Francine Bouchelle's tongue upon his own, warmly pondering the date they had set for the coming Thursday. He was startled when the clerk—a sullen and ugly young man who must have been related to someone influential—called to him.

"Richard Sterling," he said.

Dicky stopped and turned.

"You have a telegram. Delivered this morning."
There was no person from whom he wanted such
correspondence. No woman from his past
belonged in his present, and he had not been in
touch with his sisters (who now lived in
Connecticut with their husbands) since their
mother had passed away six years ago. With
trepidation, he approached the wooden counter
behind which the surly youth sat as if it were a
fortress.

Dicky asked, "From whom?"

The youth behind his lacquered ramparts said,
"A man named Lingham. Montana Territory."

Dicky's blood ran cold.

He took the proffered telegram and read it as he
walked toward the stairwell on the far side of the
lobby. He pondered the phrase "all old
acquaintances will be in attendance" as he
climbed the steps, passed by German immigrants
on their way to the pantry, put the key in his door,
twisted the lock, walked inside and isolated
himself. He thought about how his dad had died
with only forty-four years behind him and how he
was now exactly that old.

Chapter Four

Conversations with Dirt

Oswell kissed his daughter's forehead, pulled the blanket up to her chin, walked to his son's bed, patted his shoulder, walked to the oil lantern that hung upon a door hook and twisted the key in its base, ushering darkness into the room.

"Have a peaceful slumber."

"Good night, Daddy," Loretta said.

"Good night, Pa," Benjamin said.

The rancher walked into the hall and shut the door behind him, acutely aware of every detail as if he were a bug observing enormous minutiae. Tomorrow morning he would meet Godfrey at the station, take a train north to Pennsylvania, meet Dicky there (the New Yorker had wired him yesterday) and then board the continental rail and ride it to the western horizon, where his past awaited him like a dark room filled with bear traps.

As Oswell traversed the hallway, he found the house unusually still and quiet—perhaps because the unexpected chill that night had caused him to shut the windows, or perhaps because of the heightened awareness he had experienced ever since receiving the telegram. He walked to the sitting room, wherein Elinore, seated upon her mother's divan, repaired one of the quilted blankets that they threw upon the colts in winter. She still had some suds on her shoulder from when she had put the scrub brush to the children two hours earlier.

"Elinore."

"Yes?" She poked a needle into the wool.

"I'm leaving tomorrow morning. I'll be gone a while."

Elinore nodded; she pulled a red thread up through the seam.

"When should I expect you back?"

"A month," he said. He had never been away from her for more than a week in the fourteen years that they had been married.

The redheaded woman's sewing stopped; she stared at the sliver of light imprisoned within the needle and then looked up at her husband, her eyes filled with an apprehension to which she would not give voice.

"Okay," she said.

"I asked Harper to come over and deal with the cowboys when they come for the beeves. I know you're smarter than he is, but it helps to have a man around when you negotiate a price with other men. I told him to listen to you and that your word is final."

"Harper is respectful. And he always gives the kids taffy."

Oswell was pained by how selflessly, how

bravely his wife handled her life being thrown into complete upheaval. He wanted so very, very badly to put his head in her lap and tell her all of the things he had never told her, all of the things that he had done and why he and Godfrey and Dicky had put the entire width of the United States between themselves and those events (and Lingham had skittered all the way north himself).

The rancher knew that his wife would not abandon him if he confessed his misdeeds, but he also knew that she could not love a man who had done all of the things he had done. Their marriage would become a partnership, a loveless agreement in which they ran a ranch and raised two children, an agreement in which she would close her eyes when they made love as she had the first few times (though then it was simply because she was shy). Oswell did not know whether his reticence was a selfish act or a gesture of kindness, but he knew one thing for certain: he was not strong enough to risk the love, the sanctity, the escape and the peace he had found with this woman and this life that they two together had carved.

For a moment, Elinore watched him silently ruminate; she turned her eyes back down to the colt's quilt draped across her lap.

The needle moved again and she said, "There's one thing I need to know, to make this—your leaving—a little easier."

"Ask."

"Is there . . . ?" She paused, considering her words. "Does this trip somehow involve . . . another woman? Someone you knew—someone you were with before me?"

"There's no other woman. You're the only one I've ever said the words to."

Her apprehensions faded; she nodded and said, "Then you take care of what you need to take care of. And be careful."

"I will. I'll see you in bed in a bit."

Oswell kissed his wife on the mouth and walked out of the room; he loathed himself with a violence he had not felt in years.

The moon was a clipped fingernail adrift in a field of cotton, illuminating the rancher and the porch he knelt upon with blue light. Oswell slid the grooved claw of his hammer around a raised nail head, adjusted his grip and pressed his hands forward. With a creak like a fat man sitting upon a wooden cot, the old nail rose from the plank. The rancher put it beside eleven others pulled from the wood and set the hammer down. He dug his fingertips around the six-foot-by-one-foot plank and pulled; the slat came loose, revealing a rectangle of cool opaque midnight cracked by occasional cobwebs.

Oswell placed the plank in the grass, removed the adjacent one, set it aside, took a box of matches from his shirt pocket and struck a phosphorous head on grit. He set the flame to the wick of an oil lantern hung upon the porch post, illuminating the swath of exposed soil two feet below the deck.

The rancher stabbed a trowel into the earth and began to dig. He shoveled the dirt onto the porch in a neat pile so that, when finished, he could replace it beneath the house.

Oswell dug for fifteen minutes, and though he had many doubts about what he was doing, his right hand did not. It inexorably plunged, repositioned and scooped up the soil, ladling it like gravy onto the growing pile to his left. The beads of sweat that dripped from his nose momentarily hosted pinpricks of red and blue light from the lantern and moon before falling into the soil below.

Like the prow of a ship striking a reef, the trowel clunked and halted as it struck wood. He set the tool down and reached into the dirt below the porch with his right hand. His fingertips burrowed into the soil until they lit upon a rope handle. He set his knees, braced his left hand on the opposite side of the rift and dredged up his past.

The crate rose from the dirt, far heavier than he remembered it being when he had put it there more than a decade ago. As the dirt fell from the wood, he grabbed the left handle and, with both hands and a grunt, lifted the heavy burden from the soil and set it upon the porch. Benjamin could fit inside of this box, Oswell thought as he looked at the exhumed relic.

He pried the nails from the soil-dampened lid (they came loose silently) and swung it open upon its hinges. Within was a bundle two feet in diameter and almost four feet long, wrapped in a gray blanket. He set it upon the porch and carefully unrolled it, revealing the sealskin sack that lay within. The familiar smell of fish oil and leather made the home the rancher knelt in front of seem incredibly distant and the past no longer a remote, diaphanous thing.

Oswell's fingers undid the twine and pulled open the mouth of the sack. Upon the gray blanket he slid out its contents: four repeating lever-action rifles (two with bayonets), two big-caliber single-action five-round revolvers, two small-caliber single-action ten-round revolvers, three cartons of rounds (which he would replace with fresh ammunition), a canister of gun oil, a chamois, a bundle of barrel swabs (long and short), two long curved knives and four throwing knives.

The rancher checked over the guns, cleaned and oiled them for two hours: they had aged far less than he. He replaced them in the sack with the other weapons and miscellany, rolled that up in the blanket, placed the bundle in the crate and quietly nailed it shut. He replaced the porch planks and quietly tapped the nails in the extant grooves. (He would hammer a few new bits in tomorrow morning when he was not worried about waking Elinore and the kids.)

Oswell did not want to bring the burden inside his house, but he did. He put the crate in a black trunk and left it near the door; he set his boots on top of it, toes pointing west.

Chapter Five

They Chose to Eat in Silence

Iris O'Connor grew up two miles from the restaurant at which she had worked for a quarter of her twenty-four years. The Railroad Luncheonette was not the finest place one could eat in Philadelphia, but its pork-heavy scrapple enticed two scores of locals to return daily, and its proximity to the station always supplied the place with hungry travelers. Iris (daily) hoped to find a husband in the establishment—ideally, a man from a faraway place to which she had never been—but her only suitors had been fellows with whom she had gone to school who were mean to her while she was changing from an awkward girl into a fetching woman, and she would never forgive them. The O'Connors were all grudge holders, and she carried on that proud tradition.

The establishment was quiet: the customers

had finished their lunches and departed. Iris was stacking plates one atop another in the curve of her right arm when she looked through the window at the red brick train station across the street. Passengers in suits stepped into the afternoon sun; hands went up, soliciting carriages and stagecoaches; men sat upon benches and unfolded newspapers upon the right knees that they had crossed over their left knees like women. The New York train had arrived.

From the somber assemblage strode a man in a brown suit who carried a big valise in each hand. Even from a distance, Iris could tell that he was an extraordinarily handsome fellow.

The waitress hurried to the rear of the restaurant with her burden, pressed through the double-hinged door, raced past the sizzling flattop to the porcelain counter upon which were piled ninety-eight dirty dishes and set down seven more with such speed that a pork-chop bone was catapulted into the cleaning water.

The Negro dishwasher fished out the detritus, his dark hands covered with white suds and said, "This tired nigger got 'nough work. I ain't washin' no pork chop." He tossed the bone into the garbage, indignant.

"Sorry Sulky." Iris turned from the dishwasher, sped back into the dining area, snatched a menu from the wall and approached the man in the brown suit.

"Good afternoon and welcome to the Railroad Luncheonette. Will anyone else be joining you?"

"Yes. I have two associates coming in on the two-thirty."

"Let me take you to a nice private table in the rear."

The man smirked for no discernable reason, took off his maroon hat, nodded politely and followed her as she led him to a quiet corner of the restaurant. He set his two black suitcases down—they seemed very heavy—and sat upon a wicker chair facing the window that admitted a view of the station.

"My name is Iris."

"I am Dicky."

Iris giggled and said, "That's a boy's name."

"I'm eleven. I haven't aged well."

Iris smiled and presented the menu to Dicky. He perused it thoughtfully—the exact same way that her friend's husband (who was a doctor) scrutinized things as if they contained ciphers nobody else could understand.

"People like the scrapple," she suggested.

"I'm not Dutch."

"All sorts of people like our scrapple. And it comes with eggs."

"I will have the scrapple, eggs and a coffee." He returned the menu to her. "I would like the eggs with two colors, if your cook is capable."

"He can do it."

Iris nodded and lingered for a moment, admiring Dicky's clean-shaven face, square chin, girlish lips, drawn cheeks, upturned nose, grinning blue eyes, long lashes and wavy black hair.

"Perhaps you should write down my order."

Iris blushed and said, "It's only three things. I can remember seventeen menu items without writing anything down."

"You should join a circus."

When Iris placed the scrapple, eggs and coffee before Dicky, the man's smile was gone and no more japes leaped from his agile tongue. He stared through the window that faced the train station, at the flood of people who had just arrived on the two-thirty.

"Let me know if you need anything else."

The man's blue eyes did not leave the window when he succinctly replied, "I shall."

Disappointed by the man's change in humor, Iris walked over to an empty table, sat herself down and began folding napkins into little tricornered hats.

The door opened; she looked over at the new arrivals. Two men holding a big black trunk between them entered. One was a rugged, strong man with dirty-blond hair and a mustache; the other was a plump fellow with a red beard upon his cheeks and chin. They wore brown clothing and weathered boots. The trunk they carried looked very heavy.

Dicky rose from his chair; the new arrivals strode toward him. They nodded at each other, but none of them smiled.

The New Yorker said to the heavy one, "You got fat."

"You go to hell."

The brothers set the trunk down; the wooden foundations of the building creaked. Dicky shook the right hand of the strong sibling and then the proffered palm of the heavy one. The three sat around the table and looked at each other for a moment of inscrutable assessment.

Dicky sipped his coffee and broke the silence. "Don't take this personally, but I had hoped never to sit opposite the Danford brothers again in my lifetime."

The plump one said, "I'm not waxing nostalgic looking at you either."

Dicky nodded and said, "Did either of you fellows get married?"

The plump one said, "We both did. Mine left me; Oswell still has his and some fine kids too."

Dicky looked at Oswell and said, "She's a good one?"

"She is."

To the plump one, Dicky said, "Did yours depart because you got fat, or was the weight gain caused by her running off?"

"Don't talk to my brother that way," the strong one warned.

"I was just curious about his transformation."

The strong one looked at Dicky with a gaze that might have been the prelude to a gunfight and said, "I'll knock you down, Dicky. I've done it before."

"But sometimes it went the other way."

The men stared at each other, the strong one with a baleful glare, Dicky with a humorless grin. Iris snatched two menus from the wall and hurried toward the strange reunion, hoping to curtail the fisticuffs that might be one stupid remark away from beginning.

The strong one looked at her and, before she even arrived, said, "We'd appreciate two plates of scrambled eggs, some toast and some bacon."

"Crispy," the plump one requested.

"And two coffees please."

The men ate their meals in silence, paid and left.

Through the window, Iris watched them walk to the train station carrying their heavy luggage like pallbearers. The plump one said something; the men stopped and set their luggage down. The plump one placed his hands upon his thighs, bent over and vomited. Dicky offered him a maroon handkerchief, and the plump man thanked him and wiped his lips and beard clean. He offered the cloth back to Dicky, but the handsome man declined and pointed to the nascent puddle.

The plump man laid the handkerchief upon the slick of vomit, picked up his end of the trunk and—with the strong one and Dicky—departed, leaving the partially-covered mess behind them upon the cobblestone street.

Chapter Six

Old Cards

Dicky frowned at his poor hand—a motley trio and a pair of fives—and looked up from his cards.

He said, "Do you think Lingham might be working an angle on us?"

The low sun pouring in through the train window threw half of Oswell's leathery face into shadow and brightly divined the white hairs that sprouted intermittently amongst the light brown ones.

The rancher did not look up from his hand when he said, "We're playing cards."

"I can do both simultaneously—talk and play cards. Many folks can."

"We're playing cards so we don't have to talk."

"Do you think this is a setup?"

"We'll assess the situation when we get there. There's no use guessing at things out here." The train rattled.

Godfrey laughed, shook his head and said to Dicky, "What's the point of cheating when we're not even playing for stakes?"

"You saw that?"

"I saw it." Godfrey was always the more observant Danford, Dicky thought.

"I am practicing." Dicky pushed aside his napkin to reveal the slit he had earlier cut into the fabric of the tablecloth with the razor he kept in the waist hem of his trousers. He extricated three cards—an ace, a jack and a king—and flipped them into the toss pile.

Godfrey asked, "Are you still a card sharp?"

"When a wealthy fool presents himself to me, I am."

Oswell snorted, slapped his cards down, stood up and grabbed the coat slung over the back of his chair.

"No need to get ornery," Dicky said. "Sit down—I'll play straight."

Without a word, Oswell left the table and walked toward the rear of the cabin. He pulled the door wide and escaped into the rattling roar between cars.

"His kids must adore him," Dicky said to Godfrey.

"He's not like this back home. Quiet, sure, but not so grumpy. It's just . . . well . . . he's got a lot to lose. More than both of us put together."

"You want to play for money?"

"Not unless you front me the stakes and I don't have to repay you."

Dicky gathered the cards, divided the deck in half and shuffled them loudly; he dealt out two hands and asked, "What happened with you and your wife?"

Godfrey looked at his cards far longer than he needed to.

Dicky said, "You don't have to talk about it. I was just trying to pass the time—cards are boring if money and women aren't involved."

The plump man set down a pair of cards and said, "Give me two." Dicky flicked over Godfrey's replacements; the man scooped them up and slid them into his collection.

The elder Danford said, "I talk in my sleep sometimes. Night murmurs. That's why she left."

"Plenty of people talk in their sleep. That is no reason to leave a man. Did you snore as well? Society women find snoring very distasteful."

"I didn't snore. I just talked."

"She does not sound like a very tolerant woman."

"It wasn't so much that I talked, it was what I said."

Dicky's nape prickled and his eyes became hard; his cards dipped, accidentally revealing his hand, yet his focus was elsewhere.

With cold directness, the New Yorker asked, "What did you say?"

"I don't know exactly. But one morning, when

I went into the kitchen, she looked at me . . . differently. She was repulsed and . . . and she was afraid." The memory was clearly a painful one for Godfrey to recount.

He continued, his voice quiet with shame, "We never slept in the same bed together after that. A month later, she left."

"How long ago was that? When did she leave?"

"Ten years next month."

The handsome man relaxed. If Godfrey had explicitly incriminated Dicky and the rest—and had the woman intended to do anything about it—the hammer would have fallen long ago.

The New Yorker surveyed his five cards, tossed three, snatched their replacements, placed them in his hand and said, "What was her name?"

"I'm not telling you that."

Dicky laughed at the suspicious reply and said, "I'm not going after her, I was just curious."

"Just the same, I'd prefer to play it safe. You'd pull the cross off a church steeple if you needed firewood."

"Some have claimed that I am not a devout adherent to the faith of self-sacrifice."

Chapter Seven

It Bled through the Paper

Oswell had not said more than a dozen words to Godfrey and Dicky during the last two days aboard the train. As his ranch and wife and children sank behind him in the east and the thorns of his past rose up before him in the west, he found it harder and harder to make conversation and even more difficult to succumb to sleep. For the first time in seventeen years he put a gun—the single-action ten-shooter—beneath his pillow, but it did not put his mind at ease.

The rancher lay awake in a lower bunk at the rear of the sleeping car while his brother and Dicky and twenty-seven others slept around him. To Oswell, the car felt like a mausoleum peopled by breathing corpses.

After two hours of standing at the precipice of sleep without falling over into its waters, Oswell pulled his coat and trousers from his cubby, clambered quietly out, grabbed his boots from the floor, dressed himself and walked through several darkened passenger cars until he arrived in the partially lit dining car in which three Negroes sat hunched defensively over their dripping food.

"We closed," a colored woman holding a butter-soaked cob of corn said. "We 'ready cleaned up for tomorry breakfast."

"I'm not here to eat. The light in this car is better than in the others. May I sit?"

"Them tables is 'ready set. Don't mess them up none."

"I won't. Thank you, ma'am."

Oswell sat down in a cushioned chair and withdrew an envelope from his jacket. He opened it and extracted ten sheets of paper, an amount which he anticipated would be enough for his task if he did not make too many errors. He withdrew an eight-inch case of lacquered wood decorated with gold-filigree whorls and opened it, revealing an enameled fountain pen. Elinore had given this to him for their tenth wedding anniversary.

"What you got there?" asked the young male Negro seated beside the woman, most likely her son. "That a knife?"

"That's a pen," the woman corrected. She looked at Oswell and asked, "You ain't got to fill it up with ink, does you? With a eye dropper like I see some folks do? That makes a mess no nigger can clean."

"This is the kind that uses a tablet." He twisted the iridium ring at bottom of the pen; it clicked; he slid open the flap on the side of the cylinder and slid the ink cartridge in as if it were a bullet.

He held the pen up for the woman to see; he closed and locked the barrel; it clacked.

"Watch that your writin' don't bleed through none."

"I will."

Oswell pressed the heel of his right palm across the creases in the blank papers and pondered what he was about to do . . . what he was about to set down.

He intended to write "My Dearest Elinore," but his hand wrote only,

Elinore

He looked at her name alone on the blank page and knew that his hand was correct—neither affection nor sentimentality had a place in this letter. This missive should be a clear communication of what had transpired years ago, a catalog of his wrongdoings.

Below the name of his wife, he began to unravel his knotty past with the iridium tip of the fountain pen.

This letter is to be delivered to you if I die in the Montana Territory.

You have never asked me about my life before we met, you are a good wife and respectful of my privacy and moods, but I wanted to give you the choice to learn what

*killed me and so am writing it out for you
now. If you don't want to know, throw this
letter in the fire. This is your decision.*

*I am the man you married, but a long time
ago, I was not a good man. I will not
incriminate the others I rode with, because I
don't have the—*

*Sorry about that, I slipped. I am writing this
on the train and it shakes sometimes.*

*I don't want to incriminate anyone else,
though I will mention a bit about my
childhood with Godfrey so you can see the
whole story.*

Oswell read what he had written; he felt like he
was trapped within a stagecoach that had two
wheels hanging over a cliff edge. He continued
writing.

*I grew up in Pineville, Tennessee, which I
told you a little about, but not much. After my
mom died blind and without any money, the
bank took the house and Godfrey and I didn't
have any place to go. We went to the bank and
asked the manager if he would let us stay in
the house until it was sold and he said no. We
asked for a loan and he said no, he wouldn't
give a loan to two kids—I forgot to write that
I was thirteen and Godfrey fifteen when mom
died. We got angry and then the manager said*

something rude about our mother who was doing what she had to as a poor widow to feed us kids, so I broke his jaw and then Godfrey, who was solid with muscle then, picked him up and threw him against the vault door where he hit his head and cracked his skull.

Godfrey and I were locked in jail while the doctors worked on the manager. They saved him, though he was slower than he was before the injury and walked always veering to the left. We did our time in jail and, in a couple of months, Godfrey and I were run out of town, two outlaws even though we weren't even men yet. I won't write any more about my brother, I just wanted you to see how I got the anger in me when I was young.

Sorry about that smudge, the pen got stuck and I shook it too hard, though mostly it works real fine—it's the one you gave me for our tenth anniversary.

I tried being a cowboy for a while. I mentioned this to you once when I first started courting you, but I just didn't get along too well with those fellows, though I liked the animals. When the cowboys weren't riding or corraling beeves, they played horseshoes and cards and I was never much for games. Or they talked about whores and that was talk I didn't at all like hearing and threw more than a couple of fists over stuff that was said. A cowboy who fights gets his pay withheld an extra week, and the one who started it loses half his pay, and because I was unliked, I was always blamed for starting it whether I did or not. The last time I rode beeves across four states I got into so many brawls that I didn't get any pay at all. It was on this last ride that I met a guy named J.

J was a huge man nearly six and a half feet tall and with fists like two hams. J's pa saw the size of him and from an early age raised him to be a pugilist. Boxing was illegal in the state he came from, so he went with his brothers and pa to New Orleans, where people pay to see fights in a ring. J was so big it took some time to find an opponent that wouldn't make people think of David and Goliath when they were paired up together. The first fellow he fought was a swarmer six inches shorter and fifty pounds lighter. J took the fellow's blows on his arms and they didn't hurt him any. When the man got tired, J threw a big one that cracked the man's nose and eye socket and the poor guy went into shock and died right there. J didn't want to box again after that, but his pa insisted. A couple more times J stood in the ring and took punches, but he never threw any himself other than to back the other guy off.

Pretty soon his pa gave up on him and went

home. J didn't go with him. He took to drinking and working in stables for a couple of years and, eventually, doing some work as a vaquero. The first year I knew him I don't know that I ever saw him sober, but he was a quiet drunk and not at all mean to animals or women the way the cowboys were, so I rode near him and pitched tent with him. Killing that fellow in the ring had made him quiet but he didn't blubber on like some men did about things that can't be changed.

We got jobs with the railroad—cutting trees and swinging sledgehammers and putting down ties for the tracks. We tried to get in with the Oryntals because they never said anything we could understand and I wouldn't get riled listening to them go on, but they wouldn't have us in with them, so we worked with white folks and I got into brawls. The last time I mixed it up with a fellow in the rail gang some others jumped in and so J got involved and broke nine of some fellow's ribs with a sledgehammer. We were fired from the outfit and we never got our pay. I went to the foreman that night with J and we broke his hands, but still we didn't get it. Negroes and Oryntals were doing better than us. I'm not sure if that's how you spell Oryntals.

I was nineteen. We were in Alabama and didn't know where our next meal was coming from. It was getting cold at night and I said we should rob a bank and J said he thought it was a good idea and better than starving or begging. I had two guns I had taken from a cowboy who had threatened to shoot me when I was sleeping, so we had the gear to do it. We didn't plan to shoot any people, just throw a scare into them, do some yelling if we had to, grab the money and get out.

The first bank we robbed, that is exactly what happened. We walked to a small town, figuring the banks there wouldn't have any armed guards like the ones in Mobile did. We covered our faces with scarves and went into the bank, J got the door, the other fellow with us menaced the customers and I went up to the teller and told him what to do.

Oswell wondered if it would be obvious to his wife who "the other fellow" was. He supposed it did not matter as long as Godfrey's name was not written out explicitly in a way that would legally connect him to the crimes.

He pressed the iridium tip to the top of the fourth page and continued scratching away layers.

J and the other fellow and I were calm and easy the whole time we were in there. We left that Podunk bank with more money than we had ever looked at in our entire lives, even though it was not really very much. We camped out in the wastelands between towns because they were looking for us. It was cold but we didn't feel it. A couple of days later we went to another town, bought horses and clothes and more guns and ate three dinners each we were so hungry.

For the first time in my life, I was proud of something I'd done. I imagine that seems strange to you, but all my life I felt like a fellow was digging his spurs into my sides and for once I felt like I'd thrown him from the saddle.

We robbed small banks for t

"That there's bleedin' through the paper. It's gettin' on the tablecloth," the colored woman said to Oswell.

He raised his fountain pen and looked down; he was on the fourth page, which had six more beneath it; the ink was not bleeding through.

"No. That one there," the woman said, pointing to the second page he had written, drying to his left. The blot of ink from when the pen had stuck was soaking through onto the lace tablecloth.

"I'm sorry ma'am." Oswell lifted the paper and set it upon the ground.

"Sorry don't get it clean. Mr. Randolph don't care none about no 'pology and it don't get out no ink stain."

"My name is Oswell Danford. Tell Mr. Randolph I did it. If I've ruined the tablecloth, I'll pay for it."

The two adolescents at the table, who were playing dice at the time, looked over.

"Make him pay," the boy said.

"It cost fifty cents," his sister added.

"No it don't—it's two dollars."

The woman looked at her kids and eyed them angrily.

"You get on back to your dice and keep quiet," she said. "You get a wart for each fib you tell and don't neither of you know what this thing cost." She looked back at Oswell and said, "Tomorry I ask Mr. Randolph what to do. Maybe he goin' to tell us to cut it up for napkins and you won't have to pay nothin' for it."

"Thank you. What's your name?"

"Addy."

"Thank you, Addy."

"I know it was a accident and you a nice man."

Oswell was glad that she could not read the papers she had glanced at.

The woman walked back to her kids; Oswell yawned. He wanted to finish the letter, but he had a lot more to write. He figured that he had better try to get some sleep while he could. With his cramped fingers, he twisted the cap back onto his fountain pen and replaced the enameled tool in the felt bedding of the wooden case. He yawned once more while he waited for the ink to dry, watching Addy's kids throw ivory dice and do computations with their little fingers.

Chapter Eight

The Lord's Coydogs

Beatrice Jeffries walked across the grass toward Jim's home, a small A-frame at the southwestern limit of Trailspur, Montana Territory. Her titan sat upon a small stool near the north side of the house, combing Joseph's fur with a wire brush; the coydog noticed her before he did.

The twenty-nine-year-old woman was not sure whether Jim loved her more than he loved his three pets, but he did love her enough to marry her.

The first time that the six-foot-five-inch-tall blond man had asked her to dance at a church social, she was so surprised by the request that she had said, "No thank you, Mr. Lingham." To that, the tall man had said without arrogance, "I got good feet. C'mon," took her left hand gently in his big palms and pulled her out to the floor.

To her surprise, the titanic man did have abilities as a dancer . . . and was actually quite graceful. However, because he dwarfed the petite woman so substantially, the experience, though agreeable, was like dancing with a twisting redwood. Over time, Beatrice had adjusted: she grew accustomed to tilting her head back whenever she spoke to him, and soon viewed any man under six feet tall as puny.

Jim courted her for a long time before he kissed her, and she later found out that he had actually asked permission from her father to do even that. No matter where she was or what she was doing, the thought of that conversation (at which she was thankfully not present) always made her smile.

He was fairly intelligent for a fellow from Mississippi, and he was as polite as the Englishmen she read about in the periodicals and books her great-aunt sent over from Manchester, England. In fact, Jim was so courteous, he would do practically anything to avoid an argument— even apologize for things that were not his fault (though he would never tolerate anyone maligning her or his coydogs for even a moment).

Beatrice said to her seated titan, "Joseph is looking very handsome today."

"He is now. Got into some mud and had to wash him twice." Joseph's purple-black tongue lolled from the animal's long narrow snout.

"Where are Jesus and Mary?"

"They saw a rabbit this morning. Ain't seen 'em since." He looked at the basket hooked over her right arm. "What's in there?"

"This is a surprise, Mr. Lingham." He accepted the mystery and pulled his brush through Joseph's brindled brown and silver coat. She walked up to her fiancé, leaned over and kissed him; he returned the kiss, though his hands did not leave the coydog. Beatrice patted Joseph's snout, walked up the three steps onto the porch, strode through the slatted door and into the house. The dwelling still smelled like a place where a man lived alone—the odors of socks, boots, dogs, pipes and ashes dominated.

As the door shut behind her, she heard Jim call out, "Jesus! Get your nose outta that!"

Beatrice walked up the hall of the house her fiancé had built by himself for two years, and she recalled the first time she had been introduced to the coydogs. She had questioned the sagacity of the names he had chosen for the animals, but he succinctly and unswervingly defended them. She had gotten used to the supernal allusions over time—even if she did have to regularly explain the choice to others—but still she shuddered when she heard him say things like "Jesus! Mary don't want you back there. Pull that outta her."

She walked up the hallway in which hung individual daguerreotypes of Jesus, Joseph and Mary (the coydogs), one of her and one of her and Jim together (a miniature) in formal attire. She was still outnumbered.

Beatrice's jealousy was small and a source of

amusement and false quibbles more than any real tension between them. The truth was she found his devotion to the coydog trinity a comforting indictor of constancy, his good nature and how he would raise their children.

Still, when she moved in, she intended to rearrange a few things.

Beatrice pulled the apron from her dress, hung it upon a hook and called out to her fiancé. Two coydogs barked in reply, though only Jim entered the house.

"Did you scrape your boots?"

She heard Jim turn back around, open the slatted door, go outside, drag the soles of his boots on the metal bar and reenter.

"Yeah."

"You should get into the habit of doing that. We are going to have Oriental rugs in here."

"I was hopin' for kids."

She swatted his shoulder and said, "With order, we can have both."

He looked at the oven and then over at her and hopefully inquired, "Steak and kidney pie?"

"Did Joseph tell you?"

"I smelled it out myself. No peas?"

"I put carrots instead. You are slobbering."

Jim wiped his mouth, nodded his head in appreciation, threw his limbs around her and squeezed; the sensation was like being hugged by a house. He released her, sat at the table, buttoned up his shirt, tucked a red napkin into his collar and picked up his fork, holding it with the tines facing down as if it were an ice pick. There was work to be done with him for certain . . . but this was a real man, Beatrice thought with an imagined smile.

She put an errant blonde curl behind her right ear, slid her hands into kitchen mittens, opened the cast-iron oven and pulled out the savory golden-brown pie. In the corner of her eye, she saw Jim wipe his mouth a second time.

The petite blonde woman set the food upon the table; the moment her buttocks touched the chair, Jim, his fork still clasped in his left hand, tilted his head down and said, "Thank you Jesus for the food we are about to eat. If there's any left, you're welcome to it. We appreciate all that you did for us back then. Now that's it. Amen."

"Amen." Beatrice had never once elicited angry words from her fiancé, but she had hurt his feelings on several occasions by laughing at his extemporaneous grace. In all instances, she had immediately and genuinely apologized, but the damage had been inflicted. They had eaten the tarnished meal in silence, and afterward he had spent a few hours rambling through the woods with his pets. Once when he had thanked Jesus, Jesus the coydog had barked as if in reply; Jim had not seen the humor in that at all, but instead took it for a sign, which (unfortunately) turned her giggles into far louder cachinnations. After two years, Beatrice had mastered her offensive impropriety; only on rare occasions did she have to bite her tongue to suppress gestating laughter.

The titan opened his eyes and looked at the steak and kidney pie.

He said, "Let's cut off a sizable piece for you before I go in there."

After the meal, Jim put the plates and utensils in the washbasin and slapped his stomach, pleased. He leaned over like a tree falling and kissed his bride-to-be. Beatrice slid her tongue into his mouth; his answered hers for two shared heartbeats. She felt a warmth burgeon within her chest and he withdrew from her.

"Not yet, Bea. Just one more week."

Beatrice nodded, lifted a rag from the soap bucket and went back to the oak table her giant carpenter had shaped with his own tools and hands. Her heart beat fast within her.

"I love you," he said, as he often did at unexpected times.

"I can hardly wait to share the nights with you."

"I been thinkin' of that."

They both paused for a moment as they considered the intertwining they had abstained from for their two-year courtship. Soon there would be no barriers, she thought.

One of the coydogs howled. Beatrice looked over at Jim. He had a lever-action rifle in his hand, something she rarely saw except when he was hunting. His eyes were hard and inscrutable.

The coydog howled again, an awful, plaintive sound.

"That's Mary," she said, recognizing the timbre of the female crossbreed.

"She sounds hurt. I'll go see what got her. You bolt the door behind me."

"You be careful with that," she said, flicking an index finger dripping with soap at the rifle.

He nodded, walked up the hall, went through the slatted door and shut out the night.

"Bolt it," he called from outside the house.

Beatrice walked up the hallway, slid the iron latch and looked through the slats at her fiancé. He crossed through the rectangle of orange light that the lanterns cast through the dining-room window and walked into the darkness; she stared at thick night, her heart hammering. She heard footsteps on the wet grass. Mary whimpered and the males barked. Beatrice's apprehensions grew.

The moon picked Jim out, limned him in blue as he strode across the grass. Mary howled pitiably and then whimpered twice. The other coydogs barked.

"Hush fellas." The males were silent. Mary whimpered. Beatrice watched the blue-edged silhouette that was her fiancé walk toward the coppice at the northern edge of the property; the male coydogs ran to and orbited their master like houseflies, barking, agitated.

Jim stopped, looked at the ground and said, "No." His tone put a heavy lump of dread in Beatrice's stomach; she knew that something was very, very wrong. Mary whimpered and the males barked. Jim knelt down in the grass and again said, "No."

Beatrice grabbed a lit oil lantern, undid the bolt, opened the door and exited the house. She traversed the porch, descended its three steps and walked across the grass; the night dew sparkled like a constellation upon the blades and dampened the hem of her vanilla dress.

Jim, a half dozen yards away from her, looked up and said, "Get back inside."

Beatrice stopped, "Is she going to be okay?"

"Get back inside and throw the bolt."

Beatrice looked down; the light of the lantern in her right hand had illuminated the tableau. At Jim's knees, before the sniffing snouts of Joseph and Jesus, lay Mary. The prostrated coydog's hind legs and front right leg were gone. Its lone remaining limb—its front left leg—pawed spastically in the grass, digging trenches while its three stumps waggled uselessly in their sockets. Beatrice thought of a partially-eaten roasted hen and was nauseated.

Jim wiped his eyes on his shirtsleeve; Mary's

lone paw rent the grass and soil. The dog whimpered.

"Get inside," the titan said to Beatrice. "Now."

Beatrice turned away, her hands shaking; beads of sweat chilled her forehead and upper lip. She walked toward the house.

"Run off, you two—scat," he said to Joseph and Jesus; they barked and then ran past Beatrice toward the eastern wolds.

When her left foot hit the second step, she heard Jim say, "Good-bye girl." The moment Beatrice put her hand on the doorknob, a gunshot cracked across the night. Mary was silent.

Jim escorted Beatrice home to her father's house, the repeating rifle clutched in the hand with which he usually held her. He neither spoke nor wanted to be spoken to, but there were too many questions in Beatrice's mind for her to remain silent for the duration of the entire twenty-minute walk.

Once they were upon the central avenue of Trailspur and the sounds of civilization were audible, she asked, "What happened to her? How did she get like that?"

"I don't know," he said.

"If a bear or some other animal did that to her, she would have bled to death."

Jim did not respond.

"A person must have done that to her. It looked

as if her legs had been amputated, like the way a doctor removes gangrenous limbs."

Very quietly he said, "I saw."

"Do you believe that it might have been Indians?"

"I don't want to talk about it right now."

Beatrice, though nervous and agitated, realized the insensitivity of her inquiries and closed her mouth; she hooked her arm through his and walked the rest of the way in silence, allowing him to grieve.

He deposited her on the front step of her father's house; despite her ascension, he still towered over her.

"Get in and bolt it," he said. "And lock the windows. And open the door to your pa's room so he can hear if something happens."

"What are you going to do?"

"Have a look round."

Chapter Nine

No Time for Eggs

Theodore William Jeffries would certainly miss the breakfasts his daughter fixed for him, but as a widower of twenty-nine years, he knew how to scramble an egg and blacken some toast and fry up some sausages. Moreover, it was long past time for that bookish woman to devote herself to something other than reading, writing and the old man who had raised her up.

He walked out of his bedroom rubbing his bad hip, briefly wondering why his door was ajar. He slid his feet into his leather slippers and proceeded down the hall, scratching his side through his blue pajamas.

T.W. inhaled the odiferous emanations that wafted up from the kitchen and was instantly famished. Leaning on the banister far more than he had a decade ago, he descended the stairs. His slippers scuffed across the worn wood of the bottom landing, and hearing his approach, Beatrice turned to him. Her curly blonde hair, blue eyes, chin dimple and shape were so very much like her mother's, he thought. What a tragedy the two of them never knew each other, except in that horrible moment of her birth.

He castigated himself for his morbid ruminations and said, "Good morning."

"Good morning," she replied.

"Smells tasty."

"I shall have it ready in a moment."

"Thank you. Was there any particular reason that you opened my door last night?"

A loud knock precluded her reply.

T.W. recognized the familiar tattoo, turned from the face that might have been a window through three decades and called out loudly, "Is that you, Deputy?"

"It is."

"Do we have an issue?"

"We do."

"Does it trump eggs?"

"Likely."

"Come on in and eat something while I get dressed." He looked at his daughter and said, "Don't let him eat all of it."

"I shan't."

Sheriff T. W. Jeffries, a hand pressed to his aching left hip, hastened up the stairs toward his clothes, boots, badge and gun.

Deputy Goodstead, a twenty-six-year-old Texan in blue with shiny boots and the blank face of a simpleton (though he was not one), chewed the crackling remainder of a piece of toast as he walked up the central avenue of Trailspur beside the sheriff.

"What exactly has this fellow done?" T.W. asked as he slid the tongue of his belt through the brass buckle, wincing as the leather bit into his bad hip.

"Unsettled some folks."

"How so? Has he said anything offensive? Threatened somebody?"

"I don't think so. He draws pictures."

T.W. pulled out his single-action six-shooter, swung the cylinder wide and saw that it was full. He closed it and slid the pistol back into the holster on his right hip.

Straightening his hat, T.W. said, "He draws pictures?"

"That's what Rita said."

"Is this a prank?"

"She wants us to talk to him. He makes her uneasy."

"An illustrator? This doesn't trump eggs."

The two lawmen strode past Delicious Meats, Steinman's Hats, Halcyon Hotel, Fine Tailoring for Ladies (and Men Too), the unnamed blacksmith alley run by a different fellow each month, Ed's Barbershop, Big Abe's Dancehall of Trailspur, Quality Chandler and the Trailspur Apothecary. They neared the raised wooden edifice that sat at the end of the avenue; beneath the overhang, depending from three ropes, was a sign engraved in elaborate script. It read,

JUDGE HIGGINS'S MIGHTY FINE SALOON, OR SIMPLY—THE GAVEL.

The sheriff's eyes narrowed as he gazed upon the beast tied up to the front banister; he glanced at Goodstead, whose blank face had become blanker, and then back toward the creature.

"Deputy. What am I looking at?"

"Could it be a horse?"

"I'm not putting any money on that."

T.W. had seen dead horses in far, far better shape than this sorry steed; the smell of it—a pungent combination of mulch and feces—chased away his morning appetite. On his right, Goodstead closed his slack mouth, which was a rarity, and swallowed dryly.

The lawmen strode up to the horse, cautiously and slowly. Every bone of the beast's body showed through its dirty white coat, the color of which only completed the illusion that this was not a horse, but an erect, living horse skeleton. Flies inched over its ribs and vertebrae; the hairs of its tail and mane were clumped together; its sides were brown and black with scabs from the spurs that had been relentlessly applied; a yellow crust of dried tears ringed its cloudy eyes.

T.W. and Goodstead appraised the awful creature, their left hands clamped over their mouths and noses. The deputy pressed his right palm to the beast's flank.

"Don't," the sheriff yelled.

The beast whipped its head around; Goodstead jumped back; the reins tied to the banister twanged taut; the mare's mouth snapped shut inches from the deputy's nose. The horse pulled on its tether, its cracked brown teeth revealed.

The Texan stepped back from the beast. The cloud of flies startled into flight by the activity settled back to continue their survey of the horse's crenulated hide.

T.W. looked at Goodstead's blank visage and

said, "Don't touch a mistreated horse unless it's got its ears down and comes to you willing."

"I'm a fool."

Goodstead's lack of inflection always made such comments inscrutable, though T.W. would not have deputized the man if he thought he was at all a fool. The Texan was just ignorant of certain things because he was young.

"Let's introduce ourselves to this illustrator," T.W. said. He circumnavigated the maltreated and malefic mare, ascended the five steps that led to the swinging doors of Judge Higgins's Mighty Fine Saloon, or simply—The Gavel, and was joined there by his deputy.

T.W. said quietly, "From the looks of that animal, we're dealing with a mean one." The blank face opposite him nodded.

The deputy put his right palm to his revolver and pulled down the brim of his blue hat with his left, an affectation T.W. did not begrudge the young man. The sheriff threw the doors wide and entered; the doors swung outward and when they returned the deputy came with them.

T.W. looked past the mahogany bar James Lingham had built (behind which Rita stood), past the bagatelle tables that entitled the establishment to the adjective "fine" on the sign outside, past the spittoons (which seemed less fine) at which Jeremiah, Frederick and Isaac sat gestating expectorations and to the general seating area in the back that could support ninety customers, but now held only one small man in a burgundy suit and matching bowler hat. The fellow was hunched forward, drawing on a wide piece of vellum with a fountain pen.

"He's little," Goodstead said.

"Men aren't happy about being small. That horse can tell you."

The lawmen strode past the oldsters (each of whom spit a salutation and nodded politely) and entered the general seating area. The little illustrator in burgundy rolled up the sheet of vellum. T.W. sniffed the air and smelled flowers and wine.

"He's wearing perfume," Goodstead said as they closed the remaining yards.

"Good afternoon," T.W. opened.

The diminutive man looked up from under the rim of his burgundy bowler hat. His eyes were small pebbles; his mouth was a tiny slit beneath the big nose that dominated his face. T.W. was not sure if it was a line of ink or a mustache that paralleled the mouth slit. The sheriff guessed that the man was thirty, but could have been off by a decade either way.

"You have question," the man asked with a thickly accented voice; the inflection made it seem more like a statement than an inquiry.

"Are you a Frenchman?" the sheriff asked.

"Oui."

"Is that your horse outside?"

"She is mine."

"That mare needs a bath and some food."

"Thank you for advice." The little Frenchman stared at T.W., scrutinizing his face. He said nothing more; he just sat there looking up, blinking far less regularly than the lawman did.

"Go take care of that now," T.W. said. "Your mare almost bit the deputy and is mighty unpleasant to look upon. She needs some oats and a bath. And perhaps a new owner."

"And maybe a rifle," Goodstead added.

"Go tend to her," the sheriff ordered.

"She was bad. I teach her lesson."

"How long have you been teaching it to her?"

"Three years."

T.W. wanted to slap the man, but perhaps in his culture there was no consideration for the feelings of animals.

"Go take care of that horse. Now."

"I am busy," the fragrant Frenchman said.

"You don't look busy."

"You have interrupted me."

Goodstead looked at T.W. and said, "Is he telling us to scat?"

"Show us that drawing you rolled up when you saw us coming. I'd like to see what requires your precious time."

"You will not appreciate."

"We don't appreciate your perfume, but we're smelling it just the same."

"Eau de Cologne."

"Was that a threat? Did you just threaten me?" To Goodstead he said, "You heard him threaten me."

"That is untrue," the little man said, coolly.

"Are you saying that I'm not fluent in French?"

"I did not threaten."

"Show us the drawing," T.W. said, putting the palms of his hands upon the table; Goodstead set his left boot upon the chair next to the diminutive Frenchman and leaned forward like a bird of prey.

"You will not appreciate." The little man was not at all rattled by the experience. He unrolled the paper; his little ink-stained fingers clambered across the vellum like the legs of a crab. The lawmen leaned in.

T.W. looked at the drawing, and at first he did not understand what he was looking at—the thousands upon thousands of lines swirled with such density and fluidity that the confluence confused his eyes. Then he realized what he was looking at, snatched it from the table and handed it to Goodstead.

"Have Rita burn that." The deputy nodded, took the vellum from him and carried it toward the bar. "Roll it up before you give it to her. She doesn't need to see it." Goodstead rolled up the illustration as he walked.

T.W. leaned in close to the Frenchman and said, "You ever do anything like that yourself?"

"Burn other man's possessions?"

T.W. wanted to put his fist through the little man, but he stayed his temper.

"What is wrong with you? Why would you draw something like that?"

"I draw many things."

T.W. swept his left leg beneath the chair the little Frenchman sat on, dumping the man to the floor. The toppled foreigner stood up and straightened his jacket.

"Don't bother sitting. Ride out of Trailspur. If I see you again, I'll throw you in jail for being a public nuisance and I'll put down that pitiful horse of yours myself."

"The door is that way," Goodstead said, pointing his left index finger toward the exit, his right palm pressed firmly to the butt of his holstered six-shooter.

The Frenchman put his bowler hat back on his head and, without another word, left the saloon.

"I can still smell him," Goodstead remarked. T.W. nodded.

When T.W. returned to have the late breakfast he had earlier missed, he looked at the biscuits and gravy and the pork chops but saw only the thick black lines of an illustration that detailed a young girl buried up to her neck in the sand, scalp bereft of hair, nails driven into the top of her bald screaming head.

He did not eat.

Chapter Ten

Pickles and Ribbons

Pickles yawned. He was usually asleep by eight o'clock (not much happened at night in Billings, Montana Territory), but tonight his errands had kept him out until ten. He scratched his bushy hair, contemplated what he was going to say before he said it (that helped him talk to white folks), raised his left hand and gently rapped upon the hotel door.

"Who's knockin'?"

Pickles immediately forgot what he had intended to say. He looked at his old boots as though they might have the answers, but they did not. He then thought about how old these boots were (seven years—a third his own age) and how he would like some new ones with rattlesnake skin and pointy toes like the cowboys wore.

"Is that you, you dumb nigger?"

"It's Pickles," he said. "I ain't dumb."

"You get what we sent you for?"

"I got them, yes, though it took a while to find them and I got lost twice."

Pickles heard footsteps within the apartment; the tumblers in the lock squeaked as the key was turned within it.

"I gots to oil that," he reminded himself as he

had the last time he came to this apartment (and the time before that).

The door opened. Before the errand boy stood one of the sun-bronzed twins who tenanted this room: a tall man with oily black hair that fell to his shoulders, a prickly beard, mean eyes and a gun in his right hand more often than not.

The errand boy asked, "You the one that can talk?"

"Come in."

Pickles walked in; the man shut the door and twisted the key in the lock. Seated on the bed was the talker's duplicate, Arthur, a small mandolin without any strings resting in his lap.

Laid out on the three cots Pickles had brought up on Tuesday were the mule skinners who also tenanted this room; beside the youngest one laid a fat woman who had her face pressed down into a pillow and another pillow atop her head (presumably put there to muffle her snoring).

The errand boy did not like a single person that stayed in this suite, but he was polite regardless. Money from a rude man spends just as well as the stuff from nice folks. Pickles glanced furtively at the slumbering woman, hoping to glimpse something pink, but was frustrated by the dingy blanket and dingier fellow that clung to her as if beached on an island.

The talker said, "Don't get any ideas. She ain't goin' with no nigger. Not for any money."

"I was just lookin'. She just layin' there."

"Don't talk back."

"I 'pologize."

There was a gentle knock. The twins pointed their guns at the door; they were quicker than mosquitoes when they aimed their weapons.

"Who's out there?" the talker asked.

"Alphonse."

To Pickles, the talker said, "Let him in," though neither he nor his sibling lowered the barrels of the guns they had pointed at the door.

"Don't shoot me none by accident," Pickles admonished.

The errand boy turned to the door, twisted the key in the lock and opened it wide. The small foreigner in the burgundy suit and bowler cap was back. He walked past Pickles, a roll of papers wedged in his right armpit.

"Shut the door and lock it," the talker said to Pickles. He obeyed. The twins holstered their guns.

To the foreigner, the talker said, "You get a good look at 'em?"

"*Oui.*"

"You drawed 'em all like Quinlan tol' you? James and his fiancée and the sheriff?"

"*Oui.* And deputy. And minister and church."

"They accurate?"

"Very much," Alphonse replied. He handed the bundle of vellum to the talker.

The man unrolled the parchment and looked at an illustration of a pretty white woman with curly blonde hair and an adorable dimple on her chin. The talker showed the illustration to his mute brother.

"James did well for himself, that big oaf," the talker said. Arthur stared at the illustration, his face inscrutable. To Alphonse, the talker said, "She's real beautiful."

"Today," the foreigner replied.

Pickles did not understand the foreigner's answer, but the talker did and nodded.

"Why is nigger here?" Alphonse asked, pointing to—but not looking at—Pickles.

The talker said, "I was goin' to settle him when you come up. Arthur's concerned 'bout him and how he's always lurkin'."

"*Oui.*" Alphonse turned and looked at Pickles.

The errand boy said nervously to the talker, "B-But I got th-them ribbons that you asked for. That's why—that's why I come up here." He pulled a fistful of lavender ribbons with yellow polka dots from his bag and shook the iridescent strips like talismans. "This . . . this is w-what you asked me to fetch. They got the circles on 'em j-j-just l-like—"

The Frenchman jammed a rag into Pickle's mouth and swept his feet out from under him. The floor rushed up, met and smacked the back of his skull; the impact dazed the errand boy. He opened his eyes and looked up. The inside of a bowler cap covered his face; private night enveloped him (one that smelled like hair oil). Cold metal dug into his neck.

The last thing Pickles heard before he bled out was, "Mule. Wrap up that nigger before it shits the floor."

Chapter Eleven

Not Heaven

Dicky sat opposite Godfrey for the fourth and final day of their train trip across the United States. The duo had lost interest in cards a while ago and consequently spent the days drinking, watching the landscape flee.

The train was currently parked beside a water tower; engine men lathed the bellows. Dicky's view was obscured by a blanket of steam blown east by the strong western wind. For a moment, both sides of the car were aglow with roiling bright white exhaust.

"It's like we're flying. Up in the clouds," Godfrey observed.

"Enjoy the view. I'm pretty sure we don't have angels making beds for us in heaven."

"You like jokes."

"That wasn't one."

"You know what they say about clowns."

"Children enjoy their antics?"

The door at the front end of the cabin swung wide and in the billowing steam loomed two triangles. The exhaust dissipated and the shapes resolved into a pair of hoop dresses, one dark green, the other striped blue, each filled out by a fine-looking woman. Dicky's stomach sank as he looked upon the face of the black-haired, blue-eyed woman on the left—it was Allison Bayers.

Godfrey, his back to the door, saw Dicky's reaction, slid his hand under his valise where he kept his ten-shooter and said, "Are we in trouble?"

"No," Dicky said. Upon further inspection, he realized that the woman was not Allison, just a very pretty doppelganger. "I thought I recognized . . . one of the women who just boarded. It is not her."

"Some girl you got drunk and took advantage of?"

"I don't need to get a woman drunk."

Dicky watched the women sit on the opposite side of the passenger cabin; a hunched Negro with gray hair carried two valises over to them. The one who looked like Allison counted out three coins and handed them to the porter, who was so pleased with his tip that he dropped to one knee and genuflected like an English knight and departed singing about sunshine and licorice.

The raven-haired woman set her blue coat upon

the chair opposite her and yawned, covering her mouth with her gloved left hand.

"Don't," Godfrey said to Dicky.

The conductor called out indecipherably; the train lunged forward, glided a few yards, jerked abruptly and then chugged along the steel rails in earnest. With much steadier locomotion than the train's, Dicky traversed the cabin to join the two seated women. The one who looked like Allison from afar looked less like her from the distance of only one yard, but still she was lovely, and the similarity was beyond passing.

"May I sit with you for a moment?"

"My husband probably wouldn't approve of you joining us."

"Don't underestimate him."

The brunette laughed, but the raven-haired focus of his attention did not.

She said simply, "We are not looking for company at this present time. Thank you."

Rebuffed, Dicky tilted his head forward, grinned, said, "Good afternoon," swung back around the car and landed in his seat opposite Godfrey.

The plump man said, "She must have cataracts."

"Matrimonial."

The plains of Iowa undulated outside their window. Little black bugs that were animals to be someday slaughtered or men to be someday

95

buried stood at the edges of prairies, watching the locomotive roar past. The funnel belched exhaust into the blue sky and the steam domes hissed.

Dicky thought of Allison. He remembered her sleepy eyes in the morning, her long cool fingertips on his chest and the kind way she corrected words he mispronounced when he read to her in an effort to improve his powers of elocution. Something burned the edges of his eyes like the bites of fire ants; his vision began to blur.

"You're taking this a lot worse than I expected," Godfrey said. "You could always go for her friend—she's glanced this way a couple of times since the one with black hair dozed off."

"I am thinking about something else."

"You want to talk about her?"

"I do not."

Chapter Twelve

The Idiocy of Guards

Oswell sat in the illuminated dining car, the sheaf of incriminating papers laid in his lap. He glanced at Addy two tables away. The colored woman sewed holes in socks she had pulled from the feet of her two children, both of whom were absent, presumably tucked in their beds within the servants' car. The rancher looked through the window to his left: lumps of west Iowan hills crept by like turtles. The rest of the train was quiet with slumber.

The well of sleep had claimed Oswell the previous evening, but tonight he was wide awake, determined to finish the letter he had thrice contemplated burning. He removed the tablecloth and put down the newspapers Addy had given him in case the ink bled through again. He set his missive atop the old gazette and looked at the unfinished line in the middle of the fourth page.

We robbed small banks for t

Oswell twisted the cap from his fountain pen, pressed the gleaming point to the paper and wrote.

hree years.

He glanced over at Addy as if she might have been able to divine from the pen's scratching what he had written. She paid him no attention. Her eyes were almost entirely closed, and her dark digits carried a needle through worn socks with the precision of pistons. Oswell turned back to the pages in front of him.

With the iridium dagger that tipped his enameled pen, he transformed his misdeeds into curvilinear lines.

J, the other fellow and I didn't get rich, but we lived well, mostly in hotels in the big towns near the small ones we robbed. We moved on after the area was picked clean or if people were suspicious. It seemed like we'd finally figured out what to do with ourselves. If we were smart, we would've put some money in the bank or stashed it somewhere, but we were just happy to eat good meat and buy drinks and have nice guns and horses.

Then there was the first job that we did in Louisiana. We went into a bank with scarves over our faces and guns out. We were always quick when we did this. J got the door, the other fellow shouted at the customers and I showed my gun to the teller. Then some guy said, "I seen you before," to J. J told the guy to shut his mouth and turn around and face the wall. I banged my gun on the wood and thumbed the hammer to hurry the teller, but he was an old fellow and only moved two ways—both of them slow.

The oldster dropped his spectacles, and while he was looking for them, the guy with his face to the wall said to J, "I saw you box in Louisville. You went against my cousin. You just stood there like a idiot taking punches and not doing anything. I know your name too!" and before the fool could say the name, J shoots him in the back, right through his heart, and he falls to his knees and then tips over, dead.

That was the first time any of us ever killed someone in a robbery. A kid started yelling and the other fellow went over and slapped him a few times to shut him up. I got the money from the old man and we ran out of that place and got to our horses. Somebody yelled out, "With God our Vindicator!" and I didn't realize until later why he yelled that— that bag was two-thirds Confederates, which were hardly worth burning by then. We rode out of that town and were different.

Since we had killed somebody, somebody else decided to name us—the Tall Boxer Gang, which was pretty silly since only J was a boxer and tall, and I was the leader, but we couldn't change it. Drawings of us started to circulate in the South, though they didn't really know what we looked like other than that one of us was tall and was a pugilist, so sometimes they drew him wearing boxing gloves and the scarf over his face at the same time. This would have been funny if the reward wasn't more for us dead than alive. We got out of Louisiana and the South altogether and thought about disbanding, but didn't have any more options than we did three years ago, when we began it all.

We went over to Ohio. The first job we did

there went fine, though we didn't make enough to cover expenses for the winter, and that Ohio cold isn't something to go camping in. So we had to go and do another job before long. That next time, the teller pulled a gun he'd hidden under the counter and I shot him in the neck. He died. I didn't feel bad about what I did—I was angry that the fellow was going to kill me over some other fellow's money and cursed him for being a fool. I had no way to get behind the bars and get at the money so we just tore out of there no richer and down one bullet for our effort.

We rode all that day and straight through the next two out of that state and into Pennsylvania. We went into a small Dutch settlement there. We were tired and starving and held up a grocery store and got food and all the money that was in the register. They gave us no trouble and actually seemed to feel sorry for us, which made the other fellow angry so he slapped around some old fellow and then broke his nose with his elbow. We camped a little bit, robbed another store and camped some more. There was never enough liquor for J. When we ran out of liquor for him I had to tie him down for a couple of nights, but he got past it.

I was twenty-five by then and it was getting cold. The three of us went south again to

Kentucky. We were at a bar when this young slick from New York, a fellow named D, came over and sat with us. He bought us each a glass of fancy bourbon. When we were drinking, he let us know that he recognized the Tall Boxer Gang the minute we walked in, but he didn't say it like a threat, he said it like he wanted in, though he had his gun drawn under the table in case we were unfriendly. D set us up in rooms at the hotel (where it turned out he worked) and also introduced us to some women. These were the first girls I did not have to pay for, though you should know that I never said the words to any of them and was always polite. Maybe I shouldn't write about that.

It turned out that D had a Louisville bank he wanted to hold up, but needed a gang like mine to back him. Originally, my gang stayed away from big city banks because we didn't want to go up against the armed men the banks employed, but now that we had a reputation and no qualms about killing a fellow who drew on us, we decided it might be better to go for a big score instead of a bunch of small ones, even if we did have to leave a guard curled up with a bullet in his stomach.

D said that we shouldn't walk around in public with J. He said that by himself J was just a tall man, but with a group of mean-

looking fellows around him, people might wonder if he was the leader of the Tall Boxer Gang. This shows how simple I was back then that I had to have some fellow from New York point this out to me. So J stayed in the hotel room and whittled while D, the other fellow and I took a look at the bank and brought him back food. I didn't let him drink anymore.

On Thursdays the bank closed at one o'clock. Five minutes before they shut down the place, the four of us went in with our faces covered and our guns out. The two guards at the door raised up their hands without delay. J shut the door and locked it, D unfastened the guards' belts and kicked the guns away, the other fellow scared the remaining customers into a corner by yelling at them and I went to the teller.

The teller ran from behind his window into the back and I called after him to stop or I'd kill him. Then I heard a gunshot and turned around and saw the other fellow holding his side—one of the customers drew on him and fired. The other fellow shot back into the crowd and somebody fell to the ground, maybe the one who shot him, maybe not. The guard from the vault (the teller alerted him) ran out from the back and pointed his shotgun at J, but D put two bullets in his head and stopped him.

I ran past the dead guard, through the open door to the back, and D followed behind me with that key he stole from some guy he played cards with two weeks ago—that was whole reason he thought to rob this bank in the first place, I forgot to mention that earlier.

D and I ran for the vault and there's that fool teller waiting for us with a gun, like he's defending his family or something worth sacrificing himself for. I shot him and kicked his body aside. D put the key in the metal door to the vault, twisted it and yanked the handle sideways. There was a lot of money in there.

We loaded up our sacks and went back to the lobby of the bank and rondyvewed with J and the other fellow—he was hurt but could stumble along well enough. One of the guards was sitting in a chair reading a newspaper while his partner smoked a cigarette he rolled while we were cleaning out the vault. I imagine these fellows lost their jobs when the customers told the bank owner about how easily they gave up and decided to read and smoke, but those guards lived and are probably alive right now. We tore out of the bank and to our horses and rode them hard out of town.

It took time to count all of the money we had—it was more than all of the other jobs we'd done added together twice over. But now *the authorities had good likenesses of most of us. They had a drawing of D, probably a local recognized him, and the other fellow's scarf had fallen off when he got shot and he clamped it to the wound to stop the bleeding instead of covering his face back up. And of course J was so tall he always stuck out. It was time for us to cool it for a spell.*

We went to the Arizona Territory where we could be anonymous and live in adobe houses and take to the plains whether it was winter or summer if someone came after us. . . . .

Sorry about that—the train stopped for water.

We went to a town called Nuevo Pueblo and got ourselves adobe houses just beyond the limits and lived there for a while. J started to build things and apprenticed with a carpenter in town. The other fellow almost died from his gunshot wound and his experience made him gentler. He found a girl he liked, but she said no when he asked her to marry him because he wasn't Catholic and didn't speak Spanish. D was restless and didn't care for Mexican girls or even the white ones who lived there. He disappeared for three weeks and we all figured he'd left us, but then he showed up and told us about where he'd been. He did this a few times and was usually off with girls or gambling.

After a year in Nuevo Pueblo we were running out of money and getting on each other's nerves, especially me and D. I was in the saloon drinking one night when I reached into my jacket and found a note. It read, "Meet me with your gang tomorrow night at the north side of Black Cleft if you are interested in a business proposition."

I did plenty of bad and wrong things by the time I was twenty-six, but I had never been involved with wickedness, with evil, until I meet the man that wrote that note.

Oswell realized that he was going to need a lot more paper.

Chapter Thirteen
Sandwich Showdown

Dicky curled his fingers around the straps of his black suitcases, lifted and walked down the shaded stairs of the train into the bright noon sun that shone upon the Billings, Montana Territory, railway station. He set the luggage down on the bleached gravel and summarily rested the meat of his right palm upon the handle of the single-action six-shooter jutting from the corresponding hip.

He eyed the station, a wide one-story building

ten yards from where he stood amidst the rails, but saw nobody of note. He looked at the open door, a rectangle of black from which anyone from his past might emerge . . . though nobody did. He watched the Negro porter who stood on the platform atop a small crate scrape his broom across the support beams of the overhang; cobwebs dripped like milk from the bristles. He glanced at the four windows that faced the tracks, all of which were flung wide to admit a summer wind that was currently dead. He tilted his head back to look at the roof; his heart raced as the image of Quinlan and his posse flashed in his mind like a struck match . . . but nobody was up there. A bird wheeled in the distance, dropped, twisted and then flapped its wings twice to climb to the exact same spot it had moments ago vacated.

Dicky tilted his head forward and then back, a nod so slight that it raised and then dropped the rear brim of his blue hat less than a quarter of an inch from its typical position, parallel with the ground.

Two pairs of boots stepped in unison; the Danford brothers, each on one side of their heavy trunk, strode from the train; they stopped beside the New Yorker. For a space of twenty heartbeats, the three men surveyed the railway station with eyes that glimmered in the shadows of their hats like gems found in cave walls. The continual scrape of the Negro's broom across cobwebbed wood obfuscated all other sounds.

Dicky looked over at the colored man and called out to him, "You there. Would you please stop that racket for a moment?"

"I gots to clean."

"Please pause for a minute."

"I ain't work for you."

"I am planning to buy this station. If you want to keep your job, you better mind your manners."

"I don't believe you," the Negro said, though it was clear that he was not entirely sure what he believed. "I got a itch, anyhow," he added; he climbed off of the crate, sat down, set the broom on his lap and scratched his lower back.

In the nascent quiet, the three men listened. Dicky heard the trot of a lazy horse, a woman call out, a door shut twice, a girl squeal in delight, the name Robert said thrice, each time louder . . . but he heard nothing that alarmed him. He glanced over at Godfrey, who shook his head, and then over at Oswell.

The rancher said, "C'mon."

The three men walked across the stones, boot heels cracking rocks like dusty white knuckles. The trio walked onto the platform, beneath the overhang; the sweat upon Dicky's forehead grew chill the moment he entered the shade. The Negro eyed him sullenly, but said nothing.

Dicky approached the door. He surveyed the

people within the train station: several read newspapers, one ate a large sandwich, one slept on a bench and two children chased after each other, their mother observing them with a frown that was recurrent enough to put wrinkles around her mouth. Dicky and the Danfords stopped just outside of the door and set their luggage down.

To the man eating the sandwich, the New Yorker said, "Excuse me, sir."

The man looked up from the sandwich still jutting from his mouth; a large hunk of ham dangled like a stupid tongue in between the two pieces of seeded pumpernickel. Dicky tightened his grip upon the studded pommel of his revolver; the Danfords were still as trees, their hands at their hips. Two of the oldsters reading newspapers looked up; the mother ran to her children, looking over her shoulder at the trio.

Dicky asked, "Are any men standing at either side of this door or beside any of the open windows? You may nod."

The man shook his head. A drop of mustard dribbled from the ham like slobber.

The three men outside the station door relaxed, picked up their luggage and walked inside. Behind them, Dicky heard the Negro resume his slow and steady scratching of the overhang.

Oswell pointed his left index finger to the front window of the station and said, "Over there." Dicky looked through the glass and in the bottom right corner saw the rear wheel and trunk of a stagecoach.

As the three men walked from the station, one of the oldsters said, "I think Albert is choking on that sandwich."

"Nah," another replied. "He just chew so slow you can't see it happenin' all at once."

"Why does he eat like that for? Makes 'im look like a imbecile."

"He loves to eat, but ain't got much money to buy food with. You should see him wit' a boiled potato—an hour and a half to finish her off."

"It's like some sorta contest."

The sun heated Dicky's face, hat and jacket the moment he stepped into the weedy lawn in front of the station. Fifteen yards off was a stagecoach surmounted by an oldster and a short-haired teenage Indian wearing denims and a formal jacket that, sans dust, might have been worn by a white man to a society event (though his loafers could never be shined into something presentable).

The old man—a spider-shaped fellow who seemed equal parts limb and belly—turned on his coach bench to face the trio and said, "You the ones that wired for a stagecoach up to Trailspur?"

Dicky and the Danfords did not answer; they continued to approach the stagecoach in silence. The Indian leaned forward toward the rider's box.

"Don't," Oswell said.

In the time it took the oldster to blink twice, Dicky dropped his suitcases, drew, thumbed and pointed his gun at the Indian's face. The native stopped.

Oswell, drawing his own gun, said, "Raise your hands, both of you."

The two coachmen complied; their pale palms sat in the blue sky like starfish.

Oswell said, "We don't mean any harm—we just need to check. Open up the coach so we can look inside."

The Indian jumped down—he was an agile brave—and walked to the side door that faced Dicky and the Danfords. With a tattooed hand, he twisted the handle and pulled the door wide. The stagecoach was weathered and threadbare, but empty.

"You satisfied?" the oldster asked, more annoyed than angry.

"For now. But if we get ambushed by a certain party, you two catch the first bullets," the rancher said, holstering his gun.

"Maybe I shouldn't take you, threatenin' me that way."

"It's only a threat if you planned on double-crossing us," Godfrey clarified.

"Well, I'm honest."

"Then let's load up," Godfrey suggested.

The Indian, who had wholly ignored the

argument, checked the four-in-hand brace fitted to the quartet of old steeds.

Dicky said, "Are these horses upset that they're still working while their grandchildren have been put out to pasture?"

"They ain't that old. They canter good. And I'm not renegotiating the price, if that's what you're after."

Dicky placed his suitcases inside the trunk the Indian opened down and said, "We'll pay what we agreed."

"What's the likelihood of coming upon Indians?" Godfrey asked.

"A coin toss, but most of them are peaceable," the old man said, spitting. He pointed to his teenage partner. "And Chawipon knows how to talk to the ornery ones."

"Are we gonna make it to Trailspur by nightfall?"

The old man clambered up to the driver's bench and said, "Certainly not. But we're meeting up with two more coaches headed to Westland and will have their company most of the way to Trailspur. Things are safer in a caravan."

Dicky sat on one of the shabbily upholstered benches within the stagecoach and looked through the window at the mountains on the horizon and the dissolving implications of more peaks beyond those.

"It's pretty country," Godfrey opined.

"It's wild," his brother replied, the remark having neither positive nor negative intonations.

Godfrey looked at Oswell and said, "Do you think Quinlan will come at us before we get there?" The inquiry was followed by a heavy silence. The name that had not been said aloud had now been uttered.

"I don't think so. I think he intends for this to be a showdown at the wedding," Oswell said.

Above and in front of them, on the roof of the stagecoach, Chawipon snapped the reins and the car jerked forward.

The two other stagecoaches were filled with excited Orientals newly arrived from the Far East. As Dicky listened to them chatter, he thought of pigeons pecking at pieces of discarded bread.

He and the Danfords searched the stagecoaches, but found nothing they felt was worrisome. Regardless, the trio insisted that the chattering Orientals ride before them into the open landscape of the Montana Territory.

Chapter Fourteen

Grotesques

I apologize if my handwriting is not as neat as before, but I am writing this in the Montana plains by moonlight and cannot see as clear as on the train. And I can't light a lantern either, because that might attract the Indians, though they are supposedly peaceful ones out here, at least according to the driver.

Let me continue.

So there was that anonymous note I had about a business proposition and I told the fellows about it. We decided to go meet the man who wrote it at Black Cleft.

We rondyvewed the next night, J, D, the other fellow and me. We went to the gorge, walked down and saw a small cave in the cleft wall fifteen feet up from the ground that we walked on. In that raised shelf was an odd tent and beside it was a small fire. We went closer to the tent and saw that it was covered with scalps sewn into the fabric to keep out the desert chill. None of us had ever seen anything like it before and immediately I was uncomfortable. We had our guns out, ready. Then a voice from within the tent said, "Put your guns away," with an Irish accent. "I put stones all around the cleft—if anyone fires, there will be an avalanche and you'll be crushed." We looked up at the edges of the gorge and saw dozens of big stones hanging there—dragged into position and held back by branches and smaller stones that had ropes on them so they could be pulled loose. That was how Quinlan was—always thinking ahead of other fellows.

So we put our guns away and he came out of the tent into the firelight, standing on that shelf fifteen feet above us. Quinlan was almost as tall as J, but skinnier than a sick woman. His eyes were different colors—one was blue, the other green—and sunken deep in his face. He had long wavy red hair that receded to the middle of his head and brown splotches like burn marks across his cheeks. His teeth were crooked and yellow. I'm telling you all this because I have no idea what he might do after he's killed me. You should tell Sheriff Waterson to be on the lookout for a fellow of that description and shoot him on sight no matter what he says.

So Quinlan said, "I need you boys to break three of my men out of jail. They got caught in Santa Fuerte and are to be hanged on Saturday." I asked him what his men did. "They shot up a saloon and then beat the sheriff and his deputy to death with wine bottles."

I looked at J, D and the other fellow and saw that none of us felt good about this situation. I said, "Why would we want to help these brigands?"

Quinlan sat upon the ledge of his shelf and dangled his long legs down. The fire that lit him from the side made his skin look as red as his hair.

He took out an Indian knife, pointed it at us and said, "I have a business scheme that earns money, very big money for any who ride with me. I need these fellows out of jail to do it. If you rescue them, I'll include you too."

I said, "We're supposed to believe you without any more information than that?" But Quinlan didn't say anything, he just sat there, waiting. Even though he didn't tell us more, something about the way he spoke, we all believed him—this was a man who did what he said he would do.

The other fellow said, "How many guards are at this jail?"

Quinlan said, "Usually two. I don't care if you kill them as long as you get my men out of there."

I clarified that we didn't shoot a man unless he drew on us. To that, Quinlan said nothing.

Oswell stood up from the stone he had been sitting on and arched his back, eliciting a string of minute pops. He saw that he had some ink on his right hand and rubbed some spit and dirt on the stain to no avail.

The rancher glanced over at the three stagecoaches, from which emanated the alien snores of Orientals. The vehicles were lined in a row against a sheer cliff wall for protection. The Indian stood guard, rifle in hand, eyes alert.

Oswell sat back down and pressed his fountain pen to the paper laid atop the wooden plank he used as a desk. He resumed writing.

We went to Santa Fuerte, which was a few hours ride from Nuevo Pueblo. D and I cased the jail and saw that there were two guards, just like Quinlan said—an anxious teenager and an older fellow who looked sad, probably a relative of one of the victims.

D and I rondyvewd with J and the other fellow and went over the plan. We would hit late at night, when these men were slow with sleep.

There was one last discussion in our group as to whether or not we should get involved with this jailbreak and Quinlan. J was worried what business scheme a man like Quinlan would involve us in, especially since he rode with brutal murderers, which even though we'd killed people, we didn't consider ourselves (though I now see that the distinction is pretty thin). We decided to do it, though J never really said yes, he just didn't say no. He was thinking of going legitimate as a carpenter and was getting religious.

Long after midnight, we went to the jail. D knocked on the door, saying there'd been a shooting, and the younger one opened the door to find a gun in his face. The other fellow and I stormed in, guns pointed at the older guard, who raised his hands like we told him. He then told us he didn't have the keys. I asked him where the keys were and he said the deputy— the one who wasn't killed—had them at his house. This was starting to get complicated.

D and I took the older guard and had him lead us to the deputy's home, which was a fair distance away. Outside the deputy's home I looked at the old guard and told him what to say and what I'd do to him if he didn't follow the plan. D and I hid on either side of the door, pressed flat in the shadows. The old guard knocked and after a minute the deputy's wife came to the door. He told her he needed the keys because the prisoners had a scuffle and one got his arm broken in half and was screaming crazy. The deputy arrived, yawning, and said he'd go over and help deal with the prisoners. After he shut the door, I put a gun in his back and said, "Walk." D, who had his gun pressed to the old guard, followed behind.

We got to the jail and put handcuffs and gags on the old guard and the deputy like J had already done to the teenage guard. D took the keys from the deputy's belt and he and I went to the back of the jail and opened the door leading to the cells.

D and I saw the men we were about to break out of jail—a big fat fellow with blond hair who looked like an overgrown toddler and a swarthy pair of identical twins who looked like reptiles. I could tell that D was having his doubts too, but we opened the cells and let these men out. They didn't thank us or anything. They just walked into the main area and went into the drawers to fetch their guns.

We put the deputy and guards in the empty cells and locked them up. We left the jail and got to our horses—we had picked up a few extra for the fugitives—and rode out of Santa Fuerte without any problems.

We rondyvewd with Quinlan at my house in Nuevo Pueblo. The Irishman looked at the fugitives with an unfriendly gaze and said, "Don't do that again," and the twins and the big toddler (who was probably my age) nodded and turned their heads down like whipped children.

There were eight of us then, which Quinlan thought was just enough to pull off his plot.

We ate and went to sleep and the next day rode out to Indian country.

There was a tribe of Indians in southwest Arizona called the Appanuqi, and of all the Indians in the West, they were the most feared. When white men first moved into that land, the Appanuqi did not attack isolated coaches or stragglers—they swept down and raided the settlements. They killed most of the settlers, but always left a few alive, usually boys and girls, who they blinded with torches. When these children returned to the fringes of civilization, blind and sometimes mute, other people weren't quick to follow the trails of their wagon wheels. Also, the Appanuqi traveled with grotesques for entertainment, Mexicans, other types of Indians and white people they had reshaped with doctoring and stoning and torture. The Appanuqis fought the other Indians and amongst themselves and were disappearing because of it. Not much else was known about these Indians because they did not ever speak to white men.

So when Quinlan told us that we were going to an Appanuqi settlement, the Tall Boxer Gang reined in. The other four pulled their steeds around and looked at us and at our hands.

I asked why any sane fellow would go there and Quinlan said, "The toddler can speak

Appanuqi." D asked how he learned that. Quinlan answered, "He captured one two years ago. It took a few months, but he forced the words out of him with a hammer." It was then that I knew for certain we'd made a huge mistake throwing in with these men, and I saw it in the eyes of my fellows too. Just the same, we knew there'd be a gunfight if we backed away from this deal and the twins looked as fast as any of us on the draw, probably faster.

"So he can speak Appanuqi," I said, wanting to know more.

Quinlan went on, "We are going to take over a tribe I've been marking for half a year. Intimidate them and get them under our heels." He explained how he intended to do that, which was mean business. The other fellow asked him what would happen if the Appanuqi didn't go along with the scheme or if they just came at us straight away.

Quinlan said, "We have enough firepower to put a third of them down before reloading and I have plenty of grenades to finish off the rest. As long as nobody hesitates, we are in no danger." He said this last bit to my gang, as if we might be squeamish.

I mentioned to you once right after Benjamin was born that my father was killed by Indians, so you can figure I didn't object to putting some down—especially savages like these—but I knew I couldn't bring myself to shoot a child or a woman no matter what race they were or what was happening. I kept these thoughts to myself.

We rode far. The sun had set and I heard some coyotes on the wind. J talked about buying a house and getting some dogs someday, but he was nervous and didn't believe what he was saying. D, the other fellow and I were silent.

We made camp and huddled around a pit fire to make it less visible from high vantage points. Everyone kept their guns on while they chewed beans and dried beef and peanuts. The only ones who talked were the twins to each other, and I soon realized I shouldn't listen to their stories because I would get into a brawl that would probably turn into a shootout.

When the moon was halfway up the sky, Quinlan said, "It's time to conduct our interview." He pulled a strap with eight grenades over his shoulder and gave the twins two more with just as many. We climbed onto our horses and rode southwest toward a ridge of mountains.

That ride was three hours, but it felt like a week. Our horses clumb the slope, their hooves getting louder and louder as the slope got steeper and steeper. Soon that clopping *was the only sound I heard. We went up the incline, at the edge of which hung the half moon, then on its way down. When we reached the edge of the escarpment, we looked into a huge gorge. Two dozen fires burned in the settlement down below, which was by a small pond. Seventy wigwams were arranged in a large circle around a central building that was round and made of stacked flat stones. The curving wall of this structure was decorated with white pebbles, which— when I got closer—I saw were human skulls.*

Quinlan told us that he had counted two hundred and thirty Appanuqi in this settlement, which was made up of mostly warriors—the closer to white men they got, the more braves in a settlement, it seemed. A few of them sat by the fire, but most were asleep in their wigwams.

We rode down a steep switchback trail they had carved in the side of the gorge. As we descended, they starting calling out to each other. The toddler told us that they were saying "Eight white men," and some were saying "Breakfast rides in." The Appanuqi were also cannibals. Quinlan lit the cigar in his mouth, as did the twins.

By the time we reached the bottom a score of braves had gathered to meet us, hatchets out. Quinlan and the twins lit the fuses of three grenades with their cigars and lobbed them into the group—the metal balls exploded the moment they hit the ground, they timed it so perfectly. Nine Indians lay dead and six more lay dying in the dirt, their faces half blown off, their sides blackened, some limbs gone and shrapnel burning in their guts.

Quinlan looked at the toddler and said, "Tell them we want to speak to the chief." The toddler called out the words in Appanuqi.

More braves came out of wigwams, and I was thankful that I saw no women or children. J looked ill, D was covered with sweat and the other fellow clenched his teeth like he did when he was angry. A dozen braves gathered on our right to charge in, but the twins lobbed two more grenades that exploded the moment they were at shoulder level and blew off most of their heads. Most of them died instantly, but a few fell to the ground shrieking from exposed skulls. It was horrible.

D saw two Indians raise spears and I saw one with a strange bow. We put bullets in their hearts and dropped them. In the silence after those shots, none of the Appanuqi moved.

To the toddler, Quinlan said, "Tell them to send the chief out now or we'll kill every last brave and sodomize the women." The toddler called out in Appanuqi and the Indians looked amongst themselves, unsure what to do. A voice called out from the round building of flat stones and the Indians dropped to their knees and tilted their heads as if God had spoken. An Indian with a headdress made out of at least twenty bird skulls and clothing made from bear fur walked outside through the fabric door of the building. This was the chief. He held a leash attached to a Mexican with curved legs and a lumpy head who walked beside him on all fours like a pet. The Mexican's jaw was wrecked and wouldn't shut and his tongue hung out like a dog's and all of his fingers were missing. This was one of the grotesques we had heard about and it was very hard to look upon him.

The chief walked up and I saw that he was about fifty, but still strong and full of fire. He had snake spines woven into his long hair and a tattoo of a bird upon his forehead.

He looked at the toddler and said some angry words, though he did not yell, but before the toddler translated, Quinlan said, "Tell him to look at me when he talks. I am the leader." The toddler translated Quinlan's words and the chief filled up with anger like a kettle with bubbles on the fire, but he looked over at Quinlan and repeated himself.

Quinlan said, "Tell him to kneel when he addresses me," which we all knew was going to create some real trouble. J, D, the other fellow and I drew our guns; the twins dropped down from their horses. The toddler translated.

Seven braves rushed us. I put down two, D put down three and J and the other fellow each dropped one. We were scared and there was no hesitation at all from any of us.

The twins walked over to the chief. The moment he dropped his leash, the Mexican grotesque scrambled off. The twins broke a couple of the chief's ribs and his nose and then stepped back. Quinlan told the toddler to tell the chief to kneel again and this time the man did. The cowed Indian looked up at Quinlan and asked a question, something with less pride and fire than whatever he had said before.

The toddler translated, " 'What do you want of the Appanuqi?' "

"Tell him that they all must obey me. I am the new chief." The toddler translated Quinlan's demand. The chief gaped in horror. The Appanuqi nearby looked fearfully at their leader.

The chief spoke his reply. The toddler translated, " 'I am the chief.' "

Quinlan reached to the side of his saddle, where he'd hung a burlap bag earlier that day. I didn't know what was in it. He tossed it to the ground in front of the chief. One of the twins pointed his gun at the chief's head, the other one untied the bag and emptied it on the ground right in front of him. It was two pounds of horse dung. The chief began to shake as he filled up with rage.

"Tell him to eat all of that," Quinlan said to the toddler. The toddler translated. The chief started to get up, but the nearest twin pistol-whipped him three times on the ear until blood was running out.

"Eat," Quinlan said, and that didn't need to be translated. The chief put his hands in the dung and pulled up some and put it in his mouth. He gagged, but he did not vomit. The Appanuqi grew somber as they watched their god-chief desecrate himself this way for ten minutes. He ate the whole thing and I couldn't watch, nor could any of my men. He didn't vomit, which only made it worse.

Quinlan said, "Ask him who the chief is." The toddler asked in Appanuqi and the chief bowed to Quinlan in response.

"Tell your tribesmen that they must listen to me." The chief looked at his people with tears in his eyes and spoke. The toddler nodded his verification that the chief had spoken true.

That was how we got more than two hundred Appanuqi under our heels. It was the first part of the plan Quinlan had plotted but hadn't yet explained to us in full. He said if things went well from there on out, there would be no more killings, just earnings with very little in the way of personal risk. It seemed we had already done the hard part and though the Tall Boxer Gang considered leaving Quinlan after that terrible night, it would be foolish to pass up easy money after what we already went through to get it. That was what we thought, anyhow.

The next day we marched the whole tribe out of their settlement and went back east and a little to the north. If an Indian dawdled or acted up, the twins were there like gnats, throwing fists into them, giving black eyes, busted lips and broken noses to the offenders. Once they shot a brave who fought back and then urinated on his body in front of the rest. The twins seemed to enjoy doing stuff like this.

We pushed the Indians hard—they were on foot and we were up on horses—so that by the time we made camp late that day they were beat. We let them rest and also eat some of the meat they brought with them. They ate wolves and snakes mainly, though we did see some human parts in there too.

We were in a gorge about two miles from a town called Vaca Vieja, a place where people were getting into copper mining, something that would pay off big once the railway finally got there. These long-term investors were the richest kind of men, since they don't need anything and all they do is sit around and gamble and go to brothels and watch themselves get fatter. So there was a lot of money in that town, but it wasn't centralized in a bank, because it was just a bunch of rich investors staking their claims, hiring workers and setting up operations and also some tradesmen doing their own business. It seemed that nobody could rob a place like this, but Quinlan had figured out a way. Though most Irishmen I'd known drank a lot, Quinlan didn't ever—he just sat around thinking, which I guess is when these schemes came to him.

That night we led the Appanuqi to an open plain near the town. Quinlan told the chief to make the Indians do a war dance and beat their drums and holler like devils. The Appanuqi cavorted and yelled and yipped liked wild animals, and the streets of Vaca Vieja got empty real quick. After the dance we led the Indians back to the gorge.

The next morning, Quinlan and I left the other six to watch the Indians and we rode into Vaca Vieja. More buildings were being made than currently stood completed and men from the East walked around the town in suits with all sorts of flaps and unnecessary stuff dangling down. There were about three hundred people there total. Quinlan and I found the deputy and told him that we needed to speak to the mayor, quick. The deputy asked what for and we told him it was about those Appanuqi. He didn't delay after that.

The mayor was a small nervous fellow with a red face and a runny nose. Quinlan said to him, "We've been tracking those Indians since they massacred a caravan. What did they do out on that plain last night?"

"They made fires and danced crazy, yipping wild, beating drums and calling out blasphemies."

Quinlan shook his head solemnly and looked at me and I did the same, playing along. Quinlan then looked at the mayor (the fellow seemed about to cry) and said, "The Appanuqi have marked Vaca Vieja for purging."

The mayor went white as milk and asked what could be done—should he evacuate the town, or something like that. He was an Eastern tenderfoot and had never seen any real trouble in his life, it was clear. Quinlan said, "If you take to the plains, that'll make it even easier for them to slaughter you all."

"But we can't defend against a tribe of Appanuqis," the mayor said.

Quinlan told him, "I know how to drive

them off, I've done it before." The mayor's face lit up like a child's. Quinlan went on, "But it's a great risk to me and my posse." The mayor, so excited about salvation, said that the town would pay us whatever we thought fair. Quinlan said, "You'll pay us one hundred thousand now and another hundred after we send them running." The mayor had not expected such a large sum to be named and his mouth hung open for a bit before he asked if it could be less. "No," Quinlan said. "That's what it costs for us to turn them. Last time I lost seven men."

"Good men," I added for effect. And so the mayor called a meeting, got us the money and paid us the half up front.

So that night we playacted just what you'd expect—the Indians came out of the plains and at the town making so much noise nobody could hear anything and then we rode out of the town toward them, shooting in the air. We knocked some down and the twins killed a dozen, but they turned and ran back into the plains as soon as the toddler told them to scat.

We went back and collected the rest of our fee. That first time, everything went smoothly and we were treated like heroes. We divvied the spoils evenly. Quinlan was fair about it even though it was his scheme.

The thing with a plot like this is that once

the word spreads about it, it gets spoiled, so we needed to do it a few times fast to take full advantage of it. We rode the Appanuqis hard the very next day and got to a town where they did their war dance for the setup. Quinlan and I rode in the next morning and spoke to the mayor using the same lines as before and the fellow went for it, though he was a tougher man and the town was poorer so he could only give us half as much.

We pushed to another town the next day called Rope's End and the Indians were exhausted beyond telling and starting to act up and behave ornery. One came at me while I was eating and I shot him down. The twins shot holes into a couple of others who'd been making trouble and then kicked around the bodies for a bit. But the big thing was that the chief killed himself in some way we never figured out, his eyes wide open and a grin frozen on his face.

After the chief died, the tribe was different. They had that look in their eyes, that empty look like when a man has decided he's better off feeding the worms than doing any more living. D and I pointed this out to Quinlan, but the Irishman had no interest in deviating from his plan.

That night, when the Appanuqis did the war dance for the setup of our plot, it gave me chills. They beat the drums harder and louder than before and then they began to scrape their own faces with their fingernails until they were bleeding and had shreds of skin hanging down. I swear I heard a deep voice come out of that ceremony that didn't come from any man or woman, though I couldn't tell you where it did come from.

Then the Appanuqi started slapping and punching each other, getting angrier and angrier and more wild, all the while shrieking and moaning and dancing to the drums. They picked up rocks and caved in the heads of the dozen grotesques and then began to howl in unison. And then they turned to the town of Rope's End and ran directly for it, shrieking, their faces ripped up and their tomahawks out. I knew that they were going to slaughter the whole town for real.

"We've gotta stop them," I said to my men, who were beside me. We exchanged a look that said everything about how bad it was and what we had to do. We drew our guns on Quinlan and his crew, who had not seen it coming.

The Irishman did not loose his temper but stared at me calmly. "You're gonna help stop them," I said to him, but he shook his head. "Then give me those grenades," I said, waving my gun at his nose. He did and so did the twins. J and the other fellow tied them up so they wouldn't shoot us in the backs. We left them there and rode into town to do what we could.

The first thing I see when I get to the edge of Rope's End is a brave pulling the scalp from a fourteen-year-old girl. I shoot him in the head and he drops next to her. She is crying and still alive, part of her scalp still attached to her head like a tent flap. I vomit so violently tears filled my eyes, but I keep riding in, shooting Appanuqis and throwing grenades when I see a bunch of them, but since they are so scattered, a grenade isn't much better than a bullet and I am no expert with them like Quinlan and the twins. J, D and the other fellow do the same, taking down Indians, but those devils are everywhere and it is hell.

After ten minutes I can no longer tell the screams of the savages from my own. At some point, J gets knocked out and takes an arrow, so he sees less than the rest of us do. I almost shoot the other fellow by accident and I can see the madness in his eyes that's begging me to do it and end it all for him right then. D is sobbing hysterically the whole time we are defending Rope's End and I'd never once seen him cry before, no matter what.

I am sorry about the drops on the paper, I

hope you can still read through the smudges.

Houses are burning and screams are coming from all directions and the smell of burning corpses is the only smell. I run into a saloon where four Appanuqis are biting pieces off of a screaming woman's leg whose head they have covered with a spittoon. I shoot them down, but not before she bleeds out. I go out and see a teenage boy shoot a brave and then have his face split down the middle by a tomahawk so that his brain shows.

We tried to put them down, but the Appanuqis won. The townsfolk of Rope's End were massacred. Sixty or seventy Indians survived and ran back up to where we'd left Quinlan and his crew tied up. D, the other fellow and I found J, put him on a horse, and rode out the other way.

We disbanded right after that. We just wanted to get far, far way from the evil we'd been involved in. For the next two years I did a lot of drinking and thought of killing myself plenty, but I didn't for some reason and when I met you I felt you were the reason, which I still think when I ponder you and the kids.

We had thought Quinlan and the twins and the toddler were killed by the Appanuqi, but the telegram I got from J said otherwise. Quinlan never knew anything but our first names, but as I've said before, he's smart and could've figured things out somehow. You can see why I think there's a fair chance I might be killed in the Montana Territory and also why I had to go out and meet the danger, rather than let it follow me home.

I have just reread the whole thing. I know Catholics like to go and confess their sins and it makes them feel better to get it all out, but not so with me, I don't feel any better having written all of this down. I suppose the real reason I went and wrote this is that I want you to move on with your life now that I'm dead and I figured it might be easier for you to take a new husband if you knew about what I'd done. I hope you and the kids have happy lives.

Oswell

Chapter Fifteen

Arrival of the Best Men

Beatrice looked at herself in the mirror, admiring her sky blue wedding gown and the way its whorls of lace and white silk filigree conformed to her buxom figure. The sixty-six-year-old tailor took a step away from her and nodded his head in approbation.

"You look beautiful, dear. Just beautiful."

"Thank you. You have matched it to my shape perfectly."

"To be truthful, there weren't that many alterations that had to be made on it. You have the same figure as your mother—almost exactly. I just needed to open up a couple of areas to better receive your . . . ripe bounty."

"If you weren't older than my father, I might interpret that comment as a lustful one."

"Don't underestimate oldsters—we're bursting with young lust our spouses don't appreciate. Why do you think I got into tailoring in the first place? It definitely wasn't to hem men's pants."

Beatrice swatted the old man's right shoulder, eliciting a look of pure delight upon his face.

The brass bell hanging beside the door rang, and she and the tailor looked over to see who had entered. Viola, a twenty-two-year-old brunette from Louisiana who worked in the town's lone brothel, shut the door and looked at Beatrice.

"That's a real pretty dress. You gettin' married in it?"

"I am. On Sunday."

"If I got married they wouldn't allow me to say them vows in no blue dress."

Beatrice pitied the girl—who she doubted could even read—and replied equitably, "Purity may be a state of mind as well as stricture for the body. If you want to wear blue on your day, you should."

Viola scratched the tip of her button nose and nodded; she looked over at the tailor and asked, "Did you fix up my garters yet?"

"I believe so. But you'd better try them on in front of me so that we may both be sure."

Beatrice left the tailor, carrying her paper-wrapped wedding dress in both arms as if it were a boneless child. She placed the ceremonial gown in her room, upon the bed, looked at it for a moment and then walked downstairs, where her father and Deputy Goodstead were finishing their coffees.

"Goodstead wanted you to know that if James runs out on you, he'll be right there to take his place."

Beatrice looked at the blank-faced Texan and said, "Thank you."

Goodstead nodded politely, his face inscrutable.

Her father nudged him and said in a loud whisper, "Go on fella, it's your last chance to win her love. Show her that Texans don't at all know when to quit."

Goodstead dunked a corner of toast into his coffee, put it into the horizontal aperture that was his mouth, chewed, swallowed and said, "I know the vows. Just in case."

Her father laughed, clapped a hand on his back and said, "That's the way to smear mud on yourself."

Beatrice remembered the many times that Goodstead had tried to court her. He was fairly nice looking, and despite his perpetually blank visage, not unintelligent, but he was so dull that he stayed on duty even on his days off because he had so little else of interest in his life. (Unlike Jim, who was always building things, studying the Bible or fussing over his pets.)

She asked, "Have you learned anything more about that Frenchman who cut up Jim's coydog?"

Her father said, "Nope. He hasn't been back since we ran him out of town."

"We're not positive it was him that did that," Goodstead added.

"He did it," her father said.

Goodstead remarked, "You make swift convictions, T.W. Maybe you should move on up to judge. I'll be sheriff."

"What would Judge Higgins do?"

"Become my deputy."

"Why would he do that?"

"I'd be a pretty compelling sheriff."

"Good-bye," Beatrice said, kissing her father on the cheek and nodding at Goodstead. She knew they could keep nonsensical talk like that turning for hours, and she had things to do.

"I don't even get a handshake?"

Beatrice extended her right hand and the Texan took it and shook it.

He said, "Give my regards to that old man you are about to marry. Say it loud, so he can hear."

When the bride-to-be was two hundred yards from James Lingham's property line, she heard the sound of his hammer pounding nails and knew exactly where he would be. She adjusted the basket on her arm, circumnavigated his house and crept upon the laboring carpenter. Jesus and Joseph saw her approach, but did not bother to remark upon it to their owner, which she wondered if she should find comforting or insulting.

"Mary's mausoleum is coming along nicely," she said.

"Thanks Bea," Jim replied. He set his hammer down beside the little building he had toiled over for the last three days, in which he would soon deposit Mary's body. At night, while they had discussed details of the wedding, he had whittled sticks into miniature pillars and carved wood to resemble blocks of stone.

The giant man stood from his work stool, walked over to her, blotted out the sky and kissed her on the mouth; she was not sure if the salt she tasted on his lips was from sweat or tears.

"It looks just like a Grecian temple," she said, though was still unsure why he had chosen a Greek motif as the basis of his coydog's mausoleum.

"It's pretty close."

"Let's go over the vows again."

"I got it perfect last time."

"You got the words out, but you faltered a bit in a few places."

"You went and changed the vows, is why. I know the regular stuff everyone says, but you went and got fancy."

"Once more." She paused and looked deeply into his eyes. "Please."

"I can't never say no to you when you ask it like that." He clapped his hands together, arched his back and let out a terrific sigh. Her giant leaned over, curled his left arm across her shoulders and his right arm around the backs of her knees and scooped her up from the ground; her boots lifted into the air as her head dropped down. She was suspended in his arms as if in a hammock. He leaned down and kissed her on the lips.

"Let's go an' get pretend married again."

She felt like a dizzy child as the huge man carried her across the grass toward the house they would soon share.

Beatrice and Jim, holding hands, sat across from each other at the kitchen table; the titan was stiff and anxious.

"You do not need to be nervous," she said.

Jim cleared his throat and remarked, "I feel like maybe He's listening. To see if we're good enough to give His blessing to. Or maybe He's getting sick of us saying His name for practice and won't bother with the actual weddin'."

"James Lingham!" She only said his name like that when he was on a bad path.

He shut his mouth.

"Shall we?"

He nodded.

Beatrice closed her eyes, tilted her head forward in obeisance and said, "I, Beatrice Roberta Jeffries, daughter of Theodore William Jeffries and Lucinda Millington Jeffries, stand before the Lord, my family and friends on this, the twelfth day of August, eighteen eighty-eight, to join the man opposite me, James Jacob Lingham, in holy matrimony. To this one man, I pledge myself fully and unswervingly: my heart, my soul and my body are his. I ask that the Lord sanctify this pledge and accept us into His bosom for all eternity so that we may shine together in His glory in heaven."

Beatrice opened her eyes and saw that Jim was no longer looking at her; he was staring through the window. If he was watching those damn coydogs, she was not going to be very happy.

She turned her head from him and looked through the glass. Three men walked up the hill, directly toward the house. They were far off, but she could see that all of them had luggage—two carried a quite sizable trunk between them. She looked back at Jim and for a second saw a face she did not at all recognize. There was a little anger there, which she almost never saw, and more than a hint of dread.

"Who are they?"

"It's those fellows I invited. The ones I used to ride beeves with."

"You do not seem pleased to see them."

"I hated being a cowpuncher."

She glanced back through the window and watched the men draw nearer. The two bearing the trunk looked similar, though one was heavy and had a red beard while the other was very strong and sun weathered and wore a mustache. The third man walked beside the heavy one and was extraordinarily good-looking, though too feminine and swarthy for her particular tastes. Perhaps he was an Italian or a Greek or a Jew.

"They do not appear to be very happy."

"They're probably tired. They came across the whole country to get here." Jim's quick response made Beatrice uncomfortable. He was answering a question to which he did not know the answer, which was contrary to his normal way of simply waiting to learn the truth. He was agitated, for certain.

"Why are they each wearing two guns?"

Jim's eyes did not leave the approaching trio when he responded, "They don't know what to expect out here in the West."

"One gun per person is usually enough for a wedding."

Jim did not laugh. He stood up from the table and glanced at her, though she could tell that he did not at all see her, so distant were his thoughts.

"Let me introduce you to the fellas."

She stood up, put her arm through his, walked alongside him up the hall, traversed the porch, descended the steps and walked on the grass toward the visitors, using three strides to match his two. To Beatrice, Jim's past was a remote and diaphanous thing, something in which he ostensibly had no current interest. She knew that his father and brothers were mean (not one had accepted or even replied to the wedding invitations she sent out, which said plenty), and that he had been a pugilist and a cowboy and afterward had spent a lot of years alone with dogs before he finally came to Trailspur. That was almost all of the history he had shared; it seemed largely unpleasant and she had not attempted to prise more from his lips (despite her natural curiosity). These three men were the only people from his former life that she had ever even seen.

Jim raised his right hand in salutation. The strong one waved back. The heavy one nodded. The handsome one looked at her in a way that was not entirely appropriate.

"Welcome to Trailspur," Jim said.

"Thank you," the handsome one said. The others nodded.

"I'd like to introduce you to my fiancée. This is Beatrice. Beatrice, that's Oswell, his brother Godfrey, and that one is Dicky," he said, pointing as he spoke. "These are the fellows I rode beeves with."

Oswell shook her hand; Godfrey shook her hand; Dicky, holding two suitcases, bowed his head.

"Let's get it inside," Oswell said to Jim. There was something behind those words she did not like.

"That's a good idea," her titan replied.

"Pardon me ma'am," Dicky said. Beatrice looked at him. "How many people are waiting for us inside that house?"

Beatrice was confused by the question.

"Nobody is inside," she said.

"You are positive?" Dicky asked, a pleasant grin on his face. She nodded that she was.

"Ain't nobody in there," Jim said brusquely.

Dicky eyed the house momentarily, looked back to Jim and said, "Lingham. Would you please carry this bag? My right hand would appreciate some freedom."

Jim took a suitcase from Dicky; the Easterner stretched his finely manicured fingers and then rested the meat of his palm upon the revolver handle jutting from his right hip; the gesture alarmed Beatrice.

"Do not worry, my dear. My hand just likes sitting there."

"You must be exhausted from your journey. Please, follow me inside," Beatrice said, and turned toward the house. She led the four men up the three steps, across the porch and through the slatted door into the front hallway. Dicky continued past her and examined the main living area; he turned back and exchanged a look with the brothers that was too fast to interpret.

"Where should we set our stuff down?" Oswell asked Beatrice.

Did they intend to stay here through the wedding? she wondered with some apprehension. Had Jim not told them that guests in from far-off places were recommended to Halcyon Hotel? She considered herself a hospitable woman, but she would not abide these men in her home on her wedding night—that time belonged to her and Jim alone.

"You should place your luggage over there," she said, pointing beside the sofa and puzzling at the situation.

Before she could ask for the visitors' itinerary, Jim turned to her and said, "I'm gonna show 'em the property. Could you fix up something to eat?"

"Would you gentlemen like steaks with onions, biscuits and some sugar parsnips?"

"I certainly would," Godfrey said.

"Don't trouble yourself overly, ma'am. I know from experience how hectic it gets before a wedding—especially for the bride," Oswell said deferentially.

It was not at all surprising to Beatrice that the most polite one was married, though he did not wear a ring for some reason.

She said, "Why did your wife not accompany you?"

There was a momentary hesitation before he said, "She doesn't sit trains very well. And we got kids too."

Beatrice nodded, accepting—if not fully believing—his excuse.

"We'll be back in an hour," Jim said; he leaned over and kissed her.

"That's fine."

The men turned away from her and filed out of the house, oddly silent and joyless, for reunited friends. Their eight boots made the wood creak like old trees in a heavy wind.

Jim closed the slatted door and from outside said, "Throw the bolt, Bea."

Chapter Sixteen

Invitations

Lingham had done very well for himself by catching that sharp, pretty woman, Dicky thought as the Tall Boxer Gang descended three steps from the porch onto the grass. She was at least fifteen years his junior (her hair and face still retained the gloss of youth), and she was obviously a lot smarter than Jim, but likely his quiet ways and life experience evened out that discrepancy to some extent.

Oswell said, "She's pretty. And nice."

"I got lucky," the tall man said and then pointed to the side of the house; the quartet moved in that direction in silence. Two brindled dogs came running out of the woods, their snouts and paws so dirty they looked covered in fudge.

"Jesus! Joseph! What filth you been diggin' in?"

"Did you actually name them Jesus and Joseph?" Dicky asked.

"I did."

"How does the Lord feel about that honor?"

"I say those names with love in my heart every single day. I think He appreciates it."

"Any of the neighbors have a Judas? Watch out for that one."

"Shut up," Oswell barked.

They continued around the house and deeper into the property; the dogs trotted obediently beside Lingham.

Godfrey remarked, "They look like coyotes."

"They're coydogs. Half coyote and half dog. Their mothers are coyotes. If it's the other way around, where the dog is the mother, they call 'em dogotes."

"You are making this up," Dicky said.

Godfrey scratched Jesus on the top of its head and the coydog rolled out its long pink tongue. Lingham looked at his house, which was now more than fifty yards away, and reached into the back left pocket of his denims. He withdrew a folded note and handed it to Oswell.

The rancher unfolded the paper as he walked, read its contents and handed it to Dicky. The New Yorker read the handwritten script.

I'm coming to your wedding. I will be settling accounts with you and those you rode with, and will take innocent lives if they are not present or if you cancel the ceremony. I will see you all in church on 12 August.

Quinlan

Dicky felt a chill prickle his nape; he handed the paper to Godfrey.

Oswell asked, "When did you get that note?"

"Three weeks ago. I reached into my pocket one night and it was there. I can't figure how he tracked me down—he never knew our full names or anything."

"He probably figured out that we were the Tall Boxer Gang, even though we never told him," Godfrey theorized. "So he knew that your name was James and that at one time you were a pugilist. Some towns keep records on matches—he might've gotten it from those."

"But how did he find me up here?"

"How many wedding invitations and announcements did you send out?" Dicky asked.

"Near two hundred."

The New Yorker bit back the insult that came to his lips.

Godfrey nodded and said, "People like to talk about weddings, so figure each person who was invited told another ten or twenty folks. In a short while, two or three thousand people all across the country knew your name and where you lived. Quinlan probably had a reward out for information on you and eventually someone who heard about the wedding collected that reward."

Lingham did not say anything for several strides; he just looked at his feet and his coydogs.

Quietly, he admitted, "I thought he was dead. I wasn't thinkin' about him and . . . and back then no more. I got a woman who—" Lingham's voice cracked and he stopped. His big hands and his lower lip trembled; his wan eyes coruscated in the late day sun.

Oswell walked over to Lingham, put his left hand on the big man's back and patted him a couple of times as if he were a huge child with something caught in his throat. Dicky and Godfrey paused, surveying the landscape.

"I thought he was dead," Lingham repeated.

"We all did," Oswell replied.

"We all hoped," Dicky corrected.

"Doesn't really matter much how it happened," Oswell said. "He's comin' and we know why." They resumed walking away from the house, toward the woods. "Any other things happen since then we should know about?"

"One of my coydogs—Mary—was taken and . . . she was carved up. Three of her legs were amputated, done like in surgery so she'd survive, and then she got dumped on my property with just the one leg kicking out, howling in agony. Had to put her down."

Dicky felt the muscles in his neck and shoulders tighten; the violence was no longer a distant thing.

"Beatrice's father ran some small Frenchman out of town the next mornin'—the fella was drawing nasty things and treated his horse badly. Her father thinks the little guy cut up Mary for certain."

"Probably works for Quinlan," Godfrey said.

Dicky asked, "Who is Beatrice's father?"

"He's the sheriff."

Dicky and Godfrey exchanged another look of concern; the New Yorker said, "And I thought naming the dog Jesus was a foolhardy move."

"I've been a good Christian for a long time now."

"A long time is not the same as always."

The four men reached the coppice and entered it, walking upon a trail that wound between cottonwoods and maples.

Dicky watched medallions of golden sunlight flit across hats and shoulders and asked, "Where are you taking us?"

"A place I like to go when I want to be alone and think."

"I got one of those at my ranch, in a dell nearby," Oswell remarked.

Surrounded by thick trees that obfuscated the open plains of Montana, Dicky felt safer as well . . . as if the branches and leaves would contain their words from the listening winds and the watching sky.

"I don't at all know what to do," Lingham said as shadows slid across his face.

Godfrey asked, "How much does your woman know?"

"She doesn't."

"What kind of sheriff is her pa?"

"He's solid. Keeps things orderly and knows when to draw. He's put down a few in his life."

"Have you considered bringing him and his men in on this?" Dicky and Oswell looked back at Godfrey as if he had just announced that he were, in fact, a woman.

The plump man raised his hands defensively and explained, "I'm not suggesting that Lingham tell the sheriff anything he doesn't need to know. He tells him he got a threatening letter from some fellow from his past who's got a black grudge against him. Dicky could scribble something good and convincing, I'm sure. Then we'd have the law on our side."

"I think that's a very likely way to get this sheriff and some deputies killed," Oswell said. "We're not involving any innocent people in this—it's our fight. It's what we wrought. We take care of it ourselves."

Lingham said, "We can't go to T.W. If he figured out who we were, he wouldn't hesitate to throw us in jail—maybe even hang us. He ain't the kind to make exceptions." In a quieter, embarrassed voice he added, "And he knows I used to box. I didn't think to hide that from him before."

"We're not involving the law," Dicky said, knowing that would forever close the topic of going to the law or involving others.

Lingham asked, "You think he'll make a play for us before the wedding? Quinlan?"

Oswell answered, "We should be ready for it,

but no, I don't think so. He wants to do this publicly, a showdown at the ceremony. And Quinlan don't like to deviate from his plans."

"So we're gonna have a gunfight at my wedding? With innocent folks in the middle?"

"We've got to get prepared so it doesn't happen like that," Oswell said.

Lingham asked, "How can we do that?"

"Let's visit your church and size it up."

The four men reached a small creek, the water of which was as clear as glass; two iridescent fish glided by, seemingly suspended in midair. Beside the creek were flat stones covered with lichens; Lingham sat upon one, interlaced his fingers behind his head and leaned back until he was horizontal. Oswell stretched out on the rock beside him. Godfrey knelt beside the water, cupped his hands and drew some to his mouth to drink. Dicky leaned against a tree.

"You think he's gonna get us?" Lingham asked. Nobody responded to the question; the few bugs in the area departed on buzzing wings. Two birds cawed in the distance.

"You have crows out here," Godfrey remarked.

"They're usually quiet."

Chapter Seventeen

From Their Cocoons

"We've got to find you a new wife. Or at least, someone else's daughter you can borrow," Deputy Goodstead said to T.W. as he coaxed him up the moonlit avenue toward Judge Higgins's Mighty Fine Saloon, or simply—The Gavel.

"She's not even married off yet."

"Two days. That's not a lot of time to find a lady who can make two-color eggs."

"Beatrice spent a lot of time away studying, and I was perfectly capable of cooking for myself. Scrambled eggs are fine by me."

"You got a deputy to think about."

The two men strode up the street toward the raised edifice that was the Gavel, from which emanated yipping, whistling and a chipper piano melody detuned into something more somber by the intervening wind. Goodstead straightened the yellow kerchief around his neck and clapped his hands to T.W.'s shoulders to scare off the dust that had settled upon the older man's beige jacket.

"You worn this since the war?"

"Just because we're off duty, doesn't mean you can belittle me."

"That'd be the case if we were both off duty." He pointed to the deputy star pinned to his own kerchief. "I'm on duty and can talk to civilians like you with the impunity of the law."

"You don't even know what that word means."

"I do."

"And you certainly can't pin a deputy star on a yellow kerchief."

"Well, I done it."

"Why'd you put it there?"

"I didn't want to put a hole in this pretty jacket. It might upset some folks."

"If you're on duty, you can't drink," the sheriff reminded him.

"I'll take it off when I get thirsty. I prefer bagatelles to drinking anyhow."

They reached the steps, ascended and before they reached the doors were struck by a forceful gale of laughter.

"That's people happy. Don't let it scare you." The Texan pushed open the right swinging door for the sheriff (despite his blank-faced sarcasm, he was always polite) and motioned for the older man to enter.

The minute T.W. set his boots upon the carpet of the saloon, his ears rang the way they only did when he walked into a trap. Goodstead strode beside him and pointed to a table set apart from the gamblers and bagatelles at which sat a lone woman.

The Texan announced, "The Widow Evertson is waiting."

155

"You walked me into an ambush. I thought I could trust you."

"Never discount what a man will do for two-color eggs. And she's pretty besides."

"That's not the point," T.W. grumbled.

"We all know how and where her husband died. Seems like the best possible way to end it."

"I'm not ready to go under."

The Widow Evertson raised her right hand and waved at T.W.; he waved back amicably and nodded his head. A firm Texas hand pressed upon his spine and urged him forward.

T.W. muttered, "The next time Mr. and Mrs. Scalanacci are having an argument, I'm sending you to break it up." Goodstead did not reply, but just strode inexorably, pressing the sheriff before him like a shield.

The Widow Evertson watched the sheriff's coerced approach. The ash-blonde widow's raised cheekbones, strong jaw, upturned nose and high forehead were all telltales of her blue-blood origins back East, and her immaculate, iridescent silver dress woven with bright white lace made T.W. feel like he wore pauper's rags by comparison. He presumed that she was about eight or nine years his junior—not quite fifty. Even though his deceased wife had English heritage and relations, she had been born and raised in Colorado and was relatable . . . but the Widow Evertson was a lady in the West, not a lady of the West, and he had no idea what to say to her.

"Pretty dress," was the first thing that came to him as he sat in the chair opposite her, removing his beige derby, setting it upon his lap, placing it upon the table and then resting it upon a vacant chair to his right.

Goodstead said, "That's a good place for your hat. If he's havin' trouble with his victuals, you can burp him." The comment elicited a blush of embarrassment on T.W.'s face; the deputy strode off toward the bagatelles.

The widow had a smirk on her face.

T.W. said to her, "So you like expensive things?"

She examined him for a moment; he had no idea what she was thinking.

She said, "I want to offer my congratulations to you. I have seen your daughter and Mr. Lingham around town and they appear to be a very fine couple. You must be extraordinarily happy for her."

"I was worried that she was too choosy, but James is a fine fellow and a good Christian."

"I see him in church whenever I choose to go."

T.W. found the remark a bit haughty and said, "I don't see you there often."

"Is that a criticism?"

T.W. looked at his derby in the chair beside him—he knew this was going poorly. He shook his head and then looked back at the widow.

"It's an observation. Usually people go to church more often after they've lost someone close like you did. I certainly went more when my wife died. I felt it was the best way I could talk to her."

"I was and am of a different thinking. The Lord took a part of me I miss daily. That piece should suffice until I ascend myself."

"The sermons can be inspiring."

"Your derby espouses more profundities than Minister Caulding." That particular holy man had not spoken in the town church in two years—she really had been remiss in attending services, T.W. thought.

"Caulding wasn't so inspirational, but we've got a new one now. A very smart fellow, Minister Reginald Bachs. When he speaks of the Passion, it's like you are right there watching it, it's so vivid. My scalp tingles every time the thorns come down."

"It sounds very entertaining."

T.W. suppressed the ire that her condescending remark elicited and said, "Would you like something to drink? Wine? The red kind?"

"That would be nice." T.W. stretched his right hand out and garnered Rita's attention. He placed an order for a glass of red wine and a frothy beer.

T.W. asked, "So what do you do with your days?"

"I write verse and paint, though since my

husband's passing, butterfly collecting has superseded all of my other interests."

"How does that happen, exactly?"

"Are you asking how butterflies can be captured?"

"I am."

"There are nets especially constructed to extract them from the air."

"Where do you find butterflies?"

"I go wherever they feed."

"Do they eat bugs? Little ones?"

The Widow Evertson laughed at T.W.'s remark and shook her head. There was nothing remotely pleasant about her cachinnation.

She replied, "They drink nectar with their proboscises. To locate them, one only has to locate the flowers they most prefer in the correct climes and shading. I have found several other enthusiasts in the Territory who know of such places."

"You go there and swat at them with these nets?"

"You do not 'swat at them'—procuring a butterfly is a delicate art. That is why the nets are of a very fine fabric that tapers to gradually envelop the creature. You do not want to damage the integrity of the specimen in any way before you put it in the killing jar."

"That doesn't sound like a fun place."

"They must be killed before they can damage themselves."

"Why do you collect them?"

"You have seen butterflies?"

"Certainly, though I've never studied them up close."

"I find that they are beautiful beyond even the most gorgeous flowers and sunsets. I have made paintings of them, but none ever match their true splendor." T.W. watched her eyes shine with admiration and envy. "I have a glass display in my home with five hundred specimens, in front of which I can sit for hours and wonder at the patterns and colors and how such beauty could ever come to exist in this world."

The barmaid arrived, set a glass of red wine in front of the widow and placed a stein of warm beer before the widower.

T.W. reached into his jacket pocket and asked, "What do I owe you, Rita?"

"This is on me and Higgins for you coming in here the other day and clearing out that foreigner."

T.W. nodded his head politely and said, "Thank you both."

Rita squeezed his shoulder, glanced at the Widow Evertson (a look he found not entirely friendly) and returned to her station behind the bar, opposite the incessantly moving mouths of the Gavel's most loquacious regulars.

The Widow Evertson raised her glass to T.W. and said, "May your daughter and Mr. Lingham find all that they need in each other."

"Thank you." He gently tapped his stein against her glass, fearful that he was going to shatter it; the vessels clinked.

T.W. drank a swallow of beer; the hops warmed his insides. The Widow Evertson sipped her wine; her face constricted into a sour pucker. She set the glass down and slid it to the corner of the table as if it were a disobedient child.

"When the waitress returns, I would like that replaced by something that does not induce nausea."

T.W.'s ingrained courtesy almost fully suppressed his growing irritation when he replied, "These drinks were gifts. I don't feel comfortable sending one back."

"Then perhaps you might discreetly empty mine into the spittoon so that I might enjoy another beverage."

"I'm not going to do that." He looked down at the wine for a moment and then back at her. "It can't be that bad."

"I can taste the lees in it. Are you suggesting for me to drink something that I find repugnant?"

"I'm doing my very best not to make any suggestions to you at this present time."

Miss Evertson blinked as if she had been struck. T.W. drank a full swallow of beer and looked away from her, over at Goodstead, who was having far more fun at a bagatelle table than he was with this haughty widow. He watched the deputy get his seventh ball past the outer bumper and into the center hole. The Texan's blank face did not register any excitement over achieving the difficult shot, but he ebulliently skipped around the table for his next turn.

"Sheriff Jeffries," the widow said. He looked over at her.

"Miss Evertson."

"Am I no longer holding your interest?"

"Let me ask you something—why did you agree to meet me here tonight?"

"I thought it might prove to be an entertaining diversion."

"People go to the rodeo for a diversion. People sit and talk so they can learn about each other."

"I think I have learned more than enough about you this evening."

"Because I'm not allowing you to condescend as you've been doing since I sat down? Laughing at me? I may not know how to catch a butterfly or anything about wine, but strand me in the wilderness, and I can find my way back. Give me some tools, and I can build a house—I built the one I live in. Tell me to track somebody across any terrain, and I can do it. Give me a book, and I can read it the same as you. And there isn't a finer lady in the whole world than the one I raised up myself—I know that for a fact."

"What is your point?"

"There's a very big difference between being intelligent and being smart."

"Bravo."

T.W. picked up his hat and said, "You've got a lot of fine qualities, but now I understand why people avoid you. You should go to church and get rid of some of that anger you've got. Or at least make some friends with people you don't look down on."

"I am not angry."

"Your dead butterflies might disagree. They might tell you that you kill them to take back little pieces of beauty from the Lord who robbed you. Little bits of revenge."

The Widow Evertson did not respond. T.W. stood up, grimacing over the pain that lanced through his bad hip.

"I'm going to shoot some bagatelles. I'll have my deputy walk you back so you can get home safe—we've spoken plenty."

T.W. picked up his hat and placed it under his arm. To his surprise, the Widow Evertson's hand sought and took his.

"It has been . . . very difficult for me," she said, in a voice softer than any he could have imagined coming from her mouth. "Very difficult."

T.W. knew what she meant. He felt her hand tremble.

"Please sit back down," she asked.

With her free hand, she took his hat and placed it on the chair it had only moments ago vacated.

T.W. sat back down. She drank from her glass of wine without complaint.

The two of them talked until the saloon closed. Her name was Meredith.

Chapter Eighteen

Guns for the Holy Lamb

"The town was built east to west. The first permanent building they put up was the church," Lingham said as the four men on horseback traversed the Montana plain. Oswell had recommended that they circumnavigate the town for their night journey, and consequently they rode a half mile from its limits, parallel to its southern border, due east.

The horses carried them away from the lowering moon, the steeds laden with luggage and the ponderous trunk. A few coyotes howled into the chill night air; their cries and the distant white-capped mountains made the open expanse seem extraordinarily vast to Oswell.

"This is how I see it," he said as his mare trod steadily beneath him, her corded muscles causing her dark coat to shine as if splashed with white oil. "The plan is to keep Quinlan and his crew from getting inside that church. I will be at the main entrance with a ledger that has the names of all the guests written down in it. When people arrive, I'll ask their names and then check that they're invited. If they are, I'll have them sign in the ledger, saying it's a keepsake Lingham asked for. The list in that ledger needs to be perfect."

"I'll ask Beatrice to make it—she don't make mistakes with things like that."

"Good. Anyone not in that book, I keep out. Anyone who seems like trouble, I turn over to Godfrey, who will be at the door with me, but also patrolling around the building to check things out. Anybody who seems like trouble, he ties up or knocks out. Dicky will be farther off somewhere, hidden from view, depending on the setup, and with his special rifle. This sound like the correct way to approach it to you fellas?"

Godfrey said, "Yeah."

Dicky said, "Yes."

Lingham said, "I can't think of anything better."

"The important thing is to keep Quinlan and his out of that church no matter what," Oswell said. He let his words settle for a moment. The horse hooves tamped down dewy grass; the beasts' nostrils exhaled steam that the moonlight turned into silk ribbons.

He continued, "One thing I want to be clear about. If he gets in there, if it comes to a shootout in the church, with innocent people in the crossfire, I am not of a mind to do any shooting whatsoever. I'd rather be shot dead than be responsible for one more innocent person getting killed on account of my actions and misdeeds ever again."

There was a momentary silence broken by Lingham, who said, "I feel the same way. I couldn't live with myself if . . . if something happened in there."

"I'm of the same mind," Godfrey said, enervated.

Oswell turned to look at Dicky; the rancher saw only the man's clean-shaven chin beneath the opaque shadow cast by the brim of his black hat.

He prompted the New Yorker. "Dicky?"

"I don't know what I am likely to do if my life is imperiled, but I have no intention of running toward a bullet."

"That's why I put you far off. But I want to hear you say you won't throw bullets into a crowd, trying to get at Quinlan and his. I need you to say this." There was menace in Oswell's voice that carried a threat with it the same as if he had drawn his revolver. He hated when Dicky was obstinate.

"I will not fire into a crowd."

"Good," Oswell said, though he did not fully believe Dicky. He resolved that he would shoot him down himself if the need arose—better they all go under than one innocent person.

The four men continued east until Lingham pointed north, in which direction they guided their horses and rode for ten silent minutes.

From the distant moonlit grass arose a crucifix, and then two more crucifixes, and then the steeples of the church, and then the square bulk of the edifice itself. The four riders drew near the building.

"Nice church," Godfrey said.

"It's not big enough for this town anymore—they've gotta hold three services on Sunday to get everyone a turn with God. We're gonna build another one soon."

Oswell surveyed the lot surrounding it and was pleased to see that it was clear for many acres in all directions.

"It's good that the landscape is so open," he remarked.

The horses continued toward the church, the edifice continuously rising and expanding before them. Oswell noticed a small building rise up in the east; the structure was an open one with support beams that upheld its triangular top.

He pointed to it and asked Lingham, "What's that?"

"The gazebo. I built it."

"What's it for?"

"We have dances and socials out here sometimes. That's a place the kids or old folks can sit when they get tired."

"Is the dance tomorrow going to be there?"

"No. That's at Big Abe's."

167

"Is anybody going to be at that gazebo during the wedding?"

"Shouldn't be."

Oswell looked at Dicky and asked, "Does that look like a good place for you to set up with your binoculars and special rifle?"

"It should work."

The horses closed the distance to the church, the structure lit from the west by the lowering moon. The four stained-glass windows in the facade above the double doors winked like eyes.

"Quinlan could put a grenade through those," Oswell said, pointing to the colorful oblongs.

"There's metal holding the glass together," Lingham said. "I think they'd get bounced back out." The tall man grew visibly uncomfortable at the thought.

"Does this place have other windows?"

"Small ones like those—up high and reinforced with metal. The twisters out here scare folks from getting too elaborate with exposed glass, even in God's house."

"Good."

Oswell reined in his horse, grunted at his aches, slammed his left boot into his stirrup, flung his right boot over the saddle and pounded upon the dirt. The other men climbed off of their horses.

"Help me with this trunk," the rancher said to his brother.

Godfrey scratched his red beard and walked

around to the back of Oswell's mare. He put sand on his sweaty palms, slapped them together and gripped the straps of the trunk; the rancher curled his fingers around the handles on the other side. Lingham walked over and undid the belts that tied the container to the horse's haunches.

The Danfords grunted as they slid the trunk off of the horse; the mare's tail flickered into Godfrey's eyes and nose, eliciting a sneeze. The brothers set the vessel down.

Oswell fished for the key in his denims, found it with coarse fingertips and drew it forth. He knelt beside the trunk and undid the lock. He lifted the lid, revealing the contents. Inside lay the four repeating lever-action rifles wrapped in sealskin; four boxes of ammunition, each with one hundred fresh rounds; eight cases of seven-shot magazines and a dark bundle, within which Oswell had placed all of the knives and two pairs of binoculars.

"Get the shovels," Oswell said to Lingham, who was glaring at the weapons from his past. The tall man went over to his horse and unfastened the knots that bound the tools across the rear ridge of his saddle.

Oswell fished out one of the pairs of binoculars, handed it to Godfrey and said, "Put it in your valise."

Dicky reached into the trunk and withdrew one of the rifles. He pointed it at the ground and flung the trigger guard forward; the clack of the shifting chamber startled one of the horses.

"I cleaned and oiled them back home. They're good."

Dicky leaned into the trunk and took a box of one hundred rounds for his rifle and a dozen magazine tubes. Lingham, carrying the shovels to Oswell, saw the ammunition in the New Yorker's hand and mouthed a silent prayer. Dicky slung the rifle strap over his shoulder, put the cartridges and magazines in his saddlebag, remounted his horse and rode it toward the gazebo.

Lingham handed each Danford a shovel and kept the third for himself. The trio walked toward the entrance of the church; Dicky shrank to the size of the gazebo and continued to shrink further.

Oswell looked at the double doors and then at Lingham.

"These open in, or they open out?"

"They go in."

Oswell pounded the doors with his left fist. The concussions were deep thuds that echoed dimly within the enclosure.

"Thick," Oswell remarked, pleased by the solidity of the portals. That wood could take more than a few shots without shattering apart. He looked at the ground immediately to the right of the doorway and indicated it with his chin. To Godfrey he said, "That's a good place?"

"Looks fine."

With the tip of his shovel, Oswell drew a rectangle the size of the trunk into the dirt. To the immediate right of this, Godfrey unfolded and set down a large canvas tarp.

Into the circumscribed space, the three men plunged their shovels, leaned on their handles and scooped up the flesh of the earth. They emptied the soil onto the tarp.

"Be neat. This needs to look natural when we're done."

They dug. At one time during the dig, when Oswell's mind wandered and all he heard were the sounds of his brother and Lingham breathing and grunting and metal cutting the earth, the rancher vividly felt that he was nineteen again and that all the wickedness to come could still be avoided if he could just learn to get along with cowboys and not mind the things they said. If he and Godfrey and Lingham rode beeves with the other vaqueros, they would never rob banks or shoot bank guards or get involved with a man like Quinlan. Oswell's hands continued to plunge his shovel into the ground, but his mind was no longer attached to the meat.

The pile of dirt upon the tarp grew into something that was vaguely the weight and shape of a woman.

Godfrey said, "That should be deep enough, right?"

Oswell dumped more soil onto the dirt lady

171

they had exhumed and then paused to consider the hole.

"Looks good," he said.

The Danfords leaned their shovels against the church; Lingham immediately snatched the tools and set them on the ground nearby. The brothers walked to either side of the trunk, lifted and carried it to the hole; they slid it inside.

"Good." Oswell opened the trunk, reached in and withdrew one of the bayonet-tipped rifles. He looked at Lingham and said, "Get that rope."

The tall man nodded. He went to his horse and from the saddle-horn pulled off a coil of rope.

Oswell shut the trunk, gripped the rifle by its stock and stabbed the blade down into the lid, closer to the side that opened. The point of the bayonet stuck into the wood. Oswell twisted the rifle one full circuit and then a second. He withdrew the bayonet, leaving behind a hole a little over one inch in diameter.

Godfrey cut off a three-foot length of Lingham's rope; he tied a thick knot at the end of it and a second one just a little higher up, each over two inches in diameter. He knelt beside the trunk, lifted the lid and threaded the rope through the hole until it came to the knot, which was too big to pass through. He tugged on the cord to make sure it would hold; the knot thudded against the wood, unable to transgress.

Oswell removed the other guns, put them on a

172

separate blanket his brother had laid out, withdrew the ammunition and magazine tubes and with them sat down. Lingham and Godfrey seated themselves beside him.

The men slotted seven bullets into each long, spring-loaded magazine and summarily set the filled cylinders on the blanket; the rapid clicks and clacks and metallic squeaks made the area sound like a casino. They did not speak or look up from their munitions until forty-two seven-round magazines had been filled.

"Let's do it all the way," Oswell said as he slid a magazine into the aperture at the rear of the gunstock; the cylinder clicked home. He twisted his other hand, flinging the trigger guard forward—the mechanism clacked loudly and pulled a bullet into the chamber. Godfrey inserted a tube in his rifle and flipped the lever, loading the gun with a clack. Lingham reluctantly loaded and engaged the other weapon.

They placed the live guns and filled magazines inside the sunken trunk.

The rancher closed the container and put a blanket over it. He sealed up the interstices between the trunk and the edges of the hole with the fabric. Godfrey cut an aperture in the cloth and pulled the rope through. Oswell and Lingham then ladled dirt onto the blanket, covering it completely over with eight shovelfuls.

Godfrey laid the rope in a spiral that Oswell and

Lingham covered with more dirt. They then patted the soil smooth with the backs of their shovels. With errant pebbles and twigs and footprints, they decorated the ground so that it looked the same as the areas nearby. Godfrey placed a small flat stone on the dirt to mark where the rope was buried two inches below the surface.

Lingham walked beside the large mound of dirt they had excavated and said, "Let's dump this."

The Danfords lifted the tarp upon which laid more than a hundred pounds of dirt. They walked it thirty yards from the church; Lingham scattered the soil like ashes across the ground.

The rancher folded up the tarp as they walked toward their horses. He looked back at the church entrance: the place where they had hidden their guns was indistinguishable from any other area. Even if the rock was kicked away, he was confident that he and Godfrey could accurately approximate the location of the buried rope.

Oswell looked at Lingham and asked a question he had not at all looked forward to asking. "You want something . . . a pistol hidden . . . for inside?"

"I ain't of a mind to throw no bullets at anyone in a church full of Christians. We already talked about that."

Oswell looked over at Godfrey, who had understood the implication of the question and now looked morbidly at the ground, silent.

"I know," Oswell said, "I'm talking about if he gets through . . . so you'd have . . . an option. So you could end it yourself instead of being at his mercy and letting him do what ever he's got planned to do to you."

Lingham contemplated the scenario and shook his big head, his cyclopean shadow cleft in half on his horse and the church facade.

"I don't think I could do that."

"Okay," Oswell said. He climbed upon his mare, unable to look Lingham in the eye.

Chapter Nineteen

Blackie the White: The Haint of Hotel Halcyon

For the span of two heartbeats, Dicky wondered if the man was a ghost. He did not believe in apparitions (which was helpful, since once a scornful woman had claimed that she would return from the great beyond to haunt and torment him—if she died before he did), but the ancient man's pallid skin had a weird sheen that made him look rather spectral in the lantern light of the hotel lobby. The elder's hair blended perfectly with his pale dermis, and the white suit he wore only further added to his ghostly appearance. Currently, the apparition just stared at a dark window on the east wall of the hotel lobby, blinking far less frequently than most men did. He had not yet noticed the newly arrived New Yorker.

After two hours of lying awake in his room, Dicky had decided to get dressed and come downstairs into the lobby of the hotel. He did not intend to find company (the chances of happening upon the kind of company that interested him were marginal in Trailspur). He had just needed to leave his diminishing, solitary enclosure.

It was nearly four o'clock in the morning, which was late even by New York standards. The night attendant slept on a cot in a tiny room behind the front desk, his sock-covered feet visible through the partially opened door, past which the metallic solicitations of a small bell could rouse him whenever he was needed. On a green couch sat the other denizen, the white ghost.

The oldster turned his head to Dicky; the New Yorker started when he saw the blind eyes that stared up at him from the man's rugose visage like red-veined eggs.

"Did I doze?" (The New Yorker thought the man's accent indicated that he was from Ohio.)

"It is five minutes to four," Dicky replied. He then added, "In the morning."

"Dawn is taking her time tonight." He pointed to the sofa and said, "You sit."

Dicky sat on the couch beside the old man.

176

"You're one hundred an' seventy pounds."

"I am. How can you tell?"

"I sit this couch a lot. It sunk a half inch and a little bit more when you got on. The half inch is one hundred and fifty pounds, the little bit more is the other twenty."

"You are very astute."

"It's good to know the size of people— 'specially if you needs to go up against them."

The old man looked back at the dark window; despite the fact that Dicky knew he was blind, he looked over to see if something was there. Within the dark square, ephemeral imagined shapes swam before his eyes, but nothing substantial. The floorboards creaked overhead and the attendant with the exposed socks coughed in his sleep. The night seemed heavy.

The old man asked, "Had a quarrel with your wife?"

"I am not married."

"You sound like you're forty. Older maybe."

"I am. Forty-four."

"Why ain't you married?"

"I like women too much."

"What kind of answer is that? You ugly?"

"Yes. Do you know any blind women?"

"Just get a fat one. They can do stuff the same as the rest an' can cook better."

"I shall consider that. Are you married?"

"I was."

"Did she pass on?"

"She left me when I started goin' blind. She didn't want to take care o' no invalid."

"That must have been difficult," Dicky said, watching the oldster's face constrict with bitterness.

"I couldn't even find my gun when she told me, my eyes were so bad."

"There is no justice in this world."

"You tellin' this to a blind man? I know that better than anyone!"

From the room behind the front desk, the attendant's groggy voice croaked, "Somebody need something?"

"Go back to sleep, Greg," the old man said, annoyed that his yelling had awakened the man.

Dicky asked, "Do you live here—in this hotel?"

"Yeah. I stay in a room here 'cause I can't be blind an' by myself. I need help an' my wife left me, but I was too blind to shoot her."

"You mentioned that. Would you have killed her?"

"Of course not. Why would I do that? I'd've just made it so she couldn't run off. Maybe shoot her leg or flash the muzzle across her eyes so she'd know about bein' blind herself."

Dicky looked to see if the man wore a gun; he did not.

The New Yorker asked, "Do you have any children?"

"They're miserable. You can't count on them. Probably havin' square dances with their mother, laughin' at how blind I am."

Dicky wanted to guide the conversation to a happier subject; he said, "Is this your favorite room in the hotel?"

"This is the room where I'm gonna meet Miss Isabel. That's why I'm dressed up." The old man pointed to his white suit and his white shoes. "This is the outfit I meet her in. She likes the color blue."

Dicky decided not to point out the colorless nature of the man's attire, and instead asked, "Does Miss Isabel meet you at dawn?"

"In the vision she did. But I come down early to be ready."

Dicky had previously assessed the man as volatile and bitter (and amusing), though this last remark struck him as evidence of true dementia.

"You had a vision of this woman?"

"That's right I did. About two years after my wife abandoned me I burnt down a lot of my house on accident. I was burneded up some myself an' all blind by then an' angry at everything—I tried to shoot this dog that was barking one night an' T.W. takes my gun away and says, 'No sir, Blackie, you can't go shootin' up dogs when you're blind,' which made me mad back then but makes sense to me now, 'specially cause kids play with dogs. T.W. looks at my house—which is half charcoal—an' says I should move to a hotel where others can help me, and I told him I could take care of myself an' he shouldn't trouble me, I ain't robbed no banks or nothin'. He's the sheriff, if you didn't know."

"I figured that out."

"So I was in my room an' the rain is coming into the room next to me because I burneded out the ceiling in that one an' I fall asleep and see this scene in my head." Blackie raised his index finger. "That's a thing you prob'y didn't know, blind people can see in their dreams if they ever had the power of sight in their lives, which I did for fifty-three years. That's why I sleep a lot more than I used to. Didn't sleep so much when I had good eyes. What was I about to tell you?"

"About the vision," Dicky prompted him.

"Right. The most important part!"

The attendant, awakened by the old man's exclamation asked, "Somebody need something?"

"Get the hell back to sleep!"

Dicky heard the attendant resettle in his cot; within an instant, the steady noise of his susurrations resumed.

"So I sees this vision that night in the storm. In it, I'm sittin' in a hotel lobby on a green couch, wearin' a blue suit. It's dawn an' through the window you can see a royal blue sky an' just a little bit of the sun poking her head up from the grass like a gopher—pretty like in a paintin'. I'm sittin' there, drinkin' a tea"—Blackie pointed to a cup resting on the table beside him—"and I'm watchin' the sun come up an' this woman comes into the lobby. She is . . . she is . . ." The old man shook his head, the joy and sadness that struggled for control over his vocal cords made them warble. "She is beautiful. She asks the attendant for a room an' her voice reminds me of the way my mama's sounded when I was a little kid over in Hackett. I invite her to share tea with me an' she comes over an' sits right where you are now and I pour her a cup. We start talkin' about the sunrise an' things an' at some point I realize that we're sittin' close an' holdin' hands. She tells me her name is Isabel an' then I woke up."

The oldster ruminated for a moment and then said, "I wish it went on longer, but that was it. I moved into this hotel not long after, so I could be close to this room."

Dicky felt heartsick for the old man.

Blackie added, "Maybe it seems crazy to you that I come here every morning, but let me tell you somethin'. I never saw this lobby when I had good eyes—they hadn't builded it yet. But I knew the color of this couch," he said, patting the green couch. "And I knew about that window," he said, pointing to the window on the eastern wall. "And I knew about the carpet," he said, stamping his left shoe on the Oriental rug beneath him. "I knew it all without nobody tellin' me. I saw 'em in my dream, an' here they are for real. Explain that? You can't! So that's how I know Miss Isabel will come an' have tea with me an' sit close an' hold hands an' talk to me with that voice that sounds like my mama's."

"I do not know anything at all about visions, but it definitely sounds like you have had one."

"It's always disappointing when she don't turn up, but then there's another dawn comin' up before you know it." Blackie turned his blank gaze back to the window. The eastern horizon was beginning to glow.

Without warning, the old man said, "Get out of her seat. I don't want it occupied when she gets here."

Dicky stood up, shook Blackie's cold hand and left the apparition to await his spectral mate.

Halfway up the stairs, Dicky turned and looked back down at the old man; the light from the window had painted his suit blue.

Chapter Twenty

Penultimate Breakfast (and Afterward)

Beatrice sat opposite her father at the oak table; the vapors from the eggs, cheddar biscuits and panfried pork chops with onions rose up between them.

Her father inhaled deeply and said, "Smells like the best breakfast yet." (He said this about half of the time.)

"Thank you." Beatrice tilted her head forward, clasped her hands together and closed her eyes. "Come dine with us, Lord Jesus, be a guest in our home. Let these gifts to us be blessed. Amen."

"Amen."

She opened her eyes; her father looked at her and said, "I'm making breakfast tomorrow. You aren't cooking for some old man on your own wedding day."

Beatrice nodded her head appreciatively.

They ate in silence for a few minutes, T.W. lustily nodding his approbation over the food, which Beatrice agreed was particularly flavorful that morning. At one point he asked if she would set aside a chop, some gravy and a biscuit for Goodstead, and she informed him that she already had. Her mind ordered the many things that she intended to do that day prior to the social she and her father had arranged for the wedding guests (and any townsfolk not invited to the ceremony who simply wished to join in the celebration).

"There's something I wanted to get at for a moment," her father said, and then wiped his mouth.

Beatrice knew that he was going to say something about her mother. Her father rarely spoke of the woman, and whenever he did, there was a preamble.

"Pretty soon it may not be appropriate for me to talk about certain things with you. People change some when they get married and I imagine that you will too—and that's fine. So this is what I wanted to discuss now: I suppose that you and James plan on having children?"

Beatrice's cheeks suffused with warmth at the remark, but she did not look away from her father when she responded, "We both like the idea of children."

"I figured as much. You know what happened to your mother when she gave birth to you. I wanted to let you know that Bonnie, your mother's mother who you never met, also had difficulties in giving birth to your mother. Did I ever mention this to you?"

"A long time ago."

"She survived, but was always weak blooded afterward and never fully the same. I hate to tell you about this, but you should know that when you are with child, you need to take special care."

"I shall."

"For a lot of years I've saved up my extra money—all of my bonuses and those two big rewards I collected when I was a marshal—so that I could hire a private doctor from the East to watch you for the last part of your term and deliver the baby when the time came. I've got enough money to do it twice. Maybe three times."

Beatrice's eyes filled with tears. Of the many kind things her father had done for her during her twenty-nine years, this was perhaps the kindest of all.

"Don't get upset."

"I am not upset, I am—" She stood up, walked around the table, stood beside her father, leaned over and threw her arms around him. She squeezed him fiercely and kissed him on the forehead. He hugged her in return.

"Better let go. I'm full of biscuits and pork."

"Thank you, Daddy."

He grinned and said, "You haven't called me Daddy in a while. Just hearing it makes me feel younger."

Beatrice, at a loss for words, just repeated, "Thank you. Thank you so much."

The man picked up his napkin and Beatrice picked up hers; the two of them wiped tears from her cheeks, smiling.

In Beatrice's estimation, Big Abe's Dancehall of Trailspur was very far from ready for the evening's festivities. The piano was there, but the chairs and the tables and the festoons and the welcome banner she had asked for were all absent; the floor needed to be polished as well.

The only person in the area was a Mandarin woman who sat upon an overturned bucket in a corner, poking and pulling a needle through the rent crotch of a very large pair of yellow trousers that almost certainly belonged to the proprietor.

"Pardon me, ma'am," Beatrice said.

The woman looked up and said, "What!"

"Do you know where I can find Big Abe?"

The woman raised the pants and said, "Big Abe."

Beatrice said, "Do you know where he is?"

"His pants," was her reply.

Beatrice pointed east and said, "Big Abe?" The Mandarin woman shook her head. Beatrice pointed west and said, "Big Abe?"

The Mandarin pointed her needle at the ceiling and said, "Big Abe up."

Beatrice, befuddled, stared at the woman for a moment; the Oriental jabbed her needle at the ceiling a second time. A loud thump sounded on the roof and Beatrice, comprehending, nodded to the Mandarin.

"Sheh-sheh," Beatrice said, the only Chinese she knew. The woman laughed, nodded and then replied in kind.

Beatrice walked outside Big Abe's Dancehall of Trailspur and circumnavigated the gaily painted building (purple and yellow with some green) until she came upon a ladder angled against the south facade. Without hesitation, she applied herself to the rungs and climbed. When she reached the roof twenty-four feet above, she earned herself a splendid view of Big Abe's posterior, so large and looming that it looked like the back of a lavender buffalo.

"Big Abe?"

The man stood up as if poked, turned around, bowed his bald, sun-reddened head and said, "Miss Jeffries. Good afternoon."

Beatrice stepped off of the ladder and walked across the planks toward the rotund proprietor.

"What brings you to my roof?"

"Is the dance hall going to be ready for tonight?"

"You entertain doubts?"

"The space is empty, other than the piano, and the last time I heard that particular piano, it only had one octave that was correctly tuned."

"Don't trouble yourself, my dear. Everything will be organized by tonight. And correctly tuned."

"Do I have your word? By five o'clock, the floors shall be polished and the chairs, tables, welcome banner and festoons shall be artfully arranged?"

"You can have my word. Or a sentence. Or some handshakes. Or we can go to Judge Higgins and draft some forms if you'd like—if that would dispel the doubts that currently assail you."

"That is not necessary." She returned to the ladder, descended one rung, stopped and said, "Please do not put rum in the fruit punch."

"I shan't."

Beatrice climbed down the ladder, the dirt road rising up to meet her brown, two-inch-heeled boots.

When she was a yard from the ground, she heard Big Abe say, "The rum goes into the rum punch."

The lobby of Hotel Halcyon was occupied by a dozen people, one of whom noticed her and waved, though she did not immediately recognize the amiable brown-haired gentleman. He stood up from the green couch, her name on his lips; a woman and a shy teenage girl rose up beside him. The family approached her.

"You look just like your mother," the brown-haired gentleman said to Beatrice.

The woman beside him said, "We haven't seen you since you were twelve. We're the Albens, cousins of your mother's, if you don't remember us."

"I most assuredly remember you. Thank you for coming out for the celebration," she said as Mr. Alben took and kissed her hand. She then hugged the women—the mother, followed by the shy teenager. Beatrice first met the Albens when she and her father had visited Colorado (accompanied by her father's cousin Robert) when she was twelve years old, though the shy girl had not yet been born. She recalled that they were successful in oil, pleasant conversationalists and intelligent. Mrs. Alben had written several news articles for the *Rocky Mountain Tribune* (under a man's name), which had impressed Beatrice thoroughly at the time, and inspired her earliest contribution to the *Trailspur Gazette* five years later.

"Is the groom around? He must be a handsome one to win a gorgeous woman like you," Mrs. Alben said.

"Thank you," Beatrice replied, blushing for the second time that day. "He is currently showing his guests the town of Trailspur."

Two more people approached Beatrice and introduced themselves as Smith and Smiler—men who used to marshal with her father back in Arkansas. Both of them were over sixty and moved slowly—one walked with a cane—and they just stared at her smiling throughout their interaction, as if her existence was an answer to a long-posed question and the words that came from her mouth were negligible, albeit pretty, bird sounds.

"I didn't understand half what you said, but it all sounds smart," remarked the one with the gaping smile.

"I can't believe somethin' like you came outta T.W.," the one with the cane said. "He's a good man, but . . . but you're like a queen or something."

For the third time that day, Beatrice blushed.

The old marshals vied for her right hand; Smith jabbed his cane into his companion's thigh to win the privilege. He delicately clasped her fingers, raised them to his mouth and kissed her bare knuckles, the bristles of his mustache tickling her. The moment he released her hand, his peer snatched it up and pressed it to his lips so gently that she barely felt the contact.

"Tell T.W. that Smith and Smiler are here whenever you see him."

"And ask him if he knows who your real father is."

"Smiler! That ain't at all appropriate to joke about," Smith reprimanded . . . but then started to laugh himself.

Chapter Twenty~one

Enthralled by Wilfreda

Oswell, Godfrey and Dicky sat on the wide bench that furnished Lingham's porch, watching the sun fall from the sky. The slatted door behind them opened and the tall carpenter emerged, holding the handles of three tin cups of coffee in his right hand (one needed long fingers to do that) and a fourth cup in his left hand. Lingham handed each man a coffee and was thanked with a nod. The coydogs strutted from the woods toward the porch.

"Jesus has returned," Dicky remarked.

Lingham hooked a stool with his boot, slid it across the deck and sat down; he blew upon his coffee and sipped. The tall blond man scratched Jesus's nose and then Joseph's.

"This is good coffee," Godfrey remarked.

"Thanks."

The men sipped at and blew upon the steaming ebony held in their tin cups. Oswell tried not to think about Elinore and the kids.

He said to Lingham, "We should be watchful at that dance. You said anybody can come?"

"The whole town is invited. We can only get one hundred and twenty into the church, and some folks wanted to be involved with the marriage even if they couldn't hear us say the vows. That hall can hold more than three hundred." He sipped and then added, "Beatrice is popular in this town. So is her pa."

"From what we saw walking around today, so are you," Godfrey remarked.

"They like the James Lingham I showed 'em."

Oswell said, "I know how things went back then. This James Lingham is you. Bad luck and other folks made you become that other one."

"Lots of folks had troubles and didn't do what I done," Lingham said. He shook his head morosely. "It's all gonna come out one way or the other, I suppose. Things will get settled for good."

He sipped his coffee and tapped his fingers upon the tin mug.

Oswell asked, "Is the sheriff going to approach us if we're wearing guns at the dance?"

"He will. He monitors that stuff close. And you can't do no shootin' in a hall full of people anyway."

The rancher responded, "Of course we won't. Be we should be able to defend ourselves if we get called outside or get ambushed along the way." To Dicky, Oswell said, "Put a couple of ten-shooters and a couple of fives in that valise and bring it."

"I already packed them."

"Good. And give us each a knife in case the wrong fellow asks us to dance."

The quartet rode their horses from Lingham's property; the sun knelt on the earth behind them, casting their shadows forward like jet-black pillars. Oswell and his brother wore blue suits, Dicky wore his brown three-piece outfit with a maroon tie and gloves and Lingham wore a dark green suit and matching shirt. Each man held a revolver in his free hand and watched the woodlands.

"Did Beatrice pick out that suit for you?" Dicky asked.

"She did."

"Was the inspiration green beans?"

"Shut up Dicky."

"I was only joking. You look very nice."

"Thanks."

"I've never seen a vegetable ride a horse before."

"It's a wonder we never shot you," Oswell said. "Lay off of Lingham or I'm gonna get off my horse and go a round with you."

"How about you go to hell with your threats, Oswell."

Godfrey and Lingham grew tense; Oswell looked at Dicky.

The New Yorker continued, "Not one of us knows which way tomorrow is going to go—all I am trying to do is have a little fun. You have been a gloomy bastard since I met you at the train depot, as if you were the only one who has suffered for what happened back then. You are not the only one, Oswell Danford: we all have. We all have the same weight upon us—you have just decided that your burden entitles you to be an ornery louse. Well it does not entitle you to such behavior. Godfrey is civil and so is Lingham and so am I."

Dicky reined his horse close to Oswell's and continued, "And furthermore, I have seen you clamber up and down that mare. I am fairly certain that I would be standing and you would be eating dirt in any dustup between the two of us. If you want to attack me in a valiant effort to defend Lingham's dumb suit, go ahead."

The four men rode on in silence. Oswell

wondered why Dicky's japes had pricked him so deeply, angered him so much more than they ever had before. He ruminated.

After his horse had taken a dozen strides, the rancher said, "I suppose I'm not very tolerant of any of us having fun, especially at the expense of someone else. I figure that's how we all got into this mess in the first place." Oswell shook his head. "But I shouldn't come at you as I have been. You showed up for this and some men might not have. Most men, probably. You're here to own up to what happened the same as me and my brother and Lingham, and I shouldn't be all over you the way I have been."

Oswell and the rest of the crew were surprised when he extended his right hand to Dicky. The New Yorker clasped and shook it.

The four men tied their horses amid the forty-three others fastened to the posts outside of Big Abe's Dancehall of Trailspur and walked toward the large double doors, from which emanated the sounds of a piano and a mirthful throng of people. Oswell held the valise within which all of their revolvers had been placed.

"I plan on having a good time," Dicky announced. He looked at Godfrey. "I will get us some girls."

"Be respectful," Lingham admonished the New Yorker.

"That is part of the strategy."

The doors grew large in front of them; the piano music sounded like restive children stomping out block chords with their feet.

Oswell looked at Lingham and said, "It's been a long time since I saw you dance."

"Can you still do that fancy backward stepping?" Godfrey asked.

"Better than before. We have lots of socials in Trailspur and I go to all I can. That's where I met Beatrice."

Dicky asked, "She was beguiled by your footwork?"

"She liked it."

Godfrey grabbed the brass knob and pulled the door wide. Oswell winced as the volume of the celebration roared into his ears; he was not used to crowds. Faces turned to look at the new arrivals. Several people shouted out the name James. The quartet entered the vast enclosure; hands went up to solicit the groom-to-be. He waved back amicably.

The warmth and humidity of the dance hall enveloped Oswell; his boots thudded upon the newly burnished wood, another instrument added to the convivial atmosphere of chatter, stomping, laughter and clapping. The Trailspur citizens' fondness for bright colors was evidenced by the purple, green, red and yellow clothing they wore.

Oswell surveyed the individuals that comprised

the crowd. Excepting the dozen folks Lingham had introduced him to earlier that day, the guests, who already amounted to nearly two hundred people, were all strangers to the rancher. Regardless, men who rode with Quinlan—men like the twins and the toddler and the sort of fellow he used to be himself—did not settle well in an environment such as this.

He did not notice anybody that caused him concern; when he looked at Godfrey and Dicky, the pair appeared similarly at ease with the throng.

"Seems okay," Godfrey said.

A moment later, a very large bald man in a bright yellow suit and matching top hat stormed across the floor to Lingham, clasped the tall man's right hand with both of his, and shook it as if he were trying to pump water from the ground.

"Big Abe," Lingham said. "These are the fellas I used to cowboy with. This is Oswell, his brother Godfrey, and that's Dicky from New York."

The proprietor clapped his hands to each man, said "I'm Big Abe," and tried to pump more water.

The piano player, a tiny old woman with big-knuckled hands, shifted the tempo and mode of her playing, punishing the keys into giving her what she required. Oswell guessed that the woman had ninety years behind her, if not more.

"That's Wilfreda. She's a treasure in this town," Big Abe informed Oswell.

"She can play very well."

"You haven't seen a thing—she's toying with us right now, inveigling us."

Her left hand simmering with a sinister bass line, Wilfreda raised her right hand over her head and slammed it violently to the keys. Formerly inert feet began to tap the floor, seduced by the vibrations.

Wilfreda turned to look over her left shoulder, pure white hair beneath her flat, crescent-shaped hat. Beneath colorless eyebrows that looked like caterpillars, her narrow eyes assessed the crowd with a gaze that to Oswell appeared malefic. She grinned while her left hand percolated an ever-changing rhythm that the dancers tried to conform to. Wilfreda turned back to her piano keys and plunged headlong into a robust waltz, peppering it with odd accents that elicited yelps from less coordinated dancers and people with sensitive eardrums.

Big Abe said, "She says that her playing is what keeps death away from her. Scares him off."

"She's something," Oswell replied.

"I recommend the rum punch," Big Abe said. "I made it myself."

Lingham inquired, "Beatrice don't mind you putting out rum punch?"

"Both options are available. The fruit punch is in a bucket under the table if somebody wants some. The rum punch is on the table in that huge glass bowl with all the fruit in it."

"Okay."

Big Abe departed to the table upon which the punchbowl, ladles, cups, candied apples, sweet corn cakes, seed cakes and funnel cakes lay.

Wilfreda picked up the pace of her playing, her head slowly turning away from the keys to survey the movement of the crowd.

"She looks like a witch," Godfrey said to Oswell.

"I wouldn't cross her," he responded.

More people entered the dance hall; the floor thudded in time with Wilfreda's passionate machinations. The hall grew warmer.

The crowd parted to reveal Beatrice, her arm around the elbow of an older man in a brown and orange plaid suit; he had receded silver hair, a big mustache, sharp eyes and a belly jutting from his otherwise solid frame. He walked with a limp and wore a gun on his right hip.

"Is that the sheriff?" Oswell asked Lingham quietly.

"That's him."

Beatrice, her curly blonde hair pulled into a lime ribbon, wore a dress as green as Lingham's suit and a smile that barely fit upon her luminous face. She was a pretty woman and in her happiness, stunning, Oswell thought. The sheriff motioned for her to run to her fiancé, which she did instantly; she threw her arms around Lingham's neck and kissed him on the mouth with such love that Oswell felt a bittersweet empathy twist his guts.

Lingham scooped her up into his arms and asked, "Did you have any of the rum punch?"

"No! I promise. I had the one with fruit in it."

"That's the rum punch," Lingham said, laughing.

Oswell saw his brother turn away; Godfrey and Katherine had been like that before she left him.

The sheriff stopped in front of Oswell, Godfrey and Dicky and openly appraised them.

Lingham strode beside the lawman and said, "T.W., this is Oswell, his brother Godfrey and Dicky from New York."

T.W. extended his right hand, shook Oswell's and said, "It's a pleasure to finally meet some of James's friends. What's your last name?"

Oswell had not at all expected to be asked this question, and he sensed Godfrey and Dicky grow tense beside him; he said, "Danford," figuring that there was a very good chance Beatrice already knew his last name from the wedding list. Regardless, it was clear that T.W. was a perspicacious man who could ferret out a lie.

"Thank you for traveling across the country to join in the celebration, Oswell Danford. James's past remains a bit of mystery to me."

"Lingham is a good man. And from what I've seen, he's matched or bested in every way by your very fine daughter. I like the sight of them together."

"Thank you," T.W. said with a smile that covered over something unfriendly and made Oswell uncomfortable. The sheriff turned to Godfrey and clasped his hand. "You are Godfrey Danford then? His brother?"

"I am. Though since I've got two years on him, I like to consider him my possession, not the other way around." Again, T.W. smiled in a manner that hid more than it showed.

The sheriff turned to Dicky and said, "What kind of name is Dicky for an adult?"

"The humorous kind."

"What's your real name?"

"Richard Sterling." Oswell was relieved that Dicky did not lie.

T.W. shook the New Yorker's hand and said, "Thank you for coming out to join our celebration, Richard Sterling. How does Trailspur compare to New York?"

"There is no comparison."

"I agree on that score," T.W. said, subtly winning the exchange.

The sheriff took a step back and assessed the men as if they were newly arrived beeves to be priced for slaughter.

He said, "Have some of the funnel cake—my cousin made it, and his recipe is better than anyone else's. It's got nuts and cinnamon and little bits of candied ginger in it."

"I was eyeing the funnel cake," Godfrey remarked.

Wilfreda struck ten keys as if they were evil siblings, and an enormous harmony enveloped the crowd. Like a weary climber attempting steep stairs, the ancient woman pulsed a lugubrious rhythm on her ivory. The air grew heavy and warm.

An attractive ash-blonde woman approximately Oswell's age, wearing a shapely (arguably immodest) lavender dress, called out from the crowd, "T.W."

The sheriff turned to look at the woman and said, "I'll be with you in a moment."

Lingham remarked, "The Widow Evertson seems to want your company. She's sure dressed up for it."

Beatrice laughed, looked at Lingham and said, "He replaced me before I even left the house."

"No I didn't," T.W. said defensively. "She just wants some company is all."

Wilfreda's left hand trudged up a hill of keys while her right digits wove a delicate melody that never ended in the correct place. The crowd swayed, enthralled.

The widow arrived, grabbed T.W.'s right arm and said, "I'll show you how to waltz."

The sheriff looked at Oswell and said, "See you fellas around. Stay out of trouble." He glanced at the valise in Oswell's hand and then inscrutably at Lingham and was gone.

"I wish to dance too," Beatrice said, pulling her fiancé after her father to the raised area of the dance floor.

Oswell, Godfrey and Dicky stood for a moment watching the celebrants.

"He knows we've been on the wrong side," Oswell said.

"He does. Good thing he doesn't know how to deal with that widow," Godfrey remarked.

Big Abe, luminous in his yellow suit and hat, transcended the swaying crowd; he climbed a foot ladder, rising above the revelers like a cyclopean canary.

The rotund man cupped his hands, set them on either side of his mouth for amplification and yelled out, "Longways dance!"

Wilfreda picked up the tempo of her playing; the assembly divided into male and female lines, eight rows to accommodate all of the dancers. Oswell saw Lingham skip into position opposite Beatrice.

"Let's partner up," Dicky said, flung an arm around Godfrey's shoulders and walked the older Danford to a deficient line opposite two pretty young women likely half their age.

"Two steps front and two steps back," Big Abe called out. The lines advanced toward each other, halted (a yard still between them) and then retreated whence they came. Wilfreda ran her right hand up the keyboard and played a diminished trill; the notes stabbed Oswell's eardrums like icicles.

"Three steps front and six in place," Big Abe called out. The lines advanced to each other, stopped face-to-face, and marched in place. During the static stepping, a few eager couples pecked or swatted each other, Lingham kissed the top of Beatrice's head, Dicky introduced himself to a redheaded woman who had not stopped blushing since the moment he had walked opposite her in the dance line and Godfrey waved shyly to the lady with pigtails with whom he danced.

"Get on back, three steps back," Big Abe ordered, and the genders retreated from one another. "Clap your hands three times fast." The assembly brought their hands together thunderously. "Clap your hands three times fast and stomp the wood three times slow." The assembly clapped sharply and stomped loudly in time with Wilfreda's tempo. During the final footfall, Oswell heard a shriek outside the dancehall that chilled his blood.

"Three steps front and step in place." The genders reunited. Oswell stared at the front doors of the dance hall. He heard another shriek; it was a horse in agony.

"Take your partner's right hand and shake it!" Oswell glanced back at his companions. Lingham and Beatrice shook hands, both of them laughing; Dicky claimed the pale fingers of his voluptuous partner and kissed them; Godfrey shook hands with his mousy mate as if he had just sold her a doorknob. "Tell your partner, 'Howdy!' "

Seven score voices said, "Howdy," in unison.

"You sure look nice tonight."

"You sure look nice tonight," the crowd repeated.

"Why thank you."

"Why thank you!"

"Your comportment is beyond reproach."

"Your comportment is beyond reproach!"

"Now curtsy." The crowd crossed their feet and bent their knees, each gesture on the downbeats of Wilfreda's music. "Take three steps back and step in place." The genders released each other and retreated back to their homogenous lines.

Oswell walked toward the door of the dance hall, sweat running down his back; his beige shirt and blue jacket clung to his skin. He turned his head to look for the sheriff. The man was far off, wincing as he marched in place opposite the widow. From the valise, Oswell clandestinely withdrew a ten-shooter and tucked it into his belt. He opened the door an inch and looked outside.

Cool air blew upon his sweat-glazed forehead as his eyes adjusted to the darkness. In the middle of the road he saw two loose horses, each walking in circles. One groaned in agony and collapsed to the dirt, whickering. Oswell put his hand upon his revolver and went outside.

"Take three steps forward and grab your

partner's hands." The stampede of the lines converging covered over the sound of him shutting the door.

Oswell looked north and then south; other than an older couple walking toward the saloon at the end of the avenue, he saw nobody. The rancher approached the horses.

Big Abe's stentorian exhortations were audible through the shut door. The pitch of his voice mirrored the lyric when he said, "Hold those hands up so high and drop them down, so darn low. But don't you dare fall in love. No, no, no— not just yet!"

One steed lay upon the ground, kicking its hooves sideways across the dirt, its intestines strung out like steaming gray rope in all directions, a few loops tangled about one of its legs. The other horse was upright; it dragged its hanging entrails beneath it and whickered. Both of these animals were Lingham's: the white one was the steed Godfrey had ridden and the brown mare was the one Oswell himself had mounted. The fallen horse quieted; dirt thickened its spilt blood. The walking mare continued up the street; its pink and brown entrails hissed as they dragged across the soil.

The rancher took the reins of the upright beast and walked it into an alley. The mare's steps grew less stable as its blood drained out and the length of its strewn guts grew longer and longer, but the female trudged on. He walked it past the offal bins of the butcher and into a small coppice, where he withdrew a large-caliber five-shot revolver from the valise, placed the barrel to its head, thumbed the hammer and fired. The horse sank to its knees, its eyes and mouth open as if to ask a question. Oswell thumbed the hammer and fired again. The horse collapsed.

Oswell walked seven yards away from the carcass, picked up a stick, pricked the beast's dirt-encrusted intestines and dragged them back over to the rent torso. The mare's right hoof was still moving. Oswell knew that the motion was a dying reflex.

The rancher left the coppice and returned up the alley, kicking dirt over the trail the horse's guts had scored into the ground. He emerged onto the main avenue and went toward the fallen horse. Two men stood on the other side of the dead steed, limned by the light of the moon; Oswell pointed his five-shooter at them and thumbed the hammer before his heart pulsed another beat.

"We didn't do it," the man on the left said. "We're marshals."

The rancher, his gun still out, approached the duo; they were both in their sixties—one had a cane and the other a strange gaping grin on his face, even though the situation had clearly disturbed him. Oswell surveyed the environs and looked back over his own shoulder in case these two were decoys, but saw nothing. He appraised the marshals a second time and slid his revolver back into his belt, beside the ten-shooter. He trod toward the pair, his eyes and ears alert.

"This your horse?" the one with the cane asked.

"Yeah. I went after the guy who did it."

"You get him?"

"We heard shots," the other one remarked.

"No."

Across the street, two boys had arrived to stare at the dead horse; they chewed taffy. Oswell needed to get this animal off of the street before a throng gathered.

He took the reins of Dicky's and Lingham's horses and walked them over to the fallen animal. He took rope from the back of Lingham's saddlebag and went to the dead white steed's upraised hooves.

"That's a good idea. Don't want that pretty bride to come out and see this," the one with the weird smile said.

The marshals helped Oswell secure ropes around the legs of the dead horse; they pulled hard to make sure the knots were secure and could bear the weight. Oswell cut and wrapped a separate rope around the animal's entrails and then tied that coiled, viscous burden to the beast's harness in order to contain the mess.

"You see any wood?" Oswell asked the men; the trio looked around the area.

From within the dance hall, Big Abe said, "Swing your partner round and round."

Oswell saw a sign on the adjacent storefront upon which the name VICTOR'S EMPORIUM had been written and then painted over with the word "Closed." He walked to the five-foot sign, pulled it down from the hooks upon which it hung, set it on the ground, stamped his boot in the middle of it, lifted the right edge and snapped it in half. With the applied shoulders (and cane) of the marshals, Oswell slid the pieces of wood beneath the dead horse, raising it from the ground.

He took the reins of the living horses and walked them forward; the ropes that tethered them to the fallen animal snapped taut; the dead steed's white limbs jerked forward; the carcass slid across the ground on its ersatz skis. Oswell guided the horses toward the coppice in which he had disposed of the mare. The marshals walked alongside him.

The one with the weird smile said, "Should we tell T.W.?"

"His daughter's getting married tomorrow. I wouldn't want to trouble him with this business," Oswell said.

"You're right. You are right. Let's not mention it," the one with the cane said. "Smiler doesn't use his head."

"And Smith don't got no manners."

• • •

After depositing the carcass into the coppice, Oswell and the marshals went to a water pump and cleaned themselves up. The rancher thanked the duo for their aid, to which they nodded their heads. The three men entered the dance hall.

The longways dance had evolved into a wide circle of people clapping in time with Wilfreda's up-tempo polka music. In the middle of the clearing were three dozen couples, including Lingham and Beatrice, who danced with each other like birds buffeted by a gale, circling, swatting and clasping each other, trying to make sense of the tempest. A few of the woman's blonde curls came loose from the bun at the back of her head and her neckline dampened with sweat; she kicked out an inexorable riot upon the floor barely matched by her husband-to-be's backward footwork. Oswell recalled the first time he had seen Lingham dance in Alabama and grinned at the memory.

The ancient piano player raised the tempo and wove a few sinister notes into the melody. Oswell looked at Wilfreda and saw that her head was tilted back on her neck; her eyelids fluttered; her mouth moved as if she were speaking to somebody who hovered in the air directly above her. It seemed to him as if she were saying the word "murderers" over and over again.

Chapter Twenty-two

The Sheriff Ruminates (and Dances)

T.W. watched his daughter and James exercise (and possibly exorcize) themselves in the center of the platform, sweaty illustrations of Wilfreda's playing. He supposed that the devout couple used dancing as a surrogate for the physical passion they had thus far abstained from sharing.

When Beatrice was little, her belief in a heavenly reunion with her deceased mother had helped her cope with the absence more than anything else. Consequently, no matter where they lived, T.W. took his little girl to church at least twice a week. The tales and parables had been deeply impressed upon his receptive daughter at an early age and made her a far more devout Christian than he ever was himself. T.W. could not help but make extrapolations regarding what all of this suppressed desire would result in once she was married . . .

He did not like to think of his daughter that way, but her rapture on the dance platform told him more than he wanted to know.

Meredith touched his bad hip and asked, "How does it feel now?" The widow's fingertips went to the very perimeter of what was appropriate to caress on his plaid pants.

"Better. I just need to be careful. When it starts to complain, I need to listen, even when a beautiful woman wants me to quadrille."

Meredith grinned at the compliment, pointed to James and asked, "Where did he learn to move like that?"

"He was a pugilist. Footwork is important in that sport," T.W. said, now uncertain as to how much he believed about what he knew of James's past.

"He certainly is enthusiastic."

T.W. nodded and looked back at the man who would be his son tomorrow. James tapped his feet in a quick shuffle, grabbed Beatrice's hands and pulled her around; their laughter was near maniacal. Behind them, Richard Sterling lit a blush on Roland Taylor's daughter's face, though the New Yorker seemed at all times respectful. Godfrey Danford stood at the perimeter of the circle, beside Annie, each of them drinking punch.

"Your girl can dance real good," an old familiar voice said to T.W. He turned around and looked into the grinning face of Smiler and then over at Smith beside him.

The sheriff clasped and heartily shook each man's right hand. "I'm glad you fellas got out here," T.W. said.

"We promised we would. And tell us, where did you steal that angel from?" Smith said, pointing to Beatrice with his cane.

"I raised her."

"Is she marrying the giant?" Smiler asked.

"She is."

"What's he do? Snatch birds out of trees? Swat clouds away?"

"He's a carpenter. A pretty good one too. You fellas keeping Arkansas safe?"

Smiler said through his grin, "She behaves herself. The Indians over there're all friendly now, so mostly we just ride around breaking up churlishness."

"Smiler's got a squaw."

"You are a liar, Randall Smith. I just brung her some blankets and some cough syrup. Don't mean I got no squaw."

"She gave you that necklace."

"That don't mean anything. It's just beads."

"Not to her. It means something, I told you."

"It don't."

T.W. put his arm around Meredith and said, "Mrs. Evertson, this is Randall Smith and this is Randall Smiler. We used to marshal together in Arkansas a long time ago."

Smith clasped, lifted and kissed Meredith's hand; Smiler elbowed him out of the way, took the same hand, wiped off the previous kiss and then deposited his own on the very same spot.

T.W. noticed a couple of drops of blood on Smith's boots and a spatter on Smiler's left pant cuff. He was about to ask the marshals the source of the stains, when the door to the dancehall opened. T.W. looked over: Deputy Goodstead walked in, wearing far more red than a man should, and a lace tie.

"Pardon me for a measure—I've got to talk to the deputy," T.W. said.

"Are you going to send him home to change into something less abrasive?" Meredith asked.

"I should. I'll be back soon."

T.W. circumnavigated the dance platform and strode toward the deputy, his left hip tight and aching.

"Deputy."

The blank-faced Texan knew what uttering his title meant and said, "You got business."

"James's friends." T.W. pointed out and named Richard Sterling and Godfrey Danford, both at the edge of the dance platform. He surveyed the thick assemblage by the refreshments, made nearly opaque by cigar smoke, descried and marked Oswell Danford. The strong man stood in a dark corner eating a seed cake without looking at it; his sharp eyes surveyed the crowd and glanced through the front window, his mouth mechanically chewing.

"They've been watchful since they got here— Oswell Danford especially. And they hesitated giving me their full names."

"You think they've done some darkness?"

"They've done some darkness."

"Should I shoot them?"

"Big Abe doesn't like blood on his floor."

"I suppose I better not then. Want me to lock 'em up for eating too many candy apples? I bet I could scare up a witness who saw the fat one eat one hundred and nine."

"This isn't the time to go leanin' on strangers for things they might've done outside of Trailspur. We aren't detectives."

"I never told you how I became one? It's a great story."

"Just watch them—they seem to be expecting trouble. But don't hassle them. They're guests of James's, even if I have my suspicions. You understand?"

"Shoot them outside," Goodstead said, but T.W. knew that he did not need to clarify himself, that the deputy understood the boundaries. Wilfreda's right hand wove a brisk melody into the air, atop her left hand's vitriolic tattoo.

The sheriff looked over at Richard Sterling and Godfrey Danford; he looked over at Oswell Danford and saw that the man was staring directly back at him. The strong hard man, chewing his second seed cake, waved at T.W. The sheriff responded with an upraised hand.

Goodstead remarked, "Get back to your widow before she finds another man to compliment that dress she's barely got on. I'll watch these miscreants."

T.W. said, "Thank you," turned from the deputy and walked toward Meredith, who was conversing with Smith and Smiler about what subject he could not even begin to guess.

Big Abe ascended his step ladder and called out, "I've just been informed that Mayor Warren John and his wife, Mrs. Heather John, have arrived, accompanied by their son, Deputy Kenneth John." Wilfreda played a comical melody on her ivory that elicited laughs from many of the revelers.

T.W. and the crowd turned to face the front of the dance hall. The double doors swung wide, admitting a cool dry breeze into the warm humid enclosure. Standing in the portal was Mayor Warren John, wearing a striped blue and gray suit over his square frame; his silver hair was neat and looked as if it had just been cut and washed; the electric lights sparkled in his bulbous spectacles like captured stars. His wife, wearing a white and gray bell dress, firmly clasped his left arm—she had been sick for a long time and needed either a cane or her husband to get around Trailspur. She looked far older than her husband, even though she was a year his junior. Deputy Kenneth John, a pudgy twenty-seven-year-old wearing a blue checkered shirt with a black cravat and matching vest, closed the door behind his parents.

The mayor and his wife plunged headlong into a sea of outstretched hands, which the politico deftly clasped and shook with vigor while his attached wife smiled and nodded pleasantly. Deputy Kenneth John walked over to T.W. and shook his right hand.

"Congratulations."

"Thank you. How is your mother doing?"

Kenneth John looked over at the frail woman clutching the mayor and said, "Better than last month."

"I'm glad to hear it."

The deputy pulled a flask of whiskey from his slacks, twisted off the top and sucked a mouthful from it.

"Off duty," he said, preemptively.

"Enjoy yourself. Tonight's a celebration," T.W. replied, uninterested in lecturing him this evening. Three years ago Kenneth John was a solid deputy with as much promise as Goodstead had now, but then his brother got killed in Omaha by a jealous woman, and shortly after that, his mother became ill with something each doctor diagnosed differently. For the last couple of years, Kenneth drank, was moody and was tardy; he retained his title solely because his father was the mayor, but T.W. never included him in anything important. Before much more time passed, the sheriff intended to relieve him of his star.

T.W. looked at his daughter and James, a storm of limbs upon the dance floor, and then over at

Meredith (who still conversed with Smith and Smiler), and then at the Albens, who had journeyed all the way from Colorado, and then at the mayor, who helped his frail wife into a cushioned chair Big Abe stood behind, and then over at his cousin Robert, who was putting out more funnel cake, and then over at bright red Goodstead. A warmth suffused the sheriff and he let it. This was not a night to fret over strangers or ruminate upon Deputy Kenneth John's ineptitude, this was the night before he turned his daughter over to James Lingham, and he should enjoy and celebrate it with her. Everything else, all of his troubles and suspicions, could wait until after the wedding.

He walked across the hall, shook hands with Mayor Warren John (who poked a gift cigar into his pocket), kissed Mrs. Heather John on the cheek (she always smelled like roses), slapped Judge Higgins on the back and pulled Meredith onto the platform, where they danced right alongside Beatrice and James, the widow's deftly-tailored dress threatening at all times to reveal things he very much wanted to see.

T.W.'s left hip complained; he ignored it.

Chapter Twenty-three

Spilling the Future

Wilfreda paraded an ambulatory melody before the denizens of the dancehall. Dicky pulled Tara Taylor close to him; he allowed his breath to warm the side of her neck while they danced a simple three-step pattern.

"My goodness," the redheaded woman said, a scarlet blush illuminating her cheeks, nose and forehead.

Dicky placed the palm of his hand upon the satin that covered her left hip.

He asked, "May I?"

"You are."

"I am," Dicky said, nodding. He applied a little more pressure to the fleshy curve of her hip; she swallowed dryly. His sensitive fingertips were able to divine the stitching of the underwear beneath her dress. He did not look away from her.

Whenever the handsome New Yorker engaged a timid woman (Tara Taylor was one, though she was not as mousy as Godfrey's girl), he always behaved as he had this evening—making a small physical advance and afterward asking if what he had done was acceptable. It was harder for a shy woman like Tara to deny his hand upon her hip when she already felt the warmth and strength and suggestion of it there. Dicky (greatly) enjoyed convincing women to do things they ordinarily would not do, but he did not at all enjoy copulating with a remorseful woman. By the time he entered his companion, she should feel as if she were receiving a rare gift of great value.

He leaned forward. Tara's footing lagged momentarily behind the music.

With warm, moist air that he summoned from the depths of his lungs, Dicky whispered into the woman's small ear, "You are a lovely dancer." He let his clean-shaven cheek glance across hers as he drew away. The fleeting contact thrilled her.

"Thank you," she said softly.

"James told me that the women of Trailspur were something to behold." He looked at her in such a way that he did not need to complete his statement with words. A blush rose to her cheeks for the thirty-seventh time during the last two hours.

Wilfreda augmented her chords; the air thickened with cigar smoke; Dicky drew closer to Tara. She looked away, cogitating. She wanted to say something to him, something she had almost said twice earlier. From the effort it took her to produce the words, Dicky knew that it was something he did not want to hear.

"My cousin went with a man from the East. From Boston."

"Did she?"

"She did. He was an Italian. He looked a little bit like you. Talked like you talk and was . . . he was confident like you are."

Clearly, she wanted him to ask how the affair had gone, but he did not make the prompted inquiry. He knew from the way she spoke of this Italian that things had not gone well.

"He told her a lot of things, made her some promises and then just disappeared."

"I am not Italian. And I am from New York, not Boston."

"I just wanted to tell you about that. In case you wonder why my mother's been lookin' over here with the raven eye. Or why I might want things to go slow."

If Dicky had time—he estimated two weeks, possibly three—he knew that he could woo this woman. Her barriers—her naturally timid disposition, her inexperience with men (though he doubted she was a virgin) and her cousin's bad experience with the Italian—could be winnowed away with words, direct gazes, admissions of his own shortcomings and gradually escalated physical contact . . . but Dicky did not have time for these things (and this cute, simple mouse was not worth all of that effort even if he did).

When Wilfreda changed the key of her continuous playing, the New Yorker excused himself to go to the outbuilding. He glanced over at Godfrey (who tore off a piece of funnel cake and gave it to Annie), nodded at the man and retreated with apologies to Tara from the dance floor. He would not dance with her again.

When he was three yards from the door, Oswell approached him and secretively slid a gun into his belt before a single word was said.

The rancher leaned in close and whispered, "Be subtle. Some fellow the sheriff talked to is watchin' us now. A deputy maybe." Dicky straightened his maroon bow tie and then adjusted his brown suit jacket to cover over the revolver.

"They gutted two of our horses," Oswell said.

Dicky processed the comment.

"I got rid of the carcasses. I'll watch after you through the window if you're going to the backbuilding."

"I am leaving. I'll see you back at the hotel—tonight or tomorrow morning."

Oswell looked at Dicky, his weathered face wrinkled with concern.

"I'm not running off. There is something I need to do."

"We need you tomorrow."

"I will be there."

Dicky shook Oswell's hand and walked toward the door; he glanced back at the dance platform and saw that Godfrey was holding Annie's hand and grinning.

The night wind threw a chill deep into Dicky's bones that made him hunch forward. He entered the narrow outbuilding and relieved himself (he held his breath the entire time, as he always did in such fetid containers) and then walked up the avenue toward Judge Higgins's Mighty Fine Saloon, or simply—The Gavel. The New Yorker strode in the middle of the dirt road, away from the shadows that congealed on either side; he looked into each patch of darkness as if it might contain a gun with the bullet that would conclude his forty-four years of breathing.

Dicky reached the saloon, ascended the steps, traversed the deck, raked the soles of his shoes on the boot scrape, pushed past the swinging half doors and walked into the carpeted enclosure. The clacking of bagatelle balls startled him more than he would have expected.

He walked toward the somewhat masculine curly-haired brunette who tended the bar.

She turned to him and said, "The shindy is at Big Abe's Dancehall of Trailspur, just up the block. I'm closing down and going over soon."

"I just came from there."

"Are you hunting for something stronger than Abe's rum punch? We've got good whiskey here and some bourbon from Kentucky."

"I wanted to inquire after the location of Queenie's."

The barmaid did her best to conceal her distaste

when she responded, "Go back up the avenue, make a right after Ed's Barbershop and go along a bit until you see a building where the second story is painted purple. At night they put out a lantern and a placard that says 'Queenie's,' so you can't miss it." She looked at him and added, "If you can read."

"Thank you," he said, and put a coin on the table.

Dicky ascended the narrow wooden stairs to Queenie's, his eyes on the purple lantern that shone on the second-story landing. He surmounted the steps and raised his hand to knock upon the door, but the wood retreated before his knuckles made contact.

A plump madam in a silk dress and an impressionistic amount of mascara stood in the portal and appraised Dicky for a moment.

"Are you in Trailspur for the wedding?"

"I am."

"What is your name?"

"Dicky."

She grinned and nodded her head. "Of course you are. I'm Queenie. Please come in." The madam walked him into a carpeted room with red muslins, pink lace curtains over the windows and two lavender divans. She said, "Ladies, we have a guest," and motioned for Dicky to seat himself. Despite his myriad experiences with women, he had never once entered a brothel or paid for companionship; he found the situation somewhat awkward.

A door painted with the tableau of two half-nude women lying on an oversized water lily, eating grapes and sipping ambrosia, swung wide; three women filed into the den, each wearing an elaborately laced purple and black corset and silk slippers that looked as if they had been procured in the Orient. The sound of their smooth strides across the lush carpet reminded Dicky of a sluice. The women looked at the customer and were not at all unhappy.

"He's a bit more handsome than those marshals," Queenie said to the women; they nodded in unison.

Queenie sat beside Dicky, put an arm around his shoulders, motioned to the three ladies with her free hand and said, "They are all friendly and skilled in the arts of lovemaking. That is Dolores, that is Rebecca and that is Viola. If none of them are to your particular taste, you may wait and have a look at Alice and Mina—they are both working right now. I usually do not proffer myself, but in this case will make an exception if you are inclined toward the company of a more experienced woman." She placed her hand upon his left leg and squeezed.

"Please give me a moment to consider the many fine options."

"Certainly," she said, her fingertips playing up and down his left thigh like the tongue of a cat cleaning its dirty paw.

Dicky assessed the three woman standing before him. Dolores was without question the prettiest. Her face looked like a painting, but her hips were narrow and her bosom—even bolstered by the corset—was small. Rebecca was older (he presumed closer to thirty than twenty) and her figure was fuller, but perhaps because of her additional years as a whore, she looked unhealthy around her eyes and chin. Dicky surveyed Viola, who wore garters and lace stockings with her corset and slippers. She was just north of twenty, had a pleasant (if somewhat plain) broad face and a healthy complexion; her wavy brown hair still shone with the luster of youth. Her bosom nearly spilled from the top of her corset and her hips were wide and fleshy.

"I would like to get to know Viola better."

Viola's eyes lit up; Queenie and Dolores were surprised by the choice; Rebecca was openly disappointed.

Viola said, "Truly?"

"Indeed." He looked at Queenie and asked, "Do I negotiate a price with you?"

"There is a two-dollar rental fee for the room. The remainder you work out with Viola in private." Dicky assumed that Queenie would also claim a percentage of that fee.

He handed the madam four dollars and said, "I intend to take my time and I do not wish to be disturbed. If anybody comes looking for me, I am not here."

"A lot of married men come here, Mr. Dicky. They know that Queenie's is a safe and private place."

Dicky stood up walked toward Viola, who stood looking at him with a big grin. Dolores, the gorgeous favored girl, pulled a robe over her corset, sat upon a divan and opened a small book with illustrations of birds in it.

Rebecca looked at Dicky and said, "If you change your mind or want something different, I promise you won't never forget the things I can do."

Queenie said, "Rebecca. Be respectful. Mr. Dicky has already chosen his companion for this evening." The admonished woman sat upon the other divan and sulked.

Viola pressed her chest into Dicky's shoulder, slid her right arm around the small of his back and walked him to the door painted with the nymph fresco. She drew it wide, took his right hand and led him into a small hallway lit lavender by a lantern. She shut the den door behind them and calmly ushered her client past four closed rooms, to the final chamber on the left side of the passage.

"Viola is a pretty name."

"Thank you, Mr. Dicky."

She twisted a brass handle sculpted to resemble a bird's wing and pushed open the door; amber light and the smell of lilacs and cinnamon spilled out into the hall. Viola pulled him into her chamber.

An oil lantern hung behind an amber sleeve, radiating soft light that illuminated a large bed, a tall mahogany wardrobe painted with frolicking nymphs, a low bureau and a porcelain washbasin embossed with flowers. The wallpaper was brown with copper stripes and the curtains over the lone window were gold-colored lace. Viola shut the door.

"This room is very nice," he said.

"Thank you. We each take care of our own."

"Would you please lock the door?"

"We're not supposed to do that. Queenie don't like it."

"I am a nervous fellow."

"I noticed you got a gun tucked in your belt."

Dicky removed the gun and set it upon the bed.

"You may put that away if it would make you feel more comfortable."

Viola pinched the barrel as if it were the tail of a dead rat, raised and carried the revolver over to her bureau; she opened the bottom drawer, placed the weapon inside and slid the compartment closed. She walked over to the door and twisted the brass key that sat within the lock; the tumblers clicked.

The woman turned back to face Dicky, a grin on her face. She walked toward him, plunging one foot and then the other into the lush carpet; her slippers' susurrations were lascivious. She pressed the palms of her hands to Dicky's jacket and effortlessly slid the garment off of his back and down his arms, somehow also unbuttoning and removing his vest in the process. She set the apparel upon a wooden coatrack, kissed his lips, grinned (revealing a dimple on each of her cheeks) and applied her long fingers to the maroon bow tie at his neck. The ribbon came loose and dangled from his collar; her fingertips slid the buttons of his shirt through the eyelets one after another, like a sewing machine in reverse.

"May we talk for a moment?" Dicky asked.

Her hands continued down his chest, unbuttoning his shirt.

She said, "You want to tell me about your wife?" Her fingers began to unhook the bronze buckle of his belt.

"I am not married."

She looked up at him, concern in her wide hazel eyes.

"You ain't married?"

"No."

She looked at her hands clasped firmly to his belt buckle and said, "Is there . . . do you have some sort of . . . problem?" Before he could reply, she knelt before him and placed her cheek against the crotch of his pants; she rubbed her smooth face back and forth, humming deeply. He became stiff. "It works," she said, pleased. She arose and clapped her hands back onto his belt buckle.

"May we talk for a moment, please?"

"You want me to be naked for this discussion?"

"It would be easier if you remained clothed."

She ran the palm of her right hand along his engorged phallus and nodded, "Okay. But let's not do too much talking."

Dicky sat on the edge of the bed; Viola sat beside him, put her hands in her lap and interlaced her fingers as if she were in school.

He asked, "Do you like this line of work?"

"Sometimes. When a man like you comes in, I do. Most fellows, I need to imagine other stuff or close my eyes when it's happenin'." She looked at her hands, ruminated for a moment and then added, "There are some nice folks in Trailspur, I suppose. I can't do much else, and men think I am good in here, so this is what I do."

Dicky felt a bit of melancholy creep into him.

She looked at his somber face and said, "Do you want me to tell you about other men? What I do with them? Or maybe . . . maybe you want to know what they look like when it's happenin'? Some men like to hear about that stuff. It's okay."

"How much money do you make in a year?"

She looked at him, surprised by the question.

"I'm not sure—I didn't do good in arithmetic. I usually make nineteen dollars a week, though sometimes more. Once I made thirty. Dolores usually gets twice that."

Dicky tabulated and said, "You make about a thousand dollars a year."

"I believe you."

"I would like to show you something." Dicky fished into his slacks and drew out a thick billfold. "These are all one-hundred-dollar bills, legal tender."

"How many you got there?"

Dicky handed it to her and said, "Count them."

She looked at the money in her tremulous hands and said, "I ain't good with arithmetic, I told you."

"There are fifty such bills."

"How much does that make altogether?"

"Five thousand dollars."

She said, "That's a fortune." She scrutinized the bills and added, "I never held this much money all at once, not ever. And my uncle in New Orleans was a tycoon, though he's rotten mean."

Dicky put his right hand on Viola's cheek, turned her face toward his and said, "I think you are a very special woman. You are beautiful, sweet and honest."

"Thank you, Mr. Dicky. Men say nice things to me when it's happenin' or 'cause they want something extra, but it's nice to hear compliments this way."

"I would like to have a child and I would like for you to be the mother of this child."

Viola's eyes widened; she stared at him in breathless silence. He could not tell whether the look upon her broad face was of pure joy or pure terror, though he presumed it was a mixture of both.

"You're going to pay me to be your wife? You don't even know me. And I'm a whore. And I don't know you at all."

"My name is Richard Sterling. I live in New York. I have been a card sharp and a gambler and an outlaw. I have likely been with as many women as you have men."

"That's why you ain't got no wife? You runnin' around so much you can't pick one good enough to keep?"

"Precisely. But tonight I feel different. My life seems thin . . . and sheer." Dicky wished that this confession were a ruse.

"Any girl would want a man that looks like you, and you're smart and rich too. I don't know why you come to me with this notion."

"There is a good chance that I am going to be killed tomorrow."

Viola's eyes sparkled with concern, "You're gonna get killed?"

"I do not know for certain, but it is likely."

"So you want a baby?"

"Yes. If I survive, I will take you back to New

York and marry you, I promise. If I am killed—" Dicky pointed to the money she still clutched. "That will cover your living expenses throughout the pregnancy and many years afterward if you are careful with how you spend it. If you do not want the baby, you may give him or her up for adoption. The important thing to me is that a child of mine will be born into this world—that I leave behind something other than just mistakes."

"I would keep my baby, no matter what."

"Do we have a deal?"

Viola, still in shock over the proposition, nodded her head.

"I won't put in my diaphragm. Let me hide the money so Queenie don't descry it." Viola took the bills and walked over to her bureau. She opened a large drawer and from a sea of lingerie withdrew a framed daguerreotype of a family standing outside a house abutting a swamp. With trembling fingers, she slid the glass and the picture from the frame, exposing the wood beneath and twenty dollars legal tender that she had hidden there previously. She unfolded Dicky's bills, laid them flat in the niche, and then covered them over. Viola interred the daguerreotype beneath her lingerie, shut the drawer and returned to the New Yorker.

Dicky set a smaller bill upon the nightstand and said, "You can tell Queenie I paid you ten for your services." Viola nodded, pulled off Dicky's unbuttoned shirt, draped it on the coatrack, slid off his belt like it was a serpent, pulled off his boots and socks and then slid off his pants so that he wore only his maroon union suit.

She pressed herself against him, pushed him onto his back and said, "I hope this isn't a dream."

Her tongue surged into his mouth; her warm breath filled his lungs. He untied the side of her corset, slid his hands underneath the stiff fabric, teased her nipples with his fingertips and then pressed his palms firmly to her plush breasts. Her midsection began to sway. She pressed her clothed nexus against his phallus, long and stiff beneath his union suit. Her movements were serpentine and hypnotic. There were reasons beyond hard luck that this woman had become a whore, Dicky thought.

He playfully flung her off of himself, onto the far side of the bed. He came down on top of her, slid between her legs and pulled away the corset. Her freed breasts stared up at him like enormous eyes, the nipples pink pupils. He slid her underpants from her rounded hips; she withdrew his phallus from his union suit, caressed it with both hands, fingering its lines and ridges. He pressed its tip to the dampened hair between her legs and rubbed her gently. She bit her lower lip. He pulled off his union suit.

Viola opened her thighs; Dicky entered her; the

woman's silken insides soothed his heated phallus. Her bare skin was hot against his. She clamped her legs around his lower back; they found a rhythm together, even and forceful.

Tears leaked from the corners of his eyes when he shot his seed, hard and searing as if the head of his phallus had erupted. He fell asleep between her loins, still lodged deep within her.

Chapter Twenty-four

Patience, My Dear

Beatrice sat on a wooden chair beside Jim. He handed her a cup.

The titan precluded her inquiry when he said, "It's the fruit punch." She drank the juice while he dabbed a damp cloth on her warm forehead. "I think we showed 'em all who the best dancers in Trailspur are."

She surveyed the crowd, one-third the size it was four hours ago. The throng largely ignored the solicitations of Wilfreda's playing, preferring to eat the seed and funnel cakes, drink punch or smoke cigars.

"They all danced out," Jim remarked with grammar she would not allow him to pass on to their children. She kissed him on the forehead and leaned her head against his shoulder.

"Tonight has been divine. Everyone whom I

wanted to see showed up and enjoyed themselves. I hope that the ceremony and the banquet are just as wonderful."

"Yeah," was Jim's response. She looked up at his face, but it was turned away from her and darkened by shadow. He took her right hand in one of his titanic carpenter hands and gently pressed his other atop it, as if he were making a sandwich with too little meat for the bread.

"I think we should leave soon," she said. "It is fine for guests to come to our wedding tired and bedraggled, but we must be well rested. My father rented a rolling daguerreotype saloon for the banquet." Jim nodded. She added, "This is the last night that we will sleep apart from one another." Beatrice pursed her lips and gave voice to none of the twining images that raced through her mind and made her chest and nexus ache.

"Let me tell my pals when to get to church with that ledger." He leaned over and kissed her; she felt the heat of his face and tasted sweat upon his lips.

"I'll be back in a moment," the titan said. He stood up, squeezed her shoulder and walked into the cigarsmoke haze in which luminous butts glowed like the eyes of wary cats.

She watched Jim and the Danfords congregate in a dark corner and converse.

"You are running out of time to change your mind."

Beatrice looked to her left and saw Deputy Goodstead, ablaze in red clothing.

"I believe I am going to stay the course with Jim."

"Worse things have happened. The Civil War. The Alamo. Those plagues."

"Thank you for your blessing, Deputy."

"If I could give blessings, I'd be a minister—and then I'd accidentally marry the two of us."

Despite herself, Beatrice grinned at Goodstead's blunt and tireless approach.

"You will stop pestering me for my hand once I am married, I suppose?"

"I wasn't just going for the hand."

Beatrice was startled by the bold remark.

"Sorry," Goodstead said. "I had some of the rum punch. Thought it was fruit punch, deceived by all the fruit floatin' in it."

He turned his blank gaze from her over to Jim and the Danfords.

"Did Jim say where the other one went?"

"Dicky?"

"I thought his name was Richard. The swarthy one that looks like the sort of fella no girl's father wants to give a handshake."

"That is Dicky. No, Jim did not remark upon his absence."

"Funnel cake is real good," Goodstead said, unfolding a kerchief and pulling off a piece from the rather large section he had purloined.

Beatrice had noticed Goodstead and her father monitoring Dicky and the Danfords throughout the shindy.

She asked, "Are you and my father concerned about Jim's friends?"

The jaw housed in the basement of the blank facade masticated funnel cake, while the head itself shook twice in denial. She looked over at her husband-to-be and watched him part from the Danfords. The titan strode past weary dancers, cake eaters and producers of gray clouds.

Goodstead thrust his right hand at Jim and said, "You must be James's father?"

"Nope. It's me."

"Hard to tell—old folks look so alike."

"Forty-six is not that old," Beatrice defended.

Jim asked Goodstead, "You tryin' to convince Bea to call off the weddin'?"

"Certainly not. It's nice she's want to marry someone so advanced. It's like a charity."

Jim smiled at the remark. He was never threatened by Goodstead's advances and jibes, and (like her father) he found the blank-faced Texan a great source of amusement.

The titan leaned over, scooped her up in both of his arms (she gulped the remainder of her punch so that she would not spill it), nodded to the deputy and said, "See you at the weddin'."

"I make japes and all, but I wish you two the best. Honest. And if she becomes a widow, don't you worry about who's gonna take care of her: Mayor Goodstead will provide."

Beatrice inquired, "You intend to be the mayor of Trailspur?"

"Until they need me in Washington, D.C."

Beatrice waved to Goodstead as her husband-to-be whisked her away.

Jim carried her past the ebullient Mayor Warren John and his frail wife, the small gray Judge Higgins (joined an hour ago by his barmaid Rita), her father's cousin Robert (and his tall spouse), her friends Lilith Ford and Judy O'Connell (who was with her husband Izzy), Deputy Kenneth John, Wilfreda (who congratulated her with eerie cachinnations), Big Abe and his slim wife, the ribald tailor (who was staring at Tara Taylor's backside), the three Albens in from Colorado, those marshals Smith and Smiler, the Danfords (the heavy one now holding the hand of Annie Yardley) and ultimately in front of her father who sat beside the Widow Evertson (both on wooden chairs).

"Jim is going to take me home."

Her father had not seen her coming; the moment he heard his daughter's voice, he hastily removed his hand from the widow's. Beatrice thought that he looked happy and comfortable alongside the woman.

"Why are you grinning like that?" her father asked defensively.

Beatrice responded, "Perhaps you and Miss Evertson would like to stand alongside us when Minister Bachs performs the ceremony?"

"A twofer," Jim added.

"Stop that kind of talk," her father said, unable to look her or Jim in the eye.

The widow leaned forward and surveyed her father's face. "You are blushing."

"I'm not. It's just red in here."

"The lights are yellow." The woman took T.W.'s hand and squeezed it. She looked up at Beatrice, suspended in Jim's arms, and said, "Your father tells me that you have an interest in painting."

"I do."

"I know that you will be busy in the immediate future"—her eyes went up to Jim's face and then returned to Beatrice's with a grin in them—"but whenever you are so inclined, I ask that you please join me for an afternoon of painting landscapes. I have extra brushes and canvases and many, many colors from which to choose."

"Thank you Miss Evertson. Do you prefer to be called Miss Evertson?"

"In general, I ask to be called Mrs. Evertson, but I would prefer for you and James to call me Meredith."

"Thank you Meredith."

"I read that article you wrote for the *Trailspur Gazette* last month and the one in the winter edition. It would be a pleasure to have an intelligent companion to paint with. Your father thinks that I spend too much time alone." She looked at Beatrice's father with a gaze that was both wry and earnest.

"He thoroughly understands women and their needs," Beatrice remarked facetiously.

"I am pleased to hear that," Meredith responded.

"You get her to bed," T.W., discomfited and fidgety, said to Jim. "I'll be home in a little while. Need to rest my hip a bit more before I go."

Jim swept Beatrice forward; she delivered a kiss to her father's cheek and then shook Meredith's hand. The titan carried her from the room, into the cool Montana air.

The couple climbed the lone stone step at the front of the house within which Beatrice had lived for fifteen years. They paused before the door.

"I'd like to wait inside with you—'til your pa comes home."

"He may be a while, and we both need to get to sleep. You should head back to your home."

Her titan hesitated and then looked up and down the dirt road at the neighboring houses that sat like bricks against a blue-black sky. There was something nagging him that he did not voice. Beatrice had first noticed this unnamed pregnancy three weeks ago and watched it burgeon when Mary was mutilated—something he still refused to discuss with her. Since the moment his friends arrived, she had never felt as if she had all of his attention.

"What is troubling you?"

"I just want to wait until T.W. gets here is all."

She knew something was wrong, but her trust in him was absolute: if he did not wish to disclose the source of his unease, she would not pry. At some later time, he would explain it to her if there was a reason for him to do so. He did not know everything about her either—she had never once mentioned the Catholic to whom she had been secretly engaged when she was studying out East—and she would not make him uncomfortable over his discretion.

"Let's get inside," he said, surveying the environs and then pressing his left hand to the door. The wood swung wide into the dark house. She noticed for the first time that Jim had a gun tucked into his belt.

Beatrice walked into the darkness, took a match from the brass box on the wall, struck it on steel and lit an oil lantern. The warm light radiated throughout the den and connecting kitchen.

Jim shut the door. He slid the bolt across as quietly as he could; Beatrice pretended not to hear it.

She asked, "Would you like some tea?"

"That would be a salve."

Beatrice lit the tinder within the stove, put three cups of water into the kettle and added dry tea leaves. She furtively observed Jim sit, tuck his gun behind his back and recline upon the abraded throw quilt her mother had made that adorned the couch.

"I didn't see Minister Bachs there," Jim said as she poured steaming tea into two wooden mugs.

"I do not think he comes out for shindys. I doubt he would approve of the punch or the way people close-dance."

"I s'pose. And a holy man at a celebration makes people feel anxiousness."

Beatrice set the cups upon the table before the couch. He looked at her, half of his long face illumined by the lantern, half of his face in shadow.

"You looked so pretty tonight," he said. "Still do."

"Thank you."

Jim picked up his wooden cup with his left hand (even though he was right-handed) and was about to drink when she said, "Blow on it first so you do not burn yourself." He blew the steam from the small cauldron and then sipped.

"Is there enough sugar in yours?" She had given him five lumps, which was usually the correct amount.

"Just right," he said absently, his eyes fixed on her face.

Beatrice blew upon and sipped her tea (which had no sugar in it). There was a crack upstairs, and Jim hastily twisted around in his seat; his right hand slid behind his back, and his left knee knocked into her thigh. A tablespoon of tea sloshed over the lip of her unbalanced cup and splashed upon the top of her green dress; the hot liquid seeped into her corset and stung her skin.

"Oh," she exclaimed.

Jim looked at her and asked, "Are you burnt?"

"I shall be fine."

"If it's gonna blister, you should put a tomato on it, quick."

"I shall be fine. I was just startled."

Jim nodded, set his tea down and said, "I'm gonna have a look upstairs."

"There is no need—that noise was the door to my father's armoire. The wind catches it whenever he leaves his shutters open."

"I'll go have a look."

She watched Jim rise from the couch, walk across the den and ascend beyond the lantern's amber luminance into the obscurity of the second floor. She heard his weight bend the wood above her, eliciting dry creaks. There was a pause; a heavy moment later his footsteps continued, diminishing as he went down the upstairs hallway. Beatrice's heart thudded.

The footsteps halted; somewhere above her, a door opened and closed. She heard a dull thump.

Beatrice put the cup down. The silence was oppressive.

"Jim . . . ?"

"Just lookin' round, Bea," he said, his voice tinny and muted.

The skin beneath her corset scalded by spilt tea started to throb in time with her racing pulse. She needed to set something cool and moist upon it soon so that it would not blister. The footsteps above her head resumed an even tattoo.

She asked, "Is everything in order?"

"Nothing to worry about," Jim said, his voice louder, closer.

Beatrice went into the kitchen and there untied her shoulder straps; the fine-stitch cotton fabric came loose. She pulled the top of the green garment down to reveal the black corset beneath. With nimble fingers, she unfastened three of the hooks on her left side, pulled the material halfway down her breast and saw a bright red mark glowing upon the skin.

"You got a mark?"

She looked over and saw Jim descend the final stair.

"A small one."

"I'm sorry for knockin' into you. I'm just anxious 'bout the wedding. You got a tomato to put on it?"

"No."

"A raw steak maybe? Or pork chop?"

She shook her head. Jim took a hand towel from the wall and strode to the wash bucket. He plunged the fabric into the soapy water, drew it forth, wrung out the excess liquid (with his strength, it took him only one twist to get out what would have taken her three), and walked over to her.

She reached her hand out for the cloth, but he shook his head and said, "Let me get it."

He placed the chill, wet towel upon her reddened skin; immediately the prickling wound cooled.

"I am capable of holding it there," she said.

"I'm the fool that did it to you, so it's my responsibility."

He pressed the cloth more firmly to her skin. Two beads of moisture rolled from the fabric, down the top of her left breast, beneath her corset and converged upon the textured curve of her nipple. The water felt cold upon the sensitive skin and she felt a tingling within her. Jim pressed the cloth more firmly to the burn; a rivulet snaked down the swell of her left breast and sluiced across her nipple, now stiff beneath her corset. Her mouth became dry.

Jim placed his mouth upon hers, his tongue warm and tasting of tea; more cool water drained from the cloth beneath her corset, down her left breast, across her ribs, down her stomach and pooled in a whirl at her belly button. He squeezed the cloth in his fist; the weal stung in a way that pleased her. Water ran down her breast and stomach and into the blonde curls of her pubic mound.

She thrust her tongue more deeply into Jim's mouth; he released the washcloth and slid his fingertips beneath her corset and squeezed, eliciting the most exquisite ache she had ever felt in her breast. A moan that sounded like it came from a stranger emerged from her own throat.

The wall of the kitchen struck her buttocks and shoulder blades; Jim pressed himself against her front, his phallus hard and warm at an angle across her stomach. He pulled down her corset and lowered his head to her left breast; he took half of the lobe into his mouth and wrote circles with his tongue tip around her stiff nipple. She ran her fingertips through his blond hair.

"Jim," she said as the delicious agony grew in her bosom and the blonde curls at the bottom of her corset dampened with her own moisture. (She knew they should stop, but the ache in her breasts and the warm pins in her loins made it hard to speak.)

"Jim," she said again. He raised his mouth from her breast, the pale skin and red nipple of the lobe gleaming, and kissed her again with a fire he had never once before allowed himself to exhibit.

Another crack sounded—this time from outside of the house. Jim twisted from her and drew the gun he had slid down the back of his belt. He watched the front door for a moment.

Her voice quiet and dry, Beatrice said, "That was just the front door to the Meyers' house."

"Okay."

He replaced the gun beneath his belt. She raised the cups of her corset and then refastened the hooks on the side. Beatrice did not look at Jim as she pulled up and then tied the straps of her dress. She was embarrassed, yet her heart still hammered with excitement.

"I shouldn't have done that—gone an' gotten us all crazy riled up," he said. "We should wait for God's blessin'. We waited this long."

"Tomorrow night," she said. She felt certain that had Jim not been distracted by the noise, the two of them would have prematurely joined together as husband and wife.

They drank tea and talked about the shindy. She did not ask why a man who had patiently abstained for over two years had lost his self-control the night before the wedding, because she was almost certain he would not tell her the truth when he answered her.

When her father arrived, smiling and with a smear of lipstick just beneath his chin, Jim shook his hand, kissed her good-bye and departed into the night.

Beatrice, filled with myriad concerns, asked her

father if he would read her to sleep as he had up until she was eleven years old. His voice carried her from the anxieties of reality into the realm of children's stories and ultimately into the velvet domain of slumber.

Chapter Twenty-five

Victuals and Revolvers

The small room was lit blue by the dawn sky. In the middle of the narrow bed, Oswell set down a sealed envelope upon which he had written,

Should Oswell Danford go missing or perish please deliver this parcel to—

Elinore Bass Danford
13 Cutter Way
Harrisfield, Virginia

Thank you.

He left five dollars legal tender on top of the missive to cover expenses and to encourage an honest delivery.

Oswell had not slept very well, and when he walked into the hallway and looked at his brother's weary visage, he did not need to ask if Godfrey had fared any better. The rancher knocked on the door to Dicky's apartment, but received no response.

"Maybe he's in the lobby," Godfrey said.

Oswell, who wore a dark brown suit and cowboy hat like his brother's, a fresh white shirt and a new union suit beneath it, said, "Let's see if he's down there."

The Danfords descended the stairs into the quiet lobby of Hotel Halcyon. An old man wearing a white suit stared at a window on the other side of which the coming sun announced itself in swaths.

Oswell sat in a cushioned chair; he set the guest ledger upon his lap and his enameled pen case atop that. Godfrey sat next to him; he placed the valise with the revolvers on the floor beside his feet.

"You get any sleep at all?" Godfrey asked.

"A couple of hours—in slices and slivers."

"You have any dreams?"

"I had one about Elinore and the kids." His children and wife had not recognized him in the dream.

"I had one about Mr. Ferguson. You remember him?"

"The bank manager," Oswell said. "The one who took Ma's house from us."

"Yeah. I had a dream that it didn't happen like that. We didn't beat on him at all, and instead of taking the house, Mr. Ferguson hired on some special doctor who brought Ma back from the dead and fixed her eyes and everything. And afterward, he went and married her."

Oswell imagined the scene and asked, "And then what happened?"

"I had a restaurant. You became a sheriff like you always said you were going to. Things were real different."

"Sounds like we were good men."

The brothers sat in silence for a minute.

Godfrey said, "Too bad it didn't happen that way."

"Yeah." A silhouetted figure passed in front of the window. "There's Dicky," Oswell said, pointing to the front door.

The handsome man walked into the lobby, looked at the old man in white and then at the Danfords.

"Give me a moment to refresh myself," the New Yorker said to Oswell.

"It's early. You've got some time."

Dicky, his suit wrinkled and shirt stained with sweat, climbed the stairs toward the second landing.

"I guess Trailspur women aren't any cleverer than the girls elsewhere," Oswell said with a grimace.

"I liked the one that I was dancing with," Godfrey remarked.

"What's her name?"

"Annie."

"I saw you holding hands and close-dancing. She looked pretty."

"She's very pretty. Her grandfather was from Spain."

"You always liked girls like that—like that one you asked to marry you in Arizona. What was her name?"

"Consuela."

"You had some good times with her."

"I should've just told her I was Catholic. Jesus is still Jesus, no matter what the minister calls himself."

"Is Annie going to be at the wedding?"

Godfrey nodded, but did not look happy in so doing. Oswell knew that his sibling's attachment to the woman was yet another source of concern on a day ripe with peril.

A few minutes later, Dicky descended the stairs, wearing a black suit and round, broad-brimmed hat. To Oswell, the man looked refreshed and alert.

"Do we have time for breakfast?" Dicky asked.

Oswell looked at the window; the sun had not yet risen from the earth.

"Let's have some chow," he said.

"Blackie," Dicky said to the old man in the white suit.

The elder turned to face Dicky; Oswell saw that he was blind.

The old man said, "You're the one that weighs one hundred an' seventy, right?"

"You are correct."

"What do you want?"

"We are hungry. Is there a place in town you would recommend for us to breakfast at?"

"Go to Harry's Good Eats. Her coffee'll turn you into a nigger. Food's good too. Get the pork chops."

"Thank you," Dicky said. "And I hope that Isabel comes to have tea with you this morning."

"I've got a good feelin' about today. A very good feelin'," he said, and looked back at the window with blank, blind eyes.

The three men walked into Harry's Good Eats, sat upon three stools at the burnished counter and then looked at the menu that was painted in red calligraphy upon a green placard nailed to the wall. A bearish woman, wearing her blonde hair coiled like a cobra atop her head and a grease-spattered apron, walked past the diminutive Negro standing at the smoking griddle in the rear of the kitchen alley, and over to the three new arrivals.

"Do you need for me to read you the menu?" she asked with an accent that indicated to Oswell that she was German or perhaps Swedish.

"No ma'am," Oswell replied. "We can all read."

She put her hands on her hips, prompting them to order.

Oswell said, "I'd like the pork chops and scrambled eggs. And some potatoes and dark toast. And coffee too." The woman did not write the order down, but instead nodded that she had memorized it.

"That's what I want too," Godfrey said. The woman nodded.

Dicky said, "I would like a stack of pancakes, some syrup, pork chops, and eggs over easy, if your cook is capable."

"Buzzy is deft," she said.

"I would also like a steak, medium rare—New York strip if you have it—and some sausages. Coffee would also be appreciated."

The woman looked at him incredulously and then nodded. Godfrey, despite the day that loomed before him, laughed; Oswell warmed at the familiar sound of his brother's cachinnations.

"I suppose we don't have to ask what you were doing last night," Godfrey said. "It's good you can walk, at least."

"I am Harry," the woman announced and then departed. She walked over to Buzzy to relay the order; he nodded when she had told him everything. The five-foot-tall colored man stood on a crate with a long metal spatula in each hand, expertly wielding the pair as if they were metallic extensions of his own limbs. He grabbed the flour bag and flipped meat and cracked and scrambled eggs without ever once putting the tools down. Oswell could tell that he enjoyed his work.

Buzzy cooked. The smears of light, flashes of fire, clicks, cracks, clinks and sizzles mesmerized Oswell and drew him out of his weathered body and away from his worries into an incorporeal and thoughtless limbo. He wondered if this was what death was like and then abruptly returned to himself.

Harry placed the food before the three of them; Dicky's order was so large it overhung the edges of the counter and crowded into Godfrey's space. They ate their meals. Even though he knew that he consumed very flavorful victuals, Oswell was unable to taste anything; he chewed and swallowed with no more relish than if he were chopping wood for tinder.

Dicky treated them and left a tip equal to the cost of the entire meal (a gesture that Harry seemed to find evidence of stupidity rather than generosity, judging by the irritated look upon her face when she counted the bills). The Danfords thanked the New Yorker and stood from their seats.

The three men walked out and were struck by sunlight. They lowered the brims of their hats and walked east, toward the church.

Oswell, Godfrey and Dicky, three yards' distance between each man, traversed the main avenue into a rural section of town. They walked past nineteen houses, four farms, three cattle ranches and a vast fenced property adorned with six signs reading TAYLOR'S HORSE CORRAL: RUSTLERS WILL BE SHOT DEAD.

In threescore strides, the lush grass of the plain was replaced by wild weeds. A silhouetted cross, wavering in the brilliance of the rising sun, sat in the swell of land ahead of the trio. The men continued forward; two more crosses and the body of the church rose from the ground. The gazebo, four hundred yards east of God's house and fifty to the south, was the only other anomaly on the wide horizon, the last remaining tooth in an old man's jaw.

"Your special rifle can cover that gap?" Oswell asked.

"It is a shallow-groove, lead-bullet rifle made for long-range shooting. I have won competitions with it at twice that distance."

"Okay."

They walked past the church (at which no one was present) and over to the gazebo, in which Dicky had hidden his weapons. The trio climbed the five wooden steps into the octagonal shelter.

The New Yorker took his ten-shooter from his waist, set it beneath the bench, lifted up a loose plank, looked at the oblong bundle in the dirt below, withdrew a pair of binoculars, replaced the plank, sat down, took off his black hat, fanned himself with it and yawned.

Oswell asked, "You goin' to set up the special gun now?"

"It is assembled and loaded, as is the lever-action rifle you gave me."

"I suppose you shouldn't have it out while people are getting to the church," Godfrey said.

"If someone comes directly at me, I will use my revolver—it is far quieter than either rifle. Once those church doors are shut, I will get to this." He thumped the heel of his boot upon the loose plank. "Presently, I will survey these fine Montana landscapes for rogues and jackals," he said, raising his binoculars from his lap. He spoke jauntily, but Oswell could hear tension in his voice.

"You remember the old signals?"

Dicky withdrew a lady's hand mirror from his jacket pocket and redirected the sun into Oswell's eyes for a brief, blinding moment that pulsed painfully in the center of his skull.

"One flash for all clear; two flashes for a warning; three for an engagement," Oswell said.

"I remember."

Oswell looked for a moment at Dicky. He had no idea what else to say to him. He tipped the brim of his hat to the New Yorker, turned around and descended the gazebo steps, the sun and his brother at his back as he walked west and north toward the church over four hundred yards off.

"I intend to see the Danford brothers at the banquet tonight," Dicky said.

"I hope so," Godfrey said.

"Yeah," Oswell contributed.

The gazebo shrank behind the Danfords and the church swelled in front of them. Their strides synchronized—the tattoo was that of a lone man walking across the dirt. They reached the facade of God's house.

"Give me a five-shooter," Oswell said.

Godfrey withdrew and handed his brother one of the large-caliber revolvers. Oswell raised his right pant leg, slid the gun into his boot and dropped the cuff down over it.

"That can't be comfortable," Godfrey remarked.

"It isn't—but if that sheriff sees guns on us, I'm not sure what he'll do. He's got suspicions already, and we need to be here no matter what."

"You may be able to stand at the door with that, but I can't walk the patrol with a gun in my boot," Godfrey said. "I'll stash the other two in places where I can get at them—in case I can't get to the rifles we buried in time."

"Do that."

Godfrey took the valise and headed to the side of the church.

Oswell looked at his own shadow, stretched like black taffy across the dirt, weeds and stones to his right. He wondered what Elinore's face would look like when she read the letter he had written; he shook his head to clear the visage he saw.

The forty-seven-year-old rancher leaned his back against the white church he had traveled across the country to stand in front of on this day. He looked to the east: the plains were open for many, many miles before they surged and narrowed into mountaintops, from behind which the sun shone like a brilliant accusation upon his face. Oswell scanned the flat plains; he wondered what would rise up from the dirt and try to pull him and his posse down.

Chapter Twenty-six

The Biggest Day

T.W. stood in front of the polished metal mirror he had inherited from his mother two decades prior and checked for the third time that he did not look like a fool. Tails dripped like a runny nose from the rear of his navy blue jacket, the shirt's high collar poked his jaw, the double-breasted checkered vest looked like a chessboard and the frilly cravat made him feel as if he were a clown. Though he preferred the simple plaid two-piece he had worn last evening, his daughter informed him that this suit was his most—and only—fashionable attire. T.W.'s opinion on fashion was that it was a way to persuade people to wear things that were ridiculous and spend too much money in acquiring them, but this was Beatrice's day and he would wear whatever she requested without (verbal) complaint. The tailor had adjusted the suit to accommodate the extra two inches his waist had acquired since he last wore it, and looking at his reflection, he supposed that he was not an embarrassment to the Jeffries lineage.

"The circus is in town?"

T.W. turned to face the newly arrived deputy. The Texan wore a striped black and brown two-piece suit and a silk tie as thin as a shoelace; he sipped coffee.

"Don't fling any remarks at this in front of Beatrice," T.W. said as he adjusted his cravat and wiped lint from his left shoulder. "She bought it for my fiftieth birthday."

"I'm lookin' forward to what happens at sixty."

"She says it's fashionable." T.W. lifted and then dropped one of the tails.

"I don't recall you wearin' it. And I like to laugh."

T.W. turned sideways, sucked in his stomach and said, "I wore it to Lester O'Connell's funeral."

"You couldn't toss it in the coffin?"

"Do you intend to hurl insults at me throughout my daughter's wedding day?"

"I'm focused on the suit right now."

"Be polite. Today is a big day for me."

"The biggest. You need anything?"

"Beatrice said she wasn't hungry, so I didn't cook, but that coffee and toast sure smell good."

Goodstead handed the wooden mug to T.W. and then the thick, butter-soaked toast, from which not one bite had been taken.

"Brought 'em up for you, though I had a sip of the coffee. I'll go down and get some more." He paused in the doorway and said, "With Beatrice leaving, I suppose I need to familiarize myself with the particulars of your kitchen. Took me a while to find the sugar."

"I apologize for the disarray."

"My time is valuable."

"There's another option, you know," T.W. intimated.

"Does it involve my kitchen?"

"It might."

"I'm not gonna tell you to shut your damn mouth on your daughter's weddin' day. I refuse to do it."

Goodstead left the room; T.W. turned to face the mirror again. He wondered what Meredith would think of this absurd clothing.

"You look very handsome."

T.W. turned to face his daughter. Beatrice's blonde hair was pulled into two braids that circled her head like a tiara; her blue wedding gown shone with iridescent splendor, whorls of

260

lace and white silk filigree clinging to the curves of her form. Cream-colored button-up high-top boots with two-inch heels poked out from beneath the hem of her dress, spotless and delicate. She looked as stunning in that dress as her mother had on her own wedding day.

"You look beautiful, Bea. Absolutely beautiful." He walked over to his daughter and set a kiss upon her cheek; a luminous smile burgeoned across her face like sunrise.

"If James messes up, you'll have plenty of fellows ready to do it right," Goodstead said, returning with another piece of toast and a steaming coffee. "Would you like something to eat or some coffee?"

"I am too nervous," she said.

Goodstead bit into his toast and chewed. There was a knock on the door downstairs.

Beatrice and Goodstead, both surprised, looked into the hall.

T.W. grinned and said, "That is Tim Halders."

Beatrice's eyes widened; she looked at her father and said, "You hired on a carriage? It is only a ten-minute walk to the church."

"I could not risk bad weather or a dust devil tarnishing such perfection."

Beatrice threw her arms around her father (Goodstead snatched the coffee cup from his right hand) and kissed him thrice upon the cheek.

"You spoil me," she said.

"Nothing in the whole world gives me greater pleasure."

The driver knocked again; T.W. looked at Goodstead (who set the extra coffee atop the armoire) and said, "Please escort Beatrice down. I'll join you in a moment."

"Come on," Goodstead said. "Let me put you in that carriage."

Beatrice followed the deputy into the hall. When T.W. heard their feet impact the stairs he walked over to the table by his bedside and opened the top drawer. He withdrew a small metal case no larger than a playing card and opened it. Within lay a daguerreotype of him, thirty-one years younger, standing beside the woman he had buried the day after his daughter was born.

"She's getting married today. In your dress."

Lucinda's merry eyes stared up at him from the silver image in such a lifelike manner that he found it hard to return their gaze. He kissed her face (no larger than a thumbnail in the picture), closed the frame and replaced it in the table. He took special care to shut the drawer quietly, though he did this for no reason that he fully understood.

T.W. looked in the mirror, assessed that he did not look any more ridiculous than the last three times he had surveyed himself, straightened his cravat and walked to the door. He may look silly, but it did not matter overmuch to him: this day belonged to Beatrice and James.

He thought of the carpenter who would soon be his son and then his mind turned to the titan's friends. Their faces flashed into his mind. They made him uneasy, they were unsettled themselves and he made them uncomfortable. He paused.

T.W. looked at the open armoire atop which sat the steaming cup of coffee and within which hung several frock coats, several sets of suspenders, six shirts, four pairs of trousers and the holster with his six-shooter. He hated that he even contemplated bringing a weapon into the house of God, but T.W. had learned to trust his instincts over the years.

"You havin' trouble with the stairs, old man?" Goodstead asked from below.

"Give me a minute. I misplaced your muzzle."

"You can't silence this wisdom."

The sheriff decided to bring the revolver, yet knew that he could not wear it openly in church. He surveyed the room for some subterfuge until an idea came to him. He knelt beside his bed as if in prayer and reached his free hand into the darkness below.

T.W. exited his house, a shoe box tucked underneath his left arm. Within it was Lucinda's shawl, an heirloom he had intended to pass along to Beatrice. Beneath the fabric was his gun and a strap with six extra rounds.

The Texan opened the carriage door for T.W.; a dagger of pain shot through the sheriff's left hip as he climbed the step into the vehicle, but he did not verbally acknowledge the pain. Goodstead entered the vehicle behind him and shut the door. Outside, the driver snapped his reins and called out. The horses cantered forward.

Beatrice leaned her head against her father's left shoulder.

Goodstead looked at the shoe box in T.W.'s hands and said, "You bringing pets?"

"No."

"More shoes in case the ones you got on start to itch?"

"No."

"A very small addition for James's house?"

"No."

"I'm running out of clever guesses."

"This is something I want to give Beatrice at the banquet."

"Stop spoilin' her—she don't like it. I could use some spoilin'. I'm completely ready for it."

"Lilith Ford might like to spoil you," Beatrice said.

Goodstead's blank face froze for a moment; he looked over at the bride in blue.

"She noticed you at the shindy," Beatrice added.

"My red suit got her attention?"

Beatrice did not respond to the inquiry.

Goodstead watched six houses glide past the carriage window, nodded his head and said, "She looked very comely, grazin' on that funnel cake."

"When you speak to her, I recommend that you refrain from making bovine comparisons."

"But cows are pretty. Nice to pet."

T.W. watched the houses depart from the window, replaced by farms, cattle ranges and then the Taylors' corral.

The carriage wheels rolled from lush grass onto rougher terrain; stones impacted the wooden tires, clacking and snapping.

"Grab something," Tim Halders said from the driver's bench.

The carriage lurched, jostling the passengers. The revolver hidden within the shoe box slid forward; T.W. tightened his grip on the package to keep it upright and closed.

The driver slowed the horses for the rugged landscape; the church was not far off. T.W. took his daughter's hand and squeezed it; she squeezed back.

"I hope you invited Meredith," she said.

"She'll be there."

"I like her."

"So do I."

His heart quickened when he thought of the long, melting embrace he and Meredith had shared on her doorstop the night before, the sound of her breath and the taste of rum upon her lips. It had been six years since he last kissed a woman.

Open plains and northern mountains were visible on T.W.'s left, presently obscured by the white facade of the church as it slid into view. The sheriff saw Oswell Danford and his brother standing before the edifice's main entrance. The duo stood watching the carriage from beneath the shadows of brown cowboy hats; they waved.

"It appears they didn't set their watches to Mountain Railway Time," Goodstead remarked.

"They were supposed to arrive early. Jim wanted a book with all of the guests' signatures, and he put Oswell in charge of it."

T.W. doubted that James had thought of such a sentimental thing on his own, but he did not remark upon it aloud. He would not worry his daughter with his suspicions.

The carriage stopped a few yards from the church entrance; the Danfords stood against the facade like sentinels, looking into the dark interior of the carriage. T.W. wondered where Richard Sterling was.

Oswell, walking toward the carriage, said, "Good morning Miss Jeffries, Sheriff Jeffries, Deputy Goodstead."

T.W. had not introduced Oswell to the deputy; the rancher had learned the Texan's identity on his own.

"Good morning Oswell. Good morning Godfrey," Beatrice said.

"Mornin'," Goodstead said.

T.W. leaned to the window and inquired of Oswell, "Did Minister Bachs open up yet?"

"We're the first ones here."

"Is the door locked?"

"I didn't try to open it."

"Can you see if it's open? I don't want my daughter standing outside with this dress on."

Oswell walked three steps to the double door of the church; T.W. descried something anomalous in the man's stride—a slight hitch in his right leg that he had not noticed before. The rancher put his hand to the bronze knob and twisted; the cylinder did not yield. He tried the second handle with no more success.

"They're locked."

"I see the minister," Beatrice said, and pointed through the opposite window of the carriage. T.W. looked through the portal and squinted: a broad man clad in black with a bare skull and a long silver beard walked toward the church, a valise in his right hand.

"That ain't Minister Bachs," Goodstead said.

"It isn't," T.W. replied. "Minister Bachs's chin whiskers aren't that long or that white."

"That isn't your usual minister?" Oswell asked.

"It's someone else," T.W. replied, and looked at Oswell. The rancher watched the approaching man intently. For some reason, Godfrey glanced over at the gazebo and then focused his gaze upon the approaching stranger.

"I wonder if something happened to Minister Bachs," Beatrice said to her father.

The approaching minister raised his right hand and waved amicably at the assemblage of the church.

He shouted the word "howdy" across the plain.

T.W. looked at Goodstead and said, "We're getting out." To Beatrice he said, "Wait in here until we get the church door open."

The deputy exited the carriage, turned around and helped T.W. down from the vehicle. Pain lanced through the sheriff's left hip when he made contact with the dirt; he grimaced.

T.W. limped over to the driver, climbed up beside him and said in a low, barely audible voice, "Tim."

"Sheriff."

"You see me scratch the back of my head, you lay into those horses and ride the hell out of here as fast as you can."

"Uh . . ."

"You understand?"

"I understand."

T.W. climbed down the steps, thudded back upon the dirt, winced and then strode beside Goodstead. Oswell and Godfrey walked around the carriage to stand abreast the lawmen.

"You look like quite a posse," the stranger said and then cackled loudly in the way that men do when they have spent too much time alone and need to hear their own laughter to keep themselves company.

The stranger was upon them; he was a bald six-foot-tall barrel-chested man of fifty with a long silver beard, eyebrows like raven's wings and bright blue eyes; he wore black.

The sheriff stepped forward and asked, "Who are you?"

"I'm Minister Orton Bradley." He extended his meaty hand toward T.W.; the sheriff clasped and shook it. The man's grip had no yield whatsoever, as if the hand were made of stone.

"Pleased to meet you, Minister Bradley," T.W. said.

"Call me Minister Orton."

"Pleased to meet you, Minister Orton. I'm the bride's father, Sheriff Theodore William Jeffries. That's my deputy, Everett Goodstead."

The minister released T.W.'s hand, shook the Texan's and said, "Pleased to meet you, Everett."

"That's some beard. Any critters in there, or just some crosses that never see the sun?"

Minister Orton smiled, revealing big white teeth and two wooden replacements. The laugh that erupted from his belly sounded as if it originated in a tuba.

The Danfords took a step back to exclude themselves from the conversation, yet remained near enough to observe the goings-on.

T.W. appraised the minister's apparel: the man's black clothing was frayed at the edges; patches had been sewn onto his left knee and elbow.

"Sorry my vestments aren't more refined like, but I do heaps of missionary work, and they get worn down out on the plains."

"What happened to Minister Bachs?" Beatrice asked from the carriage.

"Is that the bride in there?" A smile like a child's sat upon Minister Orton's prickly face.

T.W. adjusted the shoe box beneath his left arm so that he could quickly reach into it and said, "That's my Beatrice."

Minster Orton peered at the carriage window and whistled.

"They don't get prettier than that."

"What happened to Minister Bachs?" Beatrice repeated.

"His brother got sick in Nebrasky. He sent a wire to have me come do the service for him."

"Why did he not inform us himself?" Beatrice asked; T.W. could detect mild perturbation in her voice.

"It was all of a sudden. You can look here—"

Minister Orton opened up his valise; at the edge of his vision, T.W. saw the Danfords walk in front of his daughter, protectively shielding her from the stranger. In that instant, the sheriff knew for certain that, no matter their previous

270

wrongdoings, James's friends were concerned for the safety of his girl. The holy man withdrew a card, upon which were pasted typed streamers, and handed it to T.W.

The telegram read,

MIN O M BRADLEY
CHURCH OF THE LAMB
WESTLAND, MONTANA TERR=

DEAR ORTON
MY BROTHER'S CONDITION HAS WORSENED. I MUST VISIT HIM IN NEBRASKA. PLEASE PERFORM THE WEDDING CEREMONY FOR JAMES AND BEATRICE LINGHAM IN TRAILSPUR ON 12 AUGUST. THE COUPLE WROTE THEIR VOWS AND DO NOT NEED TOO MUCH PREACHING. YOU MAY SLEEP IN MY HOME. IF YOU CANNOT COME, PLEASE FIND ANOTHER REPLACEMENT SINCE I WILL BE TRAVELING. MIN CAULDING OR TWINER MAYBE?
THANK YOU. BLESS THE HOLY LAMB=
MIN R D BACHS
TRAILSPUR, MONTANA TERR

T.W. handed the note back to Orton, relieved. Things looked legitimate. He knew for certain that Minister Bachs had an ailing brother in Nebraska.

The holy man said, "Minister Bachs set aside some passages that have special meaning to the couple, so don't worry. And I won't do too much speechifying neither, though some words should be said about His suffering and guidance." Minister Orton produced one of the worn, leather-bound Bibles to which T.W. had seen Minister Bachs add marginalia. "Let's get inside so I can discuss the service with your girl."

"You've got the keys?"

"Yup. He left them for me."

Minister Orton reached into the pocket of his black vest and withdrew a metal ring, upon which two large bronze keys dangled, clinking. He closed his valise, picked it up with his free hand and strode toward the double doors.

T.W. walked alongside the minister, followed by Goodstead; the Danfords said something to each other that he could not hear.

The holy man inserted a bronze key, twisted it (eliciting a single metallic clack) and pushed open the right door. Damp cool air that carried the scent of candles, roses and ashes swirled into T.W.'s lungs, exhaled by the holy enclosure.

"It's pretty," Minister Orton remarked. He pushed the doors open wide, admitting a view of the aisle and burnished wood pews, and beyond them the dais, the white wood lectern, the piano and the luminous multicolored slats of stained glass reinforced with iron bars.

T.W. opened the carriage door and helped Beatrice from her seat. Her cream boots clicked upon the step, pressed six footprints into the dirt, shuffled lightly upon the "Welcome to His House" doormat and walked upon the blue rug that extended the length of the central aisle like a stream. She strode toward the holy man.

The minister said to Beatrice, "We oughta discuss the passages Minister Bachs and you selected, maybe a couple I'm fond of too. Or do you want to wait for the groom to arrive?"

"Jim leaves such decisions to me."

"That's what Minister Bachs said in his notes." He grinned and motioned toward the lectern atop the dais. She followed him up the aisle.

T.W. looked from his daughter over to the rancher, now standing just outside the door. Oswell withdrew a fountain pen from a fancy case, removed its cap and handed the writing implement to him. The rancher then opened the wedding ledger, scanned the names with his index finger (his lips moved when he did this), located what he was looking for and tapped a blank space.

"Theodore William Jeffries. Please sign here, right next to where she wrote your name."

T.W. pressed the iridium tip of the fountain pen to the paper and signed his name in the tight neat cursive that he had learned in grammar school and never since adjusted.

He handed the pen back to Oswell and said, "So you're taking signatures?"

"I am. This ledger is a souvenir for James and Beatrice."

"That's very thoughtful of you."

"It was James's idea."

"Sure it was." Oswell did not acknowledge the intimation in T.W.'s words. "You going to keep out anyone not in that ledger?"

"I am. Miss Jeffries said that everyone invited to the ceremony is listed in it."

With that admission, T.W. surmised that James's friends did not know exactly who their enemy was . . . or at least what he or his accomplices looked like. Perhaps this was James's business they were handling, not their own? Clearly they intended to keep some unknown person (or people) from entering the church, which was likely the best way to handle a bad element. T.W. resolved that he would not involve himself unless he needed to—these Danfords looked as if they could handle themselves capably.

"You'll need to add the name Mrs. Meredith Evertson to that ledger. I invited her two days ago."

"She's the one you were with last night? The one in that dress?"

"That's her."

"I'll write her in." Oswell opened the ledger,

turned to the last page and wrote "Mrs. Meredith Evertson." He showed it to T.W. and asked, "Is that how you spell it?"

"That's how."

"Okay."

"It seems that you and your brother have some concerns about the minister. Should I be concerned?"

Oswell considered the question for a moment before he said, "His story seems true?"

"It checks."

"Then don't worry about him."

T.W. glanced at his daughter and the minister: they stood at the lectern, looking at and discussing an open Bible.

The sheriff said, "People in this town love Beatrice. And she is my whole life."

"She is an exceptional woman."

"This is her day. You don't foresee it getting spoiled, do you?" He looked back at Oswell.

"I do not."

T.W. put his free hand on the rancher's shoulder and squeezed; the muscles beneath Oswell's skin were tense and alive.

"You do a good job getting those signatures. I know Beatrice will appreciate all the effort you put in. So will I."

Oswell nodded. T.W. removed his hand from the man's shoulder.

The sheriff looked over at Goodstead, who was

playing cards on the driver's bench with Tim Halders.

"Deputy." The Texan looked up from his game and at T.W. "You gambling at church?"

"We're keepin' it outside. And when I play against Tim there's no real gamblin' anyhow—just me winnin' different amounts."

"I beat you before," Tim protested.

"You beat me cuttin' cards to see who'd deal. And only once."

"But I won it."

"I'm a fool to overlook that victory."

T.W. said, "Deputy. You want to come in?"

Goodstead looked at T.W. for a signal; the sheriff touched the brim of his hat and dusted it.

The blank-faced Texan understood the sign and said, "Nah, I'll stay out here for a spell. Holler when Beatrice and James get to the kissin'."

T.W. shut the doors to the church, Oswell, Godfrey and Goodstead on the other side of it, all of them alert beneath nonchalant facades.

The sheriff walked down the aisle to the foremost pew, turned left, placed the shoe box with the shawl and revolver beneath the bench and sat down, rubbing his left hip. He watched his daughter and Minister Orton discuss sin and sacrifice and redemption. When they discussed the merit of including a rather apocalyptic passage from Revelations, the door opened.

T.W. turned in his chair and saw James

Lingham walk up the aisle. The groom in blue had dark owlish circles around his eyes and a stripe of red on his neck where presumably he had cut himself shaving. When he saw the unknown minister beside his bride, he paused.

"Jim, this is Minister Orton," Beatrice said.

"What happened to ours?" the groom said, his eyes more alert than they had been when he entered the church.

"Minister Bachs was called away. Minister Orton is going to perform the ceremony."

James looked at the holy man for a moment and then said, "Okay." He walked up the aisle, nodded to T.W., climbed up the pulpit, kissed Beatrice on the lips and took the minister's proffered hand.

Surprise lit into James's eyes; he looked at his firmly clasped appendage and said, "Don't break anything—I need to get a ring on her finger with that."

The minister laughed explosively and relinquished his steely grip.

"How'd you get so strong?" Jim asked.

"I built a lot of churches. Some cabins for poor folks too."

"Did you break the logs with your bare hands?"

Another cachinnation erupted from the gaping orifice in the minister's beard, reverberated in the enclosure and rose to the belfry, where it caused the bronze bell to buzz with metallic humor.

Chapter Twenty-seven

The Wedding Marshals

At a quarter after nine, an hour after Beatrice and the sheriff had entered the church, the guests began to arrive for the ten o'clock service; Oswell took the signatures of all comers prior to their admittance. One person, an Oriental named Snappy Fa, scratched a weird glyph next to his name, and another fellow, an illiterate oldster named Paps, scribbled a cross (perhaps meaning for it to be an *X*), but all of the guests who presented themselves had names in the ledger.

"Good morning. Who are you folks?"

"Harold Alben. This is my wife, Esther, and my daughter, Alicia."

"Please sign on the line right beside where your name is printed, Mr. Alben," Oswell said. The silver-haired gentleman wrote his name in the ledger with a curvilinear flourish. His wife and daughter then signed their names with a heavily slanted cursive that looked as if it were written by the same woman. (Clearly the mother had taught her daughter how to write, not her father or some schoolmarm.)

Oswell put his hand on the bronze doorknob, twisted it and admitted the Albens into the church, in which eighty-four signatories already sat. The rancher shut the door behind the family from Colorado and looked to his left.

Godfrey rounded the corner as he did every five minutes. He shook his head, indicating that he had not seen anything noteworthy.

"I'm going to wait here for a couple of breaths and then walk back the other way. Make the patrol irregular in case someone is trying to figure out how to get past me."

"Smart."

Oswell and Godfrey looked at the carriage parked ten yards off, within which Goodstead and the driver played cards. (They had moved the game inside the vehicle after thirty minutes too long in the sun.) The Danfords then looked at the gazebo. Dicky, who was observing the whole area with his binoculars, flashed them with his mirror—a single fast reflection of the sun.

"All clear with him too," Godfrey said. "It's hard to imagine something spoiling this day." The plump, bearded Danford tended to talk more when he got nervous, whereas Oswell became even more taciturn. "Any complications with the ledger?"

"None worth discussion."

A family approached the church on foot; the women had parasols.

"Isn't the gal on the right the one Dicky danced with? Tara Taylor?"

Oswell nodded when he recognized the buxom, freckled girl, her brother and their parents.

"See you in a few," Godfrey announced, and then walked whence he came.

The Taylors reached the church; the porcine father said to Oswell, "Are you the jailer?" His wife pushed out a laugh that did not come naturally.

"James wants a ledger with signatures from all the guests. Tell me your names please."

Wilfreda began to play gospel on the piano inside; the music sounded particularly small and fragile in the open plains.

"My wife is Vanessa Taylor, my daughter is Tara Taylor, my son is Jack Taylor and I am Roland Taylor." Oswell opened the ledger, ran his finger down to the letter *T* and saw all four names listed. He handed the man the uncapped fountain pen and indicated where he was to sign.

As Roland scribbled his name, two horses emerged from the eastern perimeter of the rural part of town, riding at a strong gallop toward the church. Oswell glanced from the steeds over to the gazebo, but received no signal. The beasts moved quickly.

Oswell distractedly pointed out the spaces where the remaining Taylors were to sign the ledger and then called out, "Godfrey. I need a hand." The horses—a white one and mottled one—continued their beeline directly toward the church, a wake of dirt and dust behind them; the riders were bent low in their saddles, nearly invisible.

Godfrey jogged around the southeast corner of the church to join his brother; he adjusted the back of his jacket. (He had just secreted a gun there, Oswell knew.)

The Danfords glanced at the gazebo to see if Dicky descried anything with his high-powered binoculars. Two quick flashes shined from the remote edifice—a warning (though not a definite engagement).

"Is Dicky in the church?" Tara Taylor asked Godfrey. "He left the shindy last night and . . . and he never came back."

"He's taken ill. I don't know if he'll make it out today."

"You all should go inside," Oswell prompted.

The mirror in the gazebo flashed again—two quick winks. Oswell fixed his eyes on the onrushing horses that tore up the weedy plain four hundred yards off.

Tara inquired, "Did he mention me? Did he say anything about me?"

"He said you weren't his kind of woman," Godfrey replied, trying to close the conversation.

The brusque answer lit anger in the young woman's eyes.

"Why?" she demanded. "He danced with me all

night." The horses were three hundred yards off; Oswell needed to get the Taylors behind a closed door very quickly.

To Tara, the rancher said, "Dicky called you fickle. And uncouth."

Oswell was ashamed of the hurt expression his remarks elicited from the young woman, but he had no time to humor her. The gallop of the oncoming horses filled his ears; the steeds were two hundred yards off.

The rancher opened the door and motioned for the family to enter. Tara's mother mumbled something about "Eastern folks," glared at each Danford, put an arm around her stunned daughter's shoulders and walked her inside.

"That's not a way to talk to my sister. Or any woman," Tara's brother Jack remarked to the Danfords.

"You men need to learn some manners," Roland added. The horses were one hundred yards off; in the gazebo, Dicky flashed his mirror two more times.

"You want to go a round with us?" Oswell asked, leaning close to the father's face.

The porcine man stared back at him, but did not respond.

In a calm voice full of menace, Oswell said, "I'm not causing a disturbance at this wedding. You want to brawl, let's go behind the church right now. If not, get inside."

"I'll get the son if he wants a taste," Godfrey added.

Jack Taylor, assessing the superior strength of Oswell and Godfrey, pulled his father toward the open door. Roland resisted.

"Go with your son—he doesn't want to see you get hurt," Godfrey suggested.

The horses were fifty yards from the church.

Oswell began to unbutton his jacket; he said, "My first punch will shatter your jaw."

"It happens that way every time," Godfrey added.

The male Taylors withdrew into the church. Oswell shut the door and lifted the cuff of his right trouser leg so that he could see the butt of his five-shooter; Godfrey reached his right hand behind his back as if he were scratching an itch.

The riders sat up tall and ungraciously yanked upon their reins to slow their steeds. Oswell recognized the man on the mottled mare as the mayor's son, Kenneth John—the deputy who liked to drink. The other man—a skinny blond fellow just shy of forty with a mustache that extended beyond his face—the rancher did not know.

"We didn't miss it did we?" Kenneth asked. His voice warbled; he swayed in his saddle. "The wedding service."

"It hasn't begun yet," Oswell said, coolly.

"Pleased to see you, Deputy," Goodstead said,

283

climbing from the carriage. The look upon Kenneth John's face showed that he did not like the Texan.

"Don't pretend to be my pal."

"I'm not," Goodstead replied. "But I like havin' you around—you make me look real good."

"I don't want to hear it from you today."

"Don't get grumpy. I wanted to compliment you—gettin' drunk before ten o'clock takes real ambition."

"It's no business of yours whatsoever when I drink," the red-faced, black-haired deputy said.

"Who are you?" Oswell asked the blond, elaborately mustached man atop the other horse.

"A friend of the deputy."

"Were you invited to the wedding?"

The man hesitated, played with his long blond mustache and shrugged.

"You tell me your name or I'm not letting you through that door," Oswell said.

"Who the hell are you to say that to my guest," Kenneth John said to the rancher.

Oswell did not respond to the inquiry.

"He's not invited," Goodstead said to the Danfords. "The only invitations Turkey Bill gets are to jail cells and beatings."

"Don't throw jibes at me," the man warned.

"I ain't afraid of your turkeys."

"That's 'cause you don't know. You don't know

what I trained 'em to do!" Oswell could tell that the man was drunk as well.

"Get back to your turkey farm before I shoot myself some Thanksgiving."

"You can't talk to me that way—you ain't the mayor."

"I ain't. Still, I done it."

Turkey Bill smoldered.

"Go tend to your poultry," Goodstead advised. "They lonely."

Turkey Bill eyed the Texan and then Oswell and then Godfrey, dug his spurs cruelly into his horse's haunches, eliciting a screech, and pulled hard on the reins. The white steed dug its hooves into the dirt and lunged forward, carrying its rider north. Turkey Bill pulled his reins hard right; he sped his horse in a wide circle around the church, grinding his spurs, provoking pained yells and blood. (Godfrey flashed his mirror once at the gazebo so that Dicky would not shoot the idiot.)

"You gonna behave yourself if we let you in?" Goodstead asked Kenneth John.

"Do not talk to me like I'm a child."

"That won't happen—I like children."

Turkey Bill finished his second noisy orbit of the church and then sped his steed back toward town, yelling something Oswell could not discern that sounded like "Muckygobblerhead."

"Who are you and these others to stop me from

going in? I was invited." (Oswell checked the list: the drunken deputy was on it.)

"I happen to know for a fact that the sober Kenneth John was the one they sent that invitation to," Goodstead responded. "T.W. put me out here to make sure there isn't a problem. You gonna behave if we let you in?"

"I don't have to answer to you—but you will have to explain to the mayor why you kept his son outside if you bar my entrance."

"I'm not worried. He is a reasonable man and knows you take too much sauce."

Kenneth John looked at Oswell and Godfrey almost as if in appeal.

"Tell me that you'll sit beside your ma and pa and behave yourself," Goodstead demanded.

The sullen man said, "Leave me alone."

"Promise you'll behave and we'll let you in."

Morosely petting the brindled mane of his horse, the cowed man said, "I'll behave."

"Then go tie up that mare."

Kenneth urged his steed to the side of the church where a score of animals had been tied, his head slung low as if he had been struck on the back of the skull. He disappeared around the corner without another word.

"Thanks for helping us sort those two fellas," Oswell said to Goodstead.

"I'm just a lawman trying to help honest folks like you two get your signatures."

Oswell looked at the deputy, yet could not divine from the man's blank features whether or not the remark had been a facetious one.

"We appreciate the support," Godfrey said.

Oswell saw a green canvas carriage emerge from the southeast part of town; it was drawn by a brace of four horses.

"Do you know who's in that carriage?" Oswell asked the Texan.

"The Sallys. Their pa is in a wheelchair, so that's how they bring him around."

Oswell looked at Godfrey with a gaze that told his sibling to stay close in case the passengers were not who they were supposed to be.

Goodstead remarked, "Got somethin' against cripples? Do they put 'em down back East?"

The carriage drew nearer; the horse hooves kicked up a wake of dirt that partially obscured the vehicle behind them.

"We just don't want anybody trying to get in who doesn't belong," Godfrey explained.

"That's how me and T.W. feel about Trailspur." Though the man's face was inexpressive, Oswell could not interpret the remark kindly. The Texan walked back to the carriage, climbed inside and dealt cards to Tim Halders, who instantly cursed his bad luck.

Chapter Twenty-eight

The Anomalous Horizon

Dicky raised binoculars to his eyes and looked westwards over the waist-high wall of the gazebo. Urged by the crop of a squat driver, a brace of four horses pulled a green canvas carriage across the plain toward the church. The gazebo's location south and west of the holy edifice afforded him a view of the right side of the vehicle, traveling northeast from the center of town. In its window he saw the face of a woman and a very old person whose gender was hard to determine. Dicky knew that he never wanted to be that old.

He looked back at the Danfords, both of whom stood at the main entrance in the rear church, awaiting the newest arrival. The situation seemed mundane, though Dicky knew that a carriage was a likely place for villains to hide themselves; he raised his hand mirror, tilted it to catch the sun and flashed his concern to the Danfords.

The carriage stopped ten yards from the church facade; Oswell waved his right hand at the new arrivals, said something and looked over at his brother. Two women descended from the carriage; each was birdlike and silver haired. They said eight words to Oswell; a moment later, he and Godfrey walked to the vehicle and removed a wooden wheelchair. The Danfords then extricated the (one-legged) old man (or woman) from the vehicle and set him (or her) gently upon the high-backed rolling seat. The silver-haired women pushed the elder toward the door. (Dicky presumed that this rugose individual was their father [or mother], though it was possible that he [or she] was a grandparent.)

Oswell asked the family a question, and each person responded by opening his or her mouth a few times. He then presented his pen (itself invisible to Dicky at this distance) to the elder, who had some difficulty writing his (or her) name down. The silver-haired women set the spine of the open ledger upon the oldster's head (as if the elder were a desk) and scribbled their signatures. Oswell thanked them and opened the door. The ladies pushed the infirm individual into the church.

Dicky set down his binoculars, withdrew his watch, pressed the open button and looked at the time: it was fourteen minutes to ten o'clock. The service was supposed to begin on the hour, though Lingham had told him that they would wait until a quarter after to start. Two couples neared the entrance, laughing and talking as they strode. Dicky flashed his mirror once, indicating that he thought they were not likely to prove a threat.

For the next twenty minutes, the New Yorker

observed the remainder of the guests arrive, sign in and enter the church. At the end of this period, he watched Oswell lean beside the closed door and say something to Godfrey, who had just completed his nineteenth orbit of the building. The plump Danford shook his head—a negative response.

The main doors to the church opened up from within; the sheriff stood in the portal and called out to the parked carriage. The blank-faced deputy and the driver emerged from the vehicle and went inside. The sheriff said something to Oswell and then shut the door. Dicky looked at his watch: the service was about to begin.

A sound like a cast stone striking a cliff wall garnered the New Yorker's attention. The noise might have been an avalanche twenty miles off, a falling tree or a gunshot.

Dicky looked across the open plains, which seventy miles east rose up into cyclopean peaks that gnawed at the bottom of the rising sun. He raised his binoculars to his eyes and faced the open horizon.

The flat line of the plains he had surveyed two dozen times that morning remained undisturbed. He heard another distant crack; Dicky was almost certain that it was a gunshot.

He turned back to the church and flashed his mirror twice in warning; Godfrey returned the signal. Dicky set his long-range rifle upon the balustrade that encircled the structure and then checked its chamber—it was clean and loaded. He set the lever-action rifle Oswell had given him upon the floor and placed all of the seven-shot magazines beside it.

The New Yorker tucked his six-shooter beneath his belt and raised binoculars to his eyes. Upon the eastern horizon, black against the blue and gray mountains, stood five flecks that had not previously existed. He could not discern whether the anomalies were men or horses, though they were definitely ambulatory beings.

Dicky flashed his mirror at the Danfords and then looked back toward the eastern horizon through his high-powered binoculars. The flecks had grown to the size of fleas; even at this great distance, he knew that they were approaching very quickly. One of the dots elongated horizontally as it veered to the right, establishing it and the other similarly-sized flecks as quadrupeds. At this distance—over three miles— Dicky could not tell if the horses were mounted.

There was another distant, barely audible gunshot; one of the flecks elongated vertically (rearing up on its hind legs, Dicky surmised). If that steed had a rider, the man had most likely been thrown. The horse shrank to its normal height and galloped alongside its brethren; the sound of the charging animals did not carry across the plains.

Two more muted reports cracked on the horizon. The flecks fanned out, yet still galloped directly toward the church. The dust and dirt that the horses kicked up cut Dicky's visibility dramatically: he could no longer see the landscape behind the animals. The New Yorker realized that this was likely the purpose of their gun-motivated stampede, and his stomach sank.

Dicky flashed his mirror three times at the Danfords; he looked back at the eastern horizon.

The distant beasts pulled a gray wake of airborne grit across the plains, toward the church. The New Yorker's heart hammered in his chest; he did not doubt for a moment that Quinlan was the conjuror behind that veil of dust.

The horses stampeded across the two miles of land that separated them from the gazebo; none of them carried riders or wore saddles. Through his binoculars, Dicky saw that the beasts trailed ropes that dragged heavy objects through the soil, churning up more detritus than their hooves yielded—an ersatz (and enormous) plow.

The wave of filth that the steeds produced was a half mile wide and rose into the sky, obfuscating the plains and mountains. Dust stuck to the animals—they became less visible as they drew nearer the gazebo. The sun intermittently flashed through the expanding veil, a lecherous old man winking at a naive girl.

Dicky set down his binoculars, picked up his

long-range rifle and aimed at the central horse. He waited for the dusty beast to enter the one-thousand-yard range within which his rifle had some accuracy. He lined the distant dot in his sights, inhaled, exhaled and gently squeezed the trigger. The gun recoiled in his grip; the shot blazed across the plains, whistling, accompanied by the echo of the report. The middle horse reared, but then resumed its gallop. He had shot it in the chest, a wound that would irritate the animal yet not immediately halt its gallop.

The New Yorker knew that he needed to lance a leg if he wanted to knock a horse down, but such a shot was very unlikely at this distance. Down the sighting of his long-range rifle, the horse's limbs were currently invisible.

Dicky waited for the stampede to come into range.

When the steeds were five hundred yards off, he pointed his rifle at the middle one, aimed at the space beneath its bulk and squeezed the trigger; the muzzle cracked; the cartridge whistled across the plain; the horse tumbled forward, its hindquarters flipped into the air and the beast slammed onto its jaw, twisting its neck horribly. In a moment, the felled animal was obscured by the dust the others pulled over it like high tide.

Dicky pulled back the bolt, plucked out the warm shell and slid in a new cartridge. He aimed below the bulk of one of the four remaining horses, inhaled to steady his grip and squeezed the trigger. The muzzle cracked; the lead projectile whistled across the plain. The horse bucked—the shot had likely struck its chest—but the animal continued forward.

The New Yorker raised his binoculars to his face and looked at the pack. Two more steeds had emerged from the dust wave to replace the one that had fallen; they were both covered with grime and almost completely invisible, even through the binoculars. Like the other four, they pulled blunt objects through the soil and expanded the veil.

Dicky felt a cool wind against his forehead; his stomach sank for the second time in five minutes. He pounded his fist upon the balustrade in fury.

"No," he remarked to the breeze that blew westward, directly at him.

The wind carried the storm of dust over the hindquarters of the six steeds, up their sides and over their nostrils: it looked as if they were slowly falling into a pond of murky water. They disappeared; the gray wall advanced.

The New Yorker had not relished the execrable (and unlikely) feat of trying to put down all six horses (and however many more emerged from the dust), but now he had no choice but to sit and wait for their arrival . . . as well as those they escorted.

Dicky set his weapon down and grabbed the lever-action rifle Oswell had given him. The firearm was not accurate beyond three hundred yards, yet it could fire seven shots instead of just one . . . which was preferable, since the New Yorker was fairly certain that this showdown would not be engaged at a distance.

With the fingers of his right hand, Dicky threw the trigger guard forward; the loading mechanism clacked and pulled a cartridge from the magazine into the chamber. He sat on the gazebo bench and watched dust fill the eastern horizon. The edge of the wave was four hundred yards from the gazebo; from it emerged the noises of hooves and neighing and metal clanking upon stones.

Dicky picked up his binoculars and glanced back at Oswell and Godfrey, both standing outside the church, watching the column advance. The plump Danford's mouth was agape like a surprised child's.

The New Yorker knelt behind the waist-high wall of the gazebo (which would not withstand the rounds of a high-caliber rifle at close range, but was thick enough to stop weaker munitions) and watched the dust storm engulf the plain and swallow the sky.

Grit flew into his eyes; his long lashes fluttered up and down like butterfly wings. He inhaled some motes and sneezed thrice, unable to stifle the reflex. Dicky spat, stuffed a handkerchief into his mouth and laboriously sucked clean air through the fabric into his lungs.

The storm of dust consumed the gazebo, isolating the structure and the lone sharpshooter within it. Dicky looked back toward the church and saw only a deluge of dirt. Looking through eyes bleary with tears, the New Yorker surveyed the environs with the perspicacity of a myopic old man at latest dusk.

He heard hooves to his right and pointed the tip of his rifle in that direction. A pocket in the maelstrom opened, revealing the dark silhouette of a horse upon which a rider clung, hunched forward, face pressed to the saddle. Dicky squeezed the trigger, flung the lever forward and fired again at the dark shape. The second bullet sped through the cylinder in the dust sliced by the first, into the rider's back. The man cried out and fell from his horse. Before the pocket in the maelstrom closed, the New Yorker saw a hoof land upon the fallen rider's right shin and snap it.

A faint creaking of wood sounded behind Dicky; he spun to it. A dust-obfuscated man had his hands clasped to the balustrade—he was pulling himself up to the platform. The New Yorker pointed the tip of his gun at the climber and threw his trigger-guard forward. The metallic clack alerted the man; he reached for his hip; Dicky squeezed off a shot that splattered crimson upon the dust behind the foe's head. The agglutination of grit and blood fell like gumdrops to the ground; the man toppled a moment later.

A pocket in the dust revealed two horses carrying hunched riders toward the church. Dicky aimed his gun; dust abruptly swirled in the gap and precluded his shot.

The muzzle of a revolver pressed into Dicky's nape. Only after he felt the cold contact of the weapon did he notice that the floorboards of the gazebo had sunk an eighth of an inch.

The owner of the weapon said, "Drop it."

Dicky hesitated.

A fist pounded the right side of the New Yorker's head; his right ear rang and burned; his cheek swelled with an instantaneous bruise. Dicky gasped and then coughed the handkerchief from his mouth.

"Drop it," the man commanded.

In that moment, Dicky contemplated spinning around and firing at his assailant, an act that would likely end his foe's life and certainly call his own to a close, simply and swiftly.

Instead, the great seducer dropped his rifle; it clattered upon the gazebo planks. He did not know if this act was the result of cowardice or optimism. Clearly some part of him felt that he had a chance against Quinlan . . . or at least a chance to somehow escape this showdown alive.

The captor snatched the revolver Dicky had secreted beneath his belt and flung it to the platform, where it bounced twice.

The New Yorker glanced behind him and saw a

person he did not recognize. The man was an Indian about his age with a scarf drawn across his nostrils and mouth, and spectacle lenses pulled against his eyes by a rag with two holes in it. He wore a vest made from the skins of wolves.

"Turn around," the Indian said. The New Yorker complied.

The captor pressed his gun into Dicky's back and urged him toward the steps with a sharp jab and the word "walk." The New Yorker strode slowly across the planks, his hands in the air. When he reached the stairs, he intended to fall down them and lunge to the right . . . and hope that the dust obscured him well enough to provide an opportunity for escape.

The fickle wind languished for a moment and then blew south.

Standing outside the gazebo were three more men; all of them had guns pointed at Dicky. The New Yorker recognized none of them, but they all recognized him through the owlish lenses pressed to their eyes.

"Bind him," the Indian said just before he shoved Dicky from the gazebo. The ground slammed into the most handsome man within the Trailspur city limits. The wind burst from his lungs; when he gasped, he inhaled a small sharp rock.

Chapter Twenty-nine

A Holy Union

T.W. walked his daughter up the blue carpet that delineated the two filled halves of the church. Wilfreda enthusiastically played the hymn Beatrice had selected, an ornate composition called "He Observes His Children with Love," written by an English composer a century earlier. James stood on the podium, his hands clasped together to keep his fingers from fidgeting. In the sheriff's estimation, the groom's anxiousness had dissipated during the last hour. Perhaps the threat that worried James and his friends would not disturb this sacred day after all.

Minister Orton walked to the edge of the dais, stopped, put his hands behind his back and looked at the congregation; a toothy grin creased the beard that surged like a waterfall from his face. T.W. walked Beatrice to the holy man; the minister delicately took her left hand and led her to James. The sheriff walked away from the dais and sat in the aisle seat of the front right pew, beneath which he had earlier secreted the box containing the shawl and revolver.

Meredith took his hand, squeezed it and kissed his cheek; the affections helped dull the unexpectedly sharp pangs of melancholy that the act of handing over his daughter had engendered. Wilfreda's hands wove a difficult counterpoint upon the piano; for a moment, T.W. thought he heard a dim rumble beneath the music, but the elusive noise was covered over by the minister's explosive laughter.

"Isn't this a handsome couple," the holy man said, surveying the bride and groom. "Are you two ready to make yourselves one in the eyes of the Christ?"

"Sure am," James said.

"I know he likes the look of you two together," the minister said and clapped his hands.

Beatrice, less interested in the man's patois, nodded and said, "Thank you. Please begin the ceremony, Minister Orton."

"First I want to show you something I brung. Just the bride. It's something I only take out on special occasions like this. Follow me."

Beatrice, surprised by Minister Orton's request, walked away from James and strode alongside the holy man.

When they stood beside the lectern, the minister said to the assemblage in a cold and unfriendly voice, "I want you fools to pay attention to this."

T.W. felt a chill crawl up his spine; he rose from his chair, as did Goodstead one pew behind him. James stared at the minister, mouth open.

With his steely left hand, Minister Orton grabbed the back of Beatrice's head and slammed her face into the lectern, where the cartilage of her nose snapped. She cried out in surprise and pain.

T.W., James and Goodstead ran at the minister.

The holy man withdrew a revolver from a hollowed-out Bible and pressed the wide barrel to the back of Beatrice's head. He thumbed the hammer; the metal clicked.

T.W., James and Goodstead stopped.

The sheriff looked at his daughter; her face was pressed flat to the hard surface of the lectern; her shoulders shook; a thin moan escaped her lips that made him want to die.

The minister leaned his left elbow on Beatrice's nape and tapped the back of her skull with the butt of his revolver.

"Back off fellas." The three men withdrew.

"Leave off of my wife," James said.

"You didn't get married. And you shouldn't lie about your vows in God's house unless you want something bad to happen."

"What do you want?" T.W. said, unable to look at his convulsive daughter, his hands balled up into hard fists.

"There's still some more guests coming. All we've gotta do is wait for them to show. Quiet now."

The shocked congregation was silent. The sound that T.W. had barely discerned during Wilfreda's playing became audible to the entire congregation—it was the rumbling tattoo of hooves.

A gunshot echoed in the distant plains, followed by another and then another.

"That's them," the minister said.

Chapter Thirty

Late Arrivals

Oswell and Godfrey unhitched Tim Halders's carriage; the freed brace of horses fled from the oncoming dust storm. The Danfords pulled the coach in front of the main church doors, dug their fingers beneath the lower planks and heaved; the vehicle tipped onto its side, upraised wheels spinning.

Godfrey reached his hand into the dirt, found the coil of rope buried there and yanked hard. The trunk opened, revealing the three lever-action rifles they had earlier secreted there. He grabbed the guns by the barrels.

Oswell yanked the rope from the trunk lid, hurried to the church entrance and wound the cord tightly around the bronze doorknobs to discourage anyone within from poking his or her curious head out into the middle of a gunfight.

Godfrey stacked the loaded magazines beside the rifles on the bulge of the overturned carriage.

Oswell snatched the pair of binoculars from the

trunk and shut it. The rancher looked east: the gazebo and everything beyond it was obliterated by the dust storm, now only two hundreds yards off.

Godfrey said, "I hope Dicky got some of them."

"I recognized the sound of the lever-action. He got some shots off."

"He didn't run out on us."

"He didn't."

The Danfords, all but their heads shielded by the tipped-over carriage, watched the oncoming storm and waited.

"I didn't expect anything like this," Godfrey said. "I can't believe he did all this just to get back at us."

"He might have more than just revenge on his mind."

Godfrey ruminated for a moment and said, "Maybe we were fools to think we could outsmart a fellow like Quinlan at his own setup."

"We didn't have choice. We couldn't leave this mess to Lingham."

"Yeah."

The brothers looked at each other for a moment, then looked back at the dust storm one hundred yards off.

Godfrey said, "If you make it and I don't, will you bury me next to Ma? I said I never wanted to go back to Pineville, but I can't think of another place for you to put me."

"I'll bury you there."

"Thanks."

They watched the maelstrom inhale the sky and the ground, a filthy eclipse.

The Danford brothers pulled handkerchiefs from their pockets and tied them over their noses and mouths. They fastened the leather cords of their hats securely beneath their chins.

The brothers snatched up their rifles and trained them upon the center of the column, pressing the stocks of their rifles deeply into their armpits. Less than fifty yards separated them from the roiling grit. Oswell felt the rumble of hooves in his stomach.

The prow of the dust storm struck the Danfords. They tilted their heads down, using the brims of their hats and the butts of their guns to shield their aiming eyes. A dark horizontal shape flickered by.

"No rider," Godfrey said.

The Danfords withheld their fire.

The silhouette of a low-flying bird floated across the haze, the air's usurpation by soil leaving it befuddled. A gunshot cracked; the shadow flinched and then sank from the sky, flapping only its right wing.

"That shot came from over there," Oswell pointed.

Each Danford fired a round, threw the lever and fired a second round. A weak moan sounded from the other side of the veil.

The wind turned; a pocket of clear air opened up. Oswell saw the haunches of a horse and the edge of a saddle. He pointed where the rider ought to be (if someone was atop the horse—he could not tell) and squeezed the trigger. The muzzle cracked; the bullet whistled, scoring a groove across the dust. He threw the lever on his rifle and fired a second shot before he knew if the first one had hit its mark.

A man clasping his bleeding neck fell backward into the pocket of clear air, gurgling.

Oswell raised his binoculars and looked at the fallen rider.

"Do you recognize him?" Godfrey asked.

"No."

Godfrey snatched the binoculars and caught a glimpse of the dying man before swirling motes filled the gap.

He said, "Looks like a rough or a mule skinner."

"Quinlan's throwing cheap guns at us first. Each of these we put down is one less he has to pay when it's over."

Godfrey set the binoculars down, wiped grit from his aiming eye and nodded.

The dust swirled in a strong crosscurrent; the Danfords waited for other gaps of clarity to appear in the dingy maelstrom, but instead found themselves in an exposed pocket. Six whistling gunshots lanced through the haze at them, one of which cracked and spun the wheel beside

Godfrey's head. The Danfords returned fire until their rifles were empty, at which point they ducked behind the carriage. The duo plucked magazines from their stocks, rammed new ones in and flung the trigger guards forward to draw bullets into the chambers.

Oswell laid upon his stomach, inched across the dirt to the edge of his cover and pointed his muzzle up. At the other side of the carriage, he saw Godfrey kneel and aim his weapon out.

A gap opened up in the dust immediately before Oswell. A boot came down and stomped upon the barrel of his gun, pressing the muzzle into the dirt. A stillborn round caused the weapon to lurch in his hands. He looked up.

"Hello, Oswell," one of the twins said, the grin on his cracked bronze face framed by a prickly beard and tangled black hair. He drew his gun and pointed it at the rancher's face more quickly than the pinned man could even pull a trigger, much less draw.

Oswell turned and yelled, "Godfrey, they're at us!"

The rancher finished his sentence an instant before a boot kicked the rifle from his brother's hands; the weapon spun into the air and struck the church behind them. The other twin drew two revolvers and pressed their barrels to Godfrey's skull.

The one standing over Oswell said, "I hope there's room for all of us at the service. I love weddings, and so does Arthur—though he gets weepy sometimes."

Oswell glanced at the other twin's face; the swarthy, thorny visage was an inscrutable mask.

"He don't talk no more. After you left us to those Appanuqis we got into a predicament where the toddler got killed and my brother lost his tongue."

The talkative twin kicked the pinned rifle from Oswell's grip; it spun across the dirt until it struck a rock five yards off.

"Both of you get up," the talker said.

Oswell pressed his palms to the dirt and began to rise. The talker kicked out his left hand; he thudded back to the ground.

"Up, I said."

Oswell put his palms to the ground, waited for a boot that did not come, and stood up; the top of his head came to the talker's eyes.

"Put your hands behind your backs."

Godfrey reached behind his back; Arthur swept his legs out from under him, sending him to the dirt. The silent twin stabbed a knee into the plump man's spine, holstered one of his own guns and plucked the hidden revolver from Godfrey's belt.

"You don't have a gun back there, do you?" The talker spun Oswell around and felt his lower back for a weapon that was not there. He did not check the rancher's boot.

Arthur wove a burlap cord around Godfrey's wrists in the shape of an eight; he pulled the binding tight; the twines creaked. He sheathed his gun and tied an adamantine knot with both hands. The silent twin stood up and pointed his weapon at Oswell.

The talker said, "I'm trussin' you like your brother—if that's actually him neath all that whale blubber."

Oswell felt a piece of cord encircle his left wrist and then wind around the other. The talker yanked the binding; the twines creaked; the rancher's wrists throbbed and his fingertips became cold, yet he remained silent—he knew that an admission of pain would add to the twin's enjoyment of this act.

"Don't blame me—Arthur's the one who wants it tight. He likes it when the hands turn purple." The captor sheathed his gun and then tied a firm knot; Oswell's middle and ring fingers twitched from the constrictive binding. Arthur grabbed Godfrey by the collar and pulled him to his feet.

Oswell saw the talker turn east and wave; the rancher looked over his shoulder. The tops of four horses and the riders they carried glided across the settling dust toward him like swans on water. Slung like a rice sack over the rear of one of the steeds was Dicky, covered with grit. Oswell had presumed that the man had died at the gazebo, but seeing him captured—and neutralized for certain—dashed his last reasonable hope of regaining his freedom.

"There's only one more of you—that dumb giant—and I'm certain Orton's got him cowed with the rest of the congregation by now."

Oswell and Godfrey exchanged a morbid glance.

"Fooled you, didn't he?"

The Tall Boxer Gang's efforts as sentries had safeguarded the guests from nothing more dangerous than that idiot turkey farmer. They had trusted in Sheriff Jeffries's assessment of the minister, but the lawman had not known how cunning and dangerous the enemy was. Oswell would have wagered that Minister Orton was a real holy man (albeit one who had fallen from His graces) who could have talked at length about any section of the Bible and also performed the ceremony believably. Quinlan was a man of minutiae.

"You ain't got somethin' to say about all this?" the talker asked Oswell.

He did not respond. He knew from experience that anything he said to the misanthrope would encourage more violence.

"Look over there," the talker said.

Oswell looked east to where the man pointed. A small black square appeared in the swirling motes, though at this distance he could not identify what he was looking at.

The four men on horses, including the Indian who carried Dicky, rode up alongside the twins and the Danfords. Oswell looked at the New Yorker's face; blood ran from cuts on his bruised brow and cheek up his forehead and into his black hair, the result of being slung head down over the horse's hindquarters. Dicky was conscious, though beaten and dazed.

"Tie those horses up," the talker said to the four men.

The Indian, clothed in moccasins, trousers and a vest made from wolf skins, climbed off of his brown mare and pointed to the New Yorker slung over its haunches.

"We're taking him in," the talker clarified.

The Indian grabbed Dicky by the hair and yanked him to the ground, where he thudded like a dropped bag of laundry. The bloodied man raised his head from the dirt and looked at the Danfords; none of them said anything.

Oswell looked back at the dark square and found that it had resolved itself into the front view of a beige and green stagecoach pulled by a team of six horses at a steady canter. Godfrey looked over at the vehicle. Dicky raised his head and stared at it through bleary eyes.

They all knew who was inside.

Chapter Thirty-one

Wedding Toasts

Beatrice could not feel her face. A dagger of fire throbbed where her nose once sat, but the remainder of her visage was numb, as if emptied of blood or frozen. The taste in her mouth was of mucus, copper and the chalky grit of a broken tooth. Minister Orton's elbow lifted from her nape.

He pressed his revolver barrel to her neck, and said "Stand up. Show 'em how pretty you are."

For the first time since the minister had usurped the wedding, Beatrice raised her head from the lectern and faced the guests. Mouths opened and eyes widened; gasps and several cries issued from the assemblage. Most of the assembly looked away from her. Blood pounded through the tissue beneath her clay skin.

She looked at her father, seated in the first pew; tears poured down his face. He did not make a sound, but simply stared into her eyes. Meredith held and patted his left hand with both of hers. Beatrice turned her watery gaze to her groom. Jim sat on the far edge of the dais, his face in his hands, his shoulders heaving.

"I'm so, so sorry," he said. He looked at Minister Orton and pleaded, "Please don't. Please don't hurt her no more."

"We're just playing."

Something cracked against the back of her skull and the entire church tilted as if it were a canoe about to capsize.

Unable to control himself, Jim ran the minister. The holy man thumbed the hammer of his revolver and jammed it to her temple.

Her father cried, "No, no, no," lunged from the pews and slammed into James, knocking the titan sideways, off of his feet, farther back on the dais. The groom lay upon the floor; the sheriff doubled over and pressed his hands to his hurt hip.

"Don't be stupid," he said to Jim. "He'll shoot."

"I can't watch him hurt her."

"This isn't any easier for me!"

Beatrice had never heard him speak with that much vitriol in her entire life. She spat a fragment of a tooth into her palm and set it upon the lectern. It was the tip of her lower right canine.

There was a knock at the door; the congregation turned to look at the entrance.

"Everybody stay put," Minister Orton ordered. "Sheriff Jeffries?"

Her father looked at the bearded man who stood beside her and said, "Yes."

"Walk up to that door and knock on it four times. Do it slow so they can count it out clear."

Her father nodded; he looked at Jim and said, "Stay calm."

"Okay."

312

"Get to it," the minister prompted.

Her father limped across the dais, down two steps and up the aisle; he gritted his teeth in pain.

"Sheriff," the minister said. "Looks like you've got some discomfort."

Her father ignored the remark, reached the door, stumbled forward and placed his palm to the wood to steady himself.

Big Abe stood up from his seat to help him.

"Sit down big man or things'll get rough," the minister warned. Big Abe glared at the holy man but wordlessly returned to the large gap his absence from the pew had created. Beatrice looked over at her father. He leaned heavily on the hand he had pressed to the door, panting.

"You've gotta make a fist to knock correctly," the minister said.

The sheriff stood upright, clenched his left hand and rapped upon the door. His shifting, unsteady posture told Beatrice how much pain he was in. He waited for a moment and knocked again upon the wood; he paused and repeated the action two more times as instructed.

"Go on back to your seat now." Her father limped back toward the front of the church, holding his hip; his face was bright red with agony; he ground his teeth.

Beatrice wiped the fluid that dripped from her chin; she delicately touched her fingertips to her nose; the throbbing pain flared into a searing fire that squeezed tears from her eyes and a yell from her mouth. The congregation looked at her.

"Don't fiddle with it—it'll get worse," the minister said.

The doors to the church swung open. In the portal stood Oswell, Godfrey and Dicky, all with their hands behind their backs. The three men were covered with dust and battered.

A voice from behind the bound men said, "Get inside, you heroes."

Jim's beaten friends walked the blue aisle, where only twenty minutes ago her father had escorted her on what was to be the happiest day of her life.

Behind the captives stood two men who looked like identical twins.

"Not them," Jim muttered. "Not them."

Each twin wore a dust-covered black coat and a matching hat from which their long dusty hair hung like worms. They pointed four large revolvers at the captives.

Oswell, Godfrey and Dicky neared the dais steps, followed by the twins. The captor on the right planted the heel of his boot into Oswell's back and shoved him. The rancher stumbled forward, struck his shins on the dais stairs and landed on his chest and chin.

"Be careful," the assailant said. Oswell rolled onto his side, rose to his knees and then stood up.

"I s'pose Jesus ain't watchin out for you. Or maybe he just isn't so powerful."

"No need to blaspheme," Minister Orton said.

"Sorry, Uncle."

Godfrey and Dicky joined Oswell on the dais. They glanced at Beatrice and looked away guiltily the moment they recognized her.

The other twin pointed a gun at Jim; Beatrice's stomach dropped.

"I seen him, Arthur." To Jim, the talkative twin said, "Get up here with the rest of your posse." The groom walked up and stood next to Oswell.

"Put your hands behind your back." Her titan put his huge hands behind his back.

Arthur holstered his guns, pulled a cord from beneath his coat and wound it tightly around Jim's wrists.

"Now we got four of a kind," the talker remarked. "That's a pretty good hand in poker."

The minister grabbed Beatrice's left arm and walked her to the side of the dais where Wilfreda sat at her piano, staring at the keys as if in quiet conspiracy.

The minister tapped the ancient woman's ear with the barrel of his gun and said, "Sit somewhere else."

"I play the piano," Wilfreda said.

With his free hand, Orton grabbed the lid that overhung the keys and said, "Play something pretty."

Beatrice said to Wilfreda, "Go before he hurts you."

The ancient woman nodded, eyed the minister evilly, rose from the bench and descended from the dais. She stopped, turned around and folded her arms, monitoring the piano as if any moment she would reclaim it.

Minister Orton shoved Beatrice onto the bench and then sat beside her.

The talkative twin said, "Mule, Ralphy. Show these people your shotguns."

Tension eddied through the wedding guests. Two of the dusty men at the door walked to the head of the aisle and faced the congregation. They holstered their revolvers, grabbed the sawed-off shotguns that hung from straps on the shoulders and aimed the huge-gauge weapons at each side of the church. Two other men remained in the doorway, revolvers out.

"Would somebody like to make a speech?" the minister asked. The congregation was confused by the inquiry.

Mayor Warren John, face red with rage, stood up from his seat, but his frail wife pulled him back down, quietly muttering, "Please don't. Please, Warren."

The talker raised the pistol in his right hand and said, "I s'pose I gotta do the speeches since Arthur ain't got his tongue no more." He walked past the four bound men, eyeing each one, and stood behind the lectern. His twin stood on the dais steps, guns out.

"I would like to say somethin' to all of you here today about the groom. He might be a nice fellow now, maybe he's good at carpentry and knitting and spouting Jesus nonsense—"

"No need to blaspheme, nephew."

"Sorry. But when I met James Lingham, he rode with these other three men you see standing alongside him. They were outlaws, they were bank robbers and they were killers."

Beatrice's insides went cold.

"Jim is not a killer," she protested.

"And considering the bride's statement, I'd add liar to the catalog."

Terror hammered in Beatrice's heart; an inaudible scream rang in her mind, louder than the pain of her smashed nose, bruised face and broken tooth.

"Jim," she said.

He did not raise his head.

"Jim," she said again, her voice weak and wavering.

The talker looked at the groom and said, "Well? You gonna fib in God's house? You gonna deny that you fellas are the Tall Boxer Gang? That you robbed banks and shot up people? Any of you fellas want to deny that accusation?"

Jim looked over at Beatrice and said, "It was a long time ago."

"Dear Jesus," Beatrice said; it felt as if her entire life had just melted. Tears rolled down her bloodied face; pink drops dripped from her chin onto her trembling white hands. Nausea filled her like a bad smell.

The congregation was silent. Beatrice looked at her father: He stared with dire loathing at Jim.

The minister put his left arm around her back, patted her shoulder and said, "It'll be okay, darlin'." She faced the holy man and saw that his remark had not been a facetious one, but an earnest condolence—evidence of true psychosis.

The talker said to her father, "I can see you heard of the Tall Boxer Gang."

Her father nodded, but did not remove his baleful glare from Jim.

Oswell asked the talker, "You goin' to shoot us?"

"Don't rush me." He returned his gaze to the congregation. "There are two things happenin' in this church today, but—even though you're dressed up fancy and all—neither's a weddin'. Sorry.

"You all need to listen close and do what I say. I want to see you nod that you understand—every single one of you. Go and do it."

Her father, Meredith, her father's cousin Robert, the Albens, the Johns, the Yardleys, the Taylors, the tailor, Morton the hatmaker, Big Abe, his wife, Lilith Ford, Judy O'Connell, Judge

Higgins, Wilfreda, the barmaid Rita, Greg the clerk, Smith and Smiler, the Sallys, Snappy Fa, Paps and the remainder nodded. Everyone in the church heeded the mandate . . . except Goodstead.

Arthur pointed his gun at the deputy's head.

"I seen him abstain," the talker remarked. To Goodstead he said, "Stand up."

The Texan stood.

"Your neck broken, Deputy?"

"It's a bit stiff," he said, his eyes fixed on the one who spoke rather than the one who pointed the gun at him.

"You the kind of fellow who likes to make smart?"

"I'm wise."

"You're one smart remark away from gettin' your head blowed off, is what you are."

Arthur thumbed the hammer on his six-shooter; the click reverberated loudly in the silent church. Even with the gun pointed at his head, Goodstead's face remained blank.

"Why don't you take me for hostage instead of that lady you've been beatin' on?"

"I want to know that you're gonna do what I tell you. You nod or my brother shoots you. Go on and do it now—nod."

The people seated on the pews adjacent to the standing deputy ducked their heads down. Goodstead looked from the talker over to Beatrice; she mouthed the word "please."

He nodded.

"My brother thinks you took too long."

Arthur walked up the pew and slapped Goodstead's face. The Texan did not react, but stared back at the talker, his cheek glowing brightly.

"Sit down and don't try to save nobody else. Doin' what we say is the only way anyone is goin' to stay alive. Does everyone understand that? Go on and nod."

The congregation nodded.

"Two things are happenin' here. The first thing is the only part that involves you directly. We are robbin' you—me and my crew, not the Tall Boxer Gang who used to do this sort of thing but now go to church and have families. This is how it's gonna proceed. The church is set up in two halves. This is side one." He pointed his pistol to his left. "And this is side two." He indicated to the pews to his right. "I was gonna use left and right, but that might confuse you whether it's my left or your left, and I want this to be clear at all times.

"Side one"—again he pointed his pistol— "leaves the church. You all go home and get your valuables. All the good stuff. We want gold, we want silver, we want jewels, we want timepieces, we want paper money. Bring all of it here.

"If somebody on side one does not return, we execute somebody on side two. If ten people from side one run off, we'll execute ten people on side two. James. Oswell. Will I carry out this threat?"

"Yeah," Jim said.

"With relish," the rancher remarked.

"You all heard 'em. The minister counted you up, so we know exactly how many you are. If you think your valuables are more important than somebody's life, I don't know what kind of person you are anyways."

"Not a Christian," the minister remarked.

"Let me warn you about this. Bring us all of the valuables we asked for; don't hold out on us none. If you keep some baubles for yourself, we'll find out. We got some guys on the outside checking your houses after you leave, and if they find stuff you hid or left behind, I will execute you for doing so. This is not the time to bluff— this ain't a poker game.

"One other thing: you come back with a gun or some extra folks with brave notions like this dumb deputy, we will slaughter you by the dozen, grab a few as hostages and win our freedom. We've done that play before and we are all still here, alive to do it again.

"After side one gets back, side two goes and does the same thing. Same rules apply. Somebody skips, I execute someone in side one; somebody withholds, they get executed."

The talker surveyed the stunned crowd and

said, "Is anybody confused by anything? Raise your hand if you are."

Mr. Alben raised his hand and said, "I am in from Colorado and do not have much to offer."

"Get what you brought. All of the good stuff."

Big Abe raised his hand, "How much time does each group have?"

"Thirty minutes. If you walked here and live a ways off, take a horse from the second side. They won't mind none." To the men at the door, the talker said, "Let's get those up here!"

The sentries dragged two huge wooden trunks to the podium. They opened the vessels and walked back to their posts.

The talker pointed his pistol at the empty trunks and said, "That's where you put your stuff. Alphonse!"

The scraping sound of something being dragged through the dirt came through the doors before its source was visible. Beatrice's apprehensions grew.

A diminutive man with black hair, a thin black mustache, a burgundy suit and matching bowler cap walked into the church. In his left hand he clutched the handle of a small black valise; with his right hand, he dragged a fifteen-foot-tall folding ladder.

Beatrice and the congregation watched the little fellow pull the ladder up the aisle; it left tracks in the blue carpet like dirty skis. He did not look at anyone, though Beatrice did not think it was out of fear, but rather disinterest. This was the Frenchman her father had described.

The ladder clattered as he pulled it up the stairs toward the back of the dais.

Beatrice heard a strange metallic sound at the doorway and looked over. A very tall, oddly-shaped man dressed in a gray suit walked through the portal. The people nearest him shuddered and looked away.

"That's the boss," the talker said.

The man's left leg was made of wood and iron; the hand on the same side was covered over by a bronze gauntlet. His spine was curved—it bent him in a permanent bow. The right side of his forehead had an impression in it that looked like a crater and the eye on that side was lower than its mate and a mere slit. His bald scalp was crisscrossed with raised scars; a mass of white hair sprouted from the back of his head.

"They turned Quinlan into a grotesque," Jim said to Oswell.

"Yeah."

The boss walked up the aisle, deftly maneuvering the crutch wedged beneath his left armpit and the wooden leg that had both an ankle and a knee hinge. His blue and green eyes did not leave the Tall Boxer Gang once. He was the least human man Beatrice had ever seen: he terrified and repulsed her. Something heavy was slung over his shoulder, but she could not yet tell what it was.

Alphonse erected and then opened the ladder.

Quinlan reached the dais and walked over to the Tall Boxer Gang. He pulled the burden from his back and flung it to the floor in front of the four captives.

Upon the dais laid four nooses.

The Tall Boxer Gang said nothing.

Tears poured down Beatrice's numb face and she knew that despite what he had done, she still had some compassion for Jim. Part of him was still the man she loved.

The talker pointed to the nooses. "That's the second event. Hang the scoundrels who betrayed us."

Chapter Thirty-two

A Jew's Dilemma

The hatmaker Morton Steinman watched the talkative twin raise a golden timepiece; it swung pendulously from the chain pinched between his thumb and index finger. The congregation observed the smears of light it left in the air.

The talker grabbed the watch, clicked the release button, looked at its face and said, "Side one—get goin'. Be back by eleven thirty."

Morton Steinman was a member of side one

and rose immediately with them. The slender, finely bearded, five-foot-six, thirty-eight-year-old shuffled along the pew behind the Welt family.

The Jewish man had been to church more than a few times during the nine years that he had made and sold hats in Trailspur; he had attended five confirmations, one funeral and eight weddings. Consequently, the exacting Semite knew precisely how long the journey was—twelve minutes. A round-trip home and back would take twice that. The remainder—six minutes—was all the time he had to gather his valuables from the apartment he inhabited above Steinman's Hats.

He reached the aisle. Big Abe and his small wife paused, allowing him to exit.

"Thank you."

Big Abe nodded and said, "You have a longer walk than we do."

While striding up the aisle, Steinman put the tips of his long fingers together as if touching his hand to a mirror and organized the six minutes in his mind. Like many people in developing towns, he did not trust his savings to a bank, but kept them in his home. He had three hiding places, including a dial safe, the combination of which he knew by memory. Its tumblers were capricious in the summertime when warm air expanded metals. He hoped that they would not misbehave today.

Sunlight glared in his eyes the moment he

exited the church; he put on his brown derby and lowered the brim. In the dirt nearby laid three dead horses, their colors obscured by the gray dust that covered them and the black syrup that leaked from their cracked heads. To the east he saw two dark lumps that might have been sprawled human corpses. On the ground to his right lay a dead hawk with its claws in the air, one wing red with blood.

He pulled a timepiece from the watch pocket at the front of his trousers; the time was one minute after eleven o'clock. He hurried the pace of his strides to gain himself a little extra time should his safe behave obtusely or in case he met some unforeseen delay.

As he strode west toward the center of town, one question nagged him continually: how could these outlaws possibly have time to thoroughly search so many homes? They had claimed that they would know if a person withheld valuables from them, but how could they really determine this? If he gave over the contents of all three of his caches, he would have nothing left other than the store, his apartment, four dozen hats and the raw materials to make a few more.

When he was a child in Berlin, he, his parents and his sister had shared an apartment in which privacy was an abstract concept (possibly the source of his ambivalence in seeking a spouse as an adult). Whenever his father, a cobbler, had a slow week, little Morty knew that they would all eat fewer meals and very little meat. The lean months had deeply impressed the young man. As a successful and independent adult, Morton Steinman had no great plans for the money he had saved over the years, but he always looked at it as a net from the poverty of his childhood. If he gave over all of his savings, he lost the security that made him rest easy when business was slow, the security that forever locked the door to that apartment in Berlin where the drooping wallpaper was discolored yellow and brown, the plaster was soft with mildew, the floor was warped, the shouts of neighbors chased away the few moments of quietude and his father's Mutter Uta died slowly, wheezing for three years on a cot next to the one he and his sister shared.

Ruminating, Steinman hastily strode past corrals, ranches, barns and houses, toward the main avenue upon which his store and home sat at the far end. He looked at the other people from side one, dispersing like windblown pollen in all directions toward their homes. He wondered if his face looked as distraught as that of Judge Higgins or Rita or Lilith Ford or the Potleys or T.W.'s cousin. Steinman knew that some of them had their life savings at home and were faced with the exact same dilemma that he was.

Continuously, he returned to the question:

would the robbers be able to determine whether or not he gave them all of his valuables?

The hatmaker saw the main avenue up ahead. He removed his derby, wiped the sweat that trickled from his curly black hair and replaced his hat.

Steinman reached the main avenue, which had a few walkers upon it, and descried Dolores, his favorite of the women who worked at Queenie's. She was like the exquisite gentile Frauen he had admired as a child in Berlin, yet to whom he had never possessed the courage to talk. He waved at Dolores; she smiled politely back at him. The hatmaker had once made a French-styled hat for her as a gift; when he presented it to her, she had stared at it for a moment, blinked and thanked him politely. She had been less friendly to him ever since.

He wiped his brow, replaced his hat and looked at his watch. It was eight minutes after eleven o'clock.

"Hello, Morton," Oliver Petey said a moment before he spat a brown missile into the dirt. He obstructed Steinman's path and said, "Weren't you going to church for T.W.'s girl's wedding?"

"I forgot something."

"They wouldn't let you in, huh?"

Steinman tolerated the furrier because his wife was a good customer.

He said, "Jewish people are allowed inside."

"Yeah . . . ?"

"We don't burst aflame or anything like that. You are aware that Jesus Christ was a Jew?"

"Until you boys killed him. He sure changed his mind after that."

"I've got to hurry," Steinman said, having wasted thirty seconds too many with this cretin. "Give Jo my regards." She had excellent taste in hats, if not spouses.

The hatmaker looked away from the furrier and strode quickly off.

"Watch that the cross doesn't fall on you."

Steinman reached his store, withdrew the key to the front door, inserted and twisted it, eliciting a click. He screwed the bronze knob and entered his shop, the heels of his leather shoes snapping upon the burnished planks. The walls were covered with scalloped white wood shelves, upon which sat hats of two types: simple ones for men and artful ones for women. Men wanted to look like the other fellows with whom they played cards, and women wanted to be dazzling, unique flowers.

He walked past the shelves and the wooden hat rack upon which hung multiples of the same beige cowboy hat in every single size, and reached the back door. He inserted the key, twisted the knob and walked through. He ascended the same narrow stairwell he had climbed after more than three thousand days of work, reached the door to his apartment, unlocked and opened it.

Steinman looked at his watch: it was eleven after eleven. He walked over to the portrait of his family that hung upon the east wall (the artist had included Mutter Uta, even though she had passed on four weeks before the painting had been commissioned) and lifted it from its hook. He set the portrait down, dialed the safe's combination, twisted the bar and opened the metal door on his first try. Within sat two neat piles of legal tender; the value of the bills amounted to over sixteen thousand dollars. He took the money and put it in his jacket pockets.

The hatmaker went to his bed, raised the bottom sheet, reached his long fingers into a delicate slit in the mattress and withdrew a felt pouch, the contents of which clicked like communicating insects. Eight thousand dollars worth of diamonds sat inside, clandestinely brilliant. He slid the pouch into his vest pocket.

Steinman went to his credenza, unfolded its central three-panel door and slid out the top drawer, which was filled with suspenders and bow ties. He pressed his pinky inside a hole in the runner; the bottom of the drawer became loose. Within the hidden space laid his mother's pearls, her silver mezuzah and her engagement ring. These were bequeathed to him to offer his beloved whenever he got engaged. Each year he became more certain that he would never marry—he found the freedom and simplicity of his bachelor life too pleasing—but these artifacts were his mother's precious treasures and meant a lot to him because of what they had meant to her. He took the heirlooms and placed them in his right trouser pocket, where they seemed much, much heavier than he had expected.

He looked at his watch: it was eleven sixteen. He had enough time to return to the church, but he needed to leave presently. That meant he needed to decide. Should he give these familial treasures and the honest yield of twenty years of his life over to cutthroats because they claimed that they could find out if they had been shorted? Should he believe these *verflucht* miscreants? He had put the bills and diamonds and heirlooms inside his pockets so that he could obey these brigands, but now he needed to decide if he would.

There was a meticulous organization to the whole robbery that was undeniable and bespoke a calculating intelligence informed by empirical knowledge of the town itself. Had the robbers been gathering information for weeks or months . . . or possibly longer? Who knew what these miscreants had learned about Morton Steinman? (A few people in town knew that he owned a safe—perhaps one had offered up that datum for a fee?)

The hatmaker chewed his thick bottom lip . . . as he always did when he came upon a dilemma (which more typically involved the color of a ribbon for a woman's hat, or which steak he wanted the butcher to cut for him). He looked at the painting of his family that he had laid upon the floor; a triangle of sunlight illuminated the face of his sister, and he remembered times as a child that she and he had enjoyed playing with their friends outside of the synagogue, even in the midst of wretched poverty.

With three heirlooms and the pecuniary achievement of his entire life, the hatmaker strode from his apartment and down the stairs.

He did not bother to lock the doors behind him.

Steinman walked apace toward the church, amidst a throng of people carrying suitcases, valises, satchels, boxes, grocer's bags, crates and blankets slung like sacks over their shoulders. He thought of the tale in Exodus, though this situation was actually a return to bondage. He pulled the timepiece from his vest: it read eleven twenty-six.

He replaced the watch and closed the remaining distance to the double doors, which stood ajar though not wide open. He had made his decision to give them what they wanted and refused to ponder the dilemma anymore. Like his father, he was resolute once decided.

T.W.'s cousin Robert and the man's wife stood in front of him in the line to reenter the church. They were both silent; their eyes were red from weeping.

From within the enclosure came the clinking sound of metal striking upon metal.

Steinman entered the church, passed the sentries and stood in the aisle behind seven people. The old woman at the head of the line dumped her possessions into the open trunk—a roll of bills and about ten necklaces—and then walked back to her seat in side one, which was almost full again with returned persons.

The talkative twin, standing alongside his brother behind the trunk, called after the old woman, "We appreciate the donation. Jesus Christ thanks you for your kindness."

"Don't say that—we don't really want His attention, right now," the minister, seated on the piano bench beside Beatrice, pointed out.

"Sorry, Uncle."

The wiry marshals that had come in from Arkansas threw their watches into the trunk, a wrapped wedding gift and some dreary looking bills.

The talker motioned for them to take a seat and they did, grumbling audibly.

Big Abe and his small wife emptied a bag of jewels and bills into the trunk. The talker surveyed what they had dumped inside and then motioned for them to sit.

Robert and wife opened a valise that had necklaces, brooches and two stacks of bills. His wife picked them out of the vessel and set them in the trunk. They turned to walk into the pews, but Arthur poked the barrel of a gun into the woman's face; a few people in the church yelled.

Robert screamed, "We gave you everything! Everything!"

"No you didn't," the talker said. Arthur lowered the gun from the woman's head to her left hand, upon which still shone her wedding ring. She tried to take the jewel from her finger, but was shaking so badly that Robert did it for her and then dropped it into the trunk. Arthur lowered his gun.

"I forgot," Robert's wife said.

The talker said, "Sit down."

Steinman walked up to the trunk. He held his breath as he withdrew and tossed the sixteen thousand dollars of legal tender atop the pile of bills, gold and jewels. He did not breathe until he had added the heirlooms and dumped the diamonds inside. He pulled his timepiece from his watch pocket and cast it atop the pile, as if it were a garnish.

The talker asked, "That's it?"

"That is everything."

"No it ain't," the talker replied.

"It is. I gave you—" The butt of Arthur's pistol slammed into Steinman's forehead before he could finish his sentence.

The talker walked away from the trunk, up the dais steps and said to the entire congregation, "I want everybody to watch what happens to someone who holds out on us."

Steinman, holding his throbbing cheek, shook his head in horror and disbelief.

"I gave you everything! I promise that I gave you all of my—" Arthur cracked a pistol against the side of his skull; he felt dizzy.

An Indian with scars on his face and a vest made of wolf skins walked into the church; he stood next to Steinman.

"This is Shagawa. He's one of the agents who checks your homes," the talker announced. "What did you find in this fella's place that he kept from us?"

The Indian raised a golden necklace and a bracelet adorned with rubies; Steinman had never before seen either piece of jewelry.

The brave said, "This is what he kept for himself."

Steinman cried, "Those are not—," but Arthur struck him across the mouth with the butt of his pistol before he could finish his protest. His front teeth buckled in his gums; blood filled his mouth; he swallowed his incisors and gagged.

In his pain, the hatmaker knew the truth. The robbers did not have people on the outside checking homes . . . yet this bit of theater would convince everyone that they did. Perhaps somebody on side one had held out, but certainly nobody on side two would risk it. Steinman was to be the goat.

He was not surprised when Arthur pressed the barrel of a gun to his forehead and thumbed the trigger.

Several women screamed.

A few men called out "No!" or "Stop!" or "There's a mistake!"

The people in line behind him dropped to the floor.

Steinman did not know Hebrew, but he had learned the Jewish prayer that one was supposed to say preceding death—the Shema. He opened his bleeding mouth to begin it; a muzzle flash scorched his eyes; his head jerked back on his neck; the gunshot was lightning.

The world was dark; a coldness rushed into his head; he heard distant screams and something heavy thud upon the ground.

Chapter Thirty-three

Pendulous Boots

Oswell watched the Indian grab the dead man's ankle and drag him to the corner behind the last pew on the left. The execution had silenced the congregation. Those who wept did so quietly.

The talker looked at the remainder of the line and said, "Put your stuff in."

Terrified people dumped their jewels and watches and cash into the trunk; the vessel was heavy with wealth.

Presently, the aisle was cleared, excepting the brigands with sawed-off shotguns, who faced the pews; the pair with revolvers, who guarded the doors; and the twins, directly behind the trunks.

The talker said, "So that's it for side one. Uncle!"

"Yes," the minister said from the piano bench, his arm around Beatrice.

"Start counting. Let me know if I need to execute anyone in side two."

The minister faced side one and counted, tapping his gun barrel upon his thick fingertips for tabulation. The congregation was still and silent throughout the endeavor. The minister finished his appraisal.

The talker asked, "We got everybody?"

"We're missing one."

"Don't forget that dead fella in the back."

"Right. They're all here then."

"Glad to hear it," the talker said. He turned to the congregation and explained, "You try a setup like this in Boston or Philly, half of 'em don't come back, we learned. Lots of people get executed. But in small towns, the people know each other and are much better Christians." The talker pulled out his watch and said, "Side two, get going. You have until five after twelve."

The people in side two—including the limping sheriff, Deputy Goodstead and the mayor—filed along their pews, into the aisle and out of the church.

Oswell looked over at Quinlan, who stood leaning upon the lectern. The Irishman was almost unrecognizable with his deformities.

Lingham had been correct—the Appanuqis had turned him into a grotesque, and it looked as if he had endured a lot of doctoring to turn him back into something that was passably human after he had won his freedom. The man's wretched form was the horrible confluence of agony and determination.

The Irishman's good eye and his eye slit watched Alphonse descend the ladder rungs. The little Frenchman had secured four nooses to the central beam above the dais.

Alphonse, holding the loose end of a cord attached to the bottom rung of the ladder, walked over to Quinlan. The Frenchman gave his boss the tether; the Irishman wrapped it around his left hand, the one covered over by a bronze gauntlet.

"Merci," Quinlan said to the little man.

"De rien."

Alphonse returned to the stepladder and climbed up the close side, so that his back was to the congregation.

Quinlan turned his asymmetrical head; he looked at the captives; the sound of his breathing whistled wetly, as if he suffered from pneumonia. With his good hand, the Irishman rubbed the scars that crisscrossed his bare scalp.

To Arthur, he said, "Hang James."

Beatrice wailed. The dire, rending pain in her voice made Oswell shrink. The rancher looked at Lingham's face; he was silent and accepting.

The giant glanced at Oswell and said, "Bye."

"Bye."

Dicky said, "Good-bye, Lingham," but did not look at him.

Godfrey, head down, said, "See you."

Arthur grabbed Lingham's tie and pulled him from the quartet of captives. The man walked without protest. Lingham did not look up at his bride or anyone else, but simply stared at his boots. Oswell knew that if the giant saw Beatrice he would break.

Lingham reached the far side of the ladder; Alphonse waited for him at the top like a crow.

"Climb," Quinlan said. "Misbehave and we'll start hurting innocents."

Lingham stepped onto the ladder and leaned forward, his purple hands still tied behind his back. He climbed the rungs, his footsteps sounding like the machinations of a very large and slow clock. Godfrey and Dicky turned away from the scene; Oswell continued to watch. He heard his brother sniffle once.

The giant reached the third highest rung; the top

of the ladder was at his knees; the noose was level with his head. Beatrice was sobbing. Alphonse put the rope around his neck and cinched it tight.

The little Frenchman descended the stepladder. Lingham shut his eyes. Oswell's heart hammered in his chest and his vision grew blurry. Alphonse walked beside his boss.

The giant said, "I'm sorry."

With his bronze gauntlet, Quinlan yanked the cord attached to the bottom rung. The stepladder jerked and clattered upon the dais. Lingham fell into the rope around his neck. Beatrice shrieked; members of the congregation shouted.

The giant kicked twice at the air as he swung on the strangulating rope. His face glowed bright red. He kicked three more times. The crotch of his pants darkened with urine. His visage became as purple as his numb hands. A paroxysm bent his spine. His body relaxed.

Lingham, dead, spun on the cord that squeezed his bent neck.

Oswell looked over at Quinlan: the Irishman stared up at the twisting corpse, satisfaction—though no joy—upon his misshapen face.

Alphonse walked over to the fallen ladder and folded it up. He dragged it two yards to the left, opened the legs and erected it beneath another noose. Beatrice's sobs were long ugly moans.

The Taylors and a few other people who lived nearby entered the church, bearing suitcases, sacks and bundles that they promptly dumped into the empty trunk. Each person glanced at the hanged man for a brief moment.

The talker asked Quinlan, "Which do we string up next?"

"Godfrey."

A terrible chill crawled down the rancher's spine; he knew that he could not watch his brother climb that ladder. A small sound escaped Godfrey's mouth, but nothing more.

"I hope that the beam don't break," the talker said.

In a low voice that only the remainder of the Tall Boxer Gang could hear, Dicky said, "Stall."

In a similarly quiet whisper, Godfrey said, "How?"

"Stumble."

"Why?" Oswell asked.

Dicky did not proffer a reason, but merely repeated the word "stall."

"Okay," Godfrey said.

To Arthur, Quinlan said, "Walk him forward."

The silent twin strode over to Godfrey, grabbed his tie and pulled him from beside his brother. The plump Danford walked three steps and then spilled onto the ground.

"That's why they give elephants four legs," the talker said. Minister Orton laughed explosively.

Oswell looked at his brother, facedown upon the dais, embarrassing himself in his final moments.

The rancher looked angrily at Dicky.

"Why is he doing this?" Oswell whispered, hotly.

"Be quiet," Dicky said. He looked up at Oswell; he no longer looked weak and beaten. In that instant, the rancher knew that the New Yorker had been playing possum since the moment of his capture.

Arthur grabbed Godfrey's collar and yanked him to his feet; they walked toward the stepladder.

Oswell noticed that Dicky's arms were moving. The rancher whispered, "What are you doing?" He received no reply.

Chapter Thirty-four

Razors and Blood

If Dicky's wrists had been tied as tightly as Lingham's and the Danfords', he would not have had enough circulating blood or maneuverability to extract the hoe-guard razor from the rear waistband of his pants. Fortunately, the Indian Shagawa was not as cruel as the twins. He had bound the New Yorker's wrists in the normal manner—tight, but allowing circulation.

During the last thirty minutes, Dicky had fished for, positioned and repositioned the razor in his fingers, acutely aware that if he dropped it he would die. Three times when he had the blade in between his right index and middle fingers (the desired location), that brutish minister had looked at him, as if sensing that he was not as beaten as he pretended to be. He had just begun to cut when Lingham was hanged. During the lynching, his pulse had raced too quickly for his fingers to remain steady or reliable; he had halted his clandestine machinations, trying to calm himself while he heard the pendulous swinging of the long corpse.

Dicky intended to cut his bonds before Godfrey was hanged.

Behind him, the plump, elder Danford walked toward the stepladder, led by Arthur. The walking captive thudded to the ground again.

For the second time, Oswell whispered, "What are you doing?"

If Dicky explained his plan, the rancher would call him out. Lingham and the Danfords might have accepted the noose, but Dicky sure as hell had not. He ignored Oswell's inquiry.

Quinlan said to Arthur, "If Godfrey falls again, strip off all of his clothes and hang him naked."

With the razor, Dicky sawed through the twines of the burlap rope; his wrists jerked apart the moment his bonds were cut.

"What are you doing?" Oswell demanded, louder.

Dicky dropped the razor, knelt down, raised

Oswell's left pant leg, pulled the gun from the rancher's boot, pointed it at the back of Arthur's head, thumbed the hammer, squeezed the trigger, blinked as the big-caliber revolver boomed and flashed and recoiled, watched the silent twin's head jerk forward, spun on the talker, caught a bullet in his left shoulder, thumbed the hammer, squeezed off a second shot that knocked the talker onto his back, spun on Quinlan to see that he had ducked behind the lectern, pointed his pistol at the minister and fired into the holy man's head, splattering his thoughts in gray and pink clumps upon the piano.

Oswell yelled, "No, no, no! Damn you, goddam you!"

The New Yorker ran to Arthur, snatched one of his six-shooters and looked at Quinlan hobbling away from the lectern.

Dicky ran at the deformed man; he squeezed off two rounds with the six-shooter in his left hand. The rounds cracked into Quinlan's wooden leg; the appendage flew out from beneath the Irishman and spun into the pews, smacking the wooden bench between the two marshals from Arkansas.

The New Yorker pounced atop the fallen Irishman and pressed one of his guns to the slit on the right side of his mottled face, within which sat a milky green eye.

"Let us go or your boss gets uglier," Dicky said

to the gunmen in the aisle. The New Yorker fired a threat into Quinlan's gauntlet; the bullet clanged against the bronze.

"Slaughter everyone in this place if he doesn't release me in five seconds," Quinlan said.

The brigands at the front—the two with the sawed-off shotguns—pointed their weapons at the crowd. The men at the doors trained four ten-shot double-action revolvers upon the congregation.

Dicky knew this was not a bluff, but still he yelled desperately, "I will kill him!"

"Five," Quinlan said.

Dicky struck the Irishman's scar-covered scalp with the butt of his gun. The rugose skin bruised.

"Four."

The brigands in the aisles aimed their weapons at the heads of the hostages and thumbed their hammers; people in the pews ducked and crowded away from the barrels, yet there was no place for them to go.

"Three."

"You selfish bastard," Oswell yelled as he careened into Dicky and knocked him off of Quinlan. The New Yorker slammed upon his back, the rancher, arms still bound behind his back, atop him; Alphonse's left shoe kicked the gun from Dicky's right hand and then the gun from his left; the weapons spun across the light blue carpet like senseless birds.

Dicky looked at the enraged, gasping face of Oswell Danford directly above him.

"You selfish bastard," Oswell repeated.

"I came here to fight!"

"We've got enough blood on us!"

"You were just going to let them hang your own brother? You are okay with that?"

Oswell kneed Dicky in the side; a rib buckled and cracked. The New Yorker punched Oswell across the jaw; the rancher's head snapped sideways, but the tough man did not seem to feel it; pain flared in Dicky's knuckles from the blow.

"Stop them," Quinlan said.

Oswell kneed Dicky in the side again; another rib cracked; the New Yorker put his hands to Oswell's throat and began to choke him. Oswell twisted his head and bit into Dicky's arm.

Shagawa pulled the rancher off of the New Yorker and to his feet. Oswell kicked Dicky's broken ribs; the New Yorker could not contain the yell that ran up his throat.

Nearby, Alphonse handed Quinlan his crutch; the Irishman stood upright.

A boot slammed into Dicky's neck; he looked up and saw the talker's prickly face. The man's bronzed brow was dripping with sweat; he breathed heavily, wheezing from the bullet the New Yorker had sent him. His tangled black hair looked like leaking oil; his obsidian eyes were unblinking and reptilian.

The pressure upon Dicky's neck grew; he clamped his hands to the talker's boot, but this man had a bestial strength with which he could not contend. A constellation blinked into existence before the New Yorker's eyes; he tried to inhale but could only slap at the growing weight that patiently crushed his windpipe. The edges of his vision grew gray; he stomped the heels of his boots upon the floor in agony.

"That's enough," Quinlan said.

The talker lifted his boot from Dicky's neck; the New Yorker inhaled deeply, but coughed the air out as soon as he had captured it. His broken ribs screamed; his lungs burned.

Dicky, gasping, noticed something that looked like a child's toy in the talker's left hand. The item was a wooden fish about two inches long adorned with shiny iridescent beads and sixteen metal hooks. The talker dropped the fishing lure into Dicky's open mouth and kicked his jaw shut.

The captor yanked the fishing line taut. Hooks bit into Dicky's tongue, gums, soft palate and cheeks; his mouth felt as if it were filled with burning coals; he tasted copper and honey. He gagged upon his own blood.

The twin pulled on the line; Dicky stood up from the ground, his face wet with tears, his body trembling as if he had been thrust naked into winter. His broken ribs doubled him forward, but his captor yanked him upright by the lure in his mouth. Blood drizzled down his chin onto the floor and into the hair on his chest.

He was led beside Oswell; the rancher smoldered and stared at the ground.

The twin yanked Dicky's arms behind his back; one of his broken ribs buckled out of alignment, poking his skin; he tried to yell, but just gurgled blood. The captor wrapped the fishing line around the New Yorker's wrists and hands.

The twin searched him thoroughly for weapons and then checked Oswell; he found nothing, because they had nothing left.

Dicky saw that the right side of the church was nearly full with returned guests, including the sheriff and the deputy. The second trunk was brimming with money and jewels. Pivoting around on his feet (he could not turn his head without pulling the hooks), he looked back and saw Shagawa walk Godfrey to the stepladder, atop which Alphonse awaited him. Dicky turned away from the scene.

He saw the talker lay his dead brother beside his dead uncle on the far side of the pew. Behind the bodies, Beatrice was sprawled out on the piano bench, though she was still breathing. Gore, flecks of bone, and clayish lumps that were the minister's brains stained her shoulder and the piano.

Oswell looked balefully at Dicky; he surveyed the New Yorker's injuries and decided to withhold his black condemnation.

Dicky heard Godfrey's boots ascend the stepladder, ponderous and morbid, like the heart of a sick old man. The sound stopped.

Oswell glanced at his brother and then back down at the ground.

Dicky heard rope rub against rope: the friction of the noose being cinched. The quick footsteps of the little Frenchman descending the stepladder followed immediately after.

"See you Oswell," Godfrey said.

"See you" was all his brother could say without breaking.

Quinlan yanked the cord; the stepladder clattered to the dais; Godfrey gasped; his neck snapped; Dicky heard the creaking of wood; a few people in the congregation muttered. A wet cough was the last sound the hanged man ever made.

Quinlan, missing a leg but using his crutch in its place, ambled over to Dicky and Oswell. The Irishman stood in front of them.

"My intention was to do this setup and hang you men for betraying me back at Rope's End. That was it. I endured more than a decade of pain and take no pleasure in giving it, or in revenge. I just wanted to settle things even with us and make a profit.

"But you just killed two of my associates." Quinlan pointed his right index finger at Arthur and Minister Orton's bodies; the talker was cleaning their faces with a towel he dipped into an urn of holy water.

Quinlan looked back at Dicky and Oswell and said, "I got your names and addresses from the telegraph operator who wired you those wedding invitations. After we string you up, I'm going to send some men back east to find and kill all of your loved ones."

Dicky thought of his sisters in Connecticut he had just doomed; it would not be hard for Quinlan to find them now that he knew the name Richard Sterling.

For the first time since the massacre at Rope's End, the New Yorker saw Oswell Danford's face drained of color . . . pale with terror.

Chapter Thirty-five

To Have, To Hold and To Hurt

The moment T.W. and Goodstead had stepped from the church to retrieve their valuables, they matched strides; Kenneth John walked alongside them and had a more serious look on his face than the sheriff had ever seen there before. T.W. limped into the carriage and his deputies rode beside him as he made a plan. At one point, Kenneth had asked if it was not wiser to do what these men said rather than attempt to thwart them. The sheriff explained why they could not remain passive.

From the first moment of violence, one fact heightened the terrible dread T.W. felt: these brigands had not bothered to conceal their identities. The sheriff knew that there were three reasons why they would not wear scarves over their faces. The first possible explanation was that they intended to leave the country after this setup was completed. This hypothesis had some merit (the leader and the little man were clearly from overseas) but for T.W. that idea did not seem sound—it was unlikely that they would all vacate America. The second possible explanation was that men this deep in darkness did not fear being apprehended; they welcomed the challenge of lawmen, courted violence and relished their own infamy. This was more likely than his first guess, but still did not fit alongside the rest of Quinlan's meticulous machinations. The third possible explanation—the one that had made T.W. unswerving in his desire to act—was that these foul men did not intend to leave any witnesses alive. Considering the violence and psychosis he had observed thus far, he thought it was entirely possible that these morally decayed men intended to massacre the entire congregation once they had their take.

The lawmen of Trailspur could not draw straws or flip coins to determine the safety of their charge—they had to act. Deputies Goodstead and Kenneth John understood and agreed with the sheriff.

T.W. had returned to the church with his valuables after a twenty-one minute absence. He was brutishly searched for weapons at the door (as were Goodstead and Kenneth John) and his suitcase was taken from him. The vessel's contents—two necklaces and a brooch that had belonged to Lucinda, his wedding band, the contents of Beatrice's jewelry box, three hundred dollars, three timepieces (all gifts from his daughter), the golden star he had received in Arkansas and a silver letter opener with seven sapphires in it (a gift from the mayor)—were emptied into the trunk by a brigand.

When he looked at the dais and saw his daughter keeled over on the piano bench, her gown spattered with gore, his stomach sank. Smiler told T.W. that his girl was okay—there had been a shooting and she had fainted.

The sheriff returned to his seat, saw Lingham's long corpse (a sight that elicited equal amounts of anger and pity), and watched Godfrey Danford hang. T.W. summarily noticed a twin and the minister laid dead on the dais, near his daughter. The sheriff did not know precisely what had happened during his absence, but there were two fewer dangerous men in the church, and he surmised that his chances had just got a little better.

He watched the deformed man promise to kill the families of Oswell Danford and Richard

Sterling. Horror penetrated the remainder of the Tall Boxer Gang as their misdeeds spread like spilled ink to far-off loved ones they thought safe . . . more innocents who would be imperiled if T.W. did nothing to stop Quinlan and his crew in Trailspur.

The misshapen boss turned to the small Frenchman and said, "Set it up for Dicky."

"Oui."

The New Yorker did not at all react to the declaration of his death sentence—his mind was on whatever relatives his gambit had just inadvertently killed.

T.W., seated in the front pew, brought the heels of his boots together until they touched either side of the box beneath his bench. He slid the package forward.

The diminutive Frenchman dragged the stepladder three yards to the right, to the empty noose that dangled beside the second sagging corpse. The urine that had pooled within Godfrey's boots found holes in the toes and dripped to the rug below.

T.W. furtively glanced at the aisle: two men with shotguns stood one row behind him, each pointing their dual-barreled weapons at opposite sides of the church. The sheriff glanced at the door and saw two sentries standing there with revolvers in all four of their hands, muzzles pointed down. The surviving twin (who had not spoken since T.W.'s return, but seemed like the one who used to talk) stood behind the open trunk, monitoring the deposits the last few stragglers made.

Upon the dais, the misshapen boss leaned against the lectern and watched the little Frenchman erect the stepladder for the third time. Standing between the boss and the two captives was the Indian who wore a vest made out of wolf skins; he held a lever-action rifle in his left hand and seemed oddly peaceful.

With the toe of his boot, T.W. lifted the lid off of the shoe box. He glanced down and saw the shawl, beneath which laid his revolver. He knew that Goodstead would follow through on his part of the plan; he prayed that Kenneth John would have the courage to do what was required of him.

The last member of the congregation sat down; the second trunk was full. The sentries closed the doors to the church. The diminutive Frenchman climbed the ladder and awaited the next man to be hanged.

Rubbing a purple weal on the side of his scarred scalp, the malformed boss said to the twin, "Hang him."

The twin shut the lid of the trunk; the slam reverberated throughout the church. He turned around, ascended the pulpit steps and walked across the dais toward Richard Sterling. The handsome man was hunched and dripping with pain.

The twin grabbed the fishing line that ran into his mouth; the hooks that jutted from his cheeks glinted. The New Yorker's gurgling shriek was the sound of a drowning man. Members of the congregation gasped; a man cried out angrily and several children wept. People were not built to witness a thing like this, the sheriff thought.

The captor punched his captive in the stomach; Richard doubled over, squirting a crimson signature upon the floor.

The New Yorker's shoulders began to convulse; his body was seized by three violent paroxysms; he dropped to his knees. Vomit sprayed from his nostrils and past the fishing lure in his mouth. He moaned in dire agony, liquefying.

The twin grabbed the fishing line and yanked his captive back to his feet; the protruding hooks glinted. T.W. saw one of Richard's molars, exposed through a rent in his right cheek, and looked away. The sheriff had seen a lot of darkness throughout his life—the frontier savages he had helped make peace with had some abominable practices—yet this was the first time he felt that he stared directly at the work of the devil.

The New Yorker, his cheeks, chin and neck bearded with gore and excreta, teetered. The twin grabbed the fishing line, yanked Richard around, and walked him toward the stepladder. The captor's back was to the congregation.

T.W. reached into the shoe box, withdrew his gun, thumbed the hammer, fired a shot into the twin's ribs and lunged sideways, ignoring the pain in his hip. He slammed his free hand into the bottom of the sawed-off shotgun held by the startled man in the aisle, jammed his revolver into the soft flesh beneath his bearded chin, thumbed the hammer and squeezed his trigger, sending the man's brains up through the roof of his skull like a fountain.

Goodstead collided into the other shotgun wielder; the Texan shoved the deadly barrels toward the ceiling where one load was discharged with a thunderous boom.

Kenneth John and his father charged the sentries at the door. The son impacted and wrestled one of the sentries to the ground; a revolver flashed and the mayor's beeline was reversed; the side of his face erupted with gore as he flew backward; his frail wife shrieked. T.W. fired a shot into the neck of the man who felled the mayor.

Goodstead slammed the butt of the shotgun he had just snatched into the jaw of its former owner; the crack sounded like a tree branch breaking. Kenneth John pulled a pistol from the man he subdued. Somebody screamed and pointed to the dais.

"Drop your guns," Quinlan said.

T.W. and Goodstead turned to the dais.

Shagawa had taken Tara Taylor hostage and pressed a gun to her neck. Alphonse sat on the piano bench beside Beatrice; he had a tiny pistol in his left hand, pointed to her temple. She was still unconscious.

The fallen twin stood up; blood leaked from his mouth into his prickly beard; he had a gory, dripping revolver in each hand. The man had been shot twice in the torso—the front and the back—and still he raised his pistols.

To T.W., Quinlan said, "Drop your guns or I will have these girls sodomized right in front of you."

A poisonous silence filled the church. The sheriff's heart pounded so hard his ribs hurt.

Quinlan said, "Throw down. Now."

"No," T.W. replied. That lone syllable was the most difficult thing he had ever had to say in his entire life. "I am not giving you the reins." He pointed his gun at the malformed man's face and thumbed the hammer—the metallic click underlining his threat.

It was clear to T.W. that Quinlan had not expected this response.

As sedately as if he were ordering a drink in a saloon, the Irishman said, "If they fire, execute the girls first and start shooting into the crowd. Murder as many people as you can."

T.W. did not put down his weapon . . . but he could not fire either. If he squeezed, Beatrice and a lot of other folks would die for certain. Quinlan looked at the little Frenchman; the two exchanged some secret communication.

The Irishman said to the congregation, "We're leaving. We're taking our trunks and these hostages. Clear the aisles."

T.W., his heart slamming in his chest and his face dripping with cold sweat, kept his gun on Quinlan; the sheriff stamped down his fear and said, "No. If I let you take them, I know how I'll find them."

The Irishman ruminated for a moment.

"Put down your guns," T.W. demanded.

T.W. saw the Frenchman shut his eyes; Quinlan fell to the ground; Shagawa and the twin dropped to their knees and bowed their heads.

For a quarter of a second, the sheriff was confused.

The rear wall of the church exploded. Slats of wood, floes of plaster, shards of stone and grit filled the entirety of the enclosure, rendering everyone who faced forward—the entire con-gregation excepting the villains—momentarily blind and deaf. The blast knocked T.W. sideways into a pew and then onto his back.

The sheriff understood instantly that the robbers had put dynamite on the outside of the church. Lying upon his side, stones and dirt raining upon him, ears ringing and his lungs struggling with the filthy air, a terrible thought came to him: these scoundrels might have rigged the entire church with explosives.

A choir that was the sound of a hundred confused, frightened people sounded all around the sheriff; above them, the lawman yelled, "Get out of the church," and then coughed out grit. He shoved a woman into the aisle, inhaled dusty air and shouted, "Get out of here! Evacuate, evacuate!" He shoved more people into the aisle.

Dim pops sounded to his left; it took him a while to recognize the sound as gunfire. Bullets whistled through the smoke and dust; people shrieked as speeding rounds found, pierced and killed them.

Goodstead materialized beside the sheriff, yelling, "Everybody get out of here! Get out, get out, get out!"

The lawmen crawled up the aisle, toward the exit, through which the congregation was draining. A few gunshots sounded in the distance, though the rounds did not seem to impact the church.

On their hands and knees, T.W. and Goodstead surveyed the enclosure: nobody was standing in the pews—those who could exit had done so already. The sheriff glanced behind him. The church's front wall was sundered, as if a giant boulder had been cast through it; swaying left and right, dangling from the rafters against the blue sky were the hanged men, one of whom was supposed to become his son that day.

The surviving criminals, Tara Taylor and his daughter were gone. Racing toward the eastern mountains, T.W. saw a rapidly diminishing beige and green stagecoach.

The pain in the sheriff's hip screamed the moment he stood up; he limped forward, outside into the clear air. He put distance between himself and the church, but each step was agony.

Once he was twenty-five yards from the edifice, T.W. looked at Goodstead's dusty blank face and said, "Get strong horses, five. And ten guns. Binoculars. And a spyglass."

The deputy said, "You okay?"

"I'm not talking about that right now. Fetch that stuff."

Goodstead careened toward a horse and deftly swung himself atop it. He rode off.

The sun was not long past noon, though it felt to the sheriff as if he had lived an entire decade in the pews today.

"Big Abe," T.W. said. The large man walked over; the laceration on his round face bled so much that he could not keep his right eye open.

"Take a horse. Send a wire to Billington with a description of these men. Make sure they're prepared. Tell them to watch the trains and also the telegraph station and post office in case they try to send off a message. Let Westland know too."

Thunder shook the world; T.W. stumbled

forward; Big Abe caught his shoulder and kept him upright. The confused citizens of Trailspur screamed.

The sheriff turned around and looked at the welter of smoke and splinters and airborne stones that had just replaced the church. A rock struck the top of his head; pebbles rained down from the sky.

"Turn away from it and shield yourselves," T.W. called out. The members of the congregation hunched forward; stones pelted their backs, ribs, necks and skulls. A rock struck the sheriff's right kidney; another pebble smacked painfully upon his clavicle. A spinning plank slapped Big Abe's neck. The hail of detritus bruised the townsfolk for thirty seconds and then ended.

"I'll send the wires," Big Abe said in the same stentorian voice that had called out the steps for dances last night. He ran off toward a confused mare that walked in circles.

Behind the church, a gray horse with stones embedded in its side and a shaft of wood lodged in its neck folded up its legs, curled its head forward and stopped moving.

T.W. surveyed the remainder of the congregation; a quick count yielded a total of eighty-three people. The church pews had held one-hundred-and-twenty guests.

"You okay?" he asked Meredith, whose face was bleeding and bruised.

"Do not worry about me right now."

The sheriff saw Deputy Kenneth John hug his frail mother; she wept into his shoulder. Mayor Warren John was absent.

T.W. saw Smiler, standing alone in a sea of strangers. No grin creased his beard: the sixty-three-year-old marshal simply stared in disbelief at the pile of rubble that had been the church. The sheriff had to look away.

"Let me help you."

T.W. turned around. Oswell Danford stood in front of him. Stones and splinters jutted from his bleeding left cheek; the ear on that side looked as if it had been chewed by a wolf. His hands were still bound behind his back.

The sheriff punched the man across the jaw; the bone cracked. The rancher spat blood into the dirt.

"Please let me help," Oswell said.

T.W.'s fist throbbed from the blow, which only made him angrier.

"They got my daughter!"

T.W. punched Oswell in the stomach, doubling him over. The rancher stood there, gasping and coughing.

"If something happens to my Beatrice . . . if something happens to her . . ." This was not a sentence T.W. was able to complete.

"I can help you. I rode with Quinlan and have some idea how this'll go. And he wants me dead, so you might be able to use me for barter."

T.W. knew that there was truth in what the rancher said.

Oswell continued, "You can hang me afterward—all I want to do is stop him. You heard his threats." In a quiet voice that sounded almost like a child's, he said, "He's going after my wife. My kids. He's going after them. My family. They don't even know what I did all those years ago."

T.W. said, "You do what I say, without argument. And I will hang you afterward."

"Okay."

"Turn around."

Oswell faced his back to the sheriff. T.W. untied the knot that bound the rancher's wrists and had turned the man's hands purple. The cord slid off. Oswell rubbed his palms together, restoring circulation; he could not yet move his fingers.

Richard Sterling, a handkerchief red with blood hanging from his mouth, walked toward the sheriff. He had a revolver in his left hand, pointed at the ground.

"Drop that weapon, Richard Sterling," T.W. said.

The New Yorker set the gun upon the ground and continued forward.

"You want to help us get Quinlan's crew before I hang you?"

Richard nodded. He winced; the motion apparently caused him internal pain.

"You can ride like that?'

Richard Sterling nodded.

"He's a good shot. And fast on the draw," Oswell added.

T.W. said, "You'll follow my lead." For the exact same reasons the sheriff had allowed the rancher to join, he accepted Richard's help.

"Deputy John," T.W. called across the plain. The man, twelve yards off, kissed his mother's cheek and walked past a score of stunned and grieving people before he reached the sheriff.

"You are in charge until we get back."

"I want to go after them," the young man said.

"You stay here. We need some law in this town."

Kenneth John did not argue, which was atypical. It was clear to T.W. that the day's events had straightened the wayward man.

"You put guards on the telegraph station here. A few on the bank and post office too. Get volunteers and arm them."

"I will."

"You and your father made a big difference." T.W. pointed to the smoking mountain of tinder and broken rock that had been the church. "We could've all been in there. You did good."

"Thank you," Kenneth John said. He went back to his mother, hugged her, walked her over to Big Abe's wife for companionship, climbed onto his horse and spurred it into action.

Deputy Goodstead, atop a white mare tethered

to four other horses, rode past Kenneth John toward the church grounds; he stared at the dusty heap that had replaced the holy edifice since he departed. The beasts behind him were strong, fresh steeds.

Roland Taylor walked toward the sheriff.

"You can have my horses, but I want to come."

"Stay here with your family." The sheriff doubted that Roland had ever fired a gun at a living creature, much less a man.

"They took Tara. I have a right to come," he bristled.

"You've never been in a gunfight in your life. This isn't the time to learn how it goes."

Roland pointed at Oswell and Richard, smoldered, and said, "You're taking them? Those outlaws?"

"They know how to shoot. And if they get killed, nobody'll care. You should be with your son and your wife."

The belligerence in the man's face was replaced by fear when he said, "I haven't seen Jack since the explosion. I . . . I didn't see him get out of there." The man's eyes filled with tears.

T.W. could not watch the man break and so said, more brusquely than he meant to, "Go to Vanessa. Now." In a softer voice he added, "She needs you."

Roland, his mouth trembling, turned away from the sheriff and walked back to his wife.

Smiler walked up to T.W. and proclaimed, "I'm comin'." The man was older than T.W. by six years, but he would not panic in a showdown, and he was a good shot. Additionally, he was a lawman and had no family, two facts that made him a preferable choice over most Trailspur townsfolk.

"I'm comin' and you can't never talk me out of it neither. They got Smith. I'm comin'."

"You're the last one. I'm only taking five on this."

"You can't talk me out of it," Smiler said, refuting a comment he had anticipated but not heard.

Goodstead reined his horse beside T.W.; the four tethered steeds halted behind him.

"Get on a horse," T.W. said to Oswell, Richard and Smiler.

The Texan observed the chosen men and said, "Is this the posse?"

"It is," T.W. said, limping to a black mare.

Goodstead looked at Oswell and Richard and said, "Nice to have a couple of guys to duck behind when the shootin' starts."

The deputy rode up to T.W., leaned down and helped hoist him onto the black mare. The horse whickered. The pain in the sheriff's left hip made his thigh muscles twitch and burn.

"You got guns?" Smiler asked Goodstead.

"Yup. Bullets too."

T.W. looked at Goodstead, Smiler, Oswell and

Richard, all of whom were mounted; it was clear that the New Yorker was weakened from his blood loss, but he held himself in the saddle capably.

The sheriff snapped reins; his black mare surged forward. The other four riders followed.

As they tore off, Goodstead called out to the Yardley girl, "Annie!"

"Yes?"

"Tell Lilith Ford I'm takin' her to dinner when I get back!"

"She got killed."

Goodstead had no ready reply.

Chapter Thirty-six

The Hammer of Halcyon

Beatrice, wearing a brown dress and beige boots, her hair pulled back in two neat braids, sat on her father's living-room couch, where a little more than one year ago Jim had spilled tea on her the night before they were to be married. She took the Philadelphia Chronicler *and the* New York Observing Eye *from the table beside her and set the newspapers in her lap. Both prestigious publications had been running her serialized article for the past three months: the bride's detailed, first-person account of the harrowing event known to the people of America as the Trailspur Wedding Massacre. The conclusion of the series was printed in these issues, pressed on the one-year anniversary of the actual event. Beatrice had delivered the final installment two weeks before it was due, satisfied with her work . . . and very, very relieved that the painful and cathartic experience of detailing the tragedy was over.*

She opened the Chronicler—*she preferred the thicker type that the Philly paper used—and began to read the article.*

"Did they make any mistakes?" her father asked, using his cane as he came down the stairs, wearing a plaid robe and weathered slippers that scuffed the steps noisily.

"I just now sat down with the papers." She lifted the New York Observing Eye *from her lap and proffered it to her father.*

"You know I won't read it." He had supported her decision to write about the event, but he had never once read an episode in the series.

"This is the one where you save me. It is entitled, 'Theodore William Jeffries, My Father, My Other Savior.' "

Her father grinned at the title, entered the den and said, "I'm sure you exaggerate things." He shuffled toward her, his slippers scuffing the wood. His hair was fully white; his face was drawn, far thinner than it was a year ago.

"There is no need to exaggerate," she said.

"I can't read about it," he said. "Don't make me." He looked nervous.

"I shall not." She put the New York Observing Eye *down*.

There was a knock on the door. Beatrice folded up the Chronicler *and began to rise from her seat.*

"Let me get it. It's just Goodstead." He turned toward the door and, leaning on the cane in his left hand, moved slowly toward it.

Prior to the tragedy, the blank-faced Texan would have simply walked in and joined whatever conversation or meal the Jeffries were having, but now they kept the door locked . . . as did most people in Trailspur. She could not remember whether she or her father had first employed the bolt.

The fifty-eight-year-old man shuffled toward the door; the bottoms of his slippers scuffed the wood like sandpaper. The scraping sound grew louder in Beatrice's ears; her heart began to race. She swallowed dryly.

Her father stopped, undid the bolt and pulled the handle; the door groaned horribly upon its hinges. He peered outside, blue light ghastly upon his old face.

"Father? Who is there . . . ?"

"It's your mother."

Beatrice felt a terrible fear blossom within her and asked, "What do you mean? My mother died when I was born."

"She's coming." Her father peered into the blue dusk, squinted, nodded his head and added, "And I'm pretty sure I see James walking up the hill too."

Beatrice realized she was dreaming and woke up. She opened her eyes, but all she could see were the golden curls of her own hair, brilliantly lit by the sun. Something cold and hard slid across the top of her head, following the contour of her skull. She was jostled to the left and then forward and knew that she was in a stagecoach. Beatrice attempted to wipe the hair from her face, but her arms did not move—they were tied behind her back. She was shivering.

The cold hard thing scraped across her scalp again. The top of her head felt cool and damp. Her golden hair fell away from her eyes and upon her bare legs. She looked at the curly blonde locks in her lap and saw that she had been stripped nude.

Alphonse walked directly in front of her, a straight razor in his left hand. She tried to scream, but the cloth stuffed into her mouth strangled the cry.

On the stagecoach bench behind the little Frenchman sat the Indian with the wolf-skin vest; the native held a blood-soaked rag to his neck. Beside him sat one of the twins; his prickly beard was sticky, agleam with blood; his respirations were wet. To the right of the wheezing man sat Quinlan, his mottled face pale and dusty. She did not know who drove the stagecoach, but saw three black boots through the slat in the front wall.

Beatrice looked to her left and saw Tara on the bench beside her. The woman was completely nude; her hands were bound behind her back; her head had been shaved bald. All of the woman's long red hair had been bundled together and shoved into her mouth, from where it depended like a horse's tail. A purple bruise shone upon her right cheek; her burst lips were caked with blood; a line of crimson ran from the side of her right breast, down her torso and right hip, onto the leather bench. The woman was awake, yet silent and immobile; she stared forward, hollow with shock.

Tears filled Beatrice's eyes.

The Frenchman set the razor to the side of her head; she jerked away from the hard, cold steel.

"If you move you get cut."

Beatrice held as still as she could, barely able to inhale enough air through her nostrils to fill her lungs. The Frenchman set the razor to the right side of her head and dragged the blade forward; the metal sizzled through the thousands of fine blonde strands that sprouted there. The newly exposed skin atop her right ear tingled. He slid the razor across the other side of her head; she felt her

371

freed hair fall upon her left shoulder and thigh.

Alphonse set the razor to her nape and slid it parallel to her tendons; the stagecoach lurched; he hastily withdrew the blade. The vehicle stabilized; he applied the razor again and slid it up her neck to the rear of her skull. The myriad minute clicks of the shearing crawled along her spine. Her skin became gooseflesh.

The Frenchman collected her shorn curls with his free hand and set them with the remainder of her hair, previously arranged in a neat row on the bench to her right.

He placed a hand upon her head and rubbed her bare scalp as if it were a globe. His small eyes surveyed the skin for errant hairs.

"She looks ready," the Indian said, adjusting the bloody rag he held to his neck.

"Oui."

The stagecoach lurched. Quinlan grunted and then grimaced.

Alphonse looked at the Irishman and asked, "Want me to examine?"

Quinlan nodded. Alphonse folded his straight razor, slid it into his burgundy vest pocket and turned away from Beatrice. Her bare head tingled; she began to shiver.

The Indian slid down the bench, closer to the gurgling twin. The Frenchman sat in the nascent space, beside his boss. Quinlan extended his left arm; Alphonse carefully undid a buckle at the bottom of the gauntlet's cuff. When it snapped open, the Irishman gritted his teeth, pained.

"You want me do this later?" the Frenchman asked.

"No. Keep going."

Alphonse unfastened the second buckle. It snapped like a firecracker.

"Dammit," Quinlan said.

"I take off?"

The Irishman nodded. Alphonse put both of his small hands on the large bronze gauntlet and pulled. Quinlan gritted his teeth. The segmented metal glove slid off to reveal a long slender hand, white as milk and covered with scars; none of the fingertips had fingernails. The pinky and ring fingers dangled limply, swaying with the vacillations of the stagecoach.

Quinlan looked at Beatrice and said, "Your groom gave me this. And other things I won't show you." She had no response.

"Make fist," Alphonse said to him.

"It hurts," the Irishman replied. Sweat beaded upon his mottled forehead and scarred scalp.

"Make fist."

Quinlan's thumb and index and middle fingers closed; the loose ring and pinky fingers twitched but did not close.

"They are disconnect. Tendons." Alphonse said. "I fix when we are safe."

"I know."

The Frenchman slowly and gently slid the gauntlet back onto Quinlan's hand. The Irishman gritted his teeth, but said nothing.

Alphonse snapped the gauntlet buckles; the boss exhaled a tremulous breath, his mottled face flushed with red and purple pain.

"I have morphine," the Frenchman said.

"I can't risk being cloudy."

"I give small dose. You do not need to suffer."

"No."

The Frenchman, concern in his eyes, nodded.

Quinlan said, *"Merci beaucoup."*

"De rien." The little man grinned and added, "Accent getting better."

Alphonse turned away from his boss, collected Beatrice's hair from the bench, wrapped a lock around the bundle to secure it, pulled the cloth from her mouth and shoved the ersatz horse tail inside. It tasted like dust and sweat.

In surprisingly fluent English, the Indian said, "They look quite pretty like that. As if they were totems of some variety."

Alphonse admired Beatrice and then Tara.

He nodded in approbation of his own work and said, *"Oui.* And they will look more pretty with crowns of nails."

Beatrice began to choke on her own hair; her body convulsed, but she had no food to expel. She gagged and slammed the back of her bald head into the panel behind her.

The Frenchman grabbed her neck and sat her upright, irritation in the gray pebbles that were his eyes.

"Do not bruise," Alphonse said. He opened a valise and withdrew a hammer and a four-inch long nail.

Beatrice's vision narrowed; she toppled forward and blacked out.

Mary, Jesus and Joseph ran across Jim's lawn, up to Beatrice. They put their filthy paws on the blue dress she wore. She swatted at them and scolded them until they sat obediently around her in a circle. Her wedding gown was ruined.

Despite her irritation, she scratched the coydogs' long snouts and patted their heads; they panted past dangling tongues and woofed amicably.

Beatrice looked over at the A-frame house her fiancé was building. Jim knelt upon the roof, silhouetted against the sky. He set the tip of a nail to a shingle and, with his favorite hammer, gently tapped the iron into the wood.

Chapter Thirty-seven

The Backsides of Horses

The white stallion rumbled beneath Oswell; its hooves slammed to the grass and rebounded only a moment after contact. Wind blew against the rancher's throbbing, fractured jaw and into the lacerations he had gained during the explosion, but the pains were distant annoyances. When he compared himself to the agonized, gory mess from New York who rode the horse beside him, his wounds seemed bearable.

The horses thundered forward; a grass tapestry peppered with elongated stones rolled by beneath them. For a moment, Oswell felt as if the hooves of these five animals spun the planet, so strong and determined were their steely strides.

"They were headed due east, right at the mountains," Sheriff Jeffries yelled over the tattoo of hooves. "They'll need to turn south—they can't get a stagecoach or that cripple through nineteen miles of mountains."

Oswell looked at the position of the late day sun and saw that they were riding southeast, diagonal to their quarry.

He said, "We're going to cut them off?"

"We are. The longer they ride due east, the farther ahead we'll be."

"Couldn't they go north when they get to the mountains?" Smiler asked.

"They shouldn't. The range continues all the way up and eventually gets to water they couldn't ford. If they go that way, we'll follow them and get them pinned."

Goodstead asked, "What's the plan?"

The sheriff looked at Oswell and said, "How do you think this is going to go?"

The rancher had an idea what Quinlan would do, though did not look forward to verbalizing it; he said, "He will try to get you to throw down. He will try to cow you. He will do things to the women to make you go soft."

The lawman's face was hard; he said, "Continue."

"He might try to barter for me and Dicky, but he's not going to give up Beatrice. Maybe the other one."

"Tara," Goodstead said, his contempt for Oswell clear even in just two syllables.

"He might offer Tara in exchange for Dicky and me, though the main thing will be getting us to throw down our guns so he is in control."

"But he won't give my girl back in a trade?"

"No matter what he tells you, he won't. Bein' the sheriff's daughter, she's too valuable."

"That's what I figured."

The sheriff and Oswell looked over at Dicky; the New Yorker pulled a blood-soaked rag from his mouth, bits of it sticking to his tongue, lips and inner cheeks. He sipped, swished and spat out the liquid from a flask of whiskey; his face reddened with pain and his eyes sparkled. He shoved a plaid handkerchief into his mouth.

The lawman said, "Richard. Does that sound like how it's gonna go?"

The New Yorker nodded his head; blood dripped from two holes in his left cheek.

The terrain beneath the horses became damp; the beasts' hooves slapped into the mud and flung dark pudding in their wake.

The sheriff asked Oswell, "What do you suggest?"

"Make as if you want to barter or discuss a deal. When we get close enough, we just have it out. He won't expect you to draw with the women there, so you'll get the advantage of surprise."

The sheriff pondered the rancher's plan; mud flew pell-mell into the air.

Goodstead said, "There's gotta be a better plan. Somethin' better than just pullin' guns with Beatrice and Tara in the middle of it." The deputy thought for a moment. "There's gotta be a way to trick him."

Oswell replied, "Quinlain's been tricking people for more than thirty years, and here he is, still doing it. He won't expect us to open a gunfight when he's got hostages. That's the only advantage we've got."

The weight on the sheriff's shoulders was almost visible to Oswell. The five steeds rampaged across the wet sucking earth; they flung black debris at the blue sky.

The rancher reluctantly added, "It's best to look at it like the women are already gone and this is the one chance you have to bring them back."

"You rotten bastard," Goodstead said to Oswell. He reined his horse over to the rancher's and raised the butt of his rifle.

"Goodstead! Ease off," the sheriff said. "Danford is right."

Sheriff Jeffries chewed unsavory thoughts for a moment and said, "I need a minute. Let me figure out the assignments."

Goodstead rode his steed directly in front of Oswell; the horse's rear right hoof flung a clump of mud that splattered upon the rancher's neck. The deputy guided his black mare beside its sibling, atop which sat the sheriff.

The sun behind Oswell's left shoulder told him that it was after three o'clock. Ahead of him, the blue and gray mountains climbed into the sky; he needed to tilt his head back in order to see their peaks.

The rancher tightened the buckle on the holster the deputy had given him and withdrew one of the six-shooters that came with it. The pistol was a newer make, a double-action device that would allow him to fire more quickly, without fanning the hammer. He swung the cylinder wide and saw that it was fully loaded; he closed and holstered the weapon. When he looked forward, he saw that both Goodstead and Smiler were watching him, their hands on their guns.

The rancher looked to his right, saw Dicky sway and asked, "You going to be able to stay in that saddle?"

The New Yorker nodded and then tightened the leather strap that held a stained kerchief over the hole Arthur's bullet had rent in his left shoulder.

"You've got some sisters in Connecticut, right?" Oswell asked.

Dicky nodded.

"We gotta put Quinlan down no matter what."

Dicky nodded.

"We're going to do a crisscross," the sheriff said, his voice clear over the wet slapping of hooves. The posse looked at him. He continued, "That twin is fast. The only reason I got a bullet in him was because I shot him in the back. Richard is fast and Richard killed his brother, and he and the twin have bad history. It seems like the twin will draw on Richard."

"He will," Oswell said.

"One dollar on the twin," Goodstead remarked.

"The deputy is right—the twin will probably kill Richard. Smiler?"

"Yeah."

"You go for the twin. He certainly won't be gunnin' for you and you can put him down while he's puttin' holes into Mr. Sterling."

"I'll kill that twin," the old marshal said.

"Richard, you go for the little fellow, the Frenchman. That gun he has is small caliber and if you are killed before you can get a shot off— which seems probable—I'd rather have the little guy left standing than anyone else."

Dicky nodded.

"Goodstead gets the Indian."

The deputy said, "I'll get the savage and that Frenchman Mr. Sterling didn't get to kill."

"Good. I presume Quinlan will go for Oswell?"

"He will," the rancher said.

"That means I'm goin' for Quinlan myself," the sheriff stated.

"Just be sure to put him down," Oswell admonished.

"I will. You go for whoever else is there. Somebody was driving that stagecoach, so we know there is at least one more fellow."

"I'll get whoever is left."

The horses galloped onto dry terrain.

Sheriff Jeffries raised his voice to surmount the clacking of hooves on rocks; he said, "We aren't goin' to have time to adjust the plan, so stick to it. If your assigned man isn't there, go for Quinlan first and the twin second. If they have twenty extra men who joined up with them, stick to your assigned man, put him down and then go for the rest.

"The code is, 'We just want to talk.' When I say that, you draw and put your man down."

The hooves kicked rocks pell-mell; the wake of the running horses sounded like hail.

"Goodstead, give out binoculars. Everyone look northeast. Watch for dust, birds taking flight, birds circling, reflections, anything irregular."

"Gimme the telescope," Smiler said.

"Goodstead gets the telescope—he's got the youngest eyes," the sheriff said.

The deputy reined his horse beside Smiler's and opened his saddlebag. He extricated a pair of binoculars and handed them over to the marshal.

"Thanks, Deputy."

Goodstead slowed his mare and summarily slid in between Oswell and Dicky's galloping beasts. The Texan reached into his bag, pulled out a pair of binoculars and struck them against the sundered left side of the rancher's face; Oswell's inner ear rang and flared with pain.

"Sorry," Goodstead said.

The rancher silently took the binoculars from the Texan.

Dicky reached his right hand out for a pair of binoculars. Goodstead spat in his face; the saliva sat in the New Yorker's closed right eye like a giant coagulant tear.

"Didn't see a spittoon out here," the deputy said.

Smiler laughed, a creaky cachinnation that needed oil. The Texan handed the binoculars to Dicky and spurred his horse up alongside the sheriff's. The New Yorker wiped the expectoration from his eye, blinked a couple of times and looked through the lenses.

Oswell pivoted in his saddle, faced northeast and raised his binoculars to his face. The blue and gray mountains seemed like a giant relief etched in the sky by the lowering sun. The rancher saw nothing but empty plains between himself and the ridge.

"I see smoke," Goodstead said.

Oswell put down his binoculars and looked at the deputy. Dicky, Smiler and the sheriff watched the Texan; the blank-faced man peered through an elongated enameled spyglass, nodding.

Sheriff Jeffries asked, "Can you see what it's coming from?"

"I'd bet a fire," the deputy responded. "Can't see it though."

"How much smoke?"

"A line of it. Rising straight up like a pole," the deputy said. The horses galloped for a few silent moments before Goodstead added, "It stopped. They put it out."

"What's this Quinlan's doing? A diversion?" the sheriff asked Oswell.

"I'm not sure."

"It started again. The smoke," the deputy said. The horses' hooves stomped upon dirt and weeds and stones. "Now it stopped."

"Smoke signal," Dicky said, his words garbled by the rag and injuries in his mouth.

"Are they signaling us, or other folks?" Sheriff Jeffries asked the deputy.

"I don't know how to read it. I barely know cursive."

"I know how," Smiler said. "Gimme that spyglass."

Goodstead cut his horse to the right and sidled up alongside the marshal's galloping mustang. The Texan handed the spyglass to the senior member of the posse.

Smiler raised the telescope to his right eye, looked through it, lowered it, rubbed the glass on either end with his left cuff and raised it again. He looked through it for a moment and then placed the spyglass to his other eye.

"That's the good one," the bearded man muttered to himself. Oswell and the others watched Smiler; the marshal's mouth moved—and occasionally muttered, "That ain't it"—while he peered through the glass.

"No hurry," Goodstead remarked. "Keep it to yourself."

"Deputy," the sheriff admonished.

Smiler lowered the spyglass and said, "They're

usin' Canagwa signals and repeatin' two words. 'Trade' and 'talk.' "

"I'm feeling talkative," Goodstead said, checking his revolver. "And I got some beat-up outlaws that I won't trade for less than a nickel."

"They're callin' us over," Oswell said to the sheriff.

"So this is it," the sheriff said.

"Yeah."

The quintet did not speak often as they chased their own shadows northeast for more than an hour. Oswell's mouth was numbed by the pain of his fractured jaw; whenever he spoke, his words had a slight slur to them.

The mountains expanded before the riders until all that remained of the eastern sky were shards of blue striped with white clouds, like pieces of luminous marble. The sun continued to crawl down their spines; Oswell's back dripped with sweat.

The ground beneath them became harder and harder until the horses' hooves clacked upon crenulated stone that was the extended base of the mountain ridge itself.

Goodstead took the spyglass from his eye and returned it to his saddlebag.

"They are up about half a mile."

"Let's leave these horses here," the sheriff said. "I don't want gunfire scaring them off, and if somebody gets hurt we'll need to get back to Trailspur quickly."

"Depends on who's hurt," Goodstead added.

Oswell swung his right leg over the saddle and dropped from the steed to the blue and gray stone. The impact brought fire to his jaw; his left ear rang anew.

Dicky clambered from his mare, pulled the red rag that had been another color an hour ago from his mouth, bits of his tongue, inner cheeks and lips hesitant to relinquish it. He tossed the flesh-flecked fabric to the ground, rinsed his mouth with whiskey (some of which dribbled from the holes in his cheeks) and gently shut the ruined orifice with which he had likely seduced more women than Oswell had ever even spoken to.

"Do what he said," the rancher admonished Dicky.

The New Yorker nodded, stepped forward and winced, gripping his side where Oswell had broken two ribs during their scuffle on the dais.

Smiler climbed off of his spotted mustang and walked the beast over to the pair ridden by the outlaws from the East.

Oswell watched the deputy hop off of his mare and walk over to his boss. Sheriff Jeffries leaned on Goostead's shoulder as he dismounted his black mare. The lawman grimaced when his left foot impacted the unyielding stone.

"Let's have us a chat," Goodstead said, slotting a tube magazine into the stock of his lever-action rifle. He flung the trigger guard forward; the dry clack of the bullet being drawn into the chamber echoed ten times.

Chapter Thirty-eight
Coronations in the West

T.W. ground his teeth as he walked on the hard stone due north. He raised his binoculars and looked ahead; a column of smoke climbed high into the sky, dividing the northern horizon like the left and right pages of a book. At the bottom of the gray pillar he saw a rectangle that was a stagecoach and seven dots no larger than raisins. None of the anomalies moved.

The sheriff said, "Smiler?"

"Yeah?"

"Does that smoke say anything?"

"It's just smoke."

Sweat dripped down T.W.'s forehead, into his eyes. He wiped the bitter moisture away to clear his view. His left hip throbbed so forcefully it felt as if his heart had fallen from his chest down into his waist.

He looked through the binoculars again. The raisins had not moved since he had last checked their position.

"Jesus Christ."

T.W. turned to his right; Goodstead, walking beside him, peered north through the spyglass, his blank face pale.

"What?" Goodstead looked from the lenses to T.W. and opened his mouth to speak . . . yet said nothing. "Let me see," the sheriff said, reaching for the spyglass.

The deputy raised it beyond his fingertips and said, "Better not."

"Deputy. Give me that damn telescope."

"They stripped the clothes off of them. Beatrice and Tara."

T.W. balled up his fists; the muscles in his neck hardened; his scalp tightened; his face grew hot.

He swallowed dryly and asked, "What are they doing to them?"

Goodstead looked back through the spyglass and replied, "Nothin' right now. Just have them standin' there. Looks like their arms and legs are bound so they can't run off."

"He's going to try to make you go soft before you get there," Oswell said. "It's better not to look until you can draw on him."

T.W.'s heart hammered in his chest; his ears rang; he looked at the deputy and said, "Put that telescope away."

The blank-faced Texan collapsed the spyglass and hung it around his neck by its leather cord.

"Hold to the plan," T.W. said aloud, as much to

strengthen his own resolve as to instruct those who walked alongside him.

They walked north. The boots of the quintet clacked upon the gray and blue stone; ghostly reverberations haunted the crenulated clefts to their right.

T.W. thought about the plan, and he thought about his hip, and he thought about the destroyed church, and he thought about that horse that curled up and died after the explosion, and he thought about Jesus on the cross and His agony. He thought about everything but her.

Five dark figures and two pink ones stood in tandem against the northern sky. The lowering western sun cast huge shadows of the seven onto the mountain ridge to the right.

T.W. led his posse onward. Their gigantic shadows slid toward the waiting cluster, a meeting of wraiths.

The sheriff and his men climbed the low ridge upon which Quinlan, his crew and his two hostages stood. Fifty yards remained between the groups.

T.W. saw that Beatrice was nude and shaven bald; little red lines that looked liked string ran down her face. Her blonde hair hung from her mouth like a mop. Quinlan stood beside her, leaning on his crutch.

The little Frenchman, his left hand pressed to Tara's right shoulder, said to the sheriff, "You did not appreciate art. You burn it." He pointed to Tara's head and then Beatrice's. "Now you appreciate, *oui?*"

The terrible instant that T.W. understood what had been done to Beatrice, he doubled-over and retched his hot insides upon the stone. He wiped the bile from his mouth, stood up and continued to walk north. The lawman felt as if his body were an automaton he controlled from a great distance.

T.W. and his posse closed the distance to twenty yards. Light glimmered on the long nails that protruded from Beatrice's skull; the dozen rods encircled her head like a tiara; Tara, silent and motionless, wore the same crown.

The sheriff focused his eyes on Quinlan and said, "Your signal said you wanted to trade."

Quinlan slapped his gauntlet upon Beatrice's shoulder; she wobbled; sunlight glinted upon the nails that jutted straight out of her forehead.

T.W., Goodstead, Smiler, Oswell and Richard walked toward Quinlan, Alphonse, the wheezing twin, the bleeding Indian and a mule skinner with big black boots. Most of the opposition was in bad shape, which explained to T.W. why they had hastened the showdown.

"Au revoir," the Frenchman said. He shoved Tara; she tipped forward on her bound, bloodied feet. She fell to the stone face-first; the impact drove four nails through her skull deep into her brain. She shrieked and was seized by three violent

paroxysms. Blood and urine pooled beneath her.

Quinlan said to T.W., "Throw down your guns or your girl goes the same way." He set the palm of his bronze gauntlet to Beatrice's back.

"Wait," T.W. cried. "We just want to talk."

T.W. drew his gun, pointed it at Quinlan's heart and fired; the malformed man caught the bullet and was flung back upon the stone.

Alphonse cried out, *"Patron!"*

Richard, who had turned to his side like a duelist, caught a bullet that came from the twin's gun directly opposite him; he collapsed.

Smiler fired a bullet into the right side of the twin's head; oily tangles of black hair, flecks of skull and jewels of gore burst from the opposite side like confetti; he fell to the stone.

Goodstead and the Indian fired upon each other; their shots cracked simultaneously. Both men were lanced by bullets and fell. The deputy dropped to his knees; the Indian slammed onto his back. They fired at each other a second time: the top of the Indian's head burst like a crushed tomato upon the blue and gray stone; Goodstead fell onto his back.

The mule skinner's gun jammed; Oswell fired two rounds into his head. The rancher then sent four bullets into the stagecoach; a man groaned, stumbled out of the vehicle holding his stomach and fell to the stone.

Alphonse fled.

Richard, lying on the ground and coughing up blood, shot the Frenchman in the legs at the exact same moment that T.W. did. The little man fell to his knees. The sheriff and the New Yorker fired two bullets into his chest. Alphonse withdrew a handkerchief from his coat, blew his nose, tipped forward as if he were going to crawl into his bowler cap and died.

T.W. looked at Beatrice. The malformed Irishman, bleeding and wheezing, was directly behind her, propped up on his hands, stump and remaining knee. The only way he could have survived the sheriff's dead-on shot was if his heart were not situated where it should have been.

T.W. yelled, "No!" and ran at his bound, horribly crowned daughter.

Quinlan coughed up blood and lifted his left hand from the stone.

The sheriff bolted as hard as he could.

Quinlan extended the bronze gauntlet to push the woman forward. On the mountainside, their huge shadows merged.

The sheriff was three strides from his daughter when the tendon in his left hip finally snapped; the ground slammed into him; air was hammered from his lungs. The sprawled sheriff could neither move nor yell.

Quinlan's bronze gauntlet touched the small of Beatrice's back. She teetered, the nails in her bald head twinkling.

T.W. watched his baby, his girl, his treasure, his entire life topple forward to the stone.

Oswell caught her.

Holding the woman in his strong arms, the rancher kicked Quinlan's head; the Irishman's jaw cracked, and he collapsed to the stone, convulsive. Oswell put the toe of his boot beneath Quinlan's torso and turned him over. The rancher stomped his heel upon the man's malformed, gasping face. The man's nose shattered. Oswell brought his boot down again. The dome of Quinlan's skull cracked; the shape of his head changed; gore squirted from his left ear.

Tears were pouring from Oswell's eyes.

Richard crawled to the dying Irishman. He shot Quinlan three times, the barrel so close that the muzzle flash turned the mashed face into unrecognizable char. The New Yorker dropped his gun, pulled out another revolver and fired three shots into the twin's corpse; the prostrated body shook as if it had hiccups.

T.W. tried to stand, but his left leg refused to function; he sat upright on the stone, unable to do anything more.

He watched Oswell stand Beatrice up, take her hair from her mouth and untie the binding on her wrists. Richard removed the cord from around her ankles. Smiler walked up and put his longcoat around her shoulders.

She said, "Thank you," to the three men and

walked to her father; she sat beside him. It was hard for him to look her in the eyes—her face was striped with crimson and the nails still protruded from her skull.

He took her hand and tried to kiss it a thousand times.

"I'm so sorry this happened. I'm so sorry," he said.

"You saved me. You saved me, Daddy." She was trembling; tears ran from her eyes down her cheeks.

T.W. said, "I'm going to send for a doctor. You can't ride with those nails in you."

"I'll go," Smiler said. "You aren't going to be sending Goodstead." The old marshal pointed west; T.W. and Beatrice looked.

The deputy lay upon the stone; T.W.'s stomach sank; Beatrice said, "No."

"I'm still alive." the Texan said. "And handsome." He coughed. "Very."

"He took one in the stomach," the marshal informed them.

Quietly, so that the deputy could not hear, Beatrice asked the marshal, "Is he going to make it?"

"You bet I will. An' remember how pitiful I look right now when I ask you to dinner next time."

"I'll fetch the doctor. Do you feel safe with those two?" the old marshal asked, pointing to Oswell and Richard.

T.W. squeezed his daughter's hand and looked over at the outlaws.

Oswell and Richard faced each other; they both held guns in their clenched fists. The sheriff recognized the vitriol in their gazes: somebody was about to get killed.

Chapter Thirty-nine

So This is How it is Going to End?

"Put that goddamn gun down," Oswell said to Dicky.

With his free hand, the New Yorker pulled the rag from his mouth; flakes of himself went with the fabric.

"I am not going t—" Dicky said, the sentence's conclusion precluded by whatever just came loose from his upper gums. He spat the lump to the stone and continued, "I am not going to get hanged."

"This isn't some girl you lie to so you can bed her, or some fellow you cheat in cards. The sheriff let us save our families when he could've just executed us, and we'd never know what happened or done any good. We gave him our word what we'd do after."

"I did not give him my word," Dicky said and spat more flecks of himself to the stone. "I just nodded."

"Be honest. It's the last chance you'll ever have to do it."

"I am not going to let anyone hang me." He felt something warm slide down his cheeks; his wounds began to sting anew.

"You going to get in a gunfight with the sheriff to save yourself?"

The New Yorker did not answer the inquiry; he had not thought that far ahead. Oswell's shadow was gigantic upon the mountainside.

The rancher fired his gun twice. The bullets slammed into the New Yorker's chest, cracked his sternum, lanced his lungs, and burst through his back. He stumbled three steps to the west as if kicked by a mule.

Dicky aimed his gun at Oswell's face; the rancher did not flinch or move away, but instead stared directly into the New Yorker's eyes. Dicky lifted the barrel from Oswell's visage and pointed it at his own shadow, cyclopean upon the mountainside. He fired three shots at the wraith—echoes climbed to the peaks and scurried like rabbits across the plains—and then fell to the stone.

Cold air rushed into Dicky's lungs. Fluid bubbled in his esophagus.

Thoughts of Allison came to him, the woman he had tried for fourteen years to wipe from his mind, but whose face appeared whenever he saw a similar-looking woman (as he had on the train a week ago) or whenever he was ill or in a morbid state.

As his fingertips and toes began to tingle, Dicky remembered the day he had proposed to the raven-haired woman from Maine, the luminous quality of her smile as she nodded and his own ebullience at her acceptance. He was thirty at the time. He recalled the days he spent with her family and how well he had gotten along with her father, Garret, with whom he spent more than a dozen Saturdays playing croquet while enjoying fine gin. Allison and her family had called him Richard.

He recalled that June evening, one week before he and his fiancée were to be married—the night he had made the mistake of unburdening himself. They had made love, and afterward he felt compelled to tell her about the robberies with which he had been involved. As he recounted the heinous tale of Rope's End, he could see that she no longer loved him. In her eyes, he was not the thoughtful and gay gentleman to whom she had said, "I do," but a villain and a liar. He stopped talking. They slept on either side of the bed, a chasm between them. The next morning he had awakened to find her engagement ring and a note upon the table. He gambled the ring away in a poker game that night; he never read the note.

As the New Yorker slapped his palms against

the Montana Territory stone, the faces of various women flitted through his mind. He knew that none of them would think of him when their final hours came.

Dicky's draining blood saturated his shirt and the jagged rock beneath his spine. A diaphanous pink bubble inflated on his cold lips; its sibling burgeoned in one of the holes that pierced his chest. His hands and feet filled with ice.

Oswell Danford stood over him; the rancher's head was as high as the tallest mountain peak; he said, "You want me to put another in you?"

Dicky coughed up blood. He wheezed; frigid air blew through the holes in his lungs. The spirit that played the drum in his chest dissipated. His left leg began to twitch.

A coldness crept up from his extremities, toward his eyes. His vision began to narrow. He thought of Viola, the whore with whom he had invested all of himself last evening. He tried to imagine what his child would look like, yet saw only a blank face.

He exhaled; the drum in his chest boomed one more time and was then silent.

Chapter Forty

Dusk Trepanation

A bandaged wedding guest named Doc Earl pulled the penultimate nail from Beatrice's skull, leaving behind a hole an eighth of an inch deep; a drop of warm blood slid down the side of her head, onto her shoulder. The medical man lifted pincers from a blue fire and pressed them against the wound. Blood sizzled for one long second as the puncture was cauterized. He removed the pincers and pressed a swab to the wound.

A halo of dull pain throbbed around her head, but the morphine the doctor had given her made the experience bearable if not entirely remote. She looked at the eleven nails beside her feet; the points of the steel rods were stained with crimson.

The doctor plucked the final nail from the back of her skull and tossed it to its siblings, where it landed with a clink. He cauterized the puncture with the heated pincers; blood sizzled; the smell was nauseatingly similar to that of a panfried steak. He pressed a swab to the sterilized wound and then wrapped gauze around the pulsating dozen.

Because she found the thought of donning her wedding gown utterly abhorrent, Beatrice wore

Smiler's coat with her corset underneath. She would probably feel cold if not for the warming narcotic coursing through her veins.

Upon his arrival, Doc Earl had informed her and her father that a few people left within the church had actually survived, albeit with serious injuries, and that the trunks had been pulled from the wreckage by the townsfolk too. Everyone had reclaimed their valuables, and all of the missing persons were accounted for. Twenty-nine wedding guests had died.

Beatrice's father kept his arm around her shoulders the entire time, excepting when she had dressed and when he and Smiler had to restrain Goodstead while the doctor fished the Indian's bullet out of his stomach. The deputy was averse to surgery and had repeatedly said, "It'll come out on its own" and "I trust in my abilities to excrete," throughout the process.

Her father offered her the neck of a canteen lit gold by the scalp of the sinking sun. She took it and drank; the cool liquid wet her parched mouth and throat.

"You should try to escape," Goodstead, pale and holding a towel to his stomach, said to Oswell. He pointed to the west. "Now's your chance. Run for it."

The rancher, seated upon a stone, said nothing in response; he just stared at the gilded horizon.

"Go on Oswell, skedaddle," the Texan advised.

"I promise to any god but the one I believe in that I won't shoot you right away."

"Deputy Everett Goodstead," Beatrice's father said admonishingly; his strong voice resonated through the arm with which he held her. "My daughter's seen too much violence. Mr. Danford gets hanged like I told him."

Her father raised a damp cloth and wiped her face; with metal thread, Doc Earl secured the gauze that encircled her head.

"I still cannot believe that James was an outlaw," Beatrice said. "He was the gentlest man I ever knew." Her words were small, soft and fuzzy from the morphine. This was what she had sounded like when she was nine years old.

"He never willingly hurt another person," Oswell said.

"Don't go turnin' him into a goddamn martyr," Goodstead said to the rancher. "Don't you dare. We got twenty-nine dead people and their families, and none of them care how sweet James was back when he was robbin' banks and shootin' folks."

"None of us are martyrs. We all did bad things and deserve to hang. I just wanted Miss Jeffries to know that there was never any malice in James Lingham."

"And you?" her father asked.

"I wanted to be sheriff when I was little, but things went bad for me and I turned mean."

"That's how it happens," her father said.

At that moment Beatrice noticed that the timbre of Oswell's voice and her father's was exactly the same.

Her veins and tissues warmed by the opiate, Beatrice stared up into the sky. The moon sat on a bed of cotton; large black birds soundlessly circled the orb like dried leaves on the surface of a pond.

Smiler pointed to Quinlan, his crew and Dicky, prostrated on the stone, and said, "Them buzzards is gonna eat well."

"If they're immune to poison," Goodstead remarked.

"It's time to head back home," her father said, and kissed her on the cheek.

Chapter Forty-one

An Addendum

P.S. The sheriff of Trailspur fetched the letter so I could add this information before it goes out tomorrow with the mail. I am in jail right now.

We took down Quinlan and his crew. I am sure that there will be something about it in the papers since a lot of innocent folks got hurt and killed. I can tell you now (if you didn't figure it out already) that Godfrey was the one

I referred to as the other fellow, so you won't see him again either. He was hanged, and so was J. I wound up putting D down myself because I thought he might draw on the sheriff, though now I think D just didn't want to get hanged, which some fellows find much worse than getting shot. Either way, I am the last one of the Tall Boxer Gang and I am going to get hanged on the first of September.

If you want to tell me anything before they string me up, send a wire to Theodore William Jeffries at 10 Oak Avenue in Trailspur, Montana Territory, and he will pass the message along. If you want me to be buried in Virginia, let him know that too because he said he would send my body there. It is up to you and what you think best for the kids. Maybe telling them that I'm on a trip is better than telling them what really happened, which might affect them badly or make them ashamed. Good-bye.

Chapter Forty-two

Branches (Broken and Bent)

T.W., wearing a brown suit and leather shoes, sat on the couch in his den; the weathered throw quilt his deceased wife had made pressed familiarly into his back. With a heavy lump in his stomach, he stared at the window; he had dreaded this particular sunrise.

"Do you want sausages or bacon?" Meredith inquired.

He looked over at the woman: her black and silver hair was pulled back into a bun; the cuts and bruises upon her face from the wedding were now almost invisible.

T.W. said, "I'm not too hungry. I'll just have some eggs and biscuits." He remembered neither shoving her into the aisle during Quinlan's getaway nor shielding her when gunshots rang out, but according to her he had done both of these things.

Meredith had been cooking for him and helping him up and down the stairs the last nineteen days, encouraging him to walk, and also discouraging him from overdoing it. Oftentimes, she and Beatrice discussed Italian paintings, German music and English writers; T.W. did not at all follow these conversations, but he relished the sound of them.

The widow asked, "How is your hip doing today?"

"Better. I should be able to tackle the stairs without any help pretty soon."

"I do not at all mind escorting you to your bedroom."

Despite the fact that T.W. was a fifty-seven-year-old man who had faced peril and savagery and violence and tragedy throughout his life, a rose hue illuminated his cheeks, wrought by her intimation. Meredith and he had abstained from fornicating while his hip mended, but they had tasted each other often during the late hours.

"I appreciate the help," he said, looking to the window to conceal his blush.

Footsteps upon the stairs garnered his attention; he turned around and saw his daughter descending in her lavender nightgown and slippers. The bandages had come off of her head six days ago; her fast-growing blonde hair already covered over most of the wounds, excepting the four on her forehead.

"Good morning, Daddy," Beatrice said. She had gone back to calling him that ever since her wedding.

"Good morning, Bea," he said.

"Good morning, Meredith."

"Good morning, Beatrice. Would you like sausages or bacon with your eggs?"

"I would enjoy bacon, thank you."

Beatrice sat beside her father and kissed him on the cheek.

"How did you sleep last night?" he inquired.

She hesitated for a moment and said, "I slept well."

"How much did you get?"

"A couple of hours at night. Then I read until dawn and fell asleep again until now."

"Four hours. That's not enough."

Her face had new lines in it around the edges of her mouth and at the corners of her eyes; her cheeks and chin were sharper than they had been.

"It is more than most nights," she said. "It is easier for me to sleep after the sun has come up."

"What did you read?" Meredith inquired as she laid six strips of bacon into a heated frying pan.

"A story by an English author named Wilfred Ronald Meyerson."

"Which one?" The bacon sizzled.

Beatrice hesitated before she said, " 'Embraced by the Hands of the Beast.' "

T.W. did not at all like the sound of that story, but he waited for Meredith's response. It seemed that almost any comment he made on art was incorrect.

"That is an extraordinarily evocative chiller," Meredith said as she poked the hissing bacon with a long fork. "Did you find it frightening?"

"I did find it frightening, especially when Lynette was lost in the catacombs. I could hardly breathe when she reached into the darkness and felt that wall of fur, and those hearts beating on the other side of it."

T.W. said, "That doesn't sound like it's going to help you get to sleep."

"It occupies my mind."

T.W. looked at Meredith to see if he should say

anything more on the matter; the woman shook her head. He felt that it was valuable for his daughter to put her thoughts elsewhere while she distanced herself from the tragedy, but he found her morbid inclinations, sleeplessness and night fears troubling. He had not once seen her look at a Bible since her wedding, and when the new minister came to Trailspur (it turned out that Minister Bachs had been tortured to death by Minister Orton), she had very little interest in his spiritual guidance.

Meredith slid two-color eggs, lard biscuits and bacon onto three plates and carried them from the kitchen. T.W. snatched his cane (with his daughter's help), stood, walked to the dining-room table and sat down on the seat the widow withdrew for him. Despite his request for no bacon, she had given him two crispy strips.

"Thank you," he said to Meredith. He asked his daughter, "Do you want to say grace?"

"You may say it."

T.W. bowed his head forward and said, "Come dine with us, Lord Jesus, be a guest in our home. Let these gifts to us be blessed. Amen."

Meredith said, "Amen."

Beatrice silently raised her head.

T.W. tore off a piece of his lard biscuit and dipped it into an egg yolk; the porous pastry inhaled the yellow syrup. He put it into his mouth and chewed mechanically.

"I think I should visit my great-aunt," Beatrice remarked in a small voice.

T.W. swallowed and said, "You want to go to England?"

Beatrice turned her eyes away from her father and nodded, guiltily.

He wiped his mustache with his napkin and asked, "For a holiday?"

"I do not know for certain, but I feel that I must leave Trailspur for a little while."

Several times since the tragedy she had mentioned the idea of going away on a trip, but never before had she named such a far-off destination.

"Think on it for a couple of days," he said. "If you still want to go, I will send your aunt Grace a letter."

"Thank you."

He nodded his head. The thought of her leaving was a very painful one, but he understood why she felt the need to put space between herself and the Montana Territory. He would not attempt to dissuade her if she became fixed on the notion.

They ate their meals, T.W. eating far less than he usually did. He chewed each bite far past the point of flavor, awaiting the inevitable knock on the door that he had dreaded since dawn.

Boots clacked on the step to his front door. He swallowed the eggs almost forgotten in his mouth. A fist knocked thrice upon the wood.

"Mayor Jeffries," Goodstead said.

"Come in, Sheriff," T.W. replied.

The door opened; Meredith and the Jeffries looked toward the sunlit portal. Sheriff Goodstead, wearing a dark blue shirt, matching trousers and a silver vest, upon which he had pinned his badge, entered the house; he removed his gray hat. Deputy Kenneth John, wearing black, followed shortly after; he had thinned out and trimmed his beard since the tragedy.

"Good morning, folks," Goodstead said.

"Good morning, Sheriff. Good morning, Deputy," Beatrice replied.

"Good morning," Meredith said.

Kenneth John said, "Hello."

T.W. grimaced and nodded.

The Texan looked at Beatrice and Meredith and said, "The mayor's hoarding all the pretty ones in here." He looked at T.W. and said, "You selfish."

"How is your mother doing?" T.W. asked Kenneth John.

"She ate something," he said without elaboration.

"I'm glad to hear that," T.W. replied. The woman had never recovered from her elder son's death three years ago and was now a widow as well. If she fell ill again, the mayor doubted that she would fight to stay alive, though Kenneth John was doing his best to make her proud.

"Do you like my new vest?" Goodstead asked Beatrice. "Look at the tassels on the back." He turned around to display the ten small pendants of silver thread that hung there. He shook himself; the tassels swung pendulously and glinted.

"It definitely suits you," Beatrice said.

"Thanks," he replied, and turned back around.

Meredith said to the Texan, "You have a cheerful attitude, considering what you are about to do."

"You ever have a cold where you get better—it's almost all gone—but there's just this little bit you have left, botherin' you? Like a cough or some phlegm?"

"I have."

"That's what Oswell Danford is."

T.W. slapped his palms to the table and stood up; the legs of his chair scraped across the wooden floor. Meredith handed him his cane. He kissed her and then pressed his lips to his daughter's forehead.

The mayor looked at Goodstead and said, "Let's get it over with."

They walked to the door; the three men put on their hats the moment they crossed the threshold and were struck by the sun.

Mayor Jeffries and Sheriff Goodstead sat upon mares outside of the town jail, a squat stone edifice with four barred windows. The building was currently being expanded to accommodate the influx of strangers that the tragedy had attracted.

Seventy people were gathered on the sides of the avenue, including Big Abe and his wife,

Judge Higgins, Rita, Wilfreda (whose arm was in a sling), Roland and Vanessa Taylor (who had lost both of their children and looked wrathful), Snappy Fa (who had been caught in the collapse, survived, but lost a leg), the Sallys, a dozen other wedding guests with painful souvenirs, and more than a score of strangers. Ed the barber and a customer with a half-lathered face walked out of his shop to join the assemblage.

The door to the jail opened; Deputy Kenneth John escorted Oswell Danford outside. The rancher wore brown trousers and a beige shirt that had been cleaned yesterday for today's event; his wrists were manacled. He squinted in the bright sunlight, his face covered with a prickly beard as red as Godfrey's had been. The throng silently watched the deputy escort the man toward a saddled white horse.

An egg struck Oswell's face and cracked; clear and yellow mucoidal strands dangled from his right cheek. Kenneth John continued to walk the prisoner forward. A rock cracked against Oswell's forehead, leaving behind a red mark T.W. saw from ten yards off.

The mayor fired a pistol into the air; the report eddied through the crowd and to the plains.

T.W. yelled, "That isn't what happens in Trailspur!"

"Look what he did! Look what he did," Tara's mother Vanessa yelled, her voice raw with rage.

T.W. cantered his horse directly toward the woman and said, "He's going to pay for what he did, Mrs. Taylor, I promise you. But the Montana Territory is going be a state soon—we must be civilized. This man should and will be hanged as is proper by the laws of this country."

An onion smacked Oswell's swollen ear; the rancher winced but said nothing.

"That's enough folks," Sheriff Goodstead said. "From this moment forward, I will lock up anyone who throws somethin' solider than a dirty look."

From his wheelchair, Grandpa Sally yelled, "He should be strung up in public! We should get to see him choke!"

"That isn't the kind of town I'm the mayor of," T.W. said.

"Then we shoulda voted somebody else!"

"Maybe. But you have me for now."

Deputy Kenneth John led Oswell to the white steed; the prisoner jammed his left foot into the stirrup, grabbed the pommel with his manacled hands and hoisted himself up. A gunshot cracked the silence; everyone but T.W. and Oswell flinched. The mayor surveyed the crowd and the storefronts; he saw no shooter or smoke.

T.W. looked at Goodstead and the deputy and said, "Let's ride out."

Kenneth swung himself onto his mare; the moment he was mounted, Goodstead snapped his reins and led the way. T.W. took the tether to Oswell's horse and rode alongside him, behind the lawmen.

Several people yelled out obscenities, a handful threw vegetables and a few others anonymously discharged their guns into the air to scare the prisoner (which never even caused the man to blink), but the ride to the southwestern edge of town occurred without serious incident. Most townsfolk silently watched the quartet pass by from their porches or through their windows.

They rode past James's house toward the unsettled hills.

"What happened to Lingham's coydogs?" Oswell asked T.W.

"Beatrice tried to take them in, but they kept running back here. I suppose they're wild now."

The horses climbed a low hill; the wet grass squeaked like mice beneath the beasts' hooves.

In a quiet voice, Oswell inquired, "Mayor Jeffries?"

"Yes?"

"Did my wife get the letter?"

"She did. I confirmed it with a telegram."

"Did she wire anything back, or ask for my body?"

"No."

Oswell nodded his head, but said nothing; T.W. found it hard to look at him.

The horses descended the rise; the mayor and

the rancher leaned forward as if a hand pressed upon their backs; hooves squeaked.

"Thank you for checking," Oswell said.

"You're welcome."

The horses continued forward; a leafless oak tree with three perpendicular branches rose from the earth ahead of them. Sheriff Goodstead withdrew a noose from his saddlebag, snapped his reins and galloped ahead.

Oswell asked, "Would you send me where you sent my brother's remains?"

"Pineville?"

"Yeah."

"I will."

The horses climbed another hill; T.W. and Oswell were pushed back in their saddles by the invisible hand. Ahead of them, Goodstead threw the noose over the highest branch of the black tree and wrapped the tether around its trunk.

T.W. and Oswell tipped forward as their horses descended the hill. The mayor looked at the prisoner and said, "Thank you. For catching her. For saving her."

Oswell nodded.

The horses climbed the final hill; upon the azure canvas of the western horizon jutted the leafless black tree and the noose. The two men watched the loop grow larger and larger as they rode toward it; three distant trees, a mountaintop and an entire cloud were ensnared within its perimeter.

T.W. led Oswell's horse beneath the branch. Kenneth John jumped off of his stallion and unlocked the prisoner's manacles. Oswell put his arms behind his back; the deputy refastened the cuffs. Goodstead cantered his beast alongside the rancher, slid the noose over the man's head, past his ears, down his cheeks (where it crackled against his beard) and around his neck. The Texan tightened the loop.

"Back away," T.W. said to the lawmen.

Kenneth John swung atop his stallion; he and Goodstead rode down the hill and up the adjacent rise.

T.W. slapped the hindquarters of the white steed upon which Oswell sat. The horse bolted forward with a whinny; the rancher was yanked from the saddle. The noose cracked his neck; he swung backward and then forward, his face bright red with agony. He made no noise.

The mayor looked away from the asphyxiation. Deputy Kenneth John and Sheriff Goodstead watched. The creaking of the tree branch behind T.W. slowed and then stopped.

"Ship him to Pineville," the mayor said to the lawmen.

"We will," Goodstead replied.

Mayor Theodore William Jeffries wiped tears from his eyes, snapped his reins and rode directly at the glaring sun. For the duration of one heartbeat, his long shadow was a shroud upon Oswell Danford's body.

Center Point Publishing
600 Brooks Road • PO Box 1
Thorndike ME 04986-0001 USA

(207) 568-3717

US & Canada:
1 800 929-9108
www.centerpointlargeprint.com